Wife After Wife

Wife After Wife

Olivia Hayfield

BERKLEY

NEW YORK

BERKLEY
An imprint of Penguin Random House LLC
penguinrandomhouse.com

Copyright © 2020 by Sue Copsey
Published by arrangement with Little, Brown Book Group Limited.
First published in the United Kingdom in 2020.
Penguin Random House supports copyright. Copyright fuels creativity,
encourages diverse voices, promotes free speech, and creates a vibrant culture.
Thank you for buying an authorized edition of this book and for complying with
copyright laws by not reproducing, scanning, or distributing any part of it
in any form without permission. You are supporting writers and allowing
Penguin Random House to continue to publish books for every reader.

BERKLEY and the BERKLEY & B colophon
are registered trademarks of Penguin Random House LLC.

Extract on p. 360 from A. A. Milne and Ernest H. Shepard, *The House at Pooh Corner*
(London: Methuen Children's Books, 1979)

Library of Congress Cataloging-in-Publication Data

Names: Hayfield, Olivia, 1960– author.
Title: Wife after wife / Olivia Hayfield.
Description: First edition. | New York: Berkley, 2020.
Identifiers: LCCN 2019022989 (print) | LCCN 2019022990 (ebook) |
ISBN 9780593101834 (paperback) | ISBN 9780593101841 (ebook)
Classification: LCC PR6108.A96757 W54 2020 (print) | LCC PR6108.A96757 (ebook) |
DDC 823/.92—dc23
LC record available at https://lccn.loc.gov/2019022989
LC ebook record available at https://lccn.loc.gov/2019022990

First Berkley Edition: January 2020

Printed in the United States of America
1   3   5   7   9   10   8   6   4   2

Cover art: Image of Woman by Miguel Sobreira / Arcangel Images;
Silhouettes in glasses by Michael Sanca / Shutterstock Images
Cover design by Colleen Reinhart
Book design by Elke Sigal

For Shelagh

Who does not tremble when he considers
how to deal with his wife?

—HENRY VIII

Cast of Characters

HARRY ROSE [King Henry VIII]
Head of media giant Rose Corp. Handsome, charming, intelligent, arrogant. Women just can't help themselves.

KATIE PARAGON [Catherine of Aragon]
Classy, gentle, saintly, loved by all. A devout Catholic. Wants many babies.

ANA LYEBON [Anne Boleyn]
Designer at *Hooray!* magazine. Sexy, elegant, a style icon. Ruthlessly ambitious. Nickname Ice Queen.

JANETTE MORRISSEY [Jane Seymour]
Harry's devoted secretary. Sweet-faced, prone to blushing. Fan of Princess Diana. Bakes great cakes.

ANKI, FROM CLEVELAND, OHIO [Anne of Cleves]
Harry's partner in the online game *Alt Life*. A travel agent who looks nothing like her avatar.

CAITLYN HOWE [Catherine Howard]
Gym bunny and wild child. Fan of the Kardashians. Raised by her grandmother in a crumbling manor with other families of aging hippies. A stranger to fidelity.

CLARE BARR [Catherine Parr]
Twice-widowed nurse. Kind, understanding, intelligent. Originally from Cumbria.

(continued on page 437)

CHAPTER 1

———⊗⊗⊗———

Harry

January 2018

On a gray London morning just after Christmas, Harry Rose stood at his office window watching the Thames mooching along below. The river was brown today, as befitted London's post-Christmas mood. Except it looked pink. Harry wondered again whether it had been a good idea to clad the entire building in rose-tinted glass.

Across the river, the Rose's rivals—the Gherkin, the Cheesegrater, and the Walkie-Talkie—towered over the City, dwarfing the Tower of London. Towers had come on a bit since the eleventh century, Harry reflected, though something deep inside him disliked the way these thrusting newcomers made the Tower of London look so small.

Along the riverbank to the east, he could see the lower floors of the Shard. Unfortunately, it hadn't taken Londoners long to love-match the phallic building and the round, pink office block that had unfurled just up the road. Word had reached Harry that the Rose was now known as the Vaj.

His meandering thoughts were interrupted by a knock on the door, and he saw his new assistant, Aleesha, peering through the glass. He was glad she'd managed to find her way here. Yesterday, on her first day at Rose Corp., she'd had to report to @People (formerly human resources) first, and disappeared without trace for half an hour. It was unfortunate that the "petals" radiating from the Rose's central atrium had turned the building into something of a maze.

Harry beckoned her in. As she crossed the expanse, which was the size of a small aircraft hangar, Harry couldn't help noticing that her white shirt was just the right side of see-through, allowing a misty glimpse of her underwear, the golden hue of the tanned skin beneath. *Nice.*

"Good morning, Mr. Rose."

"Hi, Aleesha. Call me Harry, remember?"

Rose Corp.'s staff were all on first-name terms, as suited the millennial vibe Harry worked hard to maintain for the brand.

As Harry went to return to his desk, pain shot through his right leg and he winced.

"Are you all right, Mr. . . . . Harry?"

No need to share the truth, that the old war wound had been playing up again. He'd have to go back to Doc Butts. His leg had been mangled, along with his Aston Martin, when he skidded off the Guildford bypass during an impromptu race with his best friend, Charles, back in 2001. The shattered bones had been pinned back together, but recently the old injury started to ache and twinge again. A limp wasn't a good look, so he did his best to hide it.

"I'm fine," Harry snapped. "Just a touch of stiffness. Probably over-did it at tennis last night."

He saw the flash of fear on her face. His bad leg was making him tetchy. Tyrant wasn't the profile he was aiming for, so he fixed his smile back in place.

He was about to make a friendly quip about her *lovely blouse* with its perfect reveal-imagine balance, but stopped himself. She might take offense. Instead he said, "Is that an espresso I see before me? Excellent!"

Too Hugh Grant?

Had it been such a good idea to employ a millennial? At fifty-four, he hoped having her around would give him more of an insight into the target market for the Rose brand. At least, that was what he'd told himself when he chose the lovely Aleesha over more experienced candidates. And she seemed different from most of the girls—women—her age that he knew. Quieter, sweeter, less combative. For all that he loved strong women, they could be so wearing.

Aleesha reminded him of Janette.

The sudden memory hurt, but he was quickly distracted by a glimpse of cleavage as she placed his coffee in front of him. Of their own accord, his eyes swiveled.

Careful, Harry!

He swiftly returned them to her face, with another smile. Her expression faltered, and the niggle of worry prodded him again. Sexist tyrant would be even worse.

How had it come to this? It was like McCarthyism. People ratting on their workmates for behavior nobody used to bat an eyelid at. These young women were happy to Instagram photos of their bottoms in micro-bikinis to a thousand followers they'd never met "IRL," but should a colleague comment on said bottom in real life, it was harassment.

Follow me, but don't touch me. It made no sense.

He'd said as much to his daughter Eliza, who was twenty. They'd argued the toss about respect and boundaries, but their points of view were poles apart. One pole being on Venus, the other on Mars.

An appreciative comment to a female member of staff wouldn't have been a problem ten years ago, even five. But now he felt increasingly uneasy. The worm had well and truly turned. He could be just a tweet away from public disgrace.

Aleesha turned to go, then hesitated. "Um, Harry?"

Her London twang pleased him. She sounded like a Radio 1 DJ, which was nicely in line with the top-floor vibe he was aiming for.

"Yes, Aleesha, did you need to ask me something?"

"It's just . . . the cup, Harry."

"This one?" He sipped his espresso.

"Yeah, it's, like—disposable?"

Was that a question? Probably not.

"Ah. And that's not on trend, correct? This is exactly why I hired you, Aleesha. You mustn't be afraid to tell me when I'm not up to speed with the zeitgeist. So . . ."

"I can get you a reusable?"

"Sure." He ran his fingers through his hair, sweeping it back. His trademark sandy locks were draining of color quickly now, but the silver fox replacing them was pleasing. He was due for a trim. Men over fifty needed to remain vigilant; otherwise, instead of looking like an older hipster, one appeared to be going to seed.

"But we don't have a kitchen on this floor, Harry."

God forbid. Imagine being able to see staff heating their microwavable lunches through the pink glass petal-walls.

"And the coffee machines all use *plastic* cups. That's not really acceptable. Hope you don't mind me saying."

"Excellent observation."

Hugh Grant again.

"Reusables are the thing, right?"

"Yes, Harry, but it'd be difficult when—"

". . . there's no kitchen, I get it. That's why we have the Tiger Team, Aleesha. The Greenhouse's elite brainstormers. Flick them an email—ask them to blue-sky it. Could be a new brand in it for us."

"OK, Harry. On it!"

He opened up his computer calendar, and his heart sank as he saw "Latham" entered at eleven. The lawyer representing his late wife Caitlyn's father. Howe was claiming Harry's unreasonable behavior had been responsible for her death. It was ridiculous. All Caitlyn's issues could be traced back to terrible parenting. Harry's conscience was clear.

No matter what others—wives, wives' parents, mistresses, jealous lovers—might think, Harry Rose always tried to do the right thing. And if that meant putting a little spin on circumstances, massaging them until the thing to do became "right," so be it.

Some might say he was twisting the facts, but Harry had always been guided by his conscience. In turn, his conscience often needed a little guidance—after all, how can we decide what is right without considering all sides, all opinions? And if Harry was selective in which of those informed his conscience . . . well, who wasn't?

Harry put his worries aside. The bottom line was, he'd argued with his conscience and, after some fairly intense battles, had declared it clear.

CHAPTER 2

Katie

July 1985

A blackbird was singing its heart out in the apple tree outside the French doors, thrown open to let the afternoon breeze drift through the house. It brought with it the scent of new-mown grass and a whiff of the honeysuckle rambling across the Cotswold-stone walls of the cottage Harry and Katie had rented for the summer.

The blackbird was competing with Bono, who was belting out "Bad" on the TV. It was Live Aid, and they'd been watching on and off all day, between popping into Oxford to buy more baby gear.

"That chap's good," commented Harry, massaging Katie's bare feet where they lay in his lap.

"The blackbird's better," said Katie, wiggling her toes. "That tickles."

"Should I get that haircut? Do you think I'd look cool?"

Katie regarded Bono's black mullet with something blond going on at the front. "I don't think it'd work in ginger, darling."

"It's not ginger, it's strawberry blond. What the fuck's he doing?"

Bono had leaped down off the stage—a not insignificant drop—and was trying to haul someone out of the crowd.

"Language, darling. You'll have to stop that when there are little ears listening."

"Sorry. Cup of tea?"

"Lovely, thanks."

"English breakfast or mad pregnancy flavor?"

"Raspberry leaf, please."

As he gently lifted her feet off his lap, Katie wondered if the cup would runneth over. Could life be any more perfect? Her tall, golden-haired Adonis there, busy in the kitchen of this idyllic cottage. Baby kicking in its appreciation of U2.

They'd been monitoring its responses to the bands. Status Quo had provoked the liveliest reaction so far, and Harry had wondered if denim rompers were a thing. That afternoon they'd spotted a pair of denim booties in Mothercare, and those were now sitting on the mantelpiece, along with a number of invitations, all of which they'd ignored since moving into their summer bolt-hole.

One of them was, in fact, a pair of tickets to Live Aid, with a note from Harry's best friend, Charles. Like Harry, he was so well connected he could get tickets for absolutely anything: cricket at Lord's, Centre Court at Wimbledon, the Royal Enclosure at Ascot.

Katie idly wondered if Harry had missed going to the summer events this year. He wanted to go to Live Aid, but Katie, eight and a half months pregnant, had preferred to stay home and watch it on TV. They'd had a near row; apparently this was going to be *the* rock concert of the eighties. Surely she could manage a first-class train journey and a taxi ride to Wembley, Harry had said.

Katie had cursed inwardly when they'd spotted Charles and his wife, Cassandra, sitting two rows behind the Prince and Princess of Wales. Harry's jaw had tightened. He *really* hated to miss out, especially when his best mate, who was also something of a substitute older brother, was around. To distract him, she'd wondered out loud what Prince Charles and Bob Geldof might talk about between acts, but Harry had only grunted and left the room.

Charles probably considered Harry under the thumb. Katie got on well with him but suspected he wasn't in favor of Harry taking up with someone older, quieter, more sensible. Possibly boring. Someone who'd been old-fashioned enough to expect Harry to marry her when she got pregnant.

Rock concerts weren't really Katie's thing. At twenty-seven, she already felt too old. The only performer she would have enjoyed was Paul McCartney. And maybe Elton John. The argument had been the first time she felt that the five-year age gap between them mattered.

She started as Harry put the mug down in front of her.

The Beach Boys were now playing, and the baby had gone quiet.

Katie picked up her tea. "Baby's not a Beach Boys fan. I loved them when I was a girl."

"Before my time," remarked Harry, putting his feet up on the coffee table.

Katie looked sideways at him, but his face was expressionless. As he bent to sip his tea, a lock of hair fell forward—he'd let it grow longer on top, and the floppiness suited him.

The sun, now lower in the sky, slanted through the window, throwing puddles of light on the rugs and illuminating a vase of red roses she'd picked from the garden.

Katie's heart constricted as she contemplated Harry's profile. Her husband was outrageously beautiful. The sun was catching his long, thick eyelashes and his silky mane of hair, lightened by summer. Beneath fine blond hairs, the skin on his arms was sun kissed to a golden brown.

It was like sharing the sofa with a lion.

Unable to resist, she lifted a hand to stroke back the lock of hair, but Harry was already jumping up and pulling a curtain across. Then he sat down in an armchair, stretching his long legs out in front of him.

"That's better. Couldn't see before."

She felt the empty space beside her. The silence that had been so comfortable all at once felt awkward. It was as if she could sense Harry's thoughts, turning from rock concerts and lazy summer days to the responsibilities of fatherhood and supporting her, his wife of two months.

She sat up straighter, aware of her enormous bump. Oh, to have a waist again.

The beginning of their relationship had been anything but typical. No meeting down at the pub or at a university party for them. In fact, they had first met properly, as adults, at his father's funeral. Harry had been in his final year at Eton when Henry Rose unexpectedly died of a lung infection that should have been easily curable. Harry suspected his father had never recovered from losing both his wife and eldest son within a year of each other.

Harry and his two sisters had suddenly found themselves orphans, and Harry had looked like a little boy lost.

Katie had known the family from when she dated Harry's older brother, Art. Their mothers had been friends, and the two families shared a villa in the South of France in the summer of 1974. On the third day, Art had shyly asked if he could kiss her, behind the bougain-villea.

Katie remembered Harry, already wickedly good-looking at the age of eleven, full of life, cannonballing into the swimming pool. He was as tall as Art, and while the older brother had been quiet and thoughtful, the younger had been full of exuberant self-confidence.

When Art died in a freak skiing accident, Katie had been terribly sad. He'd been her first proper boyfriend. And Harry was heartbroken—she remembered him sobbing at the funeral.

Then, less than a year later, Harry's mother had died. The two fami-lies lost touch after that, and rumor had it that Harry's father, Henry, had turned to drink in his grief and rarely left his country pile. A few years later, he too had died.

Katie's family had attended Henry's funeral, and there she saw Harry, almost eighteen years old, shattered by the loss of his parents and brother. He'd turned his sad, deep blue eyes on her, and she was lost.

Sometimes she wondered if it was a sound basis for a relationship. "Are you sure you're not a mother substitute?" a friend had said at the time. She'd spent the summer of 1981, before Harry went up to Oxford, coaxing him back to life, getting him to talk about his feelings (not something he was used to doing), until the hurt began to dull, that devastating smile reappeared, and the easy charm resurfaced. And as it had, she allowed the attraction that had been building to see the light of day.

She'd been a lot older than him, but Harry was tall and broadshouldered, could pass for twenty-one or twenty-two, while she'd looked younger than her twenty-three years, being tiny and favoring the ubiquitous Lady Di hairdo and frilly collars.

Having had a sweet, celibate relationship with Art, and no boyfriends since, Katie had been poleaxed by the strength of feeling that swept through her each time she met up with this beautiful, damaged boy, all at once appalled and excited by the emotions and physical goings-on that overtook her.

"KATIE!"

"Sorry . . . what?" She'd zoned out again.

"I said, shall we walk to the pub?"

"*I . . . want . . . my . . .*" sang Sting as Dire Straits readied to rock.

"Oh, I like this one," said Katie. "Why don't we stay here and I'll cook us something. They don't have a TV in the pub. Thank goodness, actually. Dreadful trend."

But as the crowd rocked along to "Money for Nothing," Katie wondered if watching it on TV was just reminding Harry of what a good time Charles would be having without him.

"OK, we can go to the pub if you want."

Trouble was, she knew what would happen. After several weeks in this village, they now knew many of the regulars, and she'd sit there, uncomfortably wedged behind a table, sipping her sad little orange juice while Harry downed pints of Hook Norton ale and yarned with the locals. It wasn't his fault; people just liked being around Harry, and in a village you couldn't be unsociable. In less *expectant* times she'd gladly have joined in, but right now she couldn't work up the energy.

To the villagers, who'd never known her sans bump, she was just a mum-to-be. Sometimes she'd chat with a wife or girlfriend, but the older ones only wanted to share their childbirth stories, which were invariably terrifying. Did she really need to hear yet again that it was like trying to poo a watermelon? Why did women assume that just because you had a baby bump, you wanted to hear their own grisly experiences?

They'd say, "No one tells you how hard motherhood is, you're just expected to know what to do." Actually, no. *Everyone* had told her how hard it is.

Harry must have read her mind. He moved back to the sofa, put one arm around her shoulders, and gently stroked her bump.

"Sorry, I can see you're knackered." The softness in his eyes banished the negative thoughts. "Why would you want to sit in a smoky pub sipping a boring drink while your husband talks rugby with Farmer Thing from Thing Farm?" He kissed her hair, then rested his head on hers. "How about a takeaway? Chinese? Probably not Indian."

"Actually, they say a strong curry can bring on labor," said Katie. "And right now, I'd like to get it over with and drink a cider down the pub without taking up space for four people."

But that wasn't strictly true. As Harry fetched his car keys, she knew that if she could freeze time, she'd probably do so right now.

"If you hurry, you'll be back in time for Queen," she called. And then sang to herself, "*Is this the real life? Is this just fantasy?*"

CHAPTER 3

Harry

The baby was stillborn. A girl.

They called her Summer, in memory of those July days, when time had slowed and a languid torpor had settled over the cottage.

Already it felt like a lifetime ago.

Harry let himself in the front door and was met by a silence louder than any of the background sounds he'd grown used to, most often the tinny chatter of Radio 4 on the little set Katie took with her as she puttered around the cottage. He'd made fun of her premature middle age, but now he flicked on the red transistor sitting by the kettle, grateful as the evening news filled the kitchen.

Katie had gone to stay with her parents over in Gloucestershire. Germaine had insisted, and one didn't argue with Katie's formidable stepmother. It was probably for the best. Katie had been inconsolable, and all Harry had been able to do those first few days was hold her tight and cry with her. He was fairly sure Germaine didn't consider male tears at all helpful.

His mother-in-law had swept into the hospital room, shooing away a grief counselor, on a mission to move things on. She'd organized Summer's funeral, told Harry he needed to be strong for her daughter, and prescribed some time away from anything that would remind her of the baby she'd lost. Including Harry, it seemed.

"Of course it's the most terrible thing, my darlings," she'd said, "but there will be more babies; you're young and healthy, one must move on. Chin up and all that."

Harry thought Katie should be allowed plenty more chin-down days. But with a stiff smile he'd come home and packed up the denim booties, the clothes, blankets, mobiles, all the clobber they'd amassed since he'd graduated, sealing everything into cardboard boxes. Now they sat, together with the dismantled cot, in the smallest upstairs bedroom. Along with the baby things, he'd attempted to pack away his own grief, together with that for his mother, brother, and father.

He unloaded a bag of shopping onto the kitchen worktop, stabbed the lid of a meal-for-one with a fork, and put it in the microwave, turning up the radio so he could hear the news above the hum. He chuckled as the newsreader reported that production of the Sinclair C5 was to cease, as sales had been "disappointingly slow." Slow? Harry had been keeping an eye on Sinclair's invention and knew only a few thousand had been sold since its glitzy launch. The British media—and every bloke in every pub across the land—had pronounced the little electric vehicle ridiculous, so it had never stood a chance.

Harry had watched the public response with keen interest. Sinclair had made a fortune in electronics, notably personal computers. The chap should have stuck with what he was good at, although Harry wasn't convinced personal computers would ever take off.

He needed to keep abreast of trends, in his role as new business director of Rose Corp. He was due to go full-time next month, now that he was old enough to take over the shareholding he'd inherited from his father. Uncle Richard would remain as CEO while Harry learned the ropes, until one day he would run the company himself. He was looking forward to that.

Since Katie had been in Gloucestershire, he was commuting down to Rose Corp. HQ on the South Bank. Word had got around about his and Katie's loss, and people had been extra kind to the new boy. Or was it just because the new boy would one day be their boss?

Rose Corp.'s beginnings had been in print media. First, a collection of regional magazines and newspapers, soon expanding into national titles. In the 1960s, they had launched a whole new style of glossy women's magazines, aimed at the independent woman. Less about keeping good house and more about having good sex. The company continued to go from strength to strength, but Harry was keen to see what new directions they might explore.

The microwave pinged, and he took out his fisherman's pie and peeled off the plastic. He grimaced. It wasn't appealing. He missed Katie's home cooking. Flipping the top off a beer, he took his meal to the living room.

Petals from Katie's roses had dropped across the coffee table, and the water in the vase was green. For a moment he saw her coming through the French windows, a basket hooked over her arm, saying, "Roses for the Roses!"

He smiled sadly at the memory, swept the petals aside to make space for his beer, rewound the VCR, and settled down to watch the cricket highlights—hopefully. Katie was much better at setting the machine than he was.

In spite of being able to watch sports without Katie asking how much longer he'd be, Harry wasn't happy being here alone. He didn't really do *alone*. He was keen to head southward now, have a fresh start, catch up with friends recently down from Oxford. He and Katie would be moving into the Fulham terraced house they'd bought, as soon as Katie felt up to it. He couldn't wait.

As he blew on a forkful of fish and potato, there was a knock on the front door.

"Bugger," he said. Should he ignore it? But the village wasn't London. They would *know* he was in, and if he didn't answer, they'd peer through the window.

With a sigh he put down his plate and made his way into the hall.

On the doorstep was a ravishingly pretty woman, holding out a dish draped with a tea towel.

"I saw you in Waitrose," she said, "buying those sad meals for one. I thought I'd make you a lasagna, and . . . maybe you might want some company. I'm Laura. I've seen you in the pub." She smiled, cocked her head to one side, edged her right foot forward. "Can I come in?"

Looking back, Harry was never quite sure how he'd ended up in bed with Laura. He remembered breaking down as he told her about Summer and how lonely he was without Katie; he remembered her coming over and sitting on his lap, and how he'd buried his face in her chest. Then things had moved quickly, and before he could object, she was hauling him upstairs by the hand. In his weakened emotional state, he'd been unable to resist.

Katie

December 1985

Harry not home yet?" said Cassandra, wife of Harry's best friend, Charles, as she shrugged off her coat.

"Working late again," Katie replied with a rueful smile, hanging the coat on the pine stand.

She was aware of the cliché, but she believed the words to be true. Harry was putting in long hours on his new job. He wanted to prove he wasn't just a privileged Hooray Henry who'd stepped into his position by virtue of birth. Which he was, of course—but he *had* achieved a first in philosophy, politics, and economics at Oxford.

"Not a Christmas party, I hope," said Cassandra. "Dangerous times for wives. All right if I keep these on?" She indicated her black boots, the perfect accompaniment for her dark red wool dress. Her blond hair was held back in a giant black velvet bow, and pearls gleamed in her ears.

Cassandra was always so well put-together, thought Katie, trying to remember if she'd combed her hair today. She'd been painting the downstairs loo (Dulux Barley White) and was still in her decorating clothes.

"Of course," she said. "They're lovely, by the way. Are they new?"

"Gucci. I shouldn't have, but Charles owes me." She paused. "He's been playing away. Bastard."

Katie's heart sank. "Oh, Cass, surely not. Come and sit down, let's have a wine."

They went through to the brand-new kitchen, completed that week. There were stripped pine cupboards with distressed pale blue tiles on the walls between. The floor was laid with terra-cotta quarry tiles, and copper saucepans hung from a rectangular metal contraption on the ceiling. In the center was a scrubbed pine table with a bowl of pomegranates in the middle.

"Bloody hell," said Cassandra. "Fulham-en-Provence!"

"Do you think it's too much? My kitchen designer said it's all about country at the moment. Creating a rural idyll in the city, or something."

"I blame that bloody Edwardian lady and her country diary," said Cassandra. "Can't even buy a bath towel without those wretched watercolor poppies. But no, darling, it's charming, absolutely divine. Really."

"Thank you."

Katie glanced up at the saucepans before pouring them a wine. It was a devil getting them down for cooking, but they did look lovely.

"Now, where did I put the cheese board?"

"Sod the cheese, Katie. Come and sit down. How have you been? Feeling better?"

"Oh, I'm fine, really."

She wasn't. And she felt as if she never would be again. But throwing herself into home renovations had helped. Cassandra was terribly kind, but Katie knew her friend thought she needed to move forward. Her battle-on attitude was like Katie's stepmother's—well intentioned but unhelpful.

"I saw that gynecologist you recommended," she said, "and apparently all my bits and pieces are in good working order and there's no reason we can't have another baby right away. We've been trying."

"Lordy," said Cassandra with a cheeky grin. "Lucky you. You hit the jackpot with Harry, that's for sure. Bloody gorgeous. Do birds flutter down and alight upon his golden head when he stands in the garden?"

Katie giggled. Yes, Harry could charm the birds out of the trees.

It should have been wonderful, the trying. But things had been feeling . . . off-kilter. She'd put Harry's reluctance to make the most of her fertile days down to the stress of starting at Rose Corp. "Let's just do it for pleasure and see what happens," he'd said. "There's no hurry, we've got years ahead of us."

It was true. He was only twenty-two, probably too young to be a dad, and she was only twenty-seven.

But she couldn't ignore the ache, the need to fill the hole that Summer had left. Harry hated sad talk, always turning the conversation to something more cheerful. She tried to get him to open up, reminding him how talking about his parents and brother had helped him deal with their deaths, but this time he just wanted to put it all behind him.

She changed the subject. "So, what's this about Charles? What makes you think he's been . . ."

"Playing away? Darling, they're all at it, you know what they're like. Idiot boys. Two years married and he's already itching." She took a large swig of her Chablis. "I won't lie, Katie, it bloody hurt when I found out, but a word from Mama put me right. Part and parcel of marriage, she said. Grin and bear it, keep up appearances, etc., etc. Rein them in once in a while if scandal threatens. I don't want a bloody divorce, I can tell you that." She raised her glass. "This helps."

"Do you know who? How did you find out?"

"Saw them, would you believe? Just some young thing from work, nothing serious, apparently. Do you think it's better or worse when they say, 'It meant nothing'? I can't decide."

Katie reached across and squeezed her arm.

Cassandra stared at her wineglass, twizzling it around by the stem. "I confronted him and he confessed. Said he'd never do it again. I don't know if I believe him or not, but it doesn't really matter, because the trust has gone now." She sighed. "That's it, Katie. It's gone forever."

"I'm sure it did mean nothing," said Katie. "But, like you say, that's not a great deal of comfort, is it?"

"None."

They both stared at the table, then Katie said, "Do you think that's true, what your mother said? That it's the norm? I couldn't bear it if I found out Harry had been with someone else."

"Yes you could. And you'll probably have to. Let's face it, *everyone* fancies your husband, and he doesn't exactly shun female attention. More fool us for marrying a couple of compulsive flirts. But I don't think you need to worry just yet, darling, he's still besotted." She smiled. "Like I said, lucky you. But you know what? It doesn't do to sit and brood, about husbands, children, or lack thereof—any of it. I know you've been up to your neck in home decorating, but maybe it's time you got out of the house a bit more. Have you thought about going back to work?"

"Perhaps I should. Trouble is, my art history degree's quite useless, and I don't want to go back to cooking for bankers." Katie had worked for a catering company that serviced the dining rooms of several City institutions, including the merchant bank that Charles worked for. "I was wondering about training as a teacher. Primary school, maybe."

"Seriously? You'd be great, darling."

"I was thinking it'd be a good job to fit around a family. If that ever happens."

"Course it'll happen. I tell you what, though. I could probably swing you a job in an art gallery in the meantime, just to get you out of the house. Charles's brother has one on Wardour Street, and if he hasn't got anything, he might know someone who has. With your degree and general loveliness, you'd be marvelous."

"Do you think? That'd be nice, actually."

"Leave it with me."

"Thank you! You're so kind," said Katie.

Cassandra finished her second glass of wine and stood up, the pine bench scraping on the quarry tiles. "I have to dash, darling. Thanks for the wine, I'll see you on your birthday."

"Thanks for popping in, you're always a tonic."

As Katie opened the front door, Cassandra paused in buttoning up her coat. "Would you mind not discussing what I told you with Harry? I don't want him to know, if he doesn't already."

"If you want. I promise."

But Katie wondered what she would do with the information, now that she had it. She really wanted to know what Harry's thoughts would be. Would he excuse Charles's behavior? Harry looked up to his older friend, saw him as a role model. If he found out what he'd been up to, would it be more likely that he, too, might think it was OK to stray?

Cassandra's words echoed in her mind: *They're all at it, you know what they're like. Idiot boys.*

CHAPTER 4

Harry

The taxi driver cursed as a woman loaded with shopping bags stepped off the curb and into his path. "*Jesus Christ!* The crowds are mental this year. You done your Christmas shopping yet, guv?"

"No, I've only just sorted the wife's birthday," replied Harry, looking out at the throngs fighting their way along Oxford Street.

The wife? Why was he speaking like a northern comedian?

Grimly determined office workers weaved through the herds of shoppers stopping to gaze at the Christmas lights overhead. Bob Geldof had switched them on, Harry remembered. The man was having quite a year.

The wet road reflected the headlights of London double-deckers and black cabs; in the yellowy interiors of the buses, commuters sat with their noses buried in their *Evening Standard*s.

As Harry's taxi drew alongside a bus, a girl with Walkman headphones clamped onto moussed blond hair wiped a circle in the steamed-up window and peered through. She caught Harry's eye and smiled, and Harry winked back.

"Did you see the match last night?" said the driver. "What a finish."

Oh no. Harry knew if he was ever to fully understand the British man on the street, he was going to have to watch more football.

"Missed it! Christmas function." It was true. Yesterday's lunch had gone on until seven thirty.

"You a Spurs man, perchance?"

Should he be a Spurs man? It was time he chose a team. He decided to channel Charles, who was far better at all this than he was. "Chelsea, actually."

"You must be well pleased, great season so far."

"Yes, absolutely." Harry needed to change the subject before he was rumbled. "My wife's birthday is less than two weeks before Christmas. I'm never sure whether to get one big present or two smaller ones."

"I'd get two. But they could be connected. Like, a necklace, then the matching earrings for Christmas."

"Excellent idea."

The cab turned off Oxford Street and continued at its snail's pace toward Soho. Harry was meeting Katie, Charles, and Cassandra in the Dog and Duck before they headed to L'Escargot for Katie's birthday dinner. He looked at his watch; he was early. His birthday shopping in Selfridges had been a smash and grab. He'd hovered in the lingerie department but had realized anything focusing attention on the bedroom might not be wise, at present. Too loaded. Maybe she'd think he was trying to send a message—that sex was for entertainment, for pleasure. Whereas she was fixated on getting pregnant again.

She denied it, but he knew her too well. And while he wasn't against it, he was mostly in favor of giving the baby business a rest, for now. He was only twenty-two, and Katie wasn't *old* old. Not biological-clock-ticking old. There was plenty of time.

He wished they could rewind to how they'd been when they were first together. When sex was passionate, spontaneous, fun. Now there was always this unspoken question: Would it *work*?

He sighed and rested his head back. Since Summer, things had shifted. He'd done his best to reinject some of the spontaneity that had led to Katie becoming pregnant in the first place. But trying to be spontaneous was a contradiction in terms.

He'd abandoned lingerie and headed for jewelry, choosing a simple gold heart necklace with a discreet diamond. Very Katie.

The taxi had stopped. In spite of the chill December air, people were standing outside the Dog and Duck. They could well have been there since lunchtime. Harry loved the Christmas vibe of London, when normal office hours (and behavior) were abandoned, replaced by a week or two of lunches that morphed into evening drinks, parties galore, dashing out to shop between times. The sun was long gone by four, the winter darkness giving life to the Christmas lights.

"There you go," he said. "Keep the change. Happy Christmas!"

Harry's mood lifted as he entered the smoky, packed pub. He made his way to the bar, smiling at punters who lifted their drinks out of the way as he squeezed past. "Thanks . . . cheers . . . thanks very much . . ."

He was tall enough to see over most of the heads and quickly established that he was the first of the group to arrive. As well as Charles and Cassandra, Katie's school friend Gemma and her boyfriend, Jonathan, were joining them. Gemma was pleasant enough, but Jonathan was altogether wet. Worked in book publishing and tried too hard to look the part.

"Yes-what-can-I-get-you?"

Harry turned from his recce of the room to order his drink.

"Oh! It's *you*! How hilarious!" said the barmaid.

She looked familiar—petite, with Madonna-esque shaggy blond hair and accessories, including a multitude of chunky necklaces over her black top. She had a wide smile, and her blue eyes gazed directly into Harry's.

He felt a flutter of something. "Sorry? Have we met?"

"Forgotten me already? I was on the bus, you were in the taxi."

"Oh yes, of course!" Harry remembered the smile through the steamy glass.

"You winked."

"Did I?"

"I liked it."

"Good. Well, pint of best, please. And . . . one for yourself."

"Thanks! I'm Bennie. And you?"

"Harry."

She took a glass and pulled the giant pump handle toward her.

"How did you get here so fast?" asked Harry. "I'm sure we overtook you."

"I got off and cut through. I was late, stupid bleedin' Christmas shoppers—I couldn't get on the first bus."

"Do you have to come far?"

"Camden."

"Ah. I'm not familiar with the frozen north. I live in Fulham."

"Course you do!" She placed the pint on the brass drip tray. "One sixty-five, please."

Harry handed over two of the pound coins that had recently replaced the old pound notes. "What do you mean, of course I do?"

"It's where all you lot live, innit? Fulham, Clapham, Battersea."

"Nonsense. I have friends all over. Hampstead, St. John's Wood . . . um, Holland Park, Blackheath . . ."

"Sloane Square?"

"Oh well, yah," he said, parodying himself. "All the rest live there."

"But only during the week," said Bennie, "before they head to the *kent-reh* for weekends."

Harry usually found this sort of inverted snobbery tiresome, but he was enjoying sparring with Bennie. He liked the mixture of fun and challenge in her eyes.

She was also extremely pretty.

"Sorry, gotta serve the punters. It's gonna be a mad night. Will you be sticking around? Are you on your own?"

"Meeting friends."

Why hadn't he said "my wife"? Because it would have sounded like a brush-off, and he didn't want this harmless flirtation to end.

"Harry, old boy!"

He felt a hand on his shoulder and turned to see Charles looking across the bar at Bennie, who had just rolled her eyes. "Chatting up the barmaid as per? Mine's a pint, if you'd be so kind."

"This your friend?" said Bennie.

"Meet Charles. He lives in Clapham," said Harry, and they shared a grin.

"What's the joke?" said Charles.

"Bennie here seems to think I'm posh," said Harry. "Tell her I'm just your average chap, will you, Charles? Are the girls here?"

"Not yet. Cass rang—they're running late. Couldn't get a taxi."

Over the music system, the Pet Shop Boys were singing about West End girls and East End boys, and Bennie was mouthing along to the words. She passed Charles his beer. "You *are* posh boys. Where did you go to school?"

"Don't tell her," said Charles, entering into the spirit. "Where did *you* go to school?"

"The local comp. That means *com-pree-hen-sive*, by the way."

"Baha! Bet you had a better time than we did, eh, Harry?"

"Well," said Bennie, "I suppose we didn't have cold baths, or get whipped or bug—"

"I'll have you know, things have moved on a bit since Dickens," said Charles.

"Have they?" said Harry. "Were you not whipped, Charles?"

"Well? *Were* you, Chaaarles?" added Bennie, imitating Harry's drawl.

"The cane was Mr. Fotherington's punishment of choice," said Charles. "He gave great cane. Really enjoyed himself. Nothing like a good spanking, what?"

"Oh my god, public schools are so perverted. Why would anyone send a precious child to one?" said Bennie.

"It's what put the Great in Britain, sweetheart," said Charles. "Loaded us with pluck and fortitude."

"Fuck's sake."

"Hello, Charles, Harry."

Harry noticed Bennie's eyes slide down to his arm, which Katie had just hooked her hand under.

"Nice talking to you . . . *chaps*," she said with a grin, before moving off down the bar.

"Hello," Harry said, kissing Katie's cheek. "Drink?"

"I think the barmaid's gone. Must've been something I said," replied Katie. "Having fun, were you?"

The possessive tone wasn't like Katie. It was just a bit of banter with a barmaid, for god's sake.

"Yes, actually. She *was* fun."

The implication hung in the air.

He caught the hurt in Katie's eyes, and guilt rushed in. She was looking lovely tonight. He'd become used to seeing her in overalls as she rubbed down a piece of pine furniture or rag-rolled another wall on her mission to create the perfect home. Tonight, a leaf-green cashmere jumper with a string of pearls set off her creamy complexion, and her blue eyes were accentuated by a tasteful touch of mascara. Her shiny dark red hair was clipped loosely back, and a dab of gloss made her lips gleam in the cozy pub lighting.

He draped an arm around her shoulder and pulled her close, kissing her hair. "You look gorgeous. Actually, you too, Cass."

"You three, Harry," said Cassandra with a grin.

"Me four?" said Charles.

"How's your birthday been?" Harry asked.

He sensed Katie relax as Charles attempted to catch the attention of another barmaid.

"Lovely. I met Stepmama—we went up to Harvey Nicks and she bought me these." She held up a foot, on which was a red lace-up ankle boot.

"Ye gods, that's a breakaway from your usual look," said Harry.

"I thought it was time I explored my wilder side."

"Go, Katie!" said Cassandra. "No more Mrs. Nice Girl!"

"Steady on," said Charles, returning with the drinks. "Katie's the nicest girl I know. If she loses her nice, my faith in humanity will disappear."

"Here's Gemma and Jonathan," said Cassandra as a tall, thin man with thick-framed glasses pushed his way toward them, followed by a matching thin, dark-haired woman.

"Hi, everyone! Happy birthday, Katie," called Gemma, peering around Jonathan's back. "Sorry we're late, dreadful traffic."

"Terrible," said Jonathan. "Christmas should be banned."

"Happy Christmas, Ebenezer," said Harry, holding out his hand. Jonathan's felt limp and slightly damp.

"Gemma, how the devil are you?"

She blushed. "Fine thank you, Harry. Lovely to see you."

Gemma was pleasant enough, but rather boring. Harry was glad Katie got on so well with Cassandra, who was much jollier.

Although . . . he wasn't sure how much the two girls shared about their personal lives. Charles had told him how Cassandra had discovered his latest affair, and Harry hoped she hadn't told Katie. He didn't want her thinking badly of Charles, didn't want at some point to have to explain how Charles's indiscretions had nothing to do with his relationship with Cassandra, that it didn't mean he loved her any the less. Katie wouldn't understand that, he felt sure.

His eyes moved back to Bennie, who was deftly filling glasses with one hand, while dropping slices of lemon into glasses with the other.

"Well, Harry?" said Cassandra.

"Sorry, what was that?"

Cassandra's eyes fell on Bennie before narrowing and meeting his. "I asked what time the table was booked for."

"Oh, eight. Plenty of time yet."

"Jonathan, how's the book trade?" said Katie. "What should I be reading?"

"*The Bone People*, of course."

Harry bristled. The "of course" was unutterably smug. No doubt Jonathan would assume Harry and Charles were thrillers men.

"Is that the one that won the Booker?" said Katie. "I've heard it's quite a difficult read."

"Well if you want something easy, there's always Danielle Steel or Jackie Collins."

"I'm more of a Winnie-the-Pooh man," said Charles.

"I'd recommend Sidney Sheldon and Freddie Forsyth for you boys."

Good god. The man was insufferable. He knew the type—grammar school chippy.

Even Katie was looking uncomfortable now, and Harry sensed Cassandra getting hot under her turned-up collar.

"I read *The Bone People*," said Cassandra. "No way would I recommend it to someone who's been through so much this year."

"Hear, hear," said Charles. "A pox on depressing stories. Give me good old Wodehouse any day."

"You should all read the new Margaret Atwood, *The Handmaid's Tale*," said Gemma.

"Already have. Excellent if terrifying read," said Harry.

"Talking of dystopian future scenarios, did you know this pub was George Orwell's local?" said Jonathan, attempting to grab back the high-brow ground.

"Yes, but he was a bit shit really," said Harry. "I mean—*1984* is *so* last year."

Everyone laughed, except Jonathan.

"Look, quick—a table," said Cassandra.

As they made their way over, Katie took Harry's hand and squeezed it. "Game, set, and match to you, darling. And . . . thanks for organizing this." Her smile was the sweetest thing.

CHAPTER 5

Harry

Harry had just dropped Katie off at the Lisle Gallery, which was run by Charles's brother Angus. He hoped the interview would go well, though he suspected the job was already in the bag.

He'd finished at Rose Corp. for the Christmas break, and they were off to Gloucestershire that afternoon. As he nosed the TVR back onto Wardour Street, he was reminded of his last visit to Soho. He glanced at the dashboard. One o'clock. Their bags were packed and the Christmas shopping was done. Or rather, Katie had done it all and he'd bought her the matching earrings.

He had some time to kill. Maybe he'd have a quick drink before heading back to Fulham.

The noise level in the Dog and Duck was deafening as he pushed his way toward the bar. When he spotted Bennie's shaggy blond head, he was at once delighted and dismayed. He was prepared to admit she was the reason he'd come in, but had a premonition his future life would be less complicated had she not been working today.

He should turn around, right now. He stopped, and a woman crashed into his back.

"Excuse me, please." The voice was cross.

"Sorry there, I'll get out of your way." Harry smiled.

"Oh." The woman's eyes widened, and she blushed. "No problem. Happy Christmas!"

Harry changed direction, heading toward the gents.

As he came out again he was still conflicted. Go right, toward the door, or left, toward the bar? He stood still as his conscience argued the toss with his less cerebral instincts.

Then all at once it was out of his hands.

"Harry!" Bennie had appeared in front of him, several glasses in each hand. "Can't keep away, eh? I'll serve you if you can fight your way through. It's a bleedin' madhouse today."

"Hello again . . . Bennie, isn't it?" Like he didn't remember. "Great. I'll just sharpen my elbows."

Harry parked himself in the corner of the bar with his copy of the *Times* and a pint of best. Katie was taking a taxi home after her interview, so as long as he was home by three, he should be fine.

Bennie somehow managed to serve the stream of Christmas revelers and stay cheerful, and popped across to chat during occasional lulls.

She intrigued him. She was streetwise, sassy; so different from most of the girls he knew.

"You remind me of Madonna," he said. "In a good way."

She hopped onto a stool and looked up at him through lashes thickly coated in mascara. "Madonna's pretty cool. Have you seen *Desperately Seeking Susan*?"

"Can't say that I have. Not really my cup of tea."

"So what *is* your cup of Earl Grey, Harry? No . . . let me guess. James Bond? Indiana Jones? What *do* toffs watch?"

"Beware of pigeonholing. One is not a toff. I enjoyed *Out of Africa*. Have you seen that?"

"Bloody *loved* it! So romantic. I would have run off with Robert Redford like a shot. And that washing-the-hair scene was the *biggest* turn-on. Oh god, I want someone golden-haired and handsome to wash my hair like that." She blinked her long eyelashes.

"Your hair looks perfectly clean to me."

"It could be cleaner."

Harry couldn't tear his gaze from her intense blue eyes. *Look away!* screamed his conscience.

"Bennie," said a guy behind her. "Dave's here. You can go now."

"Cheers, Luke. Just as well, I'm buggered." She hopped off the stool and looked at Harry again. "Only one more shift before Christmas, thank god. Want to walk with me to the bus stop?"

He shouldn't. He was still safe while she was on that side of the bar.

"Come on, Harry. Look at everyone having a good time, and here's me on my lonesome."

"Are you going home for Christmas?"

"Course! But not until tomorrow."

She disappeared into a room behind the bar, and Harry slowly folded his newspaper and downed the rest of his pint.

He could leave now and never come back.

He folded his paper again, and then again, forming it into a manageable, neat shape he could slip under his arm, smoothing it out between each fold.

He lifted his pint, in case there was a last sip not to be wasted.

"This way, it's quicker," came Bennie's voice next to him.

She led the way out of a back door that opened into a pedestrian alleyway. Suddenly they were out of the noise and smoke and into the quiet crispness of a bright winter's afternoon.

Bennie stopped to put on her denim jacket, flicking the collar up, and took a pair of black silky gloves out of the pockets. She slipped them on, smoothing them over her hands.

She took some deep breaths. "Ah, fresh air. Jeez, it's so smoky in there. Maybe one day they'll ban smoking in pubs." She grabbed a handful of her hair and sniffed it. "Disgusting. Gonna have to wash it. Maybe you should come and do that for me, Harry? With a bowl of water and a jug, like Robert did for Meryl. Actually, you look a bit like Robert

Redford. Except you're better looking." She grinned. That direct gaze again. And now that she was out from behind the bar, he was able to fully appreciate the figure-hugging jeans tucked into boots with killer heels.

"I have to go, Bennie. We're driving to Gloucestershire this afternoon. But it was fun. Maybe I'll pop in again. I work on the South Bank, but my wife's probably going to be working in Wardour Street."

There, he'd said it. *Wife*. He'd drawn the line.

"*Glor-ster-shaar*. Should've guessed. Is that where *mater and pater* live?"

He chuckled. It wasn't a bad Harry impression. Was she choosing to ignore the part about his wife?

"My parents died, I'm afraid. It's where Katie's parents live."

"Oh my god. Your parents died? Harry, you poor bloke." She reached out and touched his arm, came closer.

It was the sympathy in her eyes that demolished his resolve. As her hand slid from his arm to his waist, he pulled her toward him, and then he was kissing her, and it was heaven. At first tentative and sweet, exploring her soft lips, then she was on her toes and pulling his head down as the kiss became urgent, hungry.

Finally they pulled apart, breathless, and Harry gently took her chin in his hand. "Happy Christmas, Bennie. And now I really have to go."

"Yes, I suppose you do, Harry. But you really have to come back."

And he did. Again and again.

At first, Katie enjoyed working at the gallery. Life was good. The staff and clients were lovely, the work was interesting, and she was thrilled to discover she was pregnant again. But after miscarrying at three months, she became increasingly down. In spite of Harry's encouragement, she abandoned all thought of teacher training. Eventually she was only going through the motions with her job—she just didn't have the energy.

Sex was loaded with unspoken emotion. They no longer seemed able to talk things through. The connection between Harry and Katie frayed, and neither knew how to weave it back together.

To Harry's dismay, Katie turned for comfort to her Catholic faith (Harry had lost any belief in God when his mother died). She shifted from lukewarm to ardent as she searched for meaning in what she'd come to regard as her pointless, childless life. After another miscarriage, nothing could shift the hopelessness.

"Why is God doing this to us?" she'd ask. "Why do I keep losing babies? Are we meant never to have a child?"

After Harry's initial attempts to help her through (and he did try, in spite of his other . . . commitment), he began spending less time at home and more at work, where his enthusiasm for the job and network of useful contacts saw him achieving success alongside Uncle Richard at the helm of Rose Corp. Work problems were easier to overcome than home ones.

And then there was Bennie, whose laughing eyes were the perfect antidote to Katie's, which were full of sadness. Katie's depression was too much for Harry. The ties that bound them were hanging by a thread.

Then, Katie got pregnant again, and this time, everything went perfectly.

Harry was a father.

CHAPTER 6

Katie

March 1988

> *"The King of Spain's daughter*
> *Came to visit me,*
> *And all for the sake*
> *Of my little nut tree."*

As Katie ended the nursery rhyme, Maria's eyes closed. Katie gazed down at her daughter and offered up a silent prayer of thanks. God had blessed them after all, and she was filled with such joy she felt reborn, as new as her four-week-old baby.

The prayer of thanks was also because said child was, at last, asleep. The silence of the darkened bedroom after a day of grizzling was exquisite.

Harry had wanted to name her Elizabeth, after his mother, but when Katie had discovered Maria meant "wished-for child," as well as being a solid Catholic name, he'd let her have her way. Katie had proposed Elizabeth as a middle name, but Harry suggested they kept it "in reserve" in case they had a second daughter. Katie smiled as she remembered his words, no longer loaded with the angst of childlessness.

Maria was lying on her back, her rosebud lips slightly parted, her head turned to one side. Katie leaned over and gently stroked her cheek. The skin was so soft it was barely there, and touching it filled her with a deep peace. She gazed at the tiny hands with their micro-nails, resting to either side of her head.

Finally moving away from the bassinet, Katie sank down onto her bed. It was seven o'clock, and she was wrung out. This new kind of exhaustion was so overwhelming it gave the older kinds a glow of nostalgia. After-work tired? Yes, please—fifteen minutes rustling up something to eat, then your time was your own. *Your own.* After-exercise tired? Delicious. A hot shower and then your feet up, for as long as you needed.

It seemed so long since she'd been able to watch TV or read a book without the menace of a baby monitor, ready to crackle to life and launch her into the next round of feeding, changing, and putting back to sleep. Then there was the emotion of it all, veering between joy and despair. In spite of her euphoria at having a healthy child, Katie was aware of her old enemy, depression, lurking in the wings. Her father had died in January, enabling it to take a few more stealthy steps toward her.

Its cousin, worry, was a constant presence too. Was Maria getting enough milk? How were you meant to know the difference between an "I'm too hot" cry, an "I'm hungry" one, and "I just want a cuddle"?

"Relax!" Harry would say as she fretted over how many layers to wrap Maria in. "Babies have been surviving too-thick cardigans for centuries."

Germaine, who seemed remarkably unmoved by the loss of her husband (but then she'd rarely seen him—Ferdie loved to travel) had come to stay after Katie's return from the hospital and had tried to persuade Katie to employ a nanny, having always had a houseful of staff herself. She'd refused. She wasn't sharing Maria with another woman.

Unfortunately, Cassandra agreed with Germaine, and she suspected Harry did too. It was the norm in their circles, after all. Cass now had two children under the age of two, looked after by a highly competent nanny installed immediately after the birth of Thing One, as Cassandra called her eldest (real name Milly). She'd advised Katie to do the same "if you ever want a life again."

But Katie had dug her heels in. *This* was life. She'd handed in her notice at the gallery; she was going to be a full-time mum.

In spite of the tiredness and the emotional roller coaster, the baby had mended things between Katie and Harry. Their apprehension that something would go wrong again, then their overwhelming joy when their perfect daughter was born—it had brought them back together.

Katie sighed in tired contentment, picturing a future of trips to the zoo and walks in the park, Maria sitting on Harry's broad shoulders, Katie perhaps pushing another baby in a buggy. Weekends in the country, summers in Tuscany with Cassandra, Charles, Thing One, and Thing Two (real name Arabella).

She ought to start preparing dinner—Harry had said he'd be home "early," by which he meant before eight—but she was inclined to sit here just a little while longer, staring at her gift from God, breathing in that delicious baby smell.

Her daydreaming was interrupted by the phone ringing downstairs.

It was Harry. "Sorry, Katie, something's come up. The viscountess isn't happy with the piece in this month's *Hooray!* The editor thinks I should be able to talk her round, one-on-one, but it's going to cost me dinner, which will no doubt consist of humble pie."

"What's her problem with it?"

"Just a lack of fawning obsequiousness. Bloody aristocrats. Sorry, have to dash—taxi's here. Give Maria a kiss for me."

"I will. She's been crying all—"

But Harry was gone. As Katie put the phone down, the silence of the house no longer felt exquisite. A long evening alone stretched ahead.

She should have welcomed it. She didn't have to worry about cooking something special, could snack in front of the TV instead. But the solitude hung heavy. Harry was out there, buttering up Viscountess Doo-dah, who was probably gorgeous and would undoubtedly think Harry the same, while the most she had to look forward to was *East-*

Enders or a video she'd already seen. Was this how things would be, now that she was a mum?

Piling a tray with dips and nibbles, she settled down on the sofa, shifting uncomfortably—her breasts were sore.

She stared past the TV at a watercolor on the wall, of an English village. As she appreciated how the artist had captured the evening sunlight, a thought came to her. Perhaps they should move to the country. Harry had the Surrey estate he'd inherited, but it was far too big for just the three of them and was currently leased to a sheik. Perhaps they could sell it and buy a pretty cottage within easy commuting distance, in a lovely village where Maria—and future brothers and sisters—could go to the local primary before heading off to a suitable boarding school.

She smiled to herself. Surely Harry would see; this could be the perfect way forward to a happy family life.

Harry

August 1989

Harry cut through St. Paul's churchyard en route to Covent Garden, where he was meeting a *Sunday Times* journalist for lunch. The ten-minute walk from the Strand was part of his more-exercise initiative, launched in response to Charles's recent ribbing about a small but definitely there paunch. He glanced down and saw the little bugger, peeping over his waistband.

He passed a group of female office workers sitting on the grass, their skirts hoisted up, making the most of the sunny lunchtime. Kylie Minogue blared from a transistor, and a curvy brunette with big hair sang along, giving him the eye.

Harry grinned back and winked. He loved London in the summer.

The article was going to be in next week's Sunday supplement. Harry the newsman was, apparently, news himself. Nigel Dempster had recently described him in the *Daily Express* as "Britain's answer to Rupert Murdoch, but far easier on the eye."

"More of a Richard Branson, but with better hair," Charles had said.

Copies of Rose's new magazine *Hooray!* (or "*Tatler* for plebs," as Charles called it) were flying off the newsstands, sharing with the British public the weddings, gracious homes, and bundles of joy of movie stars, footballers' wives, and aristocrats. Celebrity culture had begun, and it seemed Harry was part of it. A full-page photo under the heading *PROUD PARENTS HARRY AND KATIE INTRODUCE BABY MARIA TO THE WORLD* had featured in the launch issue, and as a result his office had been inundated with requests for interviews. His PR manager, Zadie, had advised him to go exclusive with the *Sunday Times Magazine*, negotiating the cover story spot.

At Maxwell's, a waitress indicated a table where a woman with sleek black hair, large-framed red glasses, and matching lipstick was sitting. She rose and held out her hand. The pointy nails were red too.

"Harry, great to meet you. Terri Robbins-More." Her accent was broad Yorkshire.

She was attractive, but he drew the line at journalists. There were enough of those back at Totty Tower, as cabdrivers called Rose Corp.'s offices. Nevertheless, he'd turn on the charm during the interview. Relationships with reporters were important.

Terri

What an up-himself upper-class twat, thought Terri, as she hailed a taxi back to Wapping. And how aggravating that the magazine editor wanted a puff piece about the new young gun in town, rather than anything insightful. Probably went to the same bloody school or university.

The taxi pulled over, and she barked her destination at the driver.

If only she could dig up some dirt. But in her background research, people had nothing but good to say about the media's current golden boy.

Harry Rose had got where he was through family money, the old-boy network, good looks, and charm. He'd married an equally posh girl from an equally rich family. He wasn't stupid, but he was no Stephen Hawking. Though, when she'd asked, "What book is on your bedside table?" he'd answered, "*A Brief History of Time*." It was the year's must-read.

"What do you make of it?" Terri had asked.

"Haven't had time to read it," Harry had said, laughing heartily at his own joke.

Arse. But she'd chuckled along because, in spite of his charm and boyish good looks, there was something unsettling about Harry Rose, and she was intrigued, wanting to probe deeper.

Was there a darker side to him? A ruthless streak? He'd probably need one to survive at the top. Perhaps bluff Harry, good bloke Harry, was a smoke screen.

He may be heir to a media empire, but he'd had little to say about current affairs. He'd talked a lot about trends, brands, target markets, rather than about anything that was actually important, like the profound changes taking place in the Soviet Union, or the fact that Margaret bloody Thatcher had been in power for ten long years now, and look at the state of the north after so many pit closures.

Harry had probably never been to the north.

Terri, from a working-class Sheffield family, had clawed her way to the top, and she wasn't going along with this upper-class bollocks, one media company rubbing another's back. When she got back to the office, she'd do a little digging, whether they liked it or not.

Harry

Harry, Katie, and Maria were en route to London Zoo. The interview a few days ago had gone well. It always helped when the journalist was female.

Katie was staring stonily out of the window of the car sent to fetch them, while Maria sat buckled between them, gabbling nonsense to her favorite fluffy rabbit toy, Tog. It was unlike Katie not to be joining in.

Harry had to admit, he hadn't handled telling Katie about the photo shoot at all well. Thanks to his burgeoning commitments, he'd spent next to no "quality time," as people were now calling it, with his little family these past few months. Katie had initially been enthusiastic about the trip to the zoo, assuming Harry was trying to make up for recent neglect. But when he'd mentioned that the *Sunday Times* wanted to follow them around, she'd accused him of needing his family "only when it was useful for PR purposes." That had hurt.

The taxi dropped them at the zoo offices, and a girl from the press office came to meet them. The photographer and his assistant were already there. They introduced themselves as Alex and Ken.

"Hi, I'm Sue," said the press officer. She wore stripy trousers and a ruffled white blouse, and her dark hair was clipped up with two pearly combs. "I thought we might go to the Children's Zoo?"

"Oh, I rather fancied being photographed with a tiger!" said Harry.

"Sorry, Mr. Rose, we don't have many animals that are handleable, I'm afraid."

"What about an elephant?" said Harry.

"Lelefant!" said Maria.

Sue crouched down. "Hello there. Who's this?" she said, pointing to Tog.

Maria hid behind Katie's legs.

"Would you like to meet a real rabbit?" said Sue, and Maria peeped around. She nodded shyly.

"Is that OK?" Sue asked the photographer.

"Could've just gone to a pet shop," he said grumpily.

"I can see if the keepers might let Harry hold a baby chimp that's being hand-reared?"

"That's more like it," said Ken.

After a quick phone call, Sue reported the chimp would be available in half an hour and suggested a visit to the Children's Zoo in the meantime.

Harry fell into step beside her as they walked. "I suppose you get a lot of twits like me asking to meet a tiger?"

"People forget they're still wild animals," Sue replied diplomatically. "Some people are adopting animals now. We sometimes have to explain they can't actually borrow them."

"Adopting?"

"You pay toward their upkeep and get your name on a plaque. Paul Young's got a fruit bat. And Simon Le Bon might be adopting a tiger—a bit of one, anyway. A whole one's expensive."

"Pop star one-upmanship! Love it. We could do a feature in *Hooray!* Can I get someone to ring you?"

"Sure, that'd be great."

"Who else have you had in?"

"We name our giraffes after British sports personalities." They were passing the giraffe enclosure. "That baby one's named after Eddie the Eagle."

"Iconic sportsman," said Harry.

Sue grinned. "Too right."

Katie, pushing Maria in her buggy, had fallen behind and was chatting with Ken and Alex.

"Sorry it's such a long walk. The Children's Zoo's across the other side," said Sue as they entered the tunnel beneath the Outer Circle.

Harry was about to reply, but his words caught in his throat. It couldn't be . . .

Like a rabbit caught in headlights, Harry halted abruptly. Then reason intervened and he stopped panicking. Bennie, coming toward him, would just walk on by. What was he worrying about?

Bennie's eyes widened in surprise. Harry gave a small shake of his head and carried on past her.

"Oh, hello there!"

What the heck? Harry stopped and half turned, looking back.

Bennie was level with Katie.

"It's Bennie, isn't it?" said Katie. "From the Dog and Duck?"

Harry took a few steps toward them, praying Bennie would find a way to move on quickly.

"I used to come in when I was at the gallery in Wardour Street. Fancy bumping into you here! I left to have this little one. And I see you've got one about the same age!"

Bennie's eyes briefly settled on Maria, then she bent down to her own buggy and pulled Henry's beanie further down over his face and tucked his blanket up around his neck. All that was visible of the little chap was his eyes and nose.

Come on, Bennie—finish it!

"Yes, I remember you," she said, "and that other bloke—Angus? Well, um, nice to see you again. Sorry, but I have to dash. Late already!"

She went to move off, but little Henry, far too warm, whipped off his hat in one swift movement, throwing it on the ground, then pulled the blanket down, revealing Maria's hair, Maria's eyes, and Maria's smile.

Then the toddler caught sight of Harry, whose eyes were flicking between the two children in horror.

"Dadda!" he cried, holding out his arms with an enormous grin.

Time stood still. Katie paled and Bennie froze, staring at her son.

Harry had no idea what to do next.

Then it was as if someone pressed Play and Bennie whirred back to life. "Hahaha, silly Henry. That's not Daddy. Sorry, um . . ."

"Harry. Actually, I think I remember you from the pub too."

"Do you? Well, sorry, Harry, he's going through this phase where he calls every bloke about your age Dadda. It's really embarrassing!" She bent down to Henry. "That's Harry, not Dadda."

Harry's laugh was forced, and he knew Katie knew. But the photographers and the press officer were laughing heartily, and Sue, bless her, said, "My little brother did that for a while. My parents love reminding him about it."

"Yeah, well, see you around maybe," said Bennie. "Enjoy the zoo!"

She set off again, little Henry craning his neck around the side of the buggy.

CHAPTER 7

Katie

The child, Henry—Harry's father's name—could have been Maria's identical twin. And Harry had turned white as a sheet. Apple White, in fact. White with a hint of nausea.

Sue, Ken, and Alex may have fallen for the "he calls everyone Dadda" explanation, but Katie knew it was a lie. She'd barely heard the words above the rushing in her ears.

How she got through the rest of the day, she'd never know. It was an out-of-body experience, smiling alongside Harry, playing at happy families. The only outward sign of the turmoil in her head was her shaking hands. As she buttoned up Maria's jacket, Harry noticed them, and his eyes briefly flew to hers and she saw the guilt.

But then he carried on laughing and joking with the press team, posing like a catalog model. No one could have guessed he was waiting for the storm to break.

Harry hadn't looked her in the eye since, and now the photographer was packing up and the press officer was saying her goodbyes.

Katie wondered how the rest of her life would be. It was about to start right now.

The three of them were alone, and Harry set off wordlessly toward the exit, pushing Maria.

Katie walked alongside. Who would speak first?

Soon they were out of the gate and on the Outer Circle, Harry scanning the road for a taxi. There were none in sight.

He flicked the brakes on the buggy and finally turned toward her. "Katie—"

"I want the truth," she interrupted. "None of your usual bullshit."

Harry looked taken aback, and Katie felt a pang of regret. She rarely used even slightly offensive language. Already, she was changed.

"How long has it been going on? Are you still seeing her?" She was surprised at the strength in her voice. As she said the words, she realized that, deep in her heart, she'd suspected something for a while now. The absences, the working late. Harry's distracted air, the distance between them.

She'd suspected *something*, but not a child.

"Since the Christmas after we lost Summer."

Nearly four years? Katie pulled her jacket tighter around her. Her hands were still shaking.

"I'm so sorry, Katie. It was . . . things weren't great between us, if you remember, and Bennie was so . . . uncomplicated and easy to be with. She made everything less painful—"

"Like I did when your parents died."

"Yes, sort of. And I'll never forget how you made me feel better." He raised his hand slightly, as if to touch her, then dropped it again.

"Go on."

"She didn't want anything from me, just my company. And we had fun, while you and I . . . we seemed to have lost that. It was wrong, I know, but I just needed somewhere to go, someone to talk to." His eyes pleaded with her to understand.

Anger was rising up Katie's gullet, like monstrous, seething black bile. She swallowed it back down. She'd wait until she was home before she let it all out.

"You haven't answered the other question. Do you still see her?"

"Sometimes. Not often, though."

"Often enough for that child to know you're its father. Were you together when we were expecting Maria? When she was born?" Katie's breathing was shallow and fast. "Has it been going on all through that time? Because, Harry, you say you needed someone who was easy to be with. And I thought we were happy then. I thought everything was good between us."

"It was. When Maria was born I was going to end it, but then . . . I couldn't abandon Bennie when she was pregnant. You can understand that?"

Katie said nothing. The days after Maria's birth had been some of the happiest of her life. Now those memories were tarnished by betrayal. Forever. Harry had ruined everything.

"I don't know what to believe. Probably nothing you say, ever again."

"Look . . ." Harry paused to wave down a taxi. "We can't do this now. Let's talk properly when we get home."

The taxi set off toward Fulham, Maria now asleep. Katie stared out of one window and Harry out of the other. Keeping the anger at bay was allowing the heartbreak in. Tears ran down Katie's face, and she didn't bother to brush them away.

The next two hours were taken up with the routines of feeding, bathing, and putting to bed. Katie was on autopilot, blocking painful thoughts as she went about the familiar tasks, taking a small degree of comfort in them.

Finally she joined Harry in the living room, where he was watching the evening news. He sat up straighter and looked up as she came in. "Katie—"

"Before you ask me what I'm going to do, I don't know. But tell me, do you love her?"

Harry looked away, stared at the floor. "Not in the way I love you."

Something inside Katie snapped. She'd never lost control in her life, until now. She picked up the nearest thing to hand, which was a copy of *Hooray!*, rolled it up, and hit Harry across his shoulders.

He raised his arms to protect himself. "Katie—for god's sake! That's not going to solve anything."

"No, but it's making me feel a whole lot better," she said, delivering more blows.

"Then hit away, if domestic abuse is your thing. Let it all out, and then maybe we can move on."

His smug comment gave Katie renewed energy, and she hit him again.

She was grimly satisfied when the stupid magazine bent into a state where it was of no further use as a truncheon. She dropped it on the floor, saying, "Piece-of-shit magazine made of terrible paper."

Harry chuckled. "True."

"I'm not laughing, Harry." She sank into an armchair.

"Shall I get us a drink?" said Harry.

"I don't want a fucking drink."

"Katie, stop it. None of this is you."

"It's what you've made me."

"Look, I'm sorry. Henry was an accident, but you of all people will understand that Bennie didn't want to get rid of the baby. What was I supposed to do? Try and persuade her to have an abortion? Abandon her? I was trying to do the right thing."

"Of course you were. You always *try to do the right thing*. You twist things until you can justify your actions. Have you never heard of contraception? Or of not sleeping around in the first place?"

"Her pills . . . she wasn't great at remembering. Quite absentminded."

The words cut like a knife. She and Harry had never used contraception. He'd suggested she go on the pill after Maria's birth, but Katie had wanted to leave matters in God's hands. Trying *not* to have a baby was a completely alien concept.

"How often did you see her?"

"Only occasionally."

"Define occasionally."

"Maybe once a month? Recently, anyway."

"And at the start?"

"A bit more. That was when things weren't great between you and me."

"So it was *my* fault you hooked up with her?"

"I didn't say that. I'm giving you a reason, not an excuse."

"So what are you going to do, Harry?"

"I'll end it, but I can't abandon her completely. Or my son. I'll give her a regular allowance for Henry."

"What's she doing for money? Does she have a job?"

Harry looked uncomfortable. "I've been covering the rent on her flat, and a bit more, until she can sort out childcare. It's difficult for her, she doesn't have any qualifications."

Another rush of anger. "She's a barmaid, for god's sake! You don't need qualifications for that. Apart from badly dyed blond hair and cheap clothes. How much have you been paying your *prostitute*?" She spat it out.

"That's not worthy of you, Katie."

"Perhaps you don't know me anymore. You've hardly been here, so that would make sense."

They seemed to have reached an impasse, and a heavy silence filled the room. Katie's eyes slid past Harry's lowered ones to the wall beyond, to the painting of the English village.

"I want to move to the country."

He looked up in surprise. "What? Why?"

"It'll be better for Maria, and it'll be a fresh start. We'll move to somewhere with a fast commuter link, have a new life, more children. I'm terribly hurt, Harry, and angry, but I don't want a divorce. I'll never divorce you. It's against everything I believe in, and . . . despite everything, I still love you."

"I don't want a divorce either, Katie. I still love you too. You believe that, don't you? But must we *really* move out of town?"

When she didn't answer, he continued. "It's difficult to explain, about Bennie. I guess I just needed someone to be with who wasn't part of my normal life."

"Isn't it more because she wasn't doing it to get pregnant? Because that's what the problem was, right? You wanted all the fun and none of the angst and responsibility. Must've been a terrible shock when you found out you were going to have not one but two children."

"Look, we're only going round in circles now. I'm not against the idea of moving, though we'd have to sell Berryhurst."

"Give the tenants notice. I don't want to wait, Harry. I'm done with London. I've been mostly unhappy here."

"Unhappy?" Harry looked stung. "Why would you have been un-happy?"

"Recovering from Summer's death? Two miscarriages? Coping with Maria by myself because you were never home? How was I supposed to be happy?"

"A comfortable life, nice job, good friends? Doesn't any of that count? For Chrissake, Katie, there's more to life than babies."

"Family is *everything* to me, Harry. Do you not understand that, af-ter all these years?"

They stared at each other, until Harry dropped his eyes.

Katie felt calmer for having released the bile. But she also felt a deep, gut-wrenching sadness that Harry had driven her to behave in a way that wasn't her. She was a kind, gentle person. Everyone said so. Now she felt the last of her old, trusting self evaporate into the ether, replaced by a person she'd never expected to be. Suspicious, angry. A little spiteful. She hadn't meant what she'd said about being unhappy. There had been plenty of good times. Those words had been squarely aimed at Harry's precious conscience, designed to hurt.

She hated that he'd done this to her. Hated that she'd never again be able to give herself, heart and soul, to Harry. From now on she'd always hold something back.

CHAPTER 8

———∞∞∞———

Katie

S top fretting, darling," Cassandra said as Katie watched the nanny pushing Maria on a toddler swing. "Look away! Look at *me*. Tell me all your gossip." She pushed her sunglasses up onto her head and widened her eyes at Katie.

Things One and Two were at their grandparents', and Cassandra had come over to have lunch with Katie, bringing her nanny, Debbie, to take care of Maria. They'd brought sandwiches and a bottle of wine to the park.

"You haven't heard, then?"

"About what?" Cassandra leaned forward across the picnic table. "You got something juicy for me?"

"Doesn't get much juicier." Katie gave a strangled laugh, then said, "Well, I can't say you didn't warn me."

Cassandra's smile disappeared. "Oh. Oh, shit."

There was something about the way she said it, about the way she sat back a little, as if taking cover from what was to come. As if she knew what that was.

"You knew. Oh my god, you knew."

"What are we talking about here?" Cassandra didn't meet Katie's eye.

Katie was silent. A thousand thoughts scrambled for attention. Cass had betrayed her too. And almost certainly Charles. An iciness was creeping through her veins.

Who else knew?

"The wife's always the last to know, so they say."

"Katie, I—"

"How long have you known?" Her voice was flat. She expected to feel anger, but there was only sorrow.

"Oh god, Katie, I'm so sorry you found out. Believe me, when Charles told me, I drove myself mad wondering what to do. He begged me not to tell you, said it wouldn't help anyone. But, Katie, I had no idea it was still going on. How did you find out? That's if he's still with . . . I've forgotten her name."

Katie wasn't fooled. Cassandra had been about to mention a name, but if it *hadn't* been whoever that was, that would mean more than one other woman. *Had* there been more than one? Katie felt the world shift beneath her feet again. All these years, no matter what they'd been through, she'd thought, deep down, she and Harry were solid as a rock. But there had been an earthquake.

"It's a barmaid," she said. "Terrible cliché, I know. And she's even a badly dyed blonde." She looked down at her hands in her lap. They were shaking. "I used to know her, actually. She worked in the Dog and Duck, left just before I stopped work at the gallery. Angus will remember her, all the guys fancied her. Obvious type. Looks like Madonna. Or at least, tries hard to." Being bitchy was helping, though Katie had in fact liked Bennie and had envied her ability to strike up an easy conversation with any old punter at the bar.

"Yes, I'd heard about her. It was Angus who told Charles; he saw them together in Soho. But that was ages ago. How come you just found out?" She opened the packet of sandwiches and held it out to Katie.

Katie shook her head. So Angus had known too. Katie's boss.

"We bumped into her at the zoo. She was there with her son—he's called Henry. He looks the same as Maria. And he called Harry 'Dadda.'"

Cassandra's sandwich made it only halfway to her mouth. "Oh my god. Shit. Oh, Katie."

"Indeed. So you didn't know about that part, then?"

"No, of course not. I would have said something. God, Katie, a child? I wonder if Charles knows."

"Would he have told you if he did?"

"I honestly don't know." She sighed. "When did we all start keeping secrets from each other, Katie?"

They were silent. Cassandra uncorked the wine and poured them both a plastic cupful. "Where would we be without this, eh?"

"It's a bit early for me. I've got to look after Maria this afternoon."

"No you haven't, Debbie's ours for the day. Darling, what are you going to do?"

"I want to leave London. Start a new life in the country. I've wanted to for a while, so this is the push I needed. Harry's agreed. He seems to want to save our marriage."

"So . . . you're not going to divorce him, or kick him out?"

"Divorce is against my faith. And, well, I can't imagine . . ." Emotion rushed in and she crumpled, resting her head on her arms, racked by sobs.

Cassandra hurried around to Katie's side of the table and rubbed her back. "There, there, darling, let it all out. Bloody men. Bloody bastard stupid fucking men."

Katie's sobs eventually subsided to hiccups, and she fished for tissues in her handbag. She blew her nose and wiped her eyes. "Sorry. I seem to have misplaced that stiff upper lip your mother said we need at these times."

"Better out than in," said Cassandra. "And my mother was talking bollocks. Here, have some wine. So, what—"

"And besides," interrupted Katie, picking up from where she'd left off, "I don't want Maria to grow up only seeing her father at weekends. I see those weekend dads here in the park. It's too sad. And I want her to have brothers and sisters. I've always wanted a big family."

Cassandra bit her lip. "Katie, sweetheart. You're still young. There's no rush for another child. Perhaps, if you want to make it work, you need to focus more on Harry?"

"I can't believe you'd say that! After what I've just told you!"

"I'm not excusing him—I'm trying to help you mend things. You're so swept up with darling Maria, sometimes men feel neglected, they don't like being second in line. Poor sausages. And I know from bitter experience what happens when men feel ignored."

"You mean—"

"Oh yes, that one all those years ago wasn't the last. He's very careful, but one develops an instinct. So . . . why don't you get a nanny, spend more time with Harry, just the two of you. Go on a few weekends away, make him feel the center of attention. It's going to be hard to forgive him, but you two have been through such a lot. You *can* work it out. I bet the affair was just for sex. Probably meant nothing."

"No. He loved her. He told me. And he won't abandon his son."

"Oh. Really? But . . . that's good too? That he's meeting his obligations? Don't move away, Katie. You have friends here, and Harry's close to work. If you bury yourself in the country, he won't be home until god knows what time. You could grow further apart."

"He's never home until late anyway. I have to face the truth. Things will never be the same. I have to make a life for myself and Maria that doesn't depend on Harry being around all the time. I really need that fresh start."

Saying it out loud gave form to the emotions and thoughts that had been whirling around in her head since Saturday. *Things will never be the same.* But she could make the most of what she had, even if that didn't include trust.

Harry and Katie reached a compromise—out of London, but not the deepest countryside. They sold Berryhurst and bought a beautiful period house in Hampton Court. It was only half an hour into Waterloo, was reasonably close to the Surrey Hills, and Maria would go to an eminently suitable Catholic school within walking distance. Life Mark II was about to begin.

CHAPTER 9

Katie

June 1991

Katie Paragon, well, I'll be damned!"

Katie turned to see a woman wearing a red Frisbee-shaped hat on a mass of frizzy brown curls. Her generous bust jiggled as she bounced up and down in excitement, holding her arms out wide.

"Good grief—Heather Althrop-Brown!" said Katie, relieved she'd managed to locate the name, filed under *Ancient History/School*. She stood to hug her old friend. "It's Katie Rose these days. How wonderful to see you!"

"Still Althrop-Brown for me. Can't be doing with the whole name-change nonsense. Can't hyphenate either—husband's surname is Hartington-Green. Also it sounds like an Essex village. That's him over there—the short bald one chatting up the redhead."

Katie introduced Harry, Charles, and Cassandra. They were seated at a round table in a marquee, at Gemma and Jonathan's wedding reception.

Maria was a bridesmaid and hadn't taken kindly to being trussed up in a froth of lemon yellow. Her vocabulary now included a disproportionate number of words for *stupid* and *no*, most of which she'd used when Katie told her the happy bridesmaid news.

She was a feisty child. "Fire in her eyes," Germaine had said. "You need a firmer hand."

Katie was enjoying herself more than she had in a long time. She'd bought a cerise suit and matching hat and shoes, and had had her hair cut in layers after Cassandra told her, "It's time to ditch the bob." Everyone said it suited her.

The noise in the marquee was increasing, in direct proportion to the number of empty wine bottles scattered across the tables.

"Come and sit with me for a bit," said Heather, linking her arm through Katie's. "We've got so much to catch up on."

Soon the pair were roaring with laughter as they knocked back champagne and reminisced about boarding school.

The music started, and the bride and groom took to the floor, slow dancing to "Lady in Red." Harry would be making some derogatory remark about Wet Jonathan's poor taste in music. He loathed Chris de Burgh.

"They're playing your shong!" Katie said, pointing at Heather's red dress. *Oh, I seem to be a little drunk. And why the bloody hell not!* "C'mon, Heather, keep up!" She topped up their glasses and raised hers toward Heather. "Chin-chin!"

"Bottoms up!" said Heather. "Hey, well done on the husband front. What a bloody dish—and rich with it!"

Katie looked over to Harry, jaw-droppingly handsome in his dove-gray morning suit, and her good mood dropped a few notches. A curvaceous blonde was sitting in Katie's seat, leaning forward toward Harry, her eyes locked on his.

Cassandra and Charles had joined the couples smooching around the dance floor, and Katie had a sudden longing to be up there with Harry. When was the last time they'd slow danced?

Nearly two years after she'd rumbled his affair, things between them had inched back to some sort of even keel. Bennie had moved to St. Albans, and last year had married the local vicar, the Right Reverend Gilbert Blunt. For some reason Harry found this hilarious. They were too far away for Harry to visit often, but he sent regular payments for Henry. Bennie's last note had suggested it might be better if Harry stopped seeing his son, as Gilbert was keen to adopt and didn't want to confuse the little lad.

The subject of Bennie and Henry now rarely came up. Which was fine by Katie.

She knew they'd never reclaim the happiness of those early years together, but as time went on she realized this was just how things were for so many people. Why had she ever thought she and Harry would be different? He probably still loved her but wasn't *in* love with her. It was enough.

She hadn't become pregnant again (yet) but, acknowledging the wisdom of Cassandra's advice, had tried not to make an issue of it. Recognizing that she needed a life of her own, she'd begun training as a counselor specializing in fertility issues. Harry didn't think it was a great career move, but if she could help others who'd been through what she had, that was good enough reason for her.

"Lord, your Harry's talking to Merry Lyebon," said Heather, her eyes following Katie's. "Red alert, Katie!"

"Who?"

"She's just back from France. Married to Will McCarey, the whisky heir. Word has it theirs is an open marriage. Let's hope she's not telling your Harry that right now. Look at her, Katie. Brazen or what?"

Merry was indeed not holding back in her appreciation of whatever Harry was telling her. Her head was slightly to one side, her enormous eyes were wide, and her red lips slightly parted. She nibbled the bottom one in a way that screamed, *Look, lips!* She kept touching Harry's arm, and her tinkling laughter reached Katie across the tables.

"Katie—off you go!" said Heather.

Neither Harry nor Merry noticed her as she stood in front of them. Time passed. Kingdoms probably rose and fell as she waited. Harry was a spaceship caught in the tractor beam of Merry's big blue eyes.

The time she spent waiting gave Katie the unwelcome opportunity to view Merry at closer quarters. To her dismay, she was even more beautiful than she'd appeared from a distance. The rosy blush on her apple cheeks was almost certainly courtesy of nature rather than Estée Lauder. It was the sort of color that said, *I am a little hot, a little excited, and it has nothing to do with the temperature in here.* But while she was certainly hot, there was no trace of shine on her creamy complexion. Her eyelashes were the length of spider legs, and the final twist of the knife—the honey-blond hair looked natural.

"Harry?" Katie said finally.

He turned to her as if waking from a coma. "Oh, Katie. Hi. Um, this is Merry. Merry, Katie."

Merry's eyes were amused, cool.

"Hello. Harry, I thought we might dance, if Merry would excuse you?" She was aware of swaying slightly as she spoke.

"Katie, it's Chris de bloody Burgh. Have a little compassion."

"Good point," said Katie, pulling up Cassandra's vacant chair and sitting down rather suddenly. "The next dance, then? As long as it's not Rick Ashley?"

"Astley," corrected Merry, in a tone that told Katie how much younger than her she was. "By the way, I love your outfit. Everyone in Paris was wearing that shade . . . last year. But we're always rather behind here, aren't we?"

"Merry's just come back from France," said Harry.

"Oh, what were you doing there?" asked Katie, giving exactly zero damn about the answer.

"My husband's in whisky, but we're expanding into wine. Tough research, but someone's gotta do it!"

Harry's guffaw was entirely out of proportion to the cliché joke.

"I was at school with Will," he said. "We called him Wilsky because of his family distillery."

Merry's peal of laughter set Katie's teeth on edge. "I didn't know that," she said.

"Oh, it wasn't for long. He had a new nickname by the sixth form," said Harry, then shut his mouth abruptly, his smile evaporating.

"Which was . . . ?" said Katie, smiling sweetly.

"I forget," said Harry.

"Gordon?" prompted Merry, looking briefly sideways at Katie before returning her headlamp eyes to Harry's.

"Yes, that was it!" said Harry, pointing upward as if God had sent him the answer.

"Why Gordon?" asked Katie.

"Um, because he's Scottish, I think," said Harry.

Chris de Burgh segued into Sinéad O'Connor's "Nothing Compares 2 U."

"Come on, Harry, come and darnsh," said Katie, grabbing his hand.

"Sorry, better do as the missus says," he said to Merry. "Catch you later."

As they made their way among the tables, Harry said, "That was rude, leaving her by herself. Are you pissed?"

"I think I am. It feels rather liberating. And something tells me that girl won't be waiting long for a partner."

They reached the dance floor, and Harry took Katie in his arms. It felt so good. She melted into his broad chest. He smelled divine, of something woody and citrusy. She breathed deeply. "Sorry, darling, about being pissed and rude."

Harry looked down at her, smiling fondly. "Maybe you should drink too much more often. It was rather fun seeing you go into bat against Merry."

Katie was taken aback. "I wasn't . . . well, she was all over you, Harry. And she's bloody married! And so are you!"

"Oh, she was just flirting. Anyway, Gordon lets her do what she wants. He needed a suitable wife for appearances. And they do make a glamorous couple. I'm going to feature them in *Hooray!* It'll be a corker.

Gordon in his kilt in front of the Scottish castle, Merry in her Barbour and green wellies, strolling across the heather."

"What do you mean, for appearances?"

"Full nickname Gay Gordon. Convenient arrangement—his family fortune, her aristocratic background. I'm pretty sure her father has a title."

"His money marrying her pedigree? Seriously? What century are we in, Harry?"

"It's still the way of the world. Gordon's not about to broadcast his sexual preferences."

"Do many people know?"

"Everyone in his circle. But otherwise he's pretty discreet, and he's such a good chap, I can't think why anybody would want to expose him. And Merry seems very happy with the arrangement."

Sinéad's soulful voice reached inside Katie and pulled at her heart. She leaned her head on Harry's chest again, closing her eyes for a moment.

Was everyone's life a sham? Full of secrets and lies?

Harry tightened his arms around her and pulled her closer.

"*Nothing compares to you,*" sang Sinéad. But as Katie opened her eyes and looked up at Harry, she saw that his were on Merry, still sitting alone at the table, a small smile playing on her lips.

CHAPTER 10

———∞∞∞———

Harry

Did you learn that in France too?" said Harry, falling back onto the sheets, a delicious exhaustion finally replacing the fire that had gripped him for the past hour. He pulled Merry's head down to his chest and she snuggled in, drawing little circles on his sweaty skin with her beautifully manicured nails.

"*Mais oui!* The French aren't at all uptight about sex," she said. "They celebrate it. Having a mistress is de rigueur, always has been. The British could learn so much from them. I certainly did."

"Well, that was *formidable*. I salute our traditional enemy," said Harry. "But I'd like you to stick with the British now—and just this one for the foreseeable."

"For now," said Merry. "You'll do just fine, Harry Rose."

Harry finally summoned the energy to sit up, and poured them another glass of champagne. "To *liaisons dangereuses*," he said, raising his glass.

"*Salut*," said Merry.

The affair had begun precisely two days after Gemma and Jonathan's wedding. Harry had put in a personal call to Merry (who'd slipped him her phone number while Katie was powdering her nose) and had organized to meet her "to discuss the *Hooray!* spread."

"I'm ready and willing to discuss a *spread*," Merry had said, and the laugh that followed was the sexiest thing he'd ever heard.

Harry had been standing at his office window, and as his secretary entered the room, he had to swiftly sit down behind his desk.

"Excellent," he'd said. "I'll have my assistant organize the meeting for later this week."

"Tomorrow would suit," came the reply. "Perhaps we should lunch in my suite at Claridge's? I'm here for the week."

Harry had paused. It was an extremely brief pause. "Right you are. Shall we say noon?"

"I'll be waiting, Harry."

Since then, Merry had arranged to spend as much time in London as possible. On their second afternoon together, Harry had suggested they jointly lease a London pad, ostensibly for her regular trips to town for McCarey's board meetings. They'd found a flat in South Kensington, and Harry became adept at inventing two-hour meetings during which he was uncontactable.

Although, the mobile phone he now owned was making life difficult. He got around the problem by telling his secretary it was too heavy to carry—the thing was the size and weight of a brick—and by claiming he'd bought it mainly for research purposes, which was true. Harry thought mobile phones might be something for Rose to expand into in the future, if they ever properly took off.

Merry was like a living embodiment of Harry's fantasies. Everything about her was curvy, soft, seductive. He wanted to eat her. She did things to him that made him lose all control, took him to a place he hadn't even known existed.

Charles had guessed what was going on immediately. They'd been sitting on the terrace at the Hurlingham Club, sipping drinks after their usual midweek game of tennis, the gentle *thock* of tennis balls carrying through the warm evening air.

"What about old Gay Gordon, then?" said Charles. "Would you

credit it? The guy who's never wanted to shag a woman ends up with the woman every guy wants to shag."

Harry knew his friend too well. He was digging.

"Indeed. Gorgeous."

"She liked you."

"Yup, she was friendly."

"Liked you *a lot*, I think. Lucky sod. Would you, Harry?"

"I'm committed to Katie."

"That's not an answer."

"Well," said Harry, "would you?"

"Resistance would be futile. It would be like saying no to Marilyn Monroe."

It was as if Charles were giving him permission. Harry had sighed. "Look, Charles. I don't want to hurt Katie. I do still love her."

"But back to Merry?"

"Yes, Merry. We're putting her and Will in *Hooray!* There's a photo shoot up in Scotland in a couple of weeks. So I've been in touch with her, yes."

"And? Look, Harry. You're like my kid brother. Don't hide important stuff from me. You might need my advice on this."

"Ah. So you're not just wanting to know what she's like in bed, then?"

In spite of his knowing questions, Charles had been taken aback. Also, it had to be said, he looked uncomfortable. And definitely jealous.

"Bugger me, Harry. That was quick work."

"Merry doesn't muck about. She lured me to her hotel room two days after the wedding, to 'talk about the shoot.'" He made quotation marks in the air.

"And you didn't think to suggest lunch at a restaurant instead?"

"Not really, to be honest. Look, I've been faithful to Katie since we moved to Hampton Court. But she's got her own life; it's all about Maria, and the church, and her counseling training. We're the proverbial ships in the night. I need more than that. Merry's made me realize I've been sleepwalking through life recently. She's made me feel alive again."

"You'll be telling me your wife doesn't understand you next."

"We've both gone into this with our eyes open. I'm not leaving Katie. Merry's not leaving Will. It's just for fun. We enjoy each other's company, but she's not remotely interested in the same things as me. It'll probably fizzle out, but in the meantime—god, I'm going to enjoy every bloody minute of it."

Charles laughed. "Message understood." Then his face turned serious. "But for Chrissake, be discreet, Harry. I'd hate for Katie to get hurt again. And Cassandra mustn't know. Those two are thick as thieves."

"Discretion will be my middle name."

They raised a glass to brotherliness.

Harry's assistant buzzed to tell him Terri Robbins-More had arrived.

"Send her in."

"Right you are, boss," came Ben's voice.

Right you are, boss? Harry made a mental note to speak to human resources about a replacement for Ben. He'd thought having a male secretary would fit with Rose Corp.'s well-publicized equality goals, but it wasn't working out.

It was two years since the *Sunday Times* cover story, and Harry had been watching Terri's journalistic star rise. She was known in press circles as Baskin-Robbins, thanks to her instinct for a good scoop.

Harry braced himself. Terri was fearless, didn't give a toss whom she upset, and in normal life he'd have gone out of his way to avoid her. He still thanked the God of Secrets she hadn't accompanied them on the zoo photo session.

Terri was a hugely popular writer, especially with the liberal left, and was a regular on *Question Time* and *Newsnight*, where she sometimes stood in for Jeremy Paxman. She was a champion of the people (especially northerners), fighting for the little guy, sniffing out corruption, exposing fat-cat chief executives and MPs with salacious secrets. She could spot bullshit from a thousand paces. Corporate and political empires had come tumbling down courtesy of Terri. Once she had you in her sights, it was like being a lumbering frigate in the crosshairs of an Exocet missile.

She still worked mostly for the *Sunday Times*, but Harry wanted Terri on his team, for two reasons. One, she had a way of finding out everything about newsworthy people. That included him, and it was only a matter of time before she turned her sharp eyes and matching pencil in his direction. He needed to keep this potential enemy close.

And two, she'd be perfect to head up the magazine he was planning to launch.

Terri strutted into the room on a pair of stilettos that could easily have served as weapons. Useful, considering how many people probably wanted to kill her. She still had her trademark sleek, jet-black bob, its razor-sharp edge mirroring her cutthroat jawline, but now there was a long fringe swept across at an angle, half hiding one eye. It gave her a piratical look.

"Terri, super to see you again. Ben, can we have coffee, please? Or tea if you'd rather, Terri?"

"Coffee," she said, sitting down on the office sofa. "It's been a while, Harry. What's all this about, then?"

"Straight to the point, I see." Harry slipped off his suit jacket and hung it on the back of his chair, then perched on the edge of his desk, crossing one ankle over the other.

"All right, let's cut to the chase. I'm starting up a new magazine, and I want you to be its editor."

"Seriously? What magazine?"

"It'll be like *Hooray!*'s evil twin, if you like. Still all about celebrities, high-profile figures, but the truth, not the airbrushed version. There'll be no spin—it'll be street-smart and hard-hitting. Most importantly, every week we'll do an in-depth cover story about someone highly newsworthy—the cool people, the movers and shakers. Movie stars, politicians, top businesspeople. The photographs will be iconic. But there'll be no helpful lighting. Raw, exposed pictures, maybe black and white. Getting to the heart of the person, like the interviews. And in return for being the lead story in the UK's hottest magazine—think a combo of *Rolling Stone* and *Vanity Fair*—there'll be no PRs allowed, and there will be no restrictions on what we can ask them. Everything will be fair game."

"Tsh!" snorted Terri. "As if anyone who matters will agree to that!"

"Oh, but they will," said Harry. "It will always be the case that the famous need us more than we need them. And if our circulation is as enormous as I intend it to be, they'll be queuing up to be in it. As you know, celebrities get to a stage where they believe their own hype. They think they're infallible; clever enough to control their image, steer things their way. But you, Terri, will be like a human truth serum."

"Everyone has secrets, Harry. And yes, I'm the one who finds them out. But people know that. So who the fook would agree to be in . . . what are you even calling it?"

"I thought the *Rack*."

Terri snorted again. "I like it. They can't complain if they get grilled, eh?"

"Right. But while it would be good to dig up the occasional skeleton, it won't be grubby. We're going to reveal the real person behind the facade. That's what Joe Public wants. They don't give a toss about Mr. Bigshot Movie Star's take on his new film, but they sure as hell care about his love life and his battle with drugs and alcohol. No checkbook journalism, though. No doorstepping, no kiss 'n' tells. This will be a whole new way of doing things, Terri."

He stopped to gauge her reaction. Terri was tapping her pencil against her notepad and frowning at the floor, her eyes all but hidden behind her dark fringe.

"Who've you got in mind for issue one?" she said finally.

"To be decided. Princess Diana would be perfect, but unlikely. Bono?

George Michael? Or that new model everyone's talking about—Kate Moss?"

The meeting went on for another hour or so. Terri was a tough nut to crack, but he could see her warming to the idea of doing pretty much what she'd done at the *Sunday Times*, but with more of a free rein—and more money.

By the time she left, Harry was fairly sure he had his new editor.

He sat back in his chair, his hands behind his head and a contented smile on his face. Rose Corp. was well and truly blooming.

CHAPTER 11

Harry

December 1991

Harry finally managed to connect the key with the keyhole. It had been a challenge. Every time his hand came close, some unseen force made his hand swing to the left or right, and he'd ended up stabbing the glossy black paint of the front door.

The door swung inward with more speed than he'd been expecting. He stumbled through it, swearing, falling sideways against the enormous Christmas wreath that had been hanging from the knocker. It fell to the floor.

"Bugger." Harry stared at it, then decided to leave it where it was. He slammed the door behind him.

"Harry?" Katie's face appeared around the living room door.

"You sshhouldn't have waited up," Harry slurred.

"I've been at carol practice, we went to the pub afterward."

"I've been at lunch," said Harry.

"Till eleven thirty?"

"It's Chrishmash, season of good beer. Cheer."

Katie pursed her lips. She was wearing her white bathrobe and slippers, ready for bed. Through the living room doorway, Harry saw a large Christmas tree strung with pretty lights and silver tinsel. Katie and Maria must have put up the decorations sometime this week. Harry hadn't been home before eleven since Monday, so had missed out on all that.

A golden star sat atop the tree, glowing in the darkened room like the star of Bethlehem, guiding Harry back to his family.

He was knocked sideways by a wave of sentimentality. Dear old Katie, with her carols and her Christmas trees and her Christmas baking. Katie loved Christmas as much as he did, although hers was a lot more Jesus and a lot less wassail.

"Come here, darling," he said, holding out his arms.

"I'm going to bed."

"Lovely idea. I'll be right with you."

"Harry, please. You're drunk; it's not appealing. I'd rather you kept to your side of the bed tonight."

"But, Katie, I want a big cuddle."

"Sorry, Harry. I don't." She turned abruptly and headed for the stairs.

"Wash wrong, Katie?" he said, following. "C'mon, it's Chrishmash!"

Ten minutes later she was sitting up in bed reading her novel, and Harry was lying on his side watching. He hadn't seen Merry for three weeks; they'd both been too busy with all the extra work and engagements this time of year brought for a supplier of alcohol and a media company. So Harry was feeling frustrated. A man had his needs. His hand crept toward Katie's body, and she swatted it away.

"Stop it, Harry. I've told you, I don't find you remotely attractive when you've been drinking." She shuffled further toward the edge of the bed.

Harry's mood shifted abruptly. "Not the right time of the month? You don't need my services this week?"

"Go to sleep, Harry."

"No, c'mon, let's talk about this. You're only interested when your charts say, 'Brace yourself, it's time for a bonk.' Am I right?"

The volume of his voice increased along with his self-pity, fueled by his indignation. "Well, what about *me*? What about—"

"Be quiet. You'll wake Maria."

"I don't give a shit. Do you realize how hard I work to keep you two in—in Chrishmash trees and this big house and—"

"Daddy, stop shouting at Mummy."

Maria had materialized in the bedroom doorway. She was staring at him intently from beneath her fringe. She looked like Damien in *The Omen*.

"We weren't shouting, sweetheart," said Katie. "We were having a discussion. I'll take you back to bed."

By the time she returned, Harry had started to drift off to sleep.

"And in case it's of any interest to you, Harry, I'm already pregnant." Katie turned her back on him and flicked off the light.

Harry and Merry were spending a glorious afternoon in the Kensington flat. After the Christmas sex drought, they hadn't made it as far as the bedroom for their first frantic reunion, bumping up hard against the hall wall. But they'd taken their time over the second, relishing every sensuous moment.

"Aaah, that's better," Harry said as they lay back, catching their breath. "First bonk in bloody weeks."

"So romantic, darling," said Merry. "What's up with wifey, then?"

"Pregnant. And with her history of problems, I guess we're just overly careful."

Merry went quiet. "Congratulations," she said finally. "I have absolutely no maternal instinct, but one would like the option."

"I can't imagine being married to you and not even wanting to give it a try." Harry ran an appreciative eye over her luscious nakedness.

"It's just as well he didn't," said Merry. Then she bit her lip and turned away, pouring two glasses of wine from the bottle on the bedside table. She handed one to Harry.

"Not ever, not even out of curiosity? I bet you could raise his interest," Harry said.

"Will doesn't have a heterosexual cell in his body, you know that."

They sipped their wine.

"What did you mean, when you said just as well you didn't?"

Merry stared ahead. "He's HIV positive."

Harry's spirits sank. The real world had finally intruded into his private fantasyland.

"He's fine," she said, "no symptoms or anything, but given his . . . well, he thought he should get tested."

"And you've definitely never . . ."

"No, Harry." She turned to look at him. "*You'll* be fine. Unlike Will."

"Poor you. What happens now?"

"We'll keep it secret for as long as we can. I don't know what the prognosis is."

"If there's anything I can do . . ."

"I doubt it. We'll just carry on as normal for as long as we can, and . . . Harry, my time with you is so important to me now. I'm going to need this escape more than ever."

"Right, of course."

"Let's not think about that now," said Merry. "I have a favor to ask you, darling."

"Does it involve more fun between the sheets before we head off once more unto the breach?"

"No, but I won't rule that out, if you're nice to me."

Harry was glad her spirits had lifted again. He had quite enough female moodiness to contend with at home. Christmas, with Germaine, Katie, and Maria, had been a trial.

He reached over and took the glass from Merry's hand, putting it down on the bedside table. Then he tucked a blond tendril of hair behind her ear and leaned over to nibble her earlobe. "Again, again," he whispered.

"Mm," she said, squirming. "Harry, how is it that you can do this to me?" Her hand moved southward as his lips traveled to her neck, where he stopped to kiss her, softly at first and then biting and sucking gently as his hand stroked her breast. He slid on top of her, kissing her deeply, and her legs wrapped around him. Soon they were moving together, and Harry was lost in her soft curves, her musky perfume.

"Darling, that was delicious," Merry said later as their pulses returned to normal. "So can I ask my favor now?"

"Strike while I'm incapable of refusing you anything," murmured Harry, his eyes still closed.

Merry giggled. "Have you met my sister, Ana?"

"Not that I'm aware of. Why?"

"She's a friend of your sister's. Megan, I mean. You've got two, haven't you?"

"Yes. Megan and Margot; confuses the hell out of people. I haven't seen Megan since she went abroad. You'd like her. Margot probably not so much."

"Is that Margot James? Married to the Scottish laird with the castle and all the moors? I think Will knows them."

"That's the one. She's gone the full Scot—she's even more dour than her husband, and she wears kilts and headscarves, like the Queen. She disapproves of me. Actually, she disapproves of everyone."

Harry missed his little sister, if not the older one. Five years his junior, Megan was pretty and sweet and full of fun, and hero-worshipped him. A young teen when their father had died, she'd gone a little wild at school, narrowly avoiding being expelled for smuggling in vodka and sneaking out to meet boys. She'd only got away with it because of the whole orphan situation.

College had been one long party for Megan, after which she'd gone to Val d'Isère as a chalet girl, working her way through the best-looking ski instructors, or so Harry had heard on the grapevine.

Margot despaired of Megan's "flightiness" and had been nagging her to come home and get a proper job. The last time Harry had spoken to Megan, she'd told him she was indeed ready to grow up and would be returning home after the season.

"Ana met Megan at Val d'Isère," said Merry. "They're both chalet girls and they've become good friends. Ana's very arty, she's been studying design in Paris."

"And?" said Harry.

"When she comes back she's going to need a job, and apparently they've been plotting to ask if you'd take Ana on in the art department of one of your magazines. Ana told me this over the phone, having no idea about me and you. I didn't enlighten her. I'm just, shall we say, paving the way for when your little sister pops the question. I reckon Ana would be great. She's incredibly stylish, sharp as a whip. Quite the Parisian."

"Does she look like you? That would help her case."

Merry batted his arm. "Not a bit. She's tall and dark, much thinner than me. Fiercely intelligent, frightens the life out of most men."

"Interesting. OK, I'll think about it," said Harry. "We're looking for people for our newest mag. I'll have a word with the art director."

"Darling, you're a star."

"I'm not promising anything. The final decision won't be up to me."

"I understand. But a carefully chosen word in the right ear, if you think she's got the talent?"

"As good as done."

CHAPTER 12

Ana

April 1992

As Ana cut through the backstreets of Covent Garden, Tears for Fears' "Woman in Chains" floated out of the open windows of the Pineapple Dance Studios above her. She sang along under her breath. She *loved* this band. She was still catching up on the British music scene after her years in France.

She reached the Lamb and Flag and made her way up the narrow staircase, ordering a spritzer at the bar. She'd come straight from her interview at Rose Corp. and was early enough to grab a table by the window. Percy was meeting her here at six, and although she didn't want to jinx her chances, she was fairly sure this was something of a celebration. The interview had gone swimmingly.

Nate Romano, art director of the *Rack*, launching later in the year, was one seriously gifted guy, and Ana had been hugely impressed with the design work he showed her. Every last detail of the magazine was being styled to within an inch of its life, and only the best-quality paper stock would serve as its canvas. It was glossy, weighty, beautiful, and even smelled divine. The cover was a work of art in itself.

Nate had seemed impressed with her CV and portfolio, and during the course of the interview Ana's take on this opportunity had gone from a fill-in job swung by a friend to a position she wanted more than anything.

Well, almost anything. She looked up, in case Percy might be coming through that doorway right now, a few minutes early. He wasn't.

Ana had met Percy North several months ago in Val d'Isère. It really had been love at first sight, something she'd always dismissed as poppycock. Her wary approach to life had been swept aside in the face of this lovely man with his shaggy blond hair and warm brown eyes. He'd walked in on her as she was cleaning the toilet (*such* a romantic meeting—how many times had they described it to friends now?), she'd turned and looked into his eyes, and something profound had happened.

By the end of his two-week skiing holiday, they were engaged.

Percy was an account director at Soho ad agency Black, White, and Green, and shared a flat in Notting Hill with a couple of friends. They were planning to marry at the end of next year, which allowed plenty of time to settle into a new job, find somewhere to live, and organize the wedding.

Ana glanced out of the window and saw Percy coming along the cobbled street, his Burberry raincoat slung over his arm. He looked up, and she waved. His face broke into a grin and he waved back, hurrying the last few steps before disappearing below.

How had he known to look up at that moment? It was as if they had some telepathic thing going on. Ana had never felt as connected to anyone in her life.

She couldn't wait for Percy to meet her family, especially Merry. It was the first time she hadn't been nervous about introducing a boyfriend to her sister, because for once she was confident he had eyes only for her. That feeling of security was sublime.

On encountering Merry, most men dissolved into something pathetic and squidgy. There was something about her—she was like a siren in a Greek myth. No doubt it was mostly to do with the generous bust, baby-blue eyes, and soft blond curls, but there was more to it—a mix of vulnerability and power, of innocence and knowledge.

Ironic, then, that Merry had chosen to marry the only man Ana knew who was completely immune to her charms, the gloriously gay Will McCarey.

Although she and Merry had always been close, Ana hadn't understood that marriage at all. Will's family was enormously rich, but surely Merry wouldn't marry someone purely for money? Then, after a few hints from Merry, she'd got it. Her sister, with her upper-class background, top-notch education, and circle of influential friends, was the perfect corporate wife. And for her part, Merry had unfettered access to his family fortune, a nice job helping promote the McCarey brand, and, importantly, a husband with the blindest of eyes when someone caught her fancy.

Ana wondered if her prospective boss, Harry Rose, was included in that last category. The interview had been organized through his sister Megan, Ana's friend and flatmate, but Merry had said something about "helping things along." It had been the way she said it, with a knowing chuckle. And then Harry had turned up during the interview.

"Hi!" said Percy, making his way over. He kissed her cheek, and she caught a whiff of his expensive aftershave. "Top-up?"

"I'm fine, thank you." She smiled up at him.

"You look lovely; I'd employ you. I'll just get a pint, be right back."

The buzz of conversation was increasing in volume as local workers filled the place up, relaxing and sharing the latest office gossip. Ana was looking forward to being part of it all, hopefully soon.

"There we go, packet of your favorite crisps. Don't say I never treat you." Percy sat down opposite her. "So? Am I looking at Rose's newest trainee designer?"

"I don't know yet, but I think it went well. The art director is *amazing*. And I actually met Harry Rose! I didn't realize he's so young."

"Yes, he's only just taken over the helm from his uncle, Richard York.

I hear good things about him, seems pretty bright. He's got all sorts of interesting ideas about where he wants to take the company."

"You seem to know a lot."

"Yeah, we're pitching for the business later in the year. It's going to be huge for us. I've been given the nod that I'll be heading up the pitch."

"Percy, that's great! But . . . if I get the job, that wouldn't matter?"

Percy laughed. "I don't think so. If you were chief exec it might be different, but a junior designer on one magazine, nah. Anyway, what's he like, Harry Rose?"

Ana thought back. It had been a brief meeting, and rather unsettling. She'd been sitting at a long table opposite three people from the *Rack*. There was the editor—a woman called Terri Robbins-More, who'd reminded her of Cruella de Vil. Then, from the art department, there had been Nate, long limbed, black, and cool, and the art editor, Lizzie, whose mousy bob and glasses belied immense talent, as became apparent as she talked Ana through some sample layouts. It was a top-notch team.

So far, so normal interview.

Then Harry had come in, pulling up a chair next to Terri. His presence in the room had charged the air; it crackled with charisma. He was tall, and his exquisitely tailored suit showed off his long legs and broad shoulders.

As he looked across the table at Ana, she saw the resemblance to Megan—red-gold hair and deep blue eyes fringed with long lashes. He was fair skinned with ruddy cheeks, and there was a faint sprinkling of freckles across his nose.

Harry Rose was remarkably good-looking. If you liked that type.

Ana didn't. His self-confidence was overpowering, and for some reason she felt a desperate urge to deflate it. Nate had been talking her through the design elements of the *Rack*, but Harry took over, pointing out things Nate had already described, using adjectives like "cool," "street," and "on trend."

His words didn't fit his persona, which was far more *Hooray!* than the *Rack.*

He'd seemed a little too interested in her, watching her in a way that made her uncomfortable. She wondered again if it was something to do with Merry. He'd fluffed his words a couple of times, repeating himself and forgetting what he was about to say. She'd had to prompt him, while she sensed the discomfort of the others in the room.

Finally he'd pushed his chair back and said, "Well, lovely to meet you, Ana. I just wanted to say hi, as you're a friend of my little sister." Then he'd looked at Nate in a way that to Ana seemed to command, *Employ her, or there will be consequences.*

"Well?" said Percy.

"He was . . . you know. Public school, family money, overconfident, probably loves rugby and cricket. Harry Rose is one big cliché."

Harry

How about Ana, my flatmate?" asked Megan. "Oh, wait. Would that be kind of inappropriate?"

Harry's feet were up on his desk, and he leaned back in his chair as he spoke to his sister on the phone. "I don't think she's started here yet."

"No, she starts next week."

"No problem, then. Can you be at the Hurlingham by six? And afterward we can talk about what you're doing with your life, over a drink."

"Give it a rest, brother dearest," said Megan. "Anyway, I have an interview with an events management company. I think I could do that."

"A party planner? How very fitting."

"No, *events.*"

"If you say so. You'll walk it. Sorry, gotta go. See you at six."

Harry experienced a strange anticipation at the thought of seeing Ana again, this time socially. Merry's sister was like a photographic negative of Merry: jet-black hair to Merry's blond, deep brown eyes to Merry's light blue, olive-toned skin to Merry's peaches and cream. And Ana was sharp where Merry was soft. Poker-straight hair framed her prominent cheekbones and square jawline en route to her waist, while Merry's shoulder-length curls were a cloud around her apple cheeks. Ana's body was androgynous and long limbed, while Merry's was all curves.

And where Merry tended to play the dumb blonde, opening her eyes wide and hanging on your every word, Ana's eyes, their irises almost as dark as the pupils, had been slightly narrowed, sizing him up. If Merry was a kitten, Ana was a cat.

Later, Harry collected his sports bag and left the office, waving a cheery goodbye to his staff. It was a beautiful summer's evening and he was on his way to play tennis with two of his favorite people and an intriguing third. Life was good.

As he hailed a taxi, he realized he'd forgotten to ring Katie. He could call her from the club. But if he did, she'd only make him feel guilty for missing Maria's bedtime yet again. He decided not to bother. He didn't need the grief.

"Bloody hell, is that . . . ?" said Charles as two women appeared out of the clubhouse doors and stood scanning the terrace. He and Harry were sipping Perrier in the evening sun, waiting for their court to become available.

Harry grinned. "I told you I had a surprise for you. We're playing doubles tonight."

Charles had always been fond of Harry's little sister, twelve years his junior, so Harry had been looking forward to surprising him. And her. Because Megan had adored Charles too.

Seeing Megan through Charles's eyes, Harry experienced a momentary misgiving. Now twenty-four, she'd grown up to be a real head-turner, with a wide smile, laughing eyes, and wavy red-blond hair.

He hoped Megan's crush was a thing of the past.

But Megan didn't hold Harry's attention for long as his eyes fell on Ana, who, in tennis whites, was all long legs and swinging ponytail.

"And who is *that*?" asked Charles, raising his sunglasses onto his head for a better look.

"Megan's flatmate. She's making up the four," said Harry, glad Charles's eyes were firmly on the girls, as he had an uncanny ability to read Harry's mind. "She's going to be working at Rose as a designer," he added, realizing they were bound to mention it.

Megan spotted them and broke into a run, squealing, "Oh my god—Charles Lisle!"

"Oh dear," said Harry, smiling. "That's not Hurlingham-appropriate behavior."

"Nutmeg!" called Charles, standing up and opening his arms.

Harry had forgotten the old nickname.

Megan threw herself into Charles's arms, and he lifted her up, narrowly missing the table of drinks.

"Calm down, you two," said Harry.

He looked over at Ana and smiled. "Hello again, Ana. May I present my overexuberant friend Charles Lisle. Charles, this is Ana—" He stopped. If he said Ana's surname . . .

"Lyebon," finished Ana. She moved to hold out a hand, but Charles and Megan were too busy laughing and hugging each other.

"Ana, nice to meet you," said Charles finally. But his eyes left Megan for only a few seconds. "Nutmeg, how dare you grow up! Look at you!"

"Whereas you haven't changed at all! But I have a serious bone to pick with you, you naughty man."

"Which is?"

"You're married! And when I was seven, you promised to marry me!"

"I did? I did! I remember. But you deserted me. You went to the dark side—France."

"That's where these two met," said Harry.

Charles finally turned his attention to Ana. "Ah, I see. Wait . . . what did you say your surname was?"

"Lyebon."

"You mean . . ." Charles looked at Harry. There was an awkward pause.

"Oh, maybe you know Ana's sister," said Megan. "She was Merry Lyebon before she got married."

"That's it. I knew the name was familiar," said Charles. He glanced at Harry, who made a show of looking across to the tennis courts.

"Ah, looks like they're just coming off. Shall we? After you, ladies." Harry downed the rest of his drink, then he and Charles set off after the girls.

Charles touched Harry's arm and slowed his walk, until Ana and Megan were far enough ahead. "Does Ana know about Merry and you?" he said. "Honestly, Harry. You might have warned me."

"Sorry. But no. I'm sure Merry hasn't said anything to Ana. Megan doesn't know, either, of course."

"Right, glad we got that one cleared up. Who's playing with who?"

"How about Megan and me, you and Ana?"

"Right you are."

They were evenly matched. Charles was more powerful than Harry, but Harry was quicker. Megan was speedy and keen, zipping around the court to pick up even the trickiest shots, while Ana was a formidable force at the net, firing volleys with blistering accuracy.

Charles and Ana won the first set 6–4. Their shadows grew longer as the game went on, falling across the mown stripes of the court. Harry hadn't enjoyed a game this much in years. He was playing well on the baseline, sending long shots fast and low across the net, where Ana would more often than not intercept them.

After a while, Megan and Charles faded into the background, and there was only Ana, standing at the net, filling Harry's vision. Every shot became about conquering her. He'd try to skim the ball past her, or lob it over her head, but she'd leap off those coltish legs and volley it back again.

"Hey, you two," called Charles finally. "Any chance of a shot here?"

The second set went to a tiebreak, and Harry was serving. He didn't hold back. Ana somehow returned the shot, but it was a weak forehand played to Harry's powerful backhand. Out of the corner of his eye he saw Ana run into the net, and he aimed the shot to pass her on the left.

He mistimed it, and the ball hit her squarely on the head.

As she gasped and dropped to the ground, Charles rushed over.

Harry vaulted the net, pushing him aside. "Jesus, I'm so sorry. Are you all right?"

She was lying on her back, her knees bent, staring up at the sky, touching the spot where the ball had hit her. "I think I'm OK."

"Let me see." Harry gently took her hand and moved it aside, then brushed her hair back, examining the reddened spot on her temple. He stroked his fingers slowly across it, then his eyes met hers, and he couldn't look away. It was like being under a spell; he was bewitched.

"I said I'm fine," she said, bringing him out of his trance.

"Thank goodness," said Charles. "That was quite a knock. I think we should adjourn to the bar for a restorative drink. What say you, team?"

"Yes, I hear Pimm's is the best thing for a blow to the head," said Megan. She linked her arm through Charles's. "Come on, Harry. I think the first round should be on you."

"You go ahead and get them in, I'll make sure Ana's OK."

Megan seemed very happy with this plan and set off back to the clubhouse. Harry saw Charles slip an arm around her waist.

He turned his attention back to Ana, who was now sitting up on the court. He held out his hand. "Up you come, let's make properly sure you're OK."

She ignored the hand and stood up. "Really, I'm fine." She brushed herself down, then put her hand up to her temple. "I might have a lump tomorrow, but no proper damage done. Good game, by the way. Your backhand's a killer."

"And that was terrific volleying," replied Harry. "Do you play a lot?"

"Not enough. I'm trying to get my fiancé more into it. He's into adventure sports. Likes skiing and rock climbing, that sort of thing."

"An Action Man. What does he do?"

"Advertising." She met his eyes for a moment. "Shall we join Megan and Charles, then?"

"If you're sure you're OK?"

"I'm fine." She grabbed her racquet cover, and Harry retrieved the remaining tennis balls.

Harry was disappointed by her change in demeanor. Their on-court combat, their tunneled focus on each other, had been intoxicating. Ana had been a blur of long limbs, flying ponytail, and dark, flashing eyes, determined not to let anything past. Now he saw it as a metaphor for her likely response to any move from him.

Which, of course, would be the worst possible direction he could take, for so many reasons.

As he followed her along the path, trying not to stare at her delectable legs, the reasons why came at him. Katie was pregnant. Ana was Merry's sister. She was about to start working at Rose. She was Megan's friend and flatmate.

Any one of those should have been enough to stop him in his tracks. It would be utterly foolhardy. And besides, she was making it patently clear she wasn't interested. She had a fiancé, and she was obviously an intelligent, talented woman. Why would she put her relationship and career at risk because the boss had taken a fancy to her?

There, he'd admitted it. To himself, at least. He was entranced. Enamored. Spellbound. And the most worrying part was, he'd never felt this way before.

They reached the clubhouse, and he saw Charles and Megan looking at each other in a way that had nothing to do with old friends reunited.

Oh dear. It had been a wonderful evening, but it seemed life was about to become even more complicated.

CHAPTER 13

—◆◆◆—

Katie

I'm dreading it, Cass," said Katie, slipping the new R.E.M. CD into the music system. She balanced a speaker on the windowsill so they could listen outside, then carried their plates of pasta onto the patio, which was radiating warmth after a hot June day.

Tonight was Charles and Harry's tennis night, so Katie had invited Cassandra over for a bite to eat. They were discussing next week's launch party for the *Rack*.

"That'll be me," Katie said as Michael Stipe sang about being in the corner. "Except I won't be losing my religion. God's a lot more reliable than Harry."

"Nonsense, darling. It'll be fine." Cassandra lifted a forkful of fettuccine to her mouth. "Mm, only you can make a simple bowl of pasta taste this divine. And it's looking so lovely out here." She picked up her glass of wine, waving it around at the terra-cotta pots bursting with color, and the neat lawn and herbaceous borders beyond.

"Nothing much else to do," said Katie. "I get quite excited when I spot a greenfly to spray."

Cassandra's glass was already empty. She poured herself another. "I use soap and water now. I'm trying to be organic. It's quite the thing." She took a large mouthful of wine. "Christ, Katie, when did we get to be old ladies discussing gardening? Anyway, don't knock boredom. You'll be longing for boredom when Sprog Two arrives."

Katie had gone on early maternity leave from the fertility clinic, because the boss thought it would be "inappropriate" for an obviously pregnant woman to be counseling clients about their fertility problems. She missed it. Maria was now at nursery school, and other than helping with the occasional church function, Katie was finding it difficult to fill the long days. June had been hot, and she'd spent much of it lying on the couch watching daytime TV, thinking far too much about how things had changed between her and Harry and what she could do about it. Maybe the baby would help.

This pregnancy hadn't been easy. There had been blood pressure problems, and her obstetrician warned her to avoid exertion and stress. This heat wasn't helping one bit. Thanks to her training, she was well aware that a previous stillbirth and miscarriages meant an increased probability of it happening again, and for that reason she took seriously the advice to spend as much time as she could resting.

But she was having trouble sleeping, and Harry had moved into the guest suite "just for the duration," as her tossing and turning had been keeping him awake. She missed the togetherness of sharing a bed. It was their time for curling up with each other and shutting the door on the world. No matter how tricky things got between them, as long as they ended the day with a kiss and a whispered "good night," Katie felt things would always be all right.

Now, they didn't even have that. And on the rare occasions they spent time together, Harry's mind always seemed to be elsewhere. It was as if he was just parking up at home before heading off to something more interesting.

So her days were lonely, and she'd found herself depending on Cassandra's battle-on optimism to see her through. Katie had been thrilled when she and Charles moved to Richmond, only twenty minutes' drive away.

"If you're worried what you'll look like, don't be," said Cassandra, returning to the subject of next week's party. "There are some fabulous maternity dresses now. We could go up to town and choose you something. It'd be fun. You can get Trevor thingy to do your hair again. You'll be radiant."

"But it's going to be wall-to-wall models and celebrities. Shiny Happy People. It doesn't matter what I wear, I'm going to feel like Mrs. Blobby from Fat Town. And Harry won't have time to talk to me, anyway."

"Darling, you're the boss's wife! You've got to enjoy your moment as Queen Katie! Everyone will be sucking up to you, and I'll be your lady-in-waiting."

Katie shivered.

"Oh, come on, it can't be that bad!"

"No, it was . . . like someone walked over my grave."

"Funny how pregnancy does that," said Cassandra.

At seven months pregnant, Katie knew she wasn't far enough along to plead incapacity as an excuse not to attend the party. And it was taking place just up the road, in a marquee in the grounds of Hampton Court Palace. Practically walking distance, even with a bump.

It had been Harry's sister Megan's idea to hold it there. She'd come around for Sunday lunch last weekend and had been full of party plans. She'd even been in touch with the National Trust, trying to locate a rack they could borrow as a focal point. But Harry had pointed out that once the drink was properly flowing, someone would be bound to try it out, and there were easier ways to extract advertising revenue. The idea had been shelved.

Katie had known Megan for many years now and had always liked her. She'd landed a job with the events company managing the launch—no doubt the fact that Harry Rose was looking for someone to organize what promised to be a social highlight of the summer had helped her secure the position.

Katie sighed. "OK, well, a shopping trip would be fun. Where's the nearest branch of Tents 'R' Us?"

Cassandra laughed. "That's more like it. You've been looking far too low recently. Are you sure everything's all right?"

"Oh, you know, mostly pregnancy stuff. And we hardly see Harry."

"But that's not surprising. Charles says Harry's been working his arse off on the launch of this new magazine. Calls it his baby."

"I wish Harry took as much interest in his actual child, or the one that's coming." Katie stroked her bump. "All he's said is that he'd like a boy."

"Every chap wants a son," said Cassandra.

"He's already got one."

"Ah. I was forgetting. Shall we change the subject? So Charles was telling me Harry's little sister is sweet. I've never met her."

"Yes, she's lovely. I remember her when she was a little girl, when our families were on holiday together in France. That was when I started going out with Harry's brother. Megan was the cutest thing. Strawberry-blond curls and rosy cheeks. It was lovely the way Harry looked after her. They've always been close. Then, apparently, when Charles went to stay at Berryhurst, Megan took a shine to him—even proposed! She made him a ring out of one of those make-your-own-jewelry sets."

"Sweet," said Cassandra. "She played tennis with them recently, did you know?"

"Did she? No, I didn't. I wonder why Harry didn't mention it. Or Megan, when she came for lunch. Honestly, Cass, Harry never tells me anything these days."

"You know what, Katie? It would be nice if *I* was invited to tennis sometimes. Ever. I'm not too shabby at it." She puffed out a long breath and drained her glass. "But like I said, Harry probably has loads on his mind. Charles said it was strange, seeing Megan all grown up. He also said she's sharing a flat with Merry Lyebon's sister; I don't remember her name. Do you remember Merry? That Marilyn Monroe wannabe at Gemma and Jonathan's wedding?"

"How could I forget?" said Katie.

Harry had always attracted women, like the proverbial moths to a flame—she was used to that. And although he rarely missed an opportunity to flirt, she hadn't been able to forget his expression as he'd talked to Merry.

Cassandra picked up the wine bottle.

"Hey, no more, Cass, you're driving."

Cassandra carried on pouring. "Can I leave the car here? Take a cab home? I feel like having a few more of these."

CHAPTER 14

Katie

It looked like the heat wave was about to end. After a week of glorious summer sunshine—or stifling, swollen-ankle-inducing heat, if you were in your third trimester of pregnancy—the clouds were building over London. Radio 4's morning weather forecast was predicting thunderstorms across the south.

As Katie prepared Maria's lunchbox, talk on the radio turned to Andrew Morton's new biography of Princess Diana, including claims of her depression. Poor Diana. Katie had met her several times and had liked her very much.

She called Maria down for breakfast. She was glad her daughter was now capable of dressing herself. Already the day was too hot for unnecessary stair-climbing.

As Maria appeared, Katie reminded her she'd have a babysitter tonight, because it was Daddy's important party at the palace.

"I wish I was going," said Maria, carefully pouring milk onto her cereal. "Will the Queen be there?"

"No, she lives in a different palace, darling. Buckingham Palace. But I think there might be a duke and a duchess there! I'll tell you all about it tomorrow."

Katie dropped Maria off at nursery school and headed home. Cassandra was coming over later, and they'd be getting ready together, like a couple of teenagers before the school disco. As she let herself in the front door, she glanced at the sky. Cumulus clouds were piling up, and there wasn't a breath of air. It looked as if the forecasters were right.

"Sure you won't have a teensy one?" asked Cassandra, popping the cork. She held a glass under the fizzing bubbles, which raced up and spilled over the sides. "Oops. No, don't answer that. Bad Cassandra for even asking. Cheers, anyway." She took a sip, leaving a bright red lipstick mark on the rim.

"Here, have some nibbles," said Katie, pushing a plate of cheese and biscuits toward her.

"Thanks. I won't sit down. Might rip the dress. It'll be a bloody miracle if it makes it through the evening without splitting. What was I thinking?"

Katie laughed. Cassandra was poured into an electric-blue satin dress and, despite a miracle-working undergarment, there had been a sticky moment when it looked as if the zip wasn't going to make it up. She'd worn the dress to a function at Charles's bank a year ago, and apparently he'd been so taken with it she thought she'd give it another whirl tonight. She hadn't realized that, in the space of a year, she'd gone up a dress size.

"How can this be?" she'd said. "I don't eat any more than I used to, and I go to the gym twice a week."

Katie hadn't wanted to dampen Cassandra's pre-party mood by pointing out the number of calories in a glass of wine. She knew a talk with her friend about her relationship with alcohol was long overdue, but tonight wasn't the night. Cassandra was hell-bent on having fun.

"Hottest day of the year, and I've got to wear constricting underwear so as not to look like the Michelin Man," said Cassandra. "Would you credit it?"

"Makes me glad to be in my tent," said Katie, sipping an orange juice. "At least the wind can waft up it."

"What wind?" They'd opened all the windows in the kitchen, but there was no breeze to encourage through.

Katie checked her face in her handbag mirror and patted at a few beads of sweat on her brow with a tissue.

"You look really lovely," said Cassandra. "That color's perfect on you."

The dress was made of deep green silk that trickled like water through her hands. It was gathered beneath the bust and then fell in soft folds. Trevor had put subtle highlights in her hair. She'd worried that the long diamond earrings were too much—after all, it was a summer party, not a ball—but they did look good against her auburn hair.

Harry had asked her to arrive at Hampton Court by a quarter to six, to greet the first guests. "Better get going," she said, sliding slowly off her barstool.

"One for the road, then!" said Cassandra, pouring herself a third glass. It had gone by the time Katie had said goodbye to Maria and the babysitter.

Harry

Harry put down the car phone as his driver neared Hampton Court. He'd been checking with Megan that everything was going to plan. It had been a big gamble, letting her organize this, but he was confident she could do as good a job as any of the event management companies out there. If anyone knew a thing or two about parties, it was Megan.

The car swept through the gates and into the car park, where a banner pointed the way to the launch party. *Proudly sponsored by McCarey's fine wines*, it said, and Harry smiled to himself. Merry had given Rose a great deal on their new range.

He stepped out into a wall of warm humid air, a shock after the Jaguar's air-con, and looked up at the sky. It was clouding over, but the cover brought no relief from the stifling heat that had been building through the day. The sun was tracking west, and beams were slicing through a gap in the clouds, hitting the brick walls and Tudor chimneys of the palace, making them glow a fiery red.

He stood looking at the magnificent building for a moment. If its walls could talk . . .

He hoped Katie was feeling more positive about the party, now that she'd bought a new outfit and had had something expensive done to her hair. He was confident she could put her best swollen foot forward on this important night. He'd asked Megan to keep an eye on her, though she'd no doubt be rushing about the place.

Just as well. If Megan was busy, she wouldn't be able to chase Charles. It was clear she still had that girlhood crush on him—since their reunion, she'd kept finding reasons to talk to Harry about him. He thought it rather odd. Megan could have her pick of much younger, unmarried men. Perhaps it was a father substitute thing.

He was also confident Merry wouldn't be a problem. Will was coming, too, and this was a big night for them as London's movers and shakers had their first taste of McCarey's new French wines. She'd be far too busy schmoozing to cause any raised eyebrows.

As he strode toward the marquee, Harry had a good feeling. This was going to be the party of the season.

He reached the covered walkway, and his eye was caught by the floral arrangements sitting on pedestals at intervals along it. Black roses, arranged with pale trailing greenery that spilled down the columns. He'd never seen anything like them before.

Entering the enormous marquee, he spotted Megan and members of the PR department talking with the catering staff.

Where was Ana? He couldn't help himself scanning the room for her and wondered again at the strange goings-on in his head . . . and heart. He'd made a concerted effort to put any thoughts of Merry's sister to one side following the compelling attraction he'd felt toward her that evening at tennis. He'd resisted the constant temptation to visit the *Rack*'s art department, only dropping in when it was unavoidable. He'd tried so hard to put her out of his mind.

But the images in his head refused to go away. Ana with her long ponytail flying, firing volleys at him, her tennis skirt flipping up as she brought the racquet down. Those lean, tanned legs . . .

"Hello, Harry."

"Ah, Zadie." Rose Corp.'s public relations manager had appeared at his side. "Everything's looking great. Well done. Those black roses are spectacular."

"Yeah, the roses were . . ." Zadie caught sight of Ana, who was entering the marquee at the opposite end. "Ana!" she called, waving her over.

Ana didn't seem at all self-conscious of the attention she was receiving as she walked, tall and straight-backed, across the wooden floor. The velvety material of her beautifully cut black dress clung to her slim figure. The neckline plunged in a deep V, and her golden shoulders were bare. Her raven hair was arranged in a high bun with a band of tiny pearls around it, adding to her already considerable height, and there was a matching pearl choker around her long neck. Artfully applied eyeliner made her dark eyes look feline.

Zadie wolf whistled. "Ana, I think I'll set you loose on our biggest advertisers. You'll have us booked up until Christmas!"

Ana smiled. "Thank you. You don't think it's too much black for June?"

"No way, it's a great look. Oh yes, and the boss likes the roses."

Ana turned to Harry. "Hello," she said, looking at him warily.

Harry couldn't remember what he was about to say. All coherent thoughts had fled.

"The roses?" prompted Zadie.

"Ah yes. Roses. The black ones. Fabulous. Do I take it you're responsible?"

"Megan wanted roses; Terri wasn't happy with red." Her tone was cool. "I just suggested a less conventional color."

"Well, they look perfect. I can see we did the right thing getting your design skills on board. I hope you'll bring that flair into the pages of the *Rack*."

"I'm glad you like them. I should . . ." She waved her hand over at the group Megan was talking to.

"Of course, you have things to do."

Ana turned to go, and Harry saw that there was a cutaway section in the back of her dress, all the way down to just below her waist. He itched to trail his fingers down her golden skin.

"Down, boy," teased Zadie. "Though I gotta say, I reckon I'd turn for her."

Harry was shocked out of his trance. "Zadie, I can't believe you just said that."

She winked. "Don't worry, Harry. I won't tell if you won't."

CHAPTER 15

Ana

Ana, Megan, and two girls from the events company were arranging goody bags on the table at the marquee entrance. The black bags, made of luxuriously thick paper, were printed in gold with the Rose logo and the words *Are You Ready to Rack?* The goodies included a box of gourmet chocolates, a half bottle of McCarey champagne, and a single-use camera.

Souvenir issues of the *Rack* were in sealed boxes in a locked van outside and would be put out after the cover reveal had taken place.

As Terri had pointed out more than once, they were paying the events people a substantial fee to make sure everything ran like clockwork, so Ana didn't need to be doing this. But until Percy arrived (he'd been invited as an advertiser), she'd stay here as moral support for Megan.

She noticed Harry's eyes on her. Again. It was making her uncomfortable. She suspected Harry Rose was something of a ladies' man. He was charming, witty, and intelligent, but there was something about him that left her cold. She couldn't put her finger on it.

Nobody else seemed to have a problem. Everyone at Rose thought he was the bee's knees, with the possible exception of Terri (who, Ana suspected, hated everyone who'd grown up south of Watford on principle, especially if they were well-spoken).

"Action stations," hissed the girl next to her. "Guests!"

A party of three had appeared on the red carpet. Ana recognized Charles Lisle, her tennis partner. He was between two women, one blond and the other with dark red hair. The blonde was wearing a too-tight dress in a loud shade of blue and was clinging to Charles's arm. Her free arm kept flying out to the side as if she were trying to regain her balance. If Ana wasn't mistaken, she was already half-cut.

As they approached, Ana saw that the auburn-haired woman had a baby bump below her gorgeous green dress. She was attractive, in an understated way, and looked a little nervous.

Megan hurried over to them. "Hi, guys! Ohmygosh, Katie, you look *gorgeous*! You're absolutely blooming!"

Katie. This was Harry's wife. Now Ana remembered Megan saying she was going to be an auntie again.

Megan turned to Charles, who was looking down at her with affection. Ana watched his eyes rove over her lacy midnight-blue dress, cut low across her bust, then move to the red-gold curls piled on top of her head, before returning to her face, framed by corkscrew tendrils. Under his scrutiny, Megan turned slightly pink. Then she playfully punched him in the stomach. "Hello, old bean."

His smile spread into a grin, and he pulled one of her curls straight, letting it spring back up. "Looking good, Nutmeg."

The blond woman gave a not very subtle cough.

"Sorry, ladies," said Charles, not taking his eyes from Megan. "Forgetting my manners. Megan, this is Cassandra. Cassandra, meet Harry's baby sister, Megan."

"*Enchantée*," said Cassandra. "I hear you've been in France. Must be nice to be back in the *bosom* of your family." Her eyes traveled to Megan's obvious cleavage.

Charles spotted Ana and came across, ushering the two women with him.

"Ana, we meet again. Ladies, this is Ana Lyebon, also recently returned from *la belle* France. She has a fearsome volley. You look *très chic*,

Ana." He kissed her on both cheeks. "Ana, this is Cassandra—Mrs. Lisle—and Katie Rose."

Ana was about to compliment Katie on her dress, when Harry appeared by his wife's side.

"Harry!" said Cassandra, rather loudly, and helped herself to a glass of wine from a nearby waiter's tray.

"Hello, Cass." Harry kissed her cheek, then touched Katie on the arm. "You look lovely, sweetheart. How are you managing in this heat?"

"Not too bad, but I don't think I'll be doing much dancing."

"Would you like a glass of water?" asked Ana. Without waiting for a reply, she waved the waiter back and handed a mineral water to Katie.

"Thanks." Katie smiled, but Ana detected a wariness.

"Ah, here comes your sister, Ana," said Harry.

Merry was sashaying down the red carpet toward them in a white 1950s-style dress, on the arm of Will, who looked a little gaunt. Ana felt a niggle of worry. Given Will's lifestyle . . .

"Oh, it's *her*," hissed Cassandra.

Ana was used to other women's reactions to her sister.

Harry frowned. "VIP guest and major sponsor, Cassandra," he said in a low voice. "And Ana's sister."

"Darlings!" called Merry.

Ana didn't miss the way she squeezed Harry's arm when he kissed her cheek. Once again she had an inkling Merry might be supplying more than Harry's wine.

"Wilsky, old chap," said Charles, shaking Will's hand. "How's the booze business?"

"Whisky's doing welski, thank you, Lisle. Jury's still out on the wine—we're hoping Merry's efforts are rewarded tonight."

Cassandra took a very obvious sip of hers. "Not bad. Notes of Tesco chardonnay."

There was an awkward pause, then Ana said, "The caterers were saying it has a lovely crispness, just right for a summer party."

"Ana, darling," said Will. "I see you're channeling Hepburn. I *adore* the look."

And she adored his soft Scottish accent.

"While everyone else is wilting," he said, "you manage to look cool as a cucumber, as always."

More guests were now arriving. Harry took Katie's arm and went to greet them.

Cassandra was swaying slightly as she sipped her wine, and her eyes kept sliding over to Megan. Ana watched her, feeling uneasy, wishing she'd ease up on the drink—they didn't want any dramas to spoil the smooth running of the evening.

"Megan," she said. "Can I just check with you about . . . our special guest?" She twitched her head toward the area behind the tables.

Thankfully, Megan remembered the real reason she was there, and followed Ana.

"Doesn't Charles look utterly *gorgeous* in a suit?" she said, gazing across at him.

"Don't, Megan. His wife's already looking daggers at you. Do you want to cause a scene at your first big event? Get professional."

Megan pouted. "OK, sorry. I'll behave. Ah, here's Percy. At least one of us will be getting some tonight."

Ana's fiancé was looking dapper in a Paul Smith suit. He shared a few words with Harry, then came over. "Ana, you look incredible. Hi, Megan. Dig the corkscrew curls. Hey, I finally got to meet your famous brother! He seems really nice."

"He's the best," said Megan. "Right, I'd better make myself useful. Ana—you're off the hook now. Go have fun with Percy. Party on!"

Ana smiled. They'd recently been to see *Wayne's World*, and Megan had adopted the battle cry.

The trickle of people turned into a steady stream, and the marquee started to buzz.

"So who's who, then?" said Percy. He looked around with interest.

Ana pointed out a few people.

"That's Katie Rose? I thought Harry would be married to someone more glamorous. And she's got to be quite a bit older than him."

"She's pregnant, in case you hadn't noticed," said Ana. "How could anyone look glamorous lugging a subcutaneous baby around in this heat? I think it's brave of her to come at all. And has it occurred to you Harry might love her for her brain?"

Percy looked taken aback. "Sorry, yes, of course. Mustn't be mean about the boss's wife."

"What's the time?" said Ana suddenly, scanning the room for Megan. She spotted her coming back with Terri.

"You're not needed," said Terri, waving Ana away.

Percy's eyes widened. "Cruella?" he muttered.

"How did you guess?"

Megan touched Harry on the arm and whispered something in his ear. He murmured a few words to the minor royals he'd been talking to and guided Katie over to the red carpet.

Ana couldn't help but gasp as David Bowie and his statuesque new wife, Iman, entered the marquee. Bowie wore a sea-green jacket over beige trousers, and a spotted red tie. Suddenly every other man in the room looked exceedingly dull.

As everyone craned their necks for a better look, Ana noticed Lizzie, the art editor, peeling the overlay off the huge poster to one side of the stage. It was a blowup of the *Rack*'s first cover, and until now there was a question mark where the image should have been.

The black-and-white photograph showed a different Bowie from the affable man on the red carpet—unsmiling, challenging, those famous eyes dominating the cover with their direct gaze. The (Pantone Rose Red) typography read, *IS IT ANY WONDER? BOWIE ON FAME, LOVE, AND LIVING IN AMERICA.*

The crowd parted as Harry ushered the couple to the stage, a few feeble flashes firing as guests attempted a snapshot with their goody-bag cameras. Terri had bollocked Megan for including them, wondering why they'd banned press photographers if "every Tom, Dick, and Harry" at the party was going to be given a camera.

"I don't think a blurred Fuji freebie developed a week after the event will be a threat to our professional," Megan had replied.

Of course, Terri had known that; she just liked having a go at Megan—who'd really pushed her luck by adding, "And I don't think you'll find Harry bothering with his disposable, even if Tom and Dick give it a whirl."

Harry introduced a couple of VIPs to Bowie and Iman along the way, all the while keeping things moving. He was a natural at this. Finally they were on the stage, and Harry tapped the microphone. The talking died down.

"My lords, ladies, and gentlemen. Welcome to the launch of the *Rack*."

He had almost (but not quite) as much onstage presence as Bowie.

"Back in the fifties, my father, the late Henry Rose, started work as a reporter on a small newspaper called the *Lancaster Chronicle*. Ten years later, this exceptional man was head of the most dynamic print media company in England, with a stable of groundbreaking newspapers and magazines.

"When I started at Rose, I took a good hard look at our titles and asked myself, 'What would Dad have done?' And it was as if he answered, *No one believes what they read in the press anymore, Harry. You should change that. Give the British people the truth. Decide who matters, and ask them the tough questions.*

"And so, ladies and gentlemen, the *Rack* was born . . ."

He thanked Bowie profusely for being their "first person on the rack" and then concluded, "Before I let you all get back to the serious business of partying, I'd like to introduce you to our editor." He beckoned Terri onto the stage. "Or as I like to call her, Torturer in Chief." There was a ripple of laughter. "Terri—short for Terrifying—will be writing our lead features herself. I think David's still talking to her?"

Bowie chuckled and nodded.

"Terri has brought to life my vision, and I'm sure you'll agree that the *Rack* is a triumph. So thanks to Terri and her team"—his eyes met Ana's—"for creating what will be Britain's coolest read. Thank you again for coming along, everyone. Now, as they say, party on!"

He must have got that from Megan.

Harry led David and Iman to a table at the edge of the dance floor, where Sting and his wife greeted them.

Now that the official part of the evening was done, staff moved the DJ's equipment forward. Waiters with platters of finger food began circulating, and the noise in the marquee rose again.

So far, so good, thought Ana. Everything was going beautifully.

CHAPTER 16

Katie

The marquee was stifling. There were pedestal fans around the sides, but they were only wafting the hot, sticky air around.

"You need to shit down—sit down," said Cassandra. "Let's grab a sheat." She pulled out a chair and waved over the nearest waiter. "Bottle of Bolly over here, and water for my friend, please."

"I don't have bottles," he said, "but I can see—"

"Please do. I'll take one of those to be going on with."

Katie lowered herself onto the chair. "Ah, that's better. Cass, maybe you should have water, too, this time round? Pace yourself a bit? We've got a long night ahead of us."

"Bugger that," said Cassandra. "This is sheriously thirshty work."

Katie looked around for Charles, thinking it might be wise to have a quiet word, but he was nowhere to be seen.

Cassandra leaned toward her. "That Merry, I don't trusht her. And Jesus, did you clock that white dress? All she needs is a grille to stand over for the full Marilyn Monroe. And her husband's *got* to be gay. I mean, how many straight blokes do you know who tell a woman she's channeling Hepburn?" Cassandra looked across to where Ana Lyebon was talking to a man wearing eye makeup, who might have been from Duran Duran. "Hepburn, my arse. Morticia Addams, more like."

"The two sisters are very different," said Katie.

"One's too hot and one's too cold."

"Like the three bears' porridge."

The DJ spun his first disc, and a group of young women, probably from Rose, hit the dance floor.

"I feel so old," said Katie. "And I hardly know anyone, apart from you and Charles. I've been so out of it all since I became a mum."

"You know Harry's sister. Christ, she's a piece of work."

Katie was finding Cassandra's drunken bitchiness tiring. She felt herself being dragged down by the oppressive heat and her friend's negativity.

"Oh, she's just a bit of a flirt. I'm sure Charles thinks of her like a little sister."

"Yeah, right. And she's only looking at him like a big brother? Like hell she is." She pushed her chair back suddenly, saying, "I'm going outside now, I may be some time." Everyone at the next table heard too.

"Why? Are you too hot?" said Katie. "Do you want me to come with you?"

"No, I need a pee, and it's going to be a major mission in this armored underwear. Stay where you are, Katie. You've done your bit, you can blob for the rest of the party if you want."

It was true. Harry didn't need her now that everyone had arrived. She glanced over to where he was talking to the Lord Mayor of London and his wife.

Cassandra staggered off toward the exit, and Katie was glad to see her make it out of the marquee without tripping up or colliding with anything.

She watched the dance floor, feeling a stab of envy at the twenty-somethings having fun. She imagined the pitying eyes seeing Katie Rose sitting alone, the pregnant wallflower sipping her sad glass of water.

Perhaps she should join Harry. She looked around again and saw him laughing heartily with a group of similarly braying men in suits.

No.

She decided to go outside for some air. Making her way to a side exit, she stepped into the gathering dusk and stopped to savor the sudden peace and the view of Hampton Court in front of her. The floodlights had been switched on, and the air was heavy with the scent of flowers from the palace gardens. A few couples were wandering along the paths, enjoying the romance of it all, and she felt very alone.

Even the baby had gone quiet. She hadn't felt it kicking since this morning.

She took some deep breaths, but the air out here wasn't much fresher than inside. It felt charged, crackling in anticipation of what the towering cumulonimbus overhead were threatening to unleash. A breeze scuttled briefly across her path as she set off walking again, trying to shake off a sudden restlessness.

Already her feet were protesting. She stepped onto the strip of lawn alongside the path and took off her shoes. It was bliss, the cool grass soothing her hot, swollen feet. She walked a little further before sinking down onto a bench.

Katie let the beauty of the Tudor palace wash over her. She looked up at the windows, thrown into black relief by the floodlights, and remembered a recent stroll in the grounds with Harry and Maria, Harry spooking them with stories about the palace ghosts. One was Jane Seymour, Henry VIII's third wife, and then there was the terrified teenager Catherine Howard, his fifth, who famously ran screaming along the Haunted Gallery after news of her arrest for treason.

Katie was brought back to the present by the sound of approaching footsteps. It was Harry's old school friend Will McCarey.

"Escaping the seething horde?" he said. "Wise move. Too hot in there for me. There are people dancing, would you believe?"

"I have the perfect Get Out of Jail Free card," said Katie, patting her bump.

"So you do. Congratulations! Mind if I join you?"

"Oh, please do. I was feeling like the biggest wallflower in the history of bedding plants."

"I was admiring your dress earlier," he said, sitting down. "Do you mind?" His hand hovered over the fabric.

"Be my guest."

"What a lovely silk." He then suggested how she could modify it into a cocktail dress later on. What a nice man.

"Quite a pad, isn't it?" he said, looking around at the palace, its colors now fading in the twilight.

"I was just thinking about its history. The ghosts. I don't really believe in them. Do you?"

Will smiled.

> *"The spirit-world around this world of sense*
> *Floats like an atmosphere, and everywhere*
> *Wafts through these earthly mists and vapors dense*
> *A vital breath of more ethereal air."*

Katie looked at him in surprise. "Oh, that was beautiful!"

"Longfellow. It goes a bit bonkers at the end, but it's one of my favorites."

"Are you a fan of poetry?"

"Had it drummed into me at school. But yes. Your Harry was good at it—he wrote it too. Wasn't half-bad."

"He can be pretty creative."

"Would you like to know a secret?"

Katie wondered what on earth this person she hardly knew was about to share. "I don't know, would I?"

"I had a big crush on your husband at school. I decided I was the only one who understood him."

"Oh. I see! Well, I had a crush on a girl. Letty Anders. Long golden hair. That's single-sex schools for you."

"Indeed," said Will, and they were quiet again.

A fat raindrop plopped into Katie's lap, making a dark blot on the silk, and they looked up at the sky just as lightning flashed over to the north, silhouetting the tall Tudor chimneys. There was a distant rumble.

"Looks like our time's up," said Will.

They were just getting up to go, Will gallantly offering his arm, when the sound of someone yelling reached them. It seemed to be coming from the maze, which was a short distance away.

"Too funny," said Will. "Someone's lost in the maze and there's going to be a thunderstorm."

"Surely the maze is out of bounds?" said Katie.

"Wouldn't you have? When you were a bright young thing?"

"That stage seemed to pass me by."

The yelling came again. It was a woman's voice.

"Perhaps we should investigate?" said Katie as more raindrops smacked into the path.

But a maze rescue wasn't necessary. Cassandra appeared out of its entrance at a run, closely followed by Charles, who was calling to her to stop. Finally, Megan appeared behind them.

"Oh no," said Katie. "Cassandra!"

"Stop her, Katie!" called Charles. "There's been a misunderstanding!"

Katie moved to block Cassandra's path. She didn't want her friend making an exhibition of herself inside the marquee.

The gravel hurt her feet.

"Katie, be careful," called Will.

Cassandra ground to a halt and turned on Charles, who had quickly caught up. Behind them, Megan slowed to a walk.

"You BASTARD!" Cassandra shrieked.

"Calm down, Cassandra, for god's sake," said Charles. "We were just fooling around in the maze."

"Fooling around? FOOLING AROUND? You were *kissing*! BAS-TARD!" She swayed, and Katie reached out to steady her.

"Cassandra, this isn't the time or place," Katie said. "You and Charles can talk when you get home. Which should probably be soon."

"It wasn't his fault," said Megan, catching them up. Her cheeks were pink and her lipstick smudged. "I'm sorry, I shouldn't have—"

"Shut up, slut," spat Cassandra. "You wheedle your way in here with your stupid non-job so you can steal my fucking HUSBAND . . ." Then suddenly she was launching herself at Megan.

Instinctively, Katie moved to pull her off, but as she grabbed Cassandra around the waist, her friend pushed her away, catching her in the stomach with her elbow.

Pain shot through Katie's abdomen, and she cried out, doubling over.

Charles hauled Cassandra off Megan, then crouched down at Katie's side, searching her face. "Katie, are you OK?"

Cassandra's hands flew to her mouth. "Katie, I'm—"

Charles turned on her, his expression full of disgust. "Fuck off, Cassandra. Just fuck the hell off."

"No, I'm not all right," gasped Katie as pain ripped through her stomach. A clap of thunder exploded over the palace, and the rain grew heavier. "I think the baby's coming, but it's too early." Despair washed over her, and she began to cry. "I'm going to lose it again, Charles, aren't I?"

"No, Katie, you're going to be all right. We'll get you straight to hospital, try not to panic."

He turned to Megan. "Find Harry—be quick."

Harry

I t's great to meet you properly at last," said the fair-haired man, pumping Harry's hand. "I've heard so much about you from Ana and Megan!"

Harry searched his memory for an ID—jacket sleeves rolled up (why didn't he just take it off?), Australian surfer hair (no way were those streaks natural).

"Percy North, BWG," prompted Surfer Boy.

Ah, that would be why Harry's hackles were raised. This was Ana's fiancé.

"Of course. Are you enjoying the party?"

"I most certainly am, Harry! The girls have done a great job, haven't they?"

"Indeed. What's your role at BWG?"

"Account director. I work on some really happening accounts."

"Oh, you're a bag carrier. What do you think of the *Rack*?"

"Haha! Yes, a bag carrier, for my sins. The *Rack* looks very cool, I'm sure we'll be queuing up to book space. I can't wait to read the Bowie article. Sounds like Terri Robbins-More is one mean interviewer."

"The best there is."

"Mean boss, too, though, apparently. Gives Ana a hard time."

This conversation was going nowhere Harry was interested in.

"I'm sure Ana's capable of looking after herself. And Terri is impressed with what the designers have been doing, even if she doesn't constantly dish out the praise."

"Megan's done a great job this evening too," said Percy. "You must be proud of your sister. She's such a fun person to be around. I love hanging out at the girls' flat. Though Ana and I will be moving in together as soon as we find a place."

What was a woman like Ana doing with this sycophantic bore?

Looking over Percy's shoulder, Harry saw Merry heading toward them. She looked pretty tonight, but there was perhaps too much of the blond bombshell going on. Other women were giving her the side-eye, while men were openly ogling her.

"Hello, boys!" she said.

Of course, she would know Ana's fiancé.

"Harry, this is—" began Percy.

"He knows who I am, silly. I'm his chosen provider of wine and . . . other things." She winked at Harry.

What the heck?

She touched Harry's arm. "Champagne too. Have you tried it?"

"The response has been good, you'll be glad to hear."

"Lordy, these shoes are killing me," said Merry, and she clung to Harry's arm as she lifted a foot and wiggled it around.

Ana appeared at Percy's side. "Has anyone seen Megan?" She did a double take at Merry, still clinging to Harry's arm. "She's wanted by the caterers." She frowned slightly at her sister.

"I was just saying what a great job Megan's done tonight," said Percy.

"I think I saw her with your friend," Merry said to Harry. "The guy with glasses."

"Charles?" said Harry sharply.

"Here she is," said Ana. "Thank goodness. I couldn't have covered for her for much longer. Oh, I guess the rain's finally here."

Harry followed Ana's gaze and saw Megan hurrying toward them, her shoes in one hand, her hair wet and sticking to her face. Her expression was panicked. His heart sank. Had something happened between her and Charles?

"Megan? What on earth?" He shook off Merry's arm impatiently.

"Harry, come quick," Megan panted. "Ana, I need you to phone for an ambulance. Katie's gone into labor."

"Oh, how exciting!" said Percy.

A wave of panic hit Harry. She was only seven months along. He knew nothing about survival rates, but this couldn't be good.

"Where?" said Harry.

"Follow me."

Outside, through the pouring rain, Harry saw Katie, supported by Charles on one side and Cassandra on the other.

"An ambulance is coming," he called.

They stopped walking, as Katie was clearly having a contraction.

"Katie!" Harry said, reaching her.

She let go of Charles's arm and grabbed his own as she doubled over with a moan. Her wet dress clung to her stomach and legs.

"I'm so sorry, Harry," Cassandra said, and he saw tears mingling with the raindrops running down her face. "I'm so—"

"Shut the fuck up, Cassandra," growled Charles. "It's not about you."

"Cass," gasped Katie, straightening up a little. "It wasn't your fault."

"The fuck it wasn't," said Charles. "If you hadn't—"

"Stop it, you two. Save it for later," said Harry.

The rain intensified, the drops slicing like shards of glass across the beams of the palace floodlights. There was a flash of lightning, and thunder crashed overhead. Harry had a momentary fancy that it was a reprimand from the big man upstairs, for not checking on his wife. What had happened to Katie while he was schmoozing VIPs and obsessing over Ana?

As thunder reverberated around the palace, Ana and Merry appeared, hurrying toward them under two big black umbrellas. Merry's white dress and platinum-blond hair stood out in the gloom.

Ana sheltered Katie as she began to move again, dragging heavily on Harry's arm. Merry held the other umbrella over Harry, but he waved her away.

"Is she . . ." said Ana.

"The baby's coming," Harry said grimly.

"Megan's waiting for the ambulance at the drop-off point."

"Harry," whispered Katie. He bent down to listen. "It's too soon. Why is God doing this to us?"

"They can do wonders," he said. "Tinier babies than ours survive. You and the baby are going to be just fine." But his voice caught, and as Megan and the paramedics appeared on the path, and Katie clung to his hand, a terrible certainty filled his heart.

CHAPTER 17

Harry

November 1992

It was seven thirty, and Harry was still at work. It had been dark for hours, and out of his office window the lights of London were blurred by the fine drizzle falling across the city.

Britain was in the grip of late-autumn gloom. The recession was dragging on, and unemployment was expected to hit three million soon. Harry was about to add to that, with a number of layoffs. Rose Corp. was doing well, bucking the trend, but Colin Hale, his bean counter in chief, was telling him they needed to cut costs, be leaner.

The Queen had just called 1992 her annus horribilis. Since June, Harry's own annus had been excessively horribilis. Five months after his baby son (they'd called him Max) had been stillborn at twenty-nine weeks, he was still regularly blindsided by grief. The universe could be so cruel.

But at least he had his work—and thoughts of Ana—to distract him.

Harry put down his pen and looked out the window, wondering again what to do about Katie. She seemed unreachable, hadn't even begun to climb out of the dark place she'd fallen into. The only spark was when she spent time with Maria, reading her books or watching her play with her toys. But she never took her out, other than to and from school, which she'd started in September. Katie constantly fretted over Maria's health, the sad legacy of her miscarriages and stillbirths. Harry knew he should talk to her about the overprotectiveness. It was turning the child into a drama queen. Maria really did stamp her foot when she didn't get her own way.

Her brattish behavior was raising eyebrows, and they'd already been contacted by the school about "Maria's issues around inclusion and space," which apparently meant not sharing, and demanding the best spot on the mat.

Before, Cassandra had always been there to help Katie out of her despair. She'd cheer her up with a shopping trip or an outing with the children.

But now poor Cass had her own demons to face.

A postmortem established that the baby's death had nothing to do with the blow to Katie's abdomen—that had just speeded up the inevitable. A chromosomal abnormality was responsible for a defect that meant the baby wouldn't have made it to full term, and Katie could have miscarried at any time. But that didn't stop Cassandra from blaming herself. And Charles hadn't forgiven her behavior that night, whatever part he may have played in provoking the drunken meltdown.

"Dry out or get out," he'd said. So Cassandra had checked into the Priory and was attempting to kick the addiction she'd finally admitted to.

Harry and Charles's friendship was strained, too, and he felt the loss of their easy companionship. Harry was livid that Charles had led Megan on that night. No matter how flighty she was, Charles was the older married man who should have known better. And now Megan imagined herself madly in love with him and had practically cheered when Cassandra was packed off to rehab. Harry was exasperated with them both.

Charles had accused him of hypocrisy. "What gives you the right to judge, with your blond bombshell tucked away in South Ken?"

But that was completely different. He and Merry both knew the boundaries, and nobody would get hurt. Besides, he rarely saw Merry now. He'd found himself making excuses, and when they did get together, he was easily bored, and . . . he admitted to himself that the only way he could lift his performance from mildly aroused to passionate was to visualize Ana's willowy body, her glossy black hair, her dark, dark eyes.

Merry had her own problems too. Will was increasingly unwell, and was holed up in his Scottish castle.

Things seemed to be going badly for all of them.

Harry began loading his briefcase with reports, his copy of the *Times*, and his Filofax. At least, in spite of the recession, Rose was continuing to bloom. Circulation figures for the *Rack* had exceeded expectations. The only downside was that Terri needed no input from him at all. She ran a tight, efficient ship and coaxed increasingly creative triumphs from her staff, in spite of her tyrannical management style.

The art editor had so far been the only one to cave, leaving for a job at *Hello!* Ana had been promoted to replace her, and Harry dropped by her office to congratulate her.

As Harry had shut Ana's office door behind him, causing her to frown slightly, he'd had the strongest compulsion to pull her into his arms and tell her the truth—that he was losing sleep over her. That he was a man possessed. That he couldn't go on like this.

Instead, as he'd met her cool, unsmiling gaze, he'd placed a bottle of champagne on her desk, saying, "A small token of my appreciation. I know you've only been with us a short while, but you've earned this promotion fair and square. Well done."

"Thank you."

"And . . . Ana. We haven't talked properly since—well, since June. But thank you for your help. Your calmness under pressure, and all that."

"How is Katie?"

"Not great. Searching for reasons why when there aren't any. It's hard to reach her when she's like this. I'm not sure that I can anymore."

"That's very sad. She should probably go back to work, take her mind off things."

"She has Maria."

"Isn't she at school?"

"Yes, she's just started."

"Then she should definitely get a job. I'm sure it would help. And commiserations on the loss of your baby. It must have been awful for you too."

"Thanks. Yes, it was. Again." He sighed. "I wish death would leave me the fuck alone."

Anna frowned, and their eyes locked for a moment.

"I hear your friend Cassandra's in rehab," she said.

"How did you . . . ?"

"Megan told me."

"Of course." His tone of voice must have said it all.

"Don't be too hard on Megan, Harry. She thinks the world of you, and this rift between you and Charles is really upsetting her."

"He needs to get his relationship back on track without any distractions."

"Maybe you don't realize how Megan feels. It's not a schoolgirl infatuation anymore. I honestly think she loves him."

An idea formed in Harry's head. "Perhaps I should come over and talk to her."

There was a pause.

"Or take her out for dinner, maybe," said Ana. "Neutral ground."

"Home turf might be better, if there are going to be tears."

So Harry was going over to Megan's flat tomorrow. He hoped Ana would be there—and he sincerely hoped that preening ponce Percy wouldn't be.

Ana

"There's *The Bodyguard*?"

"Not keen, to be honest," said Percy.

Ana had suggested a movie, to give Harry and Megan some space. "Or we could just go out to eat?"

"I had a big lunch. And I'm a bit knackered. Can't we stay in?"

The penny dropped. Percy and his team were pitching for the Rose account in two weeks' time, and Percy somehow thought hanging out in the flat while Harry tackled his sister about her relationship with Charles was going to help with that.

"Don't mind me," called Megan from the kitchen. "Ana, it'd actually be good to have you here. Harry respects you."

Percy lifted his eyebrows at Ana and smiled. "That's great. I hope Terri knows."

"I don't think I'd be much help, Megan," she replied, ignoring Percy. "You know what I think. You've got to give Charles a chance with Cassandra—there are kids involved. If rehab works, they could be all set for a fresh start."

"But what's the point? He doesn't love her anymore. He loves me. He told me."

"You've been seeing him?" said Percy. He looked shocked.

Ana knew what was going on between Megan and Charles. She'd rather not have known, and had told Megan it wasn't happening in this flat—but she hadn't shared the news with Percy.

She'd been hoping it would all go away, that Megan would move on, to someone younger, unmarried, childless. In all the time she'd known her, Megan had never stuck with a man longer than a month or two, always growing bored.

But Megan insisted on sharing every last detail of her deepening relationship. She was worryingly indiscreet, and Ana had warned her that if news of Charles's philandering reached his wife, that might set Cassandra back, and that wouldn't help anyone.

"Look, I'm not a home-wrecker," she'd replied. "Their marriage is finished. She'll just have to get over it. I've known Charles since I was a girl, and I've never really loved anyone else. It's always been him. I just had to wait to grow up. And he said he's had lots of affairs; she's even known about some of them—"

"Is that supposed to make me more sympathetic toward him?" Ana had cut in.

"Well you see, now he realizes they were all a symptom of his dissatisfaction with his marriage. She wasn't enough. He says he's never felt about anyone the way he feels about me."

To Ana, Charles just sounded weak. And that particular sort of weakness, the type that involved concocting a pathetic, self-justifying rationale for bad behavior, was the worst weakness of all. If Charles had betrayed Cassandra time after time, no wonder she'd sought comfort in the bottle.

"Sounds as if you two are serious," said Percy. "What does Harry think about it?"

"He doesn't realize how we feel," Megan replied. "I'm going to put him straight tonight. If Harry's hearing it from both Charles and me, we might be able to change his mind. He knows we've always loved each other—it's just a different kind of love now."

"How about we stay for a little while, and then go out for a drink?" said Percy. "You and Harry could come with us?"

"Harry will be going home," Ana said.

There was a knock at the door. It looked like big brother was already here.

Ana went into the kitchen to put the kettle on. She'd busy herself making tea.

She heard the murmur of voices from the next room. Mainly Percy's.

She poked her head around the door. "Would anyone like tea or coffee? Hello, Harry."

"Ana. Tea would be lovely. I'm parched."

For a moment she saw Percy through Harry's eyes. He was wearing acid-wash jeans and a crisp white shirt with the sleeves rolled up, revealing his chunky gold watch. His blond curls, much longer at the back than the front, fell over his turned-up collar. The look she'd initially found quite appealing now looked try-hard next to Harry's beautifully tailored suit. She wondered if Harry knew Percy was heading up the pitch team for the Rose account.

"Can we not have wine?" called Megan.

"Tea first," replied Ana. "Percy, can you give me a hand?"

As he came into the kitchen, she pushed the door shut. "Percy, it's really important that Megan and Harry sort this out. Don't get in the way."

"I understand. But it's important for me to network. I shouldn't waste this opportunity to get to know Harry a little better. You know what's coming up."

"Leave it, Percy! Tonight has nothing to do with business." She crashed the mugs down onto the tray and wrenched open the fridge door. "Milk! No bloody milk again. Bloody Megan."

"Calm down, Ana. What's wrong? Anyone would think it was you getting a bollocking from Harry."

She spotted the milk hiding behind a stack of ready meals.

Ana opened the kitchen door again and saw Megan in floods of tears. But Harry was talking to her gently. He had a lovely voice, low and reassuring.

"Sorry, sorry," said Ana. "I just wondered . . . milk and sugar, Harry?"

He smiled at her. "A drop of milk, thanks."

Percy carried his own and Ana's mugs out and hovered in the living room, while Ana gave Megan and Harry theirs.

"Bedroom, Percy," she said. Then added, "We're going to the pub when we've drunk these, so you can have the place to yourselves."

"That's really not necessary," said Harry, "though it's kind of you. Hopefully Megan and I will be all talked out soon."

"We could all go to the pub?" said Megan, wiping away her tears.

"Why not?" said Percy.

Harry looked at Ana. "Perhaps a quick one, but only if I can make Megan see sense first."

Percy was about to open his mouth again, but Ana pulled him by the sleeve into the bedroom.

Five minutes later the sound of Megan's raised voice reached them. Ana had been telling Percy about Terri's latest interview coup—Tom Cruise was on the *Rack*, and she was planning to grill him about his interest in Scientology.

"Sh!" said Percy.

"Stop eavesdropping!" said Ana.

They heard a door slam, and there was a tap on the bedroom door. Ana opened it to see Harry.

"Can I have a word?"

"Stay there, Percy," she said, and followed Harry into the living room, closing the bedroom door behind her.

"Thanks for your discretion," Harry said, sitting down on the sofa and shifting across so there was space beside him. He'd taken off his jacket and loosened his tie, and now leaned forward, elbows on knees. He put his chin in his hands and sighed.

Ana had been heading for the armchair but hesitated. Harry looked so dejected. She sat down next to him—and immediately regretted it. He smelled divine. *What* was that aftershave? And with his head lowered in defeat, she had a sudden urge to stroke his beautiful golden hair.

Harry glanced over at Megan's bedroom door. "She won't budge, Ana. I want Charles and Cass to have a chance to patch things up. They're a great couple, and they have two kids. Plus Cassandra's been a big help with Katie."

"I know how difficult Megan's being," said Ana, trying to concentrate on the problem at hand. "I've told her splitting up a family isn't cool, but she's kind of obsessed."

Harry looked sideways at her, his gaze intense. It reminded her of yesterday, when he'd wished death would stay away. The mask had slipped, and she'd glimpsed the emotion beneath.

"Love can be hard," he said. "I do feel for Megan. I kind of understand."

"You do?" Ana's heart was beating faster than it should have been.

He sat back and sighed again, running his fingers through his hair, not taking his eyes from hers. "We can't help what we feel. Sometimes the strongest feelings come at the worst possible time, or we fall in love with the wrong person. We don't mean it to happen; we don't choose it."

"But we can choose not to act on those feelings," said Ana, "if that would wreck others' lives. We have free will."

"When we're in love, we can lose sight of what's right and wrong. It's part of being human."

For the first time since she'd met him, Ana began to understand why Harry meant so much to Megan, and why she was desperate for his approval. He was a deep thinker. It came as a surprise.

But still, there was something deeply unsettling about him, like a scent your subconscious picks up before you're even aware it's there.

"Charles really does seem to feel the same as Megan," he continued.

As she held his gaze, she could almost see his mind changing as he processed the conversation he'd just had with his sister and let the words he'd spoken to Ana, about trying to resist the force of love, overtake his earlier words about trying to hold together a marriage, until they were left behind and a new truth filled that space.

"He's practically washed his hands of Cassandra," he said. "I don't know—maybe he *should* move on. Maybe they *are* meant to be together. If he doesn't love Cass anymore, is there really any point?"

"What are you going to say to Megan?"

"Perhaps I'll suggest some length of time, to give Cassandra a chance to get her life back on track, with Charles there to support her. He could see how he feels after that. Maybe he'll cool off, I don't know. And if not, then he'll have to find some way of leaving that doesn't send Cassandra straight back to the bottle, like an amicable separation . . . I don't know—does that ever work? Maybe then we can all move on."

"She's lucky to have you as a brother," said Ana.

Was Harry blushing?

CHAPTER 18

Ana

By lunchtime, Rose Corp. employees were calling the fourth of December Black Friday. Redundancies were happening, and staff were being called in one by one to find out whether they were to go or stay.

So far, in the *Rack*'s offices, Nate had kept his job, but their new editorial assistant, Tim, had lost his. Tim had shown promise, so they were all feeling horrible about it. Terri was staying (of course) and had already tipped off Ana that her job was safe.

"Will I still need to see Harry?" Ana asked. According to those who'd already been summoned, "Harry Rose himself" was sitting in on the interviews.

Terri was perched on Ana's desk munching a Prêt à Manger sandwich. Although it was lunchtime, nobody else seemed to be eating. The dreadful quiet was broken by the sound of someone across the office swearing viciously at their computer.

"Yes. Fook knows why."

Tim was sorting through the contents of his desk. "It's pointless him being there," he said. "Stupid. Like hearing it from the great man himself would make it sooo much easier. 'Cause it's like, *so* painful for him, but it's for the greater good. Why the fuck would I believe Harry Rose's lame reasons for axing staff when the company's doing pretty damn well?"

"What reasons did he give?" asked Ana.

"Some bollocks about 'future-proofing'—is that even an expression? Restructuring so Rose is well positioned for the 'new online age.'" He made quotation marks in the air. "Probably just wants to keep more of the profits to put toward a private Caribbean island. Branson's got one, so no doubt he wants one too."

"Tim, sorry, love, but you just need to pack up your stuff and go," said Terri.

"What?"

"My orders from inhuman resources. People who're going must leave immediately, so they don't bring down the stayers. I know this sucks, but you're best out of it. Go home and get pissed. I would. And, Tim—I'll send you a reference and it will be fookin' glowing."

Tim sat down suddenly, defeated. "I've loved it here. And I'm going to miss you all."

Nate appeared. "Ana, your turn to see the axman."

Ana made her way, along a corridor lined with framed magazine covers, to the boardroom. She passed a designer from *Hooray!* with tears running down her face. Ana didn't meet her eye.

She knocked, and a female voice called her in.

At the oval table sat Harry, in rolled-up shirtsleeves, his hair backlit by the rare winter sun shining through the window. With him was Lesley from human resources.

"Ana! Come in and sit down," said Lesley, a pleasant smile on her face.

Glancing again at Harry, Ana wondered how he could look so relaxed when he'd spent the morning wrecking lives.

Lesley had just opened her mouth to speak when Harry leaned forward and said, "Ana. How do you feel you've been getting on as part of the *Rack* team? And where do you see yourself in two or three years' time?"

Ana hadn't been expecting a performance review but had no problem letting Harry know of her ambitions. "I couldn't ask for a more inspirational art director than Nate, and working with Terri has given me invaluable experience in how innovative design can showcase the best editorial. As for the future, I'd expect to be an art director within two years, if not here, then with another leading publisher, or perhaps an ad agency."

"So you'd say you're ambitious?" said Harry.

"Absolutely."

"And which would you say was more important—your career, or your personal life?"

Ana was thrown by the question. "I've never had a problem combining the two."

"How well would you say you cope under pressure?"

"I don't cope, I thrive. Deadlines bring out the best in me."

Harry glanced at Lesley before continuing. "We've been very impressed with your work, Ana. As part of our restructuring, we're moving Tonya Teague across to *Foodie*, and we'd like you to take over the art director position at *Hooray!* We feel it's in need of a redesign. Do you think this is something you could successfully manage?"

Ana tried to hide the elation threatening to burst out of her. This was huge. Only months ago she'd been a trainee designer on a new magazine no one had heard of. Now they wanted her to head up the design team of one of Britain's most popular weeklies.

"I'd love to freshen up *Hooray!* I've had some thoughts about it for a while, in fact. So yes, I know I'd be able to come up with ideas you'd be excited about."

"Excellent. Well, I'm sure I won't be popular with Nate and Terri, but this is what Rose is all about—bringing through people who show great promise, giving them the opportunity to . . ." He grimaced. "Bloom."

Ana couldn't help a smile.

"Yes, I did just say that. I suggest after the current issue of the *Rack* has been put to bed, you move across to *Hooray!* with the aim of a soft relaunch early next year. Mia's on board and I'm sure will welcome the opportunity to work with fresh new talent."

Ana wasn't so sure. Mia had a reputation for being devious as a snake, and her venom was legendary.

"I'll be mostly hands-off," said Harry, "but I do want to have input, as *Hooray!* is one of our flagship magazines."

"Thank you for the opportunity. I'm very much looking forward to getting started."

Harry nodded to Lesley, then sat back in his chair and ran his eyes over Ana as Lesley spoke.

"There will of course be a substantial increase in your salary and benefits," she said. "You may discuss the move with your team on the *Rack*, but it would be inappropriate to talk to anyone else at Rose about your promotion today, given the sensitivity of the situation."

"I'll be discreet," said Ana.

"Then congratulations," said Lesley.

Harry stood up and held out his hand. "May I add my congratulations, Ana. My secretary will arrange a meeting next week, as I'd like to get the ball rolling on the relaunch."

She took his hand and was mortified when a thrill ran through her as he squeezed it. It must have been the excitement of the moment.

"I know how important this will be to Rose," she said, hoping he hadn't noticed her discomfort. "I'm keen to get started."

Harry smiled, still holding her hand—and her gaze—for far longer than was necessary. His eyes really were an incredible shade of blue.

As she left the room, Ana's elation subsided a little as a suspicion crept into her mind. Had Harry just engineered a way for them to work closely together? Regular meetings with an art director would raise far fewer eyebrows than if he were paying attention to a lowly design assistant.

She put the thought aside. Even if he did have a passing fancy for her, he knew she was engaged. And if it were true that he had a roving eye, well, then it could rove somewhere else. There was plenty to choose from at Totty Tower, an awful lot of it going groupie every time he made an appearance in their departments.

She remembered she was seeing Merry for a catch-up tonight, and wondered again if there was something between Harry and her sister. As well as her own suspicions, she'd caught wind of rumors via Megan.

There was always gossip about Merry. No doubt that had something to do with what their mother had once called "far too much of the come-hither." But there had been too many whispers now for Ana to reject them out of hand.

Maybe she should do a little digging.

"Ana!" called Terri as she walked past her office.

Ana backtracked.

"What did Harry say?"

She went in and shut the door. "What do you know—what has he said about me?"

"Why the cloak-and-dagger? He just said you wouldn't be leaving. But then I never thought you would, seeing as you're his personal protégée. Just as well you do a bloody good job, otherwise I'd have found a reason to sack you on principle."

"Even if I had help getting my foot in the door, I knew I was up to the job. It was just harder for me to prove it than most."

"Fair point."

"OK, well, I'm allowed to discuss it with the *Rack* team only, but Harry wants me to move to *Hooray!* as, um, art director. Tonya Teague's going to *Foodie*."

"*Jesus Christ*. How many seconds have you worked here? Are you bonking him, Ana, or what?"

She looked Terri squarely in the eye. "I won't dignify that with a reply. You know I'm engaged, and I would hope any career success is down to my ability and hard work."

"But you do live with his sister, don't you? So he's a friend."

"I wouldn't call him a friend. I've only met him once or twice outside of work."

"It still stinks. And I'm pissed off at losing you."

"But you do understand I can't turn down the opportunity."

"No, you can't." Terri leaned back in her chair and threw her pen down on the desk. "I should loathe you, Ana, but for some reason I don't. So here's a tip. Watch out for Mia Fox. *Hooray!* is her life. If Harry has presented your move as a fait accompli without consulting her, she's going to make your life hell. And if she thinks he's taking a special interest in you, you'll be toast. Mia wants *all* his special interest to be in her."

"I'd expect Mia to have studied my work before agreeing to my promotion. And my work should speak for itself."

Terri snorted. "Ana, do you really believe your own bullshit? Just tell me that. Honest answer."

"I don't know what you mean."

"Seriously? I know you're young, and therefore perhaps not up to speed with the ways of the world, but do you really believe your talent is so outstanding that you could make art director that quickly? Do you not think family connections and ulterior motives might have had something to do with it? You know I rate your work, but . . . seriously? And Mia would never say no to Harry, but that doesn't mean she didn't want to. Watch your back."

Ana's mind whirled as she made her way back to her desk. Putting aside thoughts of Harry's motivation, she wondered about Terri's for a moment. Why would she be so patronizing about Ana's promotion? Was she jealous? Did she have designs on Harry herself? Or was it just the whole tedious north-south divide business: grafting northerners having it "toof," versus privileged southerners having everything on a plate?

Wait. What had Terri said? *Family connections.* Ana had assumed she was talking about Megan, but what if she'd meant Merry? Did Terri know something about that?

It was time for a chat with her sister.

. . .

Merry waved at Ana from her table at Joe Allen. She needn't have bothered. She stood out like a poppy in a field of corn.

Over the past year or so, her hair had grown progressively lighter, from its natural honey blond to platinum, and she was wearing a white polo neck with several gold chains dangling over the precipice of her uplifted bust.

As she waved, most other people in the restaurant looked too.

"Hi," Ana said, air-kissing her sister. There was far too much red lipstick involved to risk actual touching.

As Ana sat down, she wondered if the extra makeup was hiding something. Merry looked tired. "How are you, and how's Will?"

"Been better," said Merry. She waved over a waiter. "Wine, dear sister?"

"Make it a large one."

"A bottle of Chablis, please."

"Certainly, ladies," said the young waiter. "Are you ready to order?"

"My sister needs five minutes," said Merry.

"Sisters! Wow, one so blond and one so dark. Who'd have thought?"

Ana regarded him coolly, wishing he'd go away, while Merry bestowed one of her charming smiles. The type that made men feel so very special.

He hovered, Merry's smile apparently canceling out the request for five more minutes.

"I'll have the tuna Nicoise," said Ana, smacking the menu shut and holding it out to him.

"And I'll have the pasta of the day, sweetheart." She held out her menu as if offering a ticket to paradise.

"Honestly," said Ana when the waiter finally tore himself away. "Why do you feel the need—every time?"

"Oh dear, who rattled your cage?"

Ana sighed. "Sorry. It's just . . . I'm so tired of the whole male-female politics thing, you know? I had some brilliant news today, and I was on cloud nine until my boss insinuated it was for reasons that might have nothing to do with my talent for the job."

"Welcome to my world. Take no notice. They'll just be madly jealous, you're so beautiful. And pray what is this brilliant news? Have you been promoted?"

"Yes, to art director of *Hooray!*" She loved saying the words out loud. A thought occurred to her. "Did you know?"

"No, why would I have known? But gosh, Ana, that's incredible—congratulations!" She waved the waiter back again.

"What are you doing? Leave the poor guy alone!"

"Sorry, darling," Merry said to the waiter, who snapped back to her side as if she'd yanked his lead. "Can I change our wine order—what champagne do you have?"

She ordered a bottle of Laurent-Perrier. ("It'll have to do.")

"So, you were saying. Art director!"

"Yes. More responsibility, more money—Percy and I will be able to look for a house in a better area now. We haven't found anything we like so far. Anyway, I nearly died of shock when Harry told me."

A shadow passed over Merry's face. "He personally told you? You must be doing well."

Ana explained about the redundancies, describing the strange day, such a mixture of awful and good.

The waiter popped the champagne cork and poured them each a glass.

"Here's to you, then, my super-successful sister!" said Merry, raising hers.

"Cheers," said Ana, and took a small sip.

She placed her glass carefully down on the table, wondering how to phrase her question. "Merry? Can I ask you something personal? I know it'll be difficult for you to answer, given where I work, but I feel I need to know because of things people have been saying, especially about my promotion."

Merry looked wary. "I may not be able to answer, for the same reason."

Ana took that to mean she was on the right track. "How well do you know Harry?"

"We've met a few times. He was at school with Will."

"Did you say anything to him that would've helped me get the job at Rose?"

"I might have mentioned you were back from France and looking for a job and were artistically talented. I was trying to do you a favor. Why the sourpuss face?"

"Forewarned is forearmed. Apparently the editor of *Hooray!* will make my life hell if she thinks I've had preferential treatment from Harry."

"Well, if you have, it was only that initial foot in the door. Honestly, I've hardly seen him."

They'd reached an impasse, but Ana was sure from Merry's manner that there was more to it.

"I'd stay away from Harry, actually," Merry said, finally looking her in the eye. "I don't think he's faithful to his wife. You don't want to be next on his TBB list."

"TBB?"

"To Be Bonked."

"Merry! I don't think he'd fool around with anyone at the office, he's too professional."

Their food arrived, and talk turned to their parents down in Kent, and their younger brother Georgie, who would soon finish at Harrow. Then Merry said, "Will's been . . . he's not well."

Ana's heart sank, and she lowered her fork. "What's wrong?"

"I expect you can guess."

"You mean . . . HIV?"

She nodded. "One infection after the other, each one harder to shake off. He's been laid up for weeks now and isn't getting any better. He's so thin, Ana. The prognosis is bleak."

"Poor, poor Will. This is all wrong, he's so lovely." Ana felt tears rising and took a sip of her drink to distract herself. Suddenly the champagne tasted bitter.

"His friend Darius—you remember him?"

Ana nodded. Darius was the interior designer Will and Merry had employed to turn their Scottish castle from gloomy to glorious. He'd stayed on as some sort of manager for their American visitors, but their inner circle knew he was far more of a "wife" than Merry would ever be.

"He's looking after Will. It's horrible; I can't bear to . . ." She stopped, took a deep breath. "I'm staying down here, mostly. You know I have the South Ken flat now? It was getting too expensive, staying in hotels all the time."

"No, I didn't know." Ana was diverted from the dreadful news about Will for a moment, wondering why Merry hadn't told her before. "Can I come round?"

"Sometime," Merry said vaguely. "Tell me, do you hear much about Harry's wife? Katie? I heard she was depressed after they lost that baby. Must be horrible for Harry."

"He rarely discusses his home life with me. Poor Katie, she seems nice."

"Seriously? That mouse? She is *so* not going to hold on to Harry unless she gets herself together."

Ana frowned. "They were practically childhood sweethearts, or so Megan told me. You don't turn your back on someone you've been with that long."

"Oh no?" said Merry.

Ana decided to ask again. Merry was on her third glass of champagne, and her discretion was apt to fly out the window when she'd had a few.

"Hey, Merry, come on—it's me. Be honest. Have you ever . . . you know, with Harry?"

Merry sighed. "Oh, what the heck. You're my sister, and honestly, I could do with someone to talk to about it. But for god's sake, not a word

to anyone, or your shiny new job could disappear in a puff of smoke."
She took a large swig of champagne.

"Well?"

"Yes, Harry and I have been having . . . I was going to say a fling, but
it's turned into a lot more. We're in love, actually. And we've been a great
support to each other, with our respective marriage problems. I think I'd
go mad if I didn't have my time with him."

Ana found she had no appetite. Why did she feel such dismay, when
Merry was only confirming what she'd suspected?

"Don't go all po-faced on me, just because you're marrying your
dream man. The rest of us have to make the best of our circumstances.
You know part of my understanding with Will was that I could sleep
with whomever I wanted. And I wanted Harry. Luckily he felt the same."

"And Katie?"

"He married her too young, and for all the wrong reasons. He told
me that. And he's too decent to shake her off. For now. But who knows
what the future might hold?"

Was Merry intending to marry Harry? Ana had always been aware of
her sister's mercenary streak, but this was ruthless forward planning.

"I've had enough, Merry," she said, pushing her plate away. She
wasn't sure whether she was referring to her sister or the food.

"Ana, stop being so holier-than-thou. If I marry Harry, how is that a
bad thing for you?"

Ana picked up her bag, took out her purse, and threw a few notes on
the table. "I seem to have lost my appetite. That should cover my half.
I'll see you at Christmas."

Merry glared at her, but there was hurt in there too.

Ana strode out without looking back. She found a phone box, made
a quick call, then hailed a taxi. "Notting Hill," she said to the driver,
hoping he'd pick up on the "not in the mood to chat" subtext.

He did, and she spent the journey staring out of the window, barely
registering the Christmas lights along Oxford Street.

The happiness she'd felt about her promotion had been eroded away throughout the day, firstly by Terri's insinuations and now by Merry's revelations about Will and Harry.

She needed Percy and had been so glad when he picked up the phone and told her to come on over, he was all alone.

She paid the driver and knocked on the front door, rubbing her arms against the winter chill.

"Hi!" he said as she stepped into the warmth. "What a nice surprise. What happened to dinner with Merry?"

"Cut short," said Ana, unbuttoning her coat. "I'll explain later."

"Intriguing! Glass of wine? I've got a red open."

He was wearing his acid-wash jeans again, teamed with a royal-blue V-neck sweater tucked in at the waist. Ana made a mental note to take him shopping.

"That'd be lovely," she said, following him into the kitchen, trying not to notice the laddish chaos. "I've got some good news, but can we delay the champagne until I'm feeling happy about it again?"

"Champagne-worthy news? Why the long face, then?"

As he poured the wine, she explained about the new position, then about Terri's allusions as to why she'd got the job.

"Actually, that's not such a bad thing, you know." Percy ushered her through to the living room. The only light was from a table lamp, and the coziness was soothing. Ana began to unwind as she sat on the sofa and unzipped her boots, lifting her legs across Percy's.

"What do you mean?"

"If people think you've got a special relationship with Harry, for whatever reason, they're going to treat you with respect, not the other way round, surely?"

"But I don't *want* them thinking anything like that. I want to be respected for my work. *Only* my work. And I certainly don't want them gossiping about me behind my back."

"If Harry's taking a special interest, who cares if that's because you're Megan's friend, or he likes you, or just because you're a great designer? Why would that piss you off?"

"Why would that . . . For heaven's *sake*, Percy. Women should be judged on their ability to do a good job. Nothing else. Nobody 'sleeps their way to the top' anymore, and if anyone *ever* thought that about me—or even that I'd been promoted because I was a friend of the family, I'd be mortified. I need to put Terri straight. I just wish Merry wasn't . . ." She stopped.

"Merry wasn't what?"

"Look, you mustn't repeat this, OK?"

He made a zipped-lips gesture, but Ana didn't care for the way he perked up at the scent of gossip.

"Merry's been seeing Harry, for a while now. I think she basically got me the job in the first place. And . . . Will's HIV positive and isn't well at all."

"Oh no. That's terrible news, I'm so sorry. And Merry—well, I did wonder, the way she was acting round Harry at the party."

"Her ability to be discreet seems to have declined as her hair has got blonder." Anger bubbled up inside as she remembered their conversation. "She's talking about marrying Harry, once Will's out of the way."

"Seriously? She's not at all the dumb blonde she makes out, is she?"

"Scheming blonde, more like. Can you believe it? Poor Will, with a terminal illness, and Harry's wife losing a baby and now with depression. And all the while those two shagging in their secret South Ken love nest. It's disgusting. And to think he was going on at Megan for having a thing with Charles. Bloody hypocrite."

"Love nest?"

"Yup, they leased a flat when Merry started coming down to 'stand in for Will at meetings.' It's all so seedy. I almost feel like chucking the job back at Harry."

"Nah, you're overreacting. Just be happy about it! Congratulations, you clever thing."

Percy leaned across and took the glass from her hand. Putting it down, he took Ana's face in his hands and kissed her, slowly and deeply.

"How about we forget about work for now?" he murmured, his hand moving to her breast.

The tension of the day was sent packing to be replaced by a new sort, already being wound tight.

As Percy's kiss became more demanding, and he began to unbutton her silk blouse, her body's powerful response took Ana by surprise. As his lips traveled lower, she arched herself toward him, then at once pushed him roughly away. She quickly took off the blouse and then her bra, before setting about Percy's jeans, filled with a need that refused to take things slowly. Yanking them off, and then his boxers, she wriggled out of her skirt and underwear and straddled Percy, pushing him back against the arm of the sofa. Flinging her head back, her thick black hair flying, she gave herself up to the desire that surged through her.

Afterward, as they lay on the sofa in the lamplight, Percy said, "That was incredible. You should get promoted more often."

CHAPTER 19

Katie

April 1993

Katie snipped one final tulip to add to the flowers in her basket. The garden had burst into life after the long, dark days of winter. It amazed her, how nature bounced back with such vigor. Perhaps there was a lesson for her in that.

She made a mental note to thank Mr. Mayhew for his sterling work. Since last June, she'd been unable to find the energy for gardening. Even deadheading a faded rose was beyond her. They'd employed a housekeeper too. Sadie now did everything Katie no longer could, including looking after Maria.

Harry had given her two options: send their daughter away to school, or hire someone. Katie was grateful she now didn't have to cope with the school run, playdates, children's parties—any of it. If she wanted, she could sleep until lunchtime, and often did.

She was overwhelmed by the pointlessness of everything (especially herself), and the sadness of life. The antidepressants had helped a little, enabling her to get out of bed at some point during the day. And when she did, she would walk, alone in her world, to church, where she'd light candles for her dead babies. It was soothing, but she couldn't give form or words to her thoughts. Her mind was empty, a void into which she dared not look.

Harry had work-therapied his way through his grief for Max. When Katie had failed to do the same, he became exasperated. Finally the pleas to make an effort had given way to a distance that now seemed impossible to bridge. Harry had washed his hands of her.

Cassandra had gone off to rehab with things between them unresolved. It had apparently been a success, and Katie was as pleased for Cassandra as her dull senses would allow. Tonight, she and Charles were coming for dinner (Sadie was cooking). Katie vaguely wondered why her old friend hadn't been over before. Harry and Charles's relationship had been sorely tested, thanks to whatever had gone on with Megan, but now their friendship seemed largely restored. Perhaps it was time for the four of them to properly reconnect.

"You look nice," Harry said. "Thanks for making an effort."

They were in their bedroom, changing for the evening. It was the first time he'd looked at her properly, or said anything complimentary, in weeks, but he sounded like a polite stranger.

"Thank you. I like your new haircut, by the way."

"Do you? Someone at work said it makes me look like David Beckham. That's got to be a good thing, right?"

For a moment Katie pictured Harry at work, surrounded by talented, fashionable young people, having a laugh, talking about what they'd be doing on the weekend. Then coming home to this melancholy house, quiet as the grave. Poor Harry.

"I'm so sorry," she blurted out.

"What for?"

"Being like this." She felt tears welling up. "It's taken me so long this time, but I think I might be turning a corner."

Harry busied himself with the buttons on his shirt cuffs. "It's fine.

Just try and relax tonight." He pulled on a soft gray sweater. It really suited him. "I'll go and sort the wine," he said, without meeting her eye. "See you downstairs."

Katie swallowed and stared at her reflection in the mirror. Was it worth the bother of a little lipstick? Would Harry even notice? Was it too late?

She heard the murmur of voices downstairs—Charles's and Cassandra's voices. At once she was transported back to June, and froze. She shut her eyes. *Deep breaths.*

There were footsteps on the stairs.

"Katie?"

She and Cassandra searched each other's eyes for a moment, then Cassandra's arms went out and they were crying and hugging.

"Oh, Katie, I've missed you so much," said Cassandra, sniffing and wiping her eyes.

"Me too," said Katie, passing her a box of tissues.

Her friend looked so different. Her fair hair, always blow-dried into stylish submission, had been allowed to go its own way. Curls now fizzed around her face, on which there wasn't a trace of makeup. She wore a floaty dress and suede pixie boots, and there were beaded leather bracelets on her wrists.

"Gosh, Cass, you look so different!"

"That's because I *am* different. I can't wait to tell you all about it. But . . . you first. Charles said you've been terribly down. Is that starting to get better?"

"I think it might be. I've been in a dark place for months, but . . . I don't know. Out in the garden this morning, I thought maybe I could start to pull myself out."

"I can help you with that." Cassandra's tone was earnest. "You've got to rid yourself of all the negative energy in your life, all the toxicity. I've done it, and I'm a whole new woman." She smiled. "Look, let's get dinner over and done with, and then we'll have a heart-to-heart. By the way, I'm vegetarian now, I hope Charles remembered to tell Harry."

As she followed Cassandra down the stairs, Katie smiled a little, thinking how Old Cassandra would have mocked New Cassandra. She experienced a pang of loss.

"Harry, no!" hissed Katie as she registered Harry opening a bottle of wine.

"It's all right, Katie," said Cassandra in a soothing voice. "Please, go ahead, drink wine. I'm not one of those recovered alcoholics who can't control themselves around the booze. I have coping strategies. And I'm a much better person without it, you'll see."

"I'll drink to that!" said Charles, and Harry guffawed.

"Would you like to joke about my depression too?" asked Katie, breathing quickly.

The men stopped abruptly, Charles going pink.

"No, Katie, don't get angry," said Cassandra. "Anger poisons your soul. Divert that negative energy into something positive, something helping."

"Sorry, Katie," said Charles. "Seriously, that was crass. How are you doing, sweetheart?"

"Getting through," she muttered, and poured herself a glass of water from the tap.

"Just me and you, then, old chap," said Harry, raising his glass.

"To old friends," said Charles.

"Yes, to old friends," said Cassandra, "and new beginnings."

They took their drinks through to the living room, where Maria was watching *Raiders of the Lost Ark*.

"Maria!" said Cassandra. "How are you, my pet? I haven't seen you in so long."

"I'm very well thank you, how are you?" she replied.

Charles looked at Katie in astonishment. "What's happened to your child?"

"She's been to reform school," said Harry.

Charles laughed heartily, but Cassandra shook her head. "Harry, never disrespect your child. The consequences are far-reaching."

"Maria," said Katie, "run along and put your pajamas on, then come and say good night."

"Yes, Mummy."

"So changelings are real," said Charles.

"That's Sadie," said Harry. "She's worked wonders."

"I'm loving the positive outcomes from what have been dark times for all of us," said Cassandra.

"And it seems changelings aren't restricted to children," said Harry. "What have you done with the real Cassandra?"

Frowning slightly, she said, "I'd like to share my experience with you, if you're all comfortable with that?"

Cassandra recounted her rehab journey, sharing her discovery that a lack of nurturing during childhood and then an over-reliance on Charles for emotional support had led to low self-esteem, and how the result was that she only ever felt good about herself after a few drinks. "Milly and Arabella could so easily have ended up the same," she concluded, "shunted off, away from their parents from an early age."

"Are they home?" said Harry.

"Yes, I'm homeschooling them now."

"Jesus," said Harry. "How do Things One and Two feel about that?"

Cassandra pursed her lips. "I don't use those names anymore. It was disrespectful."

Katie noticed the singular "I." "Charles, it must be nice to have them home again, to see them every night."

Charles looked across at Cassandra.

"Tell them, Charles," she said, with a gentle smile.

Charles cleared his throat and took a sip of his wine. "We wanted to tell you in person, Katie. Harry knows, but . . . Cassandra and I are separating. It's amicable, and we'll be doing everything to make sure the children aren't affected by our living apart."

Katie's heart sank. A picture came into her head, of the four of them during a snowy weekend at a cottage in Wales, sitting by a roaring fire drinking wine. After a raucous game of Trivial Pursuit, Cassandra had wondered what they would be doing in ten years' time.

"Darling," Charles had said, "you'll be bringing me my cocoa and we shall settle down in front of *Question Time* to shout at the MPs, just like my ma and pa."

I thought those times would last forever.

"We'll be divorcing as soon as is practical," continued Charles, "and . . . I'll be marrying Megan."

Katie felt her world cave in a little further. Her eyes flew to Cassandra. Her old friend maintained her serene expression, but Katie wondered how much of her newfound positive energy she'd had to deploy to cope with that announcement. She knew how deeply Cassandra had loved Charles. Maybe still did.

Meanwhile, Harry was staring out the window as if this was all old news.

The silence was too heavy. "So it really wasn't just a childhood crush, then," she said, to break it.

Harry spoke. "They're meant to be together, Katie—I can see that now. Perhaps that sort of love only comes along once in a lifetime." He smiled at Charles. "So if you're lucky enough to find it, you've got to grab it. There's no point in hanging on to a broken relationship that's making you both unhappy."

"In letting go of Charles, I'm letting go of the pain," said Cassandra.

Katie felt a deep sadness that her old friend had had to change herself so radically to cope with Charles's desertion. "Cass, I'm happy for you that you've found some inner peace. But don't turn your back on your old self completely. We all loved you very much, you know."

"But *I* didn't love me, Katie. You have your faith; I have my new life with my children. I hope you'll still be part of that. Charles and Megan too."

Charles and Megan. If everyone was moving on and happy, then why did she feel such a sense of loss?

Because Harry was Katie's once-in-a-lifetime. But the way he'd said those words told her she was no longer his.

Harry

Was that . . . ?" said Terri, joining Harry beside a gold-medal-winning Japanese garden.

"Princess Margaret? Yep. She's enormous fun. Pity you missed her, you two would get on."

"You know her?"

"She visited Berryhurst a few times when I was a boy. Tony Armstrong-Jones was a big buddy of my father's. Where've you been?"

"With Alan Titchmarsh. A darned fine Yorkshireman. Had to pretend I understood the fook about herbaceous borders. I haven't a clue—don't know my daffodils from my delphiniums."

"Same. Letting the side down rather, aren't we, Baskins? Still, certain pastimes should be saved for middle age, I feel. Gardening being one of them. And golf."

Terri was Harry's last-minute plus-one at the Royal Gala Preview of the Chelsea Flower Show. Harry had been dismayed, and not a little exasperated, when Katie rang in tears that afternoon, saying she couldn't face going out. She'd been looking forward to it so much, but her anxiety had ambushed her before she made it out the door.

"Margaret's just agreed to an interview in the *Rack*," Harry said. "You're welcome."

"Nice one, boss." They clinked glasses.

"Marilyn Monroe at four o'clock," muttered Terri. "Looks like she's got you in her sights. Where do I know her from? Ah, isn't she the other Lyebon girl?"

Harry felt an arm slip around his waist. "Harry, darling! What a delicious surprise." Merry stood on tiptoes to reach his cheek. "Mwah!

Where's wifey? Exploring? She's a bit of a gardener, if I remember correctly."

"Katie couldn't make it."

As Harry went to introduce the women to each other, he caught the look on Terri's face. No doubt she'd already slotted Merry into the pigeonhole labeled *Has never done a proper day's work in her life; lures rich men onto the two rocks proudly displayed in that too-tight blouse.*

"Terri, meet Merry. Merry, Terri. Oh, fun with rhyme. Terri, Merry's Ana's sister, married to an old school friend of mine. Merry—"

"You're Ana's boss," interrupted Merry. "Oh no, wait. She's on *Hooray!* now."

"Harry snatched her," said Terri. "He's always had an eye for . . . talent."

Merry's eyes narrowed. She looked at Harry. "Darling, have you seen the McCarey Scottish Garden? I thought it would be fun to sponsor something this year. Come see!" She hooked her arm through his and threw a chilly glance at Terri. "Would you excuse us?"

The unforgiving rays of the evening sun fell on Merry's bleached hair and heavily made-up face. Seeing her in the harsh light of day, instead of the gentle, through-the-curtain sunlight of the South Ken flat, Harry realized how much she'd changed since they began seeing each other—from soft and playful to something far more brittle.

"I've already seen it," he said, firmly removing his arm from hers. "Amazing what you can do with heather. You'll be pleased to hear Ana's doing an exceptional job on *Hooray!* Did she tell you she won an industry award? Designer of the Year, no less."

He remembered how she'd glowed at the ceremony, the touch of her skin as he'd hugged her afterward, the lightning bolt of desire that had hit him.

"Your sister is almost obscenely talented. Right, Terri?"

"Says the man who fookin' stole her from me," said Terri. "But yes, Ana's style is to die for."

CHAPTER 20

Ana

When Percy told Ana that BWG had won the Rose account, her first reaction was surprise. Swiftly followed, of course, by joy.

But then back to surprise. She'd always had the impression that Harry didn't rate Percy, and she kind of understood that. Her fiancé bought into Harry's whole rock star–businessman persona, going starry-eyed whenever he was around the great man. While she had no doubt this appealed to Harry's obvious vanity, it probably didn't encourage his respect. Ana found it embarrassing and doubled her efforts to avoid Harry when Percy was in the building.

Perhaps the others on the agency team had swung it. She had to admit their strategies were good. Percy's boss, Connor Black, had a creative background and was renowned for his edgy TV commercials. Ana guessed it was Connor's ideas that had won BWG the account, rather than Percy's efforts to communicate those.

She put aside the negative thoughts. Why had she even allowed them to intrude, as she sat here at her parents' kitchen table, daydreaming about her big day? She focused instead on the seating plan in front of her.

They were in Kent for the weekend, to go through the wedding arrangements. Her father and Percy had walked down to the King Henry VIII for a Sunday lunchtime pint. She wondered how they were getting on and hoped they'd found some common conversational ground. She'd suggested topics: "Cricket. Dad's memories of World War Two. Avoid politics. Cricket again." Her father could be rather brusque and didn't approve of advertising as a profession. Percy seemed a little terrified of him.

Meanwhile, as a leg of lamb roasted in the Aga, Ana and her mother had so far finalized the wording of the invite and made a start on the seating plan.

Ana was glad her parents had agreed to leave out their titles. Percy had wanted "Sir Thomas and Lady Lyebon request the pleasure . . ." but Ana preferred the less formal "Thomas and Elizabeth Lyebon . . ."

Now she and her mother were poring over an A3 sheet of paper with circles drawn on it, moving around slips of paper with the guests' names on.

"It's so clever, what you're doing with the themes."

"Thanks, Mum. I basically can't stop designing things."

From the flowers to the place settings to the invitations, Ana was styling it all herself. Apart from the dress, of course. That had been bought in Paris last month. Ana had suggested the trip to Merry as an olive branch, feeling a sisterly rift wouldn't be a good idea with a family wedding on the horizon. Happily they'd managed to paper over the cracks in their relationship.

Ana had now accepted that perhaps Merry and Harry's affair wasn't such a terrible thing. No doubt both needed an escape from difficult situations at home, and what was a bit of harmless sex, if no one got hurt? Because surely that was all it was, even if Merry's fantasies said otherwise.

As a further gesture of peace, she'd asked Merry to be her matron of honor, but she'd turned it down saying, "One never wants to be matronly, and there's not a lot of honor in there, frankly."

The reception would be at Hever Castle, close to the village where her parents lived. It was costing a fortune, but Ana's increased salary meant she could contribute. They could have chosen a less splendid venue, but Ana was emotionally attached to the castle where she, Merry, and their friends had played princesses and queens in the grounds, in the days before CCTV had made sneaking in impossible. Anywhere else just wouldn't have felt right.

Megan was her wedding planner. They'd spent many evenings discussing flowers and color schemes and menus, and sometimes Charles was there, reminding Megan that he fully intended for them to run away to a tropical island because he couldn't face all this nonsense.

It was fun having Charles around. Ana would miss his company when she and Percy moved into their own place. After Charles had explained the amicable agreement he'd come to with his wife, Ana had accepted that he and Megan were good together. The former wild child was now at her happiest tucked up on the sofa with Charles, watching TV.

"Ana?"

"Sorry, Mum, what was that?"

"Head in the clouds again. Ah well, if you're not daydreaming about your big day, I suppose there'd be something wrong. I said, who shall we sit Harry Rose and his wife with? Gosh, I saw him in the paper the other day. He's awfully good-looking, isn't he?"

Ana had all but forgotten Katie would be there. Megan had told her how Harry's wife was slowly recovering from her depression and was hoping to be well enough to come. "We'll sit them with Megan and Charles . . . and Merry and Will," she replied, feeling mischievous. "Will and Harry were at school together."

"Oh, Ana, I'm not sure he'll be well enough. Unless this new cancer treatment he's on can work miracles, I think Merry will be coming by herself."

Ana said nothing. Her mother surely knew the truth about her son-in-law's illness. If she couldn't bear to speak that truth in her social circles, Ana could understand that—many in her parents' generation still had a problem accepting homosexuality. But to not even acknowledge the true nature of Will's illness within her own family?

Her mother's expression told her now was not the time to talk about that.

"If Will's not coming, then we should put Merry as far from Harry as possible," she said, picking up the slip of paper with her sister's name on it. With a secret smile she slotted it in next to the vicar.

"Good idea."

Ana looked up.

"I know about Merry and Harry. She's told me everything. And from what I hear, your boss could be your new brother-in-law before too long."

"She told you that? For goodness' sake! I know Harry and Katie have been having problems, but I've heard nothing about a separation, and Megan would know. Merry's living in cloud-cuckoo-land."

"Oh. I see. Well, I'm glad you put me right. Goodness me. Is there anything else I need to know?"

"No. And what I just said—that's between you and me, OK? Things are difficult enough between Merry and me as it is."

They heard the key in the front door, then Ana's father appeared in the kitchen doorway, Percy behind him.

"Still at it?" said her father.

"We're trying to decide where to put Harry Rose and his wife," said her mother.

"Can we put them as close to the top table as possible?" said Percy.

"He's just a work person, not family," said Ana.

"Yet," said her father.

"Pardon me?" said Percy.

"It's OK, Mum and Dad know," said Ana. "But I've put Mum right. Merry won't be becoming Mrs. Rose anytime soon."

"Never say never!" said Percy. "He'd make a pretty cool brother-in-law."

Ana pushed back her chair and went to check on the roast. "Lunch in twenty minutes," she snapped.

CHAPTER 21

Harry

June 1993

Harry closed his newspaper and swiveled his chair to look out the window. A healthy number of cranes punctuated the skyline, especially above Canary Wharf. It looked as if today's headline was correct—the recession was finally over.

Unemployment had fallen below three million and was continuing to drop. Rose Corp. shares were climbing in value, and Harry was considering new areas for expansion. The internet was of particular interest. He'd ask his secretary to organize an initial brainstorming meeting with his senior executives.

He was about to buzz her when the phone rang. It was Merry.

"Hi, look, Merry, I've asked you not to—"

"Will's dead, Harry."

His stomach dropped, and for a moment he couldn't speak.

"That's terrible news. I'm so sorry. My condolences."

"Thank you. The funeral will be in Scotland next week. Will you come?"

"I expect not, Merry. It . . . it wouldn't be appropriate."

"But I *need* you, Harry. How can I get through this by myself?" Her tone was pleading. It made him go cold.

"The guy at the castle—Darius? He can handle things, surely."

"Darius is in bits; he's incapable of organizing anything."

"Well. I'm sure you'll manage."

"But, Harry—"

"Look, I'm sorry but I'm late for a meeting. And again, Merry, I'm so sorry. Will was a lovely chap. One of the best."

He put the phone down.

Harry thought back to their school days, when Will had been the driving force behind Poetry Club, writing spectacularly bad Romantic odes for the school magazine. He hadn't even made thirty. Harry was due to reach that milestone himself in a couple of weeks. He was too young to be confronting his own mortality.

Restless, he left his office and took the lift down to *Hooray!*'s floor. Striding down the corridor, causing a flurry of raised heads, he made his way to Ana's office. He was glad to see she was alone, her dark head bent over contact sheets.

"Ana," he said, closing the door behind him.

She looked up and blushed charmingly. "Harry. What can I do for you?"

Kiss me? Take me to bed? Love me?

"I just heard about Will. Merry rang."

Ana looked taken aback, and he wondered if it was because this was the first time in all these months he'd mentioned her sister.

"I heard this morning too," she said. "We're all so sad."

"He was one of life's good guys, heart of gold." Harry pulled up a chair and sat down opposite her. "Merry thinks I should go to the funeral, but I'm not intending to. I wasn't a close friend, and I bloody hate funerals. Too hard . . ." He took a deep breath.

Ana regarded him steadily. He tried to read the expression in her dark eyes but found it impossible. She was difficult to fathom.

"Why does she think you should go?" she said finally.

"Support, I suppose. But it wouldn't be appropriate."

"No."

"Ana—"

"Harry, it's best you don't discuss Merry with me. I'd prefer to keep things—well, work only."

Harry ran his fingers through his hair and sighed. "Fair enough. You'll be going to the funeral, I suppose?"

"Yes. I can support Merry, you don't need to worry."

"I wasn't. God, Ana, I can't believe he's gone. He wasn't even thirty. The death of a friend—it makes you take stock of your life, your relationships. Like Charles, starting over with Megan. At least he's got it right."

"How's your wife doing? Megan told me she's feeling brighter."

Harry made a dismissive gesture. "Katie's had these problems forever. She gets better, then something sets her back. She relies a lot on her faith—I'm not sure I'm much help. We got together years ago. Now it just feels like a habit."

Ana fiddled with a pen, clicking the nib in and out, not meeting his eyes. "She seems lovely. I hope she's better soon."

"Are you still marrying Percy?"

Her eyes flew to his. "I—yes. Of course!"

He grinned. "Just wondered. Can't let my most promising member of staff marry any old idiot, can I?"

Ana chuckled.

"Honest opinion? Not good enough for you."

"So you're my dad now?"

"If I was, I'd send him packing."

"Wouldn't work. Forbidden love is the best kind."

"Isn't it just?"

Ana's smile faded. "Are you going to marry Merry?"

What should he say about the affair? His conscience told him to be honest. "No. It was only ever a casual thing. She knows that."

"Actually, Harry, she doesn't."

"Oh? Then I need to talk to her. But let's get through the funeral first. She'll have an awful lot on her plate."

"She told me you two are in love."

Harry was filled with dismay. It was going to be harder to extricate himself from the Merry situation than he'd imagined. He'd tried to ignore her increasing clinginess, her neediness. That wasn't what he'd signed up to at all. He should have ended it sooner. Now Ana would think he was a cad for dumping her when she was at her most vulnerable. And what Ana thought was all that mattered.

"Merry's delightful, but it isn't . . . it never was, serious. We've just—"

"Harry, please don't share this with me. She's my sister and you're my boss; you're putting me in a difficult position."

"Ana . . ." He leaned forward, holding her gaze. His heart was in his mouth. "I can't keep . . . I need to tell you. I want to be more than your boss."

He'd said it.

Ana's beautiful eyes widened, and he saw her intake of breath.

"Totally inappropriate boss behavior," he said, in a lighter tone. "Wrong on so many levels. I've tried ordering my heart to behave, but . . . Ana, every time you're near, I feel like I'm under a spell."

"I—"

"You're getting married, I know. Just be sure you're making the right decision."

The hesitance, the uncertainty in her eyes, gave him the encouragement he needed to carry on. "It's over between Katie and me. Life's too short. Don't get married unless you're one hundred percent sure. Promise me that."

"I will. And—I am."

But her eyes betrayed the lie.

Harry made his way back to the top floor, going over their conversation—every nuance of Ana's words, every fleeting expression.

He'd done it. He'd told her how he felt.

Now he could start the serious business of wearing her down, until, like every woman he'd ever wanted, she'd be his.

Step one: deal with the opposition.

As the lift doors opened, he saw Connor Black waiting in the reception area. "Connor, sorry if I've kept you. Come on through."

"Harry, mate."

Connor was a hugely talented and precocious adman who was true to his East End roots. His TV ads had won all the awards going, and he'd already been offered feature-length films to direct.

They each took a sofa in Harry's office, on either side of a low glass table.

"So, Harry, you said you had something important to discuss? Is it about the new campaign? I'm not happy with it myself yet."

"No, Connor, I'm afraid it's not. It's about something a little more delicate."

Connor's self-confident gaze faltered. And so it should. Rose's business was a huge part of their portfolio.

"Oh?"

"Percy North. You know he's seeing a senior member of my staff?"

"Yes, Ana. Lovely girl. Very stylish, very posh."

Harry ignored the comment.

"Through Ana, Percy has had . . . access to sensitive information. I'm afraid that information has reached ears it shouldn't have, and Rose's position has been somewhat compromised as a result."

"Really? In what way? Can you be more specific?"

"No. Like I say, it's sensitive. North should never have shared that information with your staff. He should have known better. I have zero confidence it won't happen again."

"I'll give him a bollocking, mate. You can count on it."

"Not good enough." Harry sat back and crossed his legs, waiting.

"A written warning?"

"Won't cut it."

"So . . . what are you saying?"

"I need him off the business. From today."

"Can do. I'll move him across—"

"And out of London."

"You what? Seriously?"

Harry leaned forward again. "Connor . . . mate. Percy North's motor-mouth has caused me serious grief. I should really sack the agency." He was gratified to see Connor turn pale.

"But if you send Percy North north, or west, or preferably overseas, I'm willing to continue our otherwise wholly satisfactory relationship. I'm happy with your work, Connor, but lose the bag carrier, OK?"

CHAPTER 22

Ana

Ana rewound the answerphone as she kicked off her shoes, sighing with pleasure as her bare feet met the tiled floor of the hallway. It had been another hot day in London, and people who were strangers to deodorant seemed to have been overrepresented on the tube home to Holland Park.

"*Hi, Ana.*" The voice was Percy's. "*Can I come over? I've got some news. Good news! We need to talk about it, though. Call me back.*"

She went through to the kitchen and opened the fridge, enjoying the cold blast of air. Idly wondering when the weather would break, she had a sudden memory of the storm at last year's launch party. Had it really been a year ago?

She poured herself a glass of Sancerre, then returned to the phone and dialed Percy's number. "It's me."

"Ana! Finally you're not working late. Can I come over? I've got some news."

"You said. Why so mysterious? Can't you just tell me over the phone?"

"I'd rather tell you in person. It's major, and I need to . . . why don't I just leave now? Shall I bring wine?"

"I have wine. Bring food, though, I'm starving."

"What sort?"

"Indian would be good."

"OK, Indian. What sort?"

"Percy, just get our usual. See you in a bit."

Ana changed into a T-shirt and chinos, then took her drink into the living room and switched on the TV, flicking through the channels. She switched it off again. She couldn't settle. Harry's softly spoken words kept coming back to her: *I want to be more than your boss.*

She closed her eyes for a moment, and his image swam before her.

Dealing with unwanted advances wasn't a new experience. She'd batted them off throughout her time in France. But Harry? A married man, her boss, her sister's lover. How could he even think she'd consider going down that path?

She enjoyed his company, his quick wit; she'd admit to that. Sparring with him, whether verbally or over a tennis net, was strangely compelling. There was no denying his . . . lord, but he was beautiful. And his charisma, which threw every other man in the room into the shade. But then, the sun was dangerous, especially if you flew too close.

Ana had a horrible feeling that Merry was about to have an Icarus moment.

He was *so* arrogant, and he'd been dreadfully rude about Percy. How had he thought belittling her fiancé would make himself more attractive in her eyes? But she also had to admit that Harry brought out the worst in Percy.

Her fiancé arrived, wearing the new Calvin Klein jeans she'd bought for him, teamed with a black T-shirt. He looked cute, and she gave him a big hug. "You have no idea how pleased I am to see you."

"Same, and I can't wait to tell you what's gone down today!"

They laid out the cartons on the table, spooning rice and curry onto their plates, unwrapping naan bread.

"Mm," said Ana, tucking in. "Too busy to eat today. OK, international man of mystery. What's the breaking news?"

Percy leaned in. "I told you it's big."

"You did. Now tell me what's big."

"OK. The big three at the agency, Connor, Matt—"

"I know who the big three are."

"Right. They said that, apparently, in the next year or so, Ireland's going to boom."

"What?"

"Connor says it's going to be the powerhouse of Europe. All sorts of investment is heading that way. Innovative new businesses, tech companies, start-ups. EU money will be sloshing about the place. So they want to be right in there, ready for when it all kicks off. And they've asked me to head it up. I'm going to be MD of BWG Dublin! Can you bloody believe it?" He sat back again, a huge grin on his face.

Ana looked away as she tried to interpret her feelings. Dismay. Annoyance. A sense of her destiny being messed with.

But none of the joy Percy was so obviously expecting.

"I realize it's a *massive* thing for us," he continued, finally picking up her consternation. "So I said I'd need to discuss it with you first. But the money's a lot more than I'm on now, and there's a relocation allowance. Have you ever been to Dublin? Apparently it's a nice city. So—"

"So no."

"What?"

"If you take the job, I won't be coming."

"Why not? You'll be my wife! It'll be a great start to our married life."

"And my career? What would I do while you were MD'ing all over Dublin?"

"There are magazines in Ireland. And book publishers, ad agencies. You'd find a job easily with your experience."

"It would be a step backward for me."

"But we'd be together, and maybe, you know, we could start a family?"

Did he understand her *at all*?

"Percy, I love my job here. I'm doing well at Rose, and I don't want a family for many, many years. I don't want to live in Dublin. I'm sorry, I really am. It does sound like a good opportunity for you."

"It is. And if I turned it down, they'd think I wasn't serious about my career. I probably wouldn't get another opportunity like it."

"So take it, and we'll see each other at weekends. Other couples do it, we'll manage."

"But, Ana, that's no way to start a marriage. I want you there with me."

Suddenly, Ana felt very tired. "It's your choice, Percy. Take the job and we'll see each other at weekends, or stay here. I'm not coming."

"Whatever happened to supportive wives?" His tone was petulant. "Come on, Ana. It'll be fun." Wheedling now. "A new start. Ireland's amazing."

"Ireland's wet. And I don't know anyone there."

He pushed back his chair and came around to her side of the table. Ana recoiled slightly as he dropped to one knee. "Ana, you're everything to me. I can't live without you. I'm begging you, come with me to Dublin."

"If you can't live without me, then stay here. And please get up."

"To be honest, I don't think I have a choice." He stood up, brushed the knees of his Calvin Kleins, and went back to his side of the table.

"Of course you have a choice. You can turn it down and stay in the position you're in now, can't you?"

"The way they presented it to me, it was like they just assumed I'd go. And—well, I *want* to. I know winning the Rose account was great, but Connor's so . . . he treats me like I'm his minion. I haven't been happy for a while."

"Well why didn't you say? You should have told me! Maybe you should just leave."

"Why would I move agencies when I've been given this opportunity?"

"Look, obviously Connor rates you, even if he doesn't dish out the praise. So you could just turn it down, be more assertive? Demand to stay where you are."

Percy now looked wholly uncomfortable. "Let me think about it. I'm not going to lie, I'm really disappointed. I thought this would be fantastic for us."

"You weren't to know. Look, let's sleep on it, shall we?"

"Together?" said Percy hopefully.

"Of course."

Ana had no appetite for the rest of her curry. It had been the most unsettling of days. The terrible news about Will. Harry's visit to her office, the memory of which was crowding out the far more pressing problem Percy had just landed on her.

When they headed upstairs, Ana found she had little appetite for Percy's kisses either.

"Early night, was it?" Charles winked at Ana from over by the toaster as she shuffled across to the kettle. It was six thirty, and she wondered how Charlie-boy could be so cheerful.

"What time did you two get in?"

"God knows. Megan fancied trying some new underground club in Camden. I'm too old, Ana. I'll be underground myself if I try and keep up with her." He peered at the toaster knob as smoke began to appear. "Without my bloody glasses, I can't read the numbers on the knob." He pushed a button, and two black pieces of toast popped up. "Bugger."

Ana smiled. "Percy came over—he's been offered a promotion. In Dublin." Why was she telling Charles? Somehow he invited confidences.

"Has he? Jaysus, Joseph, and Mary!" His Irish accent was terrible. "Are you going?"

"No. But Percy might. We didn't get far trying to decide."

Charles dropped his voice. "Look, Ana, you're marrying Percy, so I take it you're madly in love. He's the one, yes?"

"Of course," said Ana, but for some reason she shivered a little.

"Don't put love on hold while you chase your career goals. If it's a good opportunity for Percy, go with him. Get a job in Dublin—it's a cool place. It doesn't matter if it's not as highfalutin as art director at

Rose. You're really talented; you'll always do well. Go with Percy, make a life in Dublin, have a nice job and babies and new Irish friends. Don't have a half-arsed weekends-only marriage."

Megan appeared, wiping the sleep from her eyes. "Morning, Ana. I'm glad I caught you before work. Are you around Monday the twenty-eighth?"

"That's more than two weeks away. How would I know what I'm doing on a Monday more than two weeks away?" Ana was still reeling from Charles's pep talk.

"It's Harry's thirtieth. Katie's not up to organizing anything, but we can't let it go without a celebration. I thought a dinner? Close friends, family—me, basically—and a few work people. If I sort it, can you tell me who to invite from his work?"

"No—have you never heard of office politics? And I don't even know Harry that well. Talk to his secretary, Janette."

As Ana left the kitchen, she heard Megan mutter, "What's eating her this morning?"

CHAPTER 23

————❧————

Ana

It was past ten o'clock when the sun finally relinquished its hold on the long day and dipped behind the shadowy moors of Sgurr Shelagh to the west. The walls of Kindrummon Castle glowed orange in farewell, and a golden mirror image was reflected in the still waters of the loch on which the ancient fortification stood.

"It's so beautiful," said Ana as she and Merry stopped to watch the sun go down.

The twilight chill intensified, and the mountains were thrown into relief. From below the horizon, the sun streaked the clouds with washes of gold and pink, as if to make up for leaving.

They set off again, watching their step as darkness crept across the boggy ground. The plaintive cry of a water bird pierced the silence. Will's setter, McTavish, loped along, happy to be out and about after being cooped up during the funeral.

"What will happen to Kindrummon?" said Ana.

"Will left it to me, and he wanted Darius to stay on to run the estate. It was doing well—the Americans paying for the 'Scawtish experrrience'— before Will became ill."

After the funeral, poor Darius had drifted around, white-faced, like a tragic ghost haunting the ancient rooms, ignored by many of Will's older relatives who, like Ana's parents, hadn't been willing to acknowledge the true nature of his illness.

"I hope he'll stay," continued Merry. "Kindrummon will have to be run as a business, otherwise it's too much of a drain on the whisky side of things. Also, Harry has plans for it."

"*Harry?* How do you mean?"

"He's talking about a golf course. Says Kindrummon could be another Gleneagles."

Ana was silent. Had Harry been misleading her when he'd said Merry wasn't in his future plans?

"I wish he was here," said Merry. "How long do you think a widow—goodness, that sounds grim . . . how long should a widow wait before being seen out and about with a new man?"

"If he's married, never."

"Oh, not this again. He'll be separated soon."

"Did he tell you that?"

"It's only a matter of time."

Ana pulled ahead, increasing her stride. "Today probably isn't the day for this conversation," she called over her shoulder. "Let's have a little respect for Will."

"You started it."

"Sorry." She stopped, waiting for Merry to catch up again. "Everything was lovely, by the way. Well done on the arrangements."

"I didn't do much. The hardest part was finding something to wear. I don't normally do black. Maybe I should, though. Looks good with the lighter hair, don't you think?"

Ana said nothing. People were often surprised to find out they were sisters, "one so fair, one so dark." Sometimes she wondered herself. Was it really possible they shared the same genes?

The next morning, Ana avoided the other guests catching the London train. All she wanted to do was stare out the window, thinking. She had an important decision to make.

Percy was taking the Dublin job. It seemed he didn't have a choice, if he wanted to stay with the firm. He was convinced she'd go with him and was full of his new role. He couldn't say "MD of BWG Dublin" often enough. Megan had started rolling her eyes.

Then there was Charles and his "follow your heart" speech.

She'd tried to picture herself living in Dublin, but it couldn't match up to the image she'd carried with her this past year, of the two of them buying a place in a leafy London suburb, enjoying weekends away in the countryside. The English countryside.

And then there was her own career. Since the successful redesign of *Hooray!*, which had won two industry awards, she'd been consulted on other Rose projects, and after all this time as "Harry's protégée" had finally proved her worth and was able to let her work speak for itself. She was Rose Corp.'s top designer.

Mia Fox wasn't, after all, the nightmare boss Terri had predicted, perhaps because she was wary of being reported back to Harry. Terri had been on the nail when she said *Hooray!* and Harry were Mia's life. She was single and seemed to have no interests outside of work. So far she'd been polite and complimentary, if not exactly warm, friendly, and let's-do-lunchy.

So, career-wise, Ana was in the best place possible.

If she didn't go to Dublin, could she and Percy still make it work? Or would she end up being a Mia, or a Terri? Tough, career-driven women, with no life outside of the office?

Percy, or work? Or both? Surely if she truly loved him, the decision shouldn't be this hard.

Harry

June 1993

Harry was walking the short distance to Hampton Court station, on his way to catch the seven twenty-five into Waterloo. Already the day was warm; it looked like his thirtieth birthday was going to be a scorcher.

Katie had still been asleep when he left. She'd almost kicked the anti-depressants and sleeping pills, but it still took her a while to get out of bed in the mornings.

He bought a copy of the *Times* and stood in his usual spot on the northbound platform. Dotted around were other commuters, the men in similar suits to his own (cheaper versions, obviously), reading the same newspapers they read every day. Many faces were familiar—they were the same people he saw each time he caught the seven twenty-five. The only difference today was that most had taken the risk of going umbrella-free.

He had a sudden memory of driving to work from the Fulham house in his red TVR, top down, music blaring. Now look at him, like Mr. Banks from *Mary Poppins*. All that was missing was the bowler hat.

He was thirty.

The train clattered into the station and he made his way to his usual seat, then read the same paragraph on the front page of the newspaper three times before registering he was taking none of it in. He lowered the paper and stared out the window.

Thirty years old.

What was he doing with his life? Work-wise, everything was going swimmingly. He was pleased with his teams, leaner and meaner after last December's purge. Company profits were now so healthy they were looking at diversifying, and Harry was considering moving Rose Corp. to brand-new premises. He'd be hands-on with the design. Maybe a tower. Something like Canary Wharf. But taller.

His personal life was a shambles, however. He needed to do something about it. Katie would always hold a special place in his heart, but the love was gone. All that remained was a vague fondness, which gave way to exasperation whenever they attempted a "where to next" conversation. Katie wanted them to have relationship counseling (and prayed for guidance, which made Harry more annoyed). He wanted to move on, but Katie became so upset when he suggested living apart for a while that inevitably he backed down, fearing sending her back to the darkest days of her depression. So things stayed as they were. Going nowhere.

As for Merry, the sooner he could shake her off, the better. The breathy voice he'd once found so alluring now set his teeth on edge.

Meanwhile, his obsession with Ana had strengthened its grip. He'd been biding his time. Would his gamble pay off? He'd felt sure Percy's exile to Dublin would be the catalyst for a meltdown in that relationship. Ana was hugely ambitious; any fool could see that. She wasn't going to give up her skyrocketing career for art editor of *Catholic Weekly*, or *Irish Homes and Gardens*, or whatever the good people of Dublin liked to read.

Would she and Percy go the long-distance relationship route, only meeting up on weekends? Harry's guess was they'd give that a try. If they did, he'd intensify his campaign. She'd be bored during the week. Perhaps they could make up a regular four with Charles and Megan on the tennis court again. And he'd instigate plenty of late nights at the office. Late nights with . . . input from himself.

He shifted in his seat as the image of Ana's deep brown eyes and willowy body filled his head. She'd be his, he was certain. He just needed to time it right, plan it carefully.

Harry smiled. There really was nothing like the thrill of the chase.

There was a quiet knock on the door of Harry's office. He was an open-door man, but his secretary, Janette, always knocked first and waited to be called in.

She was half-hidden behind an enormous bunch of red roses.

"Blooming hell," said Harry. "Someone's gone to town."

Janette giggled. "There are thirty. I counted them. Happy birthday, Harry! Oh, but . . . no, they're not from me." She blushed. Janette did that a lot.

She lifted the bouquet higher in an attempt to hide her embarrassment. "Shall I put them in water?"

"Keep them, sweetheart," he said. "I'm not much of a flower man, in spite of the name."

She pulled off the card, passing it to Harry. "Thanks! And . . . can I double-check you don't have any plans for lunchtime?"

Harry knew something was being organized. Janette had blocked it off in his diary weeks ago. Probably staff drinks in the boardroom with a glass of el cheapo champagne, a cake, and the oversized card he'd spotted doing the rounds yesterday.

"I'll be here."

He opened the envelope as she left. The card read:

> *My love is like a red, red rose.*
> *Happy birthday, my love. So sorry I can't be with you today.*
> *With all my love forever, Merry X*

He dropped it in the bin.

At noon, Janette knocked again. Harry looked up from his team's report on how best to take advantage of the new information age. It blew his mind. In twenty years' time, it said, not only would almost every household in the Western world have a computer linked to the World Wide Web, but magazines and newspapers would be losing swathes of readers, not to mention advertisers, as news and gossip went online. People would be getting their fix on their computers.

Really?

"Yes, Janette?"

"We wondered if you could come to the boardroom, Harry." She gave a little giggle. "I'm sure you can guess why."

"I'll be there in ten. And by the way, you look nice today."

She blushed, of course, and mumbled, "Gosh, thank you!" before scuttling away.

It didn't hurt to throw her a compliment every now and again. Janette was worth keeping sweet—easy on the eye, worked like a dog, excellent at fielding troublesome phone calls, and probably a little in love with him.

As he entered the boardroom, Harry's senior staff greeted him with a loud chorus of "Happy Birthday."

"Thanks, all," he said, grinning. "I am officially grown up, I suppose. Nice of you to mark the occasion."

As Mia Fox made a beeline for him, holding out a glass of champagne, he quickly scanned the room and saw Ana standing with Terri. Deftly he moved, just in time to escape Mia, and joined a group close to the two women.

"Harry, welcome to the thirtysomething club," said Nate. "It sucks, by the way. People expect you to behave, settle down, all the boring things."

"I did all of those already," said Harry. "I'm living life backward. So here's to the dawning of my decade of bad behavior."

Mia caught him up and handed him the champagne.

"Cheers, everyone," he said, taking it off her.

"To bad behavior," said Nate loudly.

Ana turned toward them, and Harry caught her eye and smiled mischievously, raising his glass in her direction.

An hour passed, then two, with only nibbles to soak up the free-flowing wine. Voices increased in volume; staff became loose-tongued. They knew they could carry on partying until Harry left, and it looked as if that wouldn't be anytime soon.

Harry hadn't yet spoken to Ana, but every second of every minute, he'd been aware of her. She looked delectable, dressed in a buttery-yellow dress that set off her dark hair and eyes.

He ached to touch her.

According to Janette, Ana's nickname at Rose was Ice Queen, and it was no doubt well earned. She was inscrutable and detached, and it was often a challenge to make her smile.

He intended to melt her. It was time to turn up the heat.

He excused himself from Mia's leechlike attentions and finally joined Ana, who was chatting with Kevin Mould from accounts.

"Ana," he said, sending a "dismissed" vibe in Kevin's direction. "Sorry it's taken me so long to ask, but how was the funeral?"

"I'll just . . . get another . . ." said Kevin, scurrying away.

"How do you do that?" said Ana, looking at Kevin's back. "Please teach me so I don't waste another half hour of my life."

Harry laughed. "Poor old Mouldy. I'll try and make the next half hour one you'll look back on with delight."

"Happy birthday, then. You don't look a day over forty."

Ana never did cheeky. Was she a little drunk? Was that fearsome self-control compromised?

"The funeral was nice. Very Scottish. Wow, that castle. It's stunning. Fancy inheriting a bloody castle."

"Will left it to Merry, then?"

"Yep. Darius is staying on to run it, and she seems to think you have plans for it. For when you two are . . . official."

Harry glanced around, then put his hand on Ana's arm, guiding her away from the others. The touch of her skin sent a delicious thrill through him.

"Ana," he said, his voice low, "Merry's got the wrong end of the stick. Sod it, there isn't even a stick. We had a fling. It was fun, but it's over. I haven't told her properly yet; I was hoping the fact that I've been avoiding her would send a message. Obviously I need to have it out with her. But, well . . . with Will dying, it wasn't the right time."

"She thinks you're going to divorce Katie and marry her."

It was worse than he'd thought.

"That's nonsense. I don't know where this is coming from. I thought we understood each other."

"I believe you. Merry's always been a fantasist. But please let her down gently. I think she genuinely loves you."

Harry shook his head and sighed. "Ana—it's important to me that you understand." He looked around again and noticed people noticing them. He stepped back a little. "I need to talk to you about it. Can I drop by your office later?"

Ana regarded him steadily, and her dark eyes sucked him in. Every part of him, every cell, was buzzing with desire.

"OK. We'll talk later." She didn't drop her gaze.

"Percy," he said finally, attempting to get a grip. "When's he off to Dublin?"

A cloud crossed her face. "Soon. He's lined up some places to view. Dublin's expensive, but the agency's being generous."

"So . . . you'll be visiting at weekends?"

"Yes. I'm looking forward to seeing Dublin. At weekends." Her voice was flat.

"I hope all this isn't affecting your wedding plans? Not the greatest timing by BWG, was it?"

"The plans are coming along just fine. And the way I see it, we've got a lifetime ahead of us, so if a little of that is weekends only, that's OK. Hopping on a plane will be exciting. And I guess it'll keep things interesting. We won't turn into one of those couples who eat dinner in front of *Coronation Street* every night."

He smiled. "Ana, I can think of nothing lovelier than snuggling up with you on the sofa. I'd gladly suffer a soap of the north for that pleasure."

"Oh, I should warn you," said Ana, ignoring his comment, "Megan has plans for tonight."

"I thought as much. Whatever it is, I hope you're coming along."

"It's just close friends and family, I think."

Harry dropped his voice. "Come. You can't deny me on my birthday." Her eyes told him she understood the double meaning. "I'd better circulate now; Mia's looking daggers at you. I'm surprised you can't feel them. I'll drop by later."

"OK, I'll look forward to it." She smiled before turning away.

CHAPTER 24

Ana

The effects of the wine were wearing off, leaving a bitter aftertaste that wasn't all physical. What had she been thinking, flirting like that? She'd crossed a line. And on the other side was Harry—her boss.

She stared at the layouts on her desk. It was no good; she couldn't concentrate. The air in the office felt heavy, and she had the beginnings of a post-champagne headache.

She rubbed her temples, trying to focus on the photos of a footballer she'd never heard of and his wife, but her head was too full of Harry's words, the heat in his eyes. As she remembered the touch of his hand on her arm, a jolt of electricity pulsed through her, followed swiftly by a rush of shame.

How could she let herself be beguiled by Harry? What was he doing—a married man acting this way with an engaged woman, a member of his own staff? It was completely unprofessional. And, she reminded herself, he was preparing to dump her sister in cold blood, apparently not caring a jot if Merry was in love with him. He just wanted to be rid of her.

As her eyes wandered off from her work again, she spotted a Post-it note stuck to her phone. *Percy rang 3:30, ring back.*

It was now past six. She punched out his number.

"Percy North."

"It's me."

"Hi, gorgeous. How's your day been?"

"Fine. Yours?"

"Busy, busy. Trying to delegate everything before I leave. I might be a bit late coming round tonight."

"Don't worry, I've got to stay late myself."

That wasn't true. Why had she said that? Was she intending to go out with Harry, knowing what that could lead to?

"I can come round about ten?" said Percy.

"I've got a headache coming on. Let's just postpone. Tomorrow?"

"Aw, I want to see you tonight!"

"No. Look, I have to go. Bye, Percy."

"But, An—"

She cut him off.

She felt irrationally annoyed with him, though he'd done nothing wrong. Except to make her feel guilty. He'd held up a mirror, and in it was the reflection of a woman who seemed to be losing control.

This *never* happened. She was the Ice Queen. (Ana was proud of her nickname, even though staff had tried to keep her from finding it out.)

She really shouldn't drink at lunchtime.

She returned to the layouts.

Ten minutes later, she still had nothing useful to say about the spread in front of her.

"Cake?"

Ana jumped at the sound of Harry's voice behind her. She turned to see him holding two plates, each with a slice of birthday cake on it.

"Or are you on one of those pre-wedding diets? You shouldn't be, by the way. You're like Mary Poppins—practically perfect in every way."

Ana rolled her eyes but couldn't help a smile. Or the heat rising in her cheeks.

"Unlike me." He put down the plates. "Do you know, I've put on almost a stone in the past year." He looked down at his stomach and gave it a poke. "Got to do something about this."

From where she was sitting, Ana could see nothing at all wrong with Harry's body. Except . . . his legs were too long, his shoulders too broad, his face too beautiful.

"Fancy another game of tennis sometime?" he said. He wheeled a chair over and sat down, then broke off a piece of cake, popping it into his mouth.

She tried not to look at his lips.

"Go on, it's great cake," he said. "Janette made it herself." He licked his fingers, a little too slowly and suggestively.

She couldn't look away.

"Bye, Ana!" called Nate through the glass wall of her office. He did a double take. "Oh. Bye, Harry, good party."

Ana glanced up, trying not to look guilty, then raised a hand.

Now that Nate had left, the department was empty, silent. Desk lamps were off, computer screens dark, chairs tucked in. Ana's office took on a sudden intimacy.

"Megan rang, as you foretold," Harry said. "She and Charles will be turning up soon. I've switched my phone through to yours. Come out with us. It's my birthday." He leaned forward, his hands clasped in front of him, and smiled. "You can't possibly say no."

The golden highlights in his hair glinted in the glow of Ana's desk lamp.

She swallowed. "I don't know. Maybe." She broke off a small piece of cake and put it in her mouth. "Did you want to talk about Merry?"

"Not especially. I'll sort it."

Harry brought his chair closer to Ana's. Their knees were almost touching, and she caught again the subtle scent of his aftershave. She fought an overwhelming desire to close her eyes and breathe him in.

He broke off a piece of icing. It had an *A* on it.

"Look. *A* is for Ana. Open wide," he said softly.

His eyes were the same deep blue as the loch at Kindrummon. She couldn't look away. She was Mowgli in *The Jungle Book*, hypnotized by Kaa the snake. Her lips parted, and he put the cake on her tongue. His fingers stayed still, and she closed her lips around them.

He withdrew his fingers slowly, not taking his eyes from hers.

"More?" His voice was husky.

She nodded, and swallowed.

He broke off another piece. Again he placed it on her tongue, and his pupils dilated as she closed her lips around his finger.

Her last vestiges of resistance crumbled as Harry's finger slowly left her mouth and then traced a path down her jawline, coming to rest under her chin. He tilted her face up, and Ana closed her eyes as his lips met hers with the softest of touches.

A shock wave raced through her body. The kiss deepened, and it was like none she had ever known. It was like dancing with the devil; it was wrong, but she was helpless, her defenses breached. A tsunami of longing swept over her. Of their own accord, her hands reached up, her fingers entangling themselves in his hair, making sure he couldn't leave, would never end this kiss.

Then the phone rang.

"Leave it," whispered Harry.

Ana wasn't sure she'd have the strength to pick it up. Her limbs had turned to jelly.

The phone continued to ring, and Harry finally pulled away and grabbed it.

He spoke a few words, then replaced the receiver. "Megan and Charles are downstairs. I'll just nip back to the office." He stood up. "I'll meet you back here in five."

How could he be talking like nothing had happened? Her world had just been turned upside down.

He noticed her stupefied expression and perched on the edge of her desk. He reached out, stroked her hair. "Our lives are about to get pretty complicated," he said. "But we'll find a way. You're the one, Ana."

She was grateful for the time by herself, and sat breathing deeply, trying to compose herself. But her mind was racing and her body fizzed with desire that had nowhere to go.

"Coming?" Harry was back and holding out his hand to her.

She collected her bag and went over to where he stood in the doorway. Her knees went weak at his closeness; she felt like some vaporous Victorian heroine. He wrapped her in his arms and the kiss was fierce and hungry, leaving her limp and breathless.

"Come on," he said, slipping an arm around her waist. "This will have to wait. If that's even possible."

"Harry, I can't do this. I can't come out with you tonight, not like this."

"Sure you can. It's my thirtieth! You can't say no to a man who's having a milestone."

The lift arrived and Harry pushed the ground-floor button, then took her hand. "We should be discreet tonight, though. I think Charles may have twigged I've got a thing for you, but I'm not sure about Megan."

He released her hand as the doors opened.

As Ana focused on the group of people in front of her, she received another shock. Standing in the reception area with Megan and Charles were Harry's wife and daughter.

Katie visibly flinched as her eyes flew from Harry to Ana.

"Daddy!" cried the little girl, flying across the polished floor toward him. She was all bouncing curls and big blue eyes, and was wearing her very best dress for her father.

The night guard smiled. "Happy birthday, Mr. Rose!" he called.

"Thank you," replied Harry, sweeping his daughter up into a hug. "Hello, Miss Maria. And what are you doing in the big city at this time of night, hm?"

"We're going to the Hard Cafe!" she said. "For burgers!"

"The Hard Rock Cafe, darling," corrected Katie. "We thought we'd surprise Daddy, didn't we?"

And boy, had Harry looked surprised.

Ana thought quickly. "Hello, Katie," she said. "I haven't seen you since . . . oh, since the launch party. It's lovely to see you again. Harry and I have just polished off the birthday cake his secretary made him, so I hope he still has room for that burger!"

Even to Ana, it sounded forced.

She turned to Harry. "Good night, Harry. Have a lovely evening."

Nobody suggested she come with them.

"Good night," he said. "Thanks for staying late to help."

Ana was so deep in thought she went two stops past Holland Park. Coming out of her trance as the train doors were shutting, she quickly exited and made her way up the steps and across to the eastbound platform. As the trance took hold again, she stared unseeing at a mouse darting about beneath the tracks.

Moments from the day circled in her mind, in a loop that refused to pause. Harry locking eyes with her across the boardroom, raising his glass as he toasted his decade of misbehavior. His hand on her arm as he guided her away from the others. The intensity in his eyes as he trailed a finger down her face, the waves of heat rippling down her body.

A whoosh of hot air rushing out of the tunnel signaled the arrival of the train.

You're the one, he'd said. But what had he meant? The next casual fling? More than that?

She tried to wrangle her feelings into coherent thoughts. Was it just a physical thing? Although . . . could the way she was feeling be described as "just"? It was overwhelming. Perhaps it was his power and charisma that had fired her response. Was she just flattered to be the latest object of desire? Or was she falling for the man behind the image? And what about that dangerous streak that had initially repelled her? She was still aware of it, and if he tired of her, what of her future at Rose? Or even beyond Rose—Harry's tentacles stretched far and wide. If things went bad, he could ruin her career.

And then there was Percy. How could she be obsessing about another man when she was about to marry the love of her life? Had her feelings for Percy changed?

Percy had been everything to her, until Harry came along. Harry's sharp wit and easy charm had somehow exposed Percy's . . . mediocrity.

Where had that thought come from? Wouldn't *any* man look a little average next to Harry? She shouldn't compare them. Percy was thoughtful, cute, hardworking. Faithful. Harry was arrogant, entitled, a stranger to self-doubt. He was far too full of himself.

She made an effort to conjure up Percy's image as she stepped into the carriage. But he was saying, "MD of BWG Dublin," again.

Percy was a poseur, there was no denying it.

Harry was the real deal.

Percy was lovely but, right now, he seemed second best.

Katie

Katie knew it was finally over the second the lift doors opened. She saw the way Harry was looking at Ana. Katie knew that look, but it hadn't been directed her way in years.

All her therapy, finally coming off the medication—it had been for nothing.

Harry's thirtieth should have been a turning point. She'd worked through her anxiety and could now face going up to London, being out and about in society. This dinner in town, with the four people who meant the most to Harry, would be a major step back to happiness and reconciliation.

But Harry had been with them only in body. His mind had been somewhere else entirely, and she knew exactly where.

Katie remembered Ana from the launch party. She'd made such an effort to block that terrible night from her memory, but now it came rushing back. How Ana's cool, lithe, stylish beauty had made her feel like an overheated whale. How the floaty silk dress she'd loved suddenly felt like a giant green tent.

Harry had hardly taken his eyes off Ana that hot summer night. But Ana had appeared oblivious, wholly focused on making sure the event ran smoothly.

The woman who'd appeared out of the lift was a different creature, her eyes glittering, her face flushed. And her expression when she'd seen Katie and Maria said it all.

Guilty.

Now Harry wanted to talk. He was reading Maria a bedtime story, and then would be telling Katie what she didn't want to hear. More on the subject of "moving on," which until now she'd managed to talk him out of.

She had a feeling it would be different this time.

"Asleep already," he said, coming into the room carrying two glasses of red wine. "Here, we may as well help this along as best we can."

She preempted him. "Harry, I've been difficult to live with, I know that. But I'm almost there. I've accepted we're unlikely to have any more children, and I'm ready to focus on our relationship—"

"Stop, Katie. Please." He sat down. "I know you're doing so much better, and that's why I think you're ready to accept it's time to move on. I'm not the same person I was when we married. I was so young, wanting to fill that space left when my parents and Art died. And you're not the same person either—"

"But, Harry—"

"Let me finish. You haven't been happy these past few years, you know that. You deserve another go too. I'll always love you, but you're more like a sister to me now. It's over, Katie. Please, let me go."

It was hopeless. *Let me go.* Katie's world was caving in again. "I know there's someone else," she said as tears welled up.

Harry dropped his eyes. "There has been, yes. But it's over now. She's not the reason why. I think . . ." He looked up again. "Turning thirty has made me take a good look at my life. I'm going through the motions, I need it to have meaning."

"It's over?" Her voice was shaky. "How long was it going on?"

"It started just after Gemma's wedding."

"Gemma's wedding?"

"When I first met Merry."

"Merry? But—"

"You remember? Blond. Very blond, in every way."

"I thought . . . the other sister."

"What?" Harry flushed and looked away. "No, no, Ana's my art director. She's getting married soon, might be going to live in Dublin. Tonight, when you met her, I'd been trying to persuade her to stay."

Was he telling the truth? Could that have been all it was? Her instincts told her he was lying, but Harry could be so persuasive.

"Katie, darling. We need to do this amicably, for Maria's sake. But I want a divorce. I'll do everything properly—you and Maria won't want for anything. We've been through so much, I'm not going to turn my back on you."

"But you did, when you had those affairs." Katie wiped at the tears on her cheeks.

Harry fetched a box of tissues from the kitchen. "I didn't instigate either of them," he said, handing them over and sitting back down. "And they wouldn't have happened if you and I hadn't been having problems."

Katie hadn't felt emotion in a long time, thanks to her medication. But now anger took hold. "I *won't* divorce you, Harry," she said, her voice rising. "It's against my Catholic faith. If your affair is over, we *must* try again. And if you can only love me as a sister—well, many marriages survive on far less."

"For god's sake, Katie!" The conciliatory tone was gone, and now there was only exasperation. "Stop flogging this dead horse. If you won't agree to a divorce, I'll move out and wait for however long it takes. Why do you have to be so bloody difficult?"

"I still love you, even after your betrayals. I'm trying to understand, to come to terms with it." Her voice was calmer now. "My counseling training has taught me a lot. You were shunted off to boarding school, then you lost your parents and Art. I wasn't enough—"

"Will you stop analyzing me!" Harry smacked his glass down and left the room.

CHAPTER 25

—◦◦◦◦—

Ana

The morning after Harry's thirtieth, Ana attempted "business as usual" vibes during the weekly editorial meeting. It was as much for her own benefit as anyone else's. Each time Harry's name was mentioned, she fought to remain impassive, staring at the notebook in front of her for fear that if she met anyone's eyes, they'd *know*.

Back in her office, a small parcel was sitting on her desk. On it was written *Ana—Private*. As she picked it up, her eyes fell on the chair Harry had been sitting on yesterday, still pulled up close. Having so far managed to divert all thoughts of the cake incident, she now allowed herself to remember, and a thrill ripped through her, starting at her heart and zipping downward.

She tore the paper off the package, revealing a red box with *Cartier* in gold lettering on the lid. Opening it, she gasped. Inside was an exquisite bracelet, made of two intertwined bands of gold that spiraled around her wrist as she slipped it on. The end nearest her hand finished in a curly flourish on which sat a tiny dragonfly.

There was a small folded note:

Ana—

I can't sleep, eat, or think straight. Fault is entirely yours.
In NYC for a few days, put me out of my misery on return,
please?
H x

At lunchtime, Merry phoned. She was almost hysterical, and it took Ana a while to calm her down enough to find out why.

"Harry says it's run its course, that it was never meant to be serious. How could he treat me this way?" Her voice rose to a wail again. "What am I going to do, Ana? I love him; I can't live without him. He's everything to me. *Everything.* Oh my god, how do I carry on?"

Ana tried her best to soothe her—*deep breaths; pour yourself a brandy; take the dog for a long walk*—promising to go up to Scotland as soon as she could. But she knew she'd be making her excuses.

She was summoned to Harry's office a week or so later. It was after five, and Janette had left for the day. He showed her in, indicating the couch, and kept his distance, sitting on the edge of his desk. But the look in those deep blue eyes scorched her retinas.

He came straight to the point. "I've told Katie I want a divorce. And . . . maybe you know. I've ended things with Merry."

Ana didn't respond immediately. Her eyes briefly settled on a framed photo of Maria on his desk.

"I'm still marrying Percy."

"Really?"

"I'm sorry. I shouldn't have . . . you know. Kissed you. We'd both had too much to drink."

"Perhaps. No regrets here."

Neither looked away, and the silence lengthened.

"Thank you for the bracelet," she said, to fill it. "It's beautiful. But I can't keep it. You must see . . . me working here, and I love my job. I can't . . ."

His intense gaze was making her incoherent. She dropped her eyes but somehow became entranced by the way the golden hairs on his lower arms contrasted so beautifully with the pale blue of his shirt, and there were little freckles beneath them . . .

"It's OK, Ana. I understand. Katie won't divorce me because of her Catholic faith, so I'll have to move out and we'll be separated for however long it takes. Sorting out the move will take time; there's Maria to consider. It probably wouldn't be wise for you and me to be together publicly while I'm still living with Katie. Company gossip, media interest, and all that."

She remembered little Maria, flying across the reception area into her daddy's arms. And Katie, with her sad eyes.

Why was he assuming she wanted this? She'd just told him she was marrying Percy. The arrogance of the man!

"And going straight from one sister to another while I'm still married probably wouldn't be a good look either. I wouldn't trust Merry to keep quiet. We need to give her time."

"So . . ." began Ana.

"So until that's all sorted, we'll need to be extremely discreet. Snatch a moment when we can."

"I'm not risking my future for a few stolen moments, Harry."

"Of course not. If you'd rather I left you alone until I've moved out, I understand. Some things are worth waiting for."

Ignoring the warnings firing from her brain, her heart soared. But she kept her gaze steady.

"You're supposed to be marrying at Christmas, right?" he said.

"Yes."

"So you've got some time to work out what it is you want. I know what I want. I meant it when I said you're the one. If you break it off with Percy, I'll work things out so we can be together without it harming your career. I promise you that."

"I understand."

His intentions seemed serious, genuine. But how well did she really know this man?

She got up to leave, and he walked with her over to the door. Pausing with his fingers on the handle, he looked down at her, and she caught the exquisite scent of him, now familiar. What his blue eyes had started, the pheromones finished, and her resolve was demolished like a tower block brought down by a ton of dynamite.

"Ana . . ." He pulled her close and kissed her, his passion taking hold, his arms encircling her, tighter, until her hips were pressed against his. He bit her bottom lip gently before moving down to her neck, planting soft kisses down its length.

She arched her back, desire sweeping aside coherent thought, but somehow, eventually, she found the strength to pull away.

"No," she said, her hands on his chest, breathing fast. "I'm engaged. I can't do this."

He took her hands in his and raised them one at a time to his lips, creating little pools of heat on her skin. "Admirable," he said. "But if you loved him enough to marry him, you wouldn't be kissing me like that."

"Don't—"

"Ana, I'm in love with you. Desperately." He gently tucked a lock of hair behind her ear. "I'll wait for you for as long as it takes. Now you'd better go, before my good intentions leave in disgust."

Percy moved to Dublin, and Ana was dismayed to discover how many hours of the day would pass without a single thought of him. As for the nights, while she phoned Percy before bedtime, conjured up his face as she drifted off to sleep, her dreams were sabotaged by Harry. Dreams so intense that she'd wake up on fire, unable to banish the image of his eyes, the sensation of his hands on her body, his skin against hers.

September 1993

Ana's heart was heavy as she boarded the plane at Dublin Airport. She'd given it her best shot. It was only the second visit she'd managed since Percy's move to Ireland in June, and she'd been determined this one would be a success.

She'd failed, though Percy had no idea she saw it that way.

The first visit, back in July, was disappointing. His phone calls since he'd left had been upbeat, but she discovered that, in reality, he was dispirited. BWG Dublin consisted only of himself and four others, two of them part-time, and the important decisions were all made in London. Percy had no real power. Ana had put her own worries aside and spent the weekend bolstering his confidence, reminding him he'd been tasked with preparing for the influx of business and money. No doubt BWG was anticipating a surge in clients, and then he'd be able to take on new staff and more responsibility.

It had been exhausting, but she nudged him back on track, made him believe in himself again.

This weekend's visit had been just as awful, but this time it was her fault.

She strapped herself into her seat, avoiding the eye of the man next to her. She sensed him ogling and opened her *Irish Times*, blocking his view of her head.

She marveled that Percy hadn't read her mind, given it was so full of Harry. This weekend in his Dublin flat, she'd been on fire, like a rampaging tiger, after weeks of pent-up sexual longing. Visions of Harry drove her on, no matter how hard she tried to block them.

"Grrr!" Percy had said as she pulled him to her the minute they got through the front door, dragging him toward the kitchen worktop, yanking off his T-shirt and hopping up, wrapping her legs around him, and sending a bowl of green apples flying.

"You've missed me, then?" he'd said when she allowed him to breathe for a moment.

"You have no idea."

Between visits to the bedroom, Percy had asked how the wedding preparations were coming along; each time he did, a cold panic had crept along her veins, dousing the fire.

She was paralyzed with indecision. Her rational self told her (while waggling a finger) that this was just a massive crush on her boss, and she'd be the stupidest of stupid idiots (or "eejits," as Percy had taken to saying) if she risked her entire future, both personal and professional, for it.

But her heart, and the parts of her that didn't have to respond via her head, told her to end things with Percy and wait for Harry.

Was she in love with Harry?

When she'd met Percy, it was a meeting of souls, a deep friendship. Sex had been slow, sweet, sensuous, controlled.

With Harry, it was all about excitement, abandon, secrets, passion; a physical attraction that left her reeling. And self-control was noticeably absent.

Which of those relationships would form the basis for a happy life, a contented future? Good, safe Percy, or bad, dangerous Harry?

As the plane was swallowed into the low cloud over Dublin, she attempted to look at her future objectively. Harry was a glittering prize, but she was under no illusions—he could be one of those trophies you had to give back after a year. She wouldn't break off her engagement or risk her career for that. If she chose Harry, it would have to be for the long haul.

She dared herself to think the thought. Maybe she could one day be Mrs. Ana Rose, a queen of London society with a seat at Rose Corp.'s boardroom table.

Dublin disappeared below her, and she knew she wouldn't be back.

. . .

On Monday, Ana left the office on time for once, admitting to herself she couldn't produce work to her usual standard until she'd decided on a course of action. Already she knew the wedding wasn't going to happen.

She needed someone to talk to before she imploded with the stress of it all.

She'd phoned Megan. "I need to unload before I go mad."

"Pre-wedding jitters?"

"Something like that. A bit more than jitters, actually."

"I'm your man. I'll chill the wine."

Megan poured them both a large glass. "So, Nervous Nellie, what's up?"

Where to start? "It's more than nerves. I don't think I can go through with it."

Megan came to sit next to Ana on the sofa. "You're bound to feel nervous, sweetie. Everyone does. Same bloke for your entire life? It's a huge deal."

"I don't want a part-time marriage, but I don't want to live in Dublin."

"He'd come back here for you, you know that. He should look for something in London."

Ana sighed. "Honestly? I don't think I want him to. I'm not sure I love him enough. Having this distance between us, it's made me realize. I was swept up by it all, it was a holiday romance. The excitement hasn't transferred to real life."

"Well, how could it? Real life isn't all romance and flowers. Percy's solid. He's a good guy, and he loves you so much, Ana."

"It's not like you and Charles. He's always been the one for you. You're so sure. I'm not sure anymore. You have to be sure."

"True."

Saying the words out loud was helping Ana resolve things in her mind. "I'm going to call it off, Megan. I can't take the risk."

Megan was quiet for a moment. "God. I can't believe this. All the plans."

"I know—I'm so sorry."

"And you haven't told him yet?"

Ana shook her head. Now it was hitting her anew, the leap of faith she was taking. A leap from loyal, good-natured Percy, to a man who'd broken the hearts of two lovely women already this year. And probably more in the past, if she was honest with herself.

"Ana," said Megan. "Will you tell me the truth, if I ask a big question?"

"Big question?"

"Is there someone else? You've been so distracted. I thought it was because of the wedding, but these past couple of months . . . it's as if your mind's off somewhere else."

Megan's eyes, usually sparkling with fun, were now so earnest, and the temptation to off-load was overwhelming.

She looked away. "No."

"You're lying. Who is it, Ana? What's going on?" Her voice was so gentle, so full of compassion, that Ana's self-control finally crumbled and the floodgates opened. Megan gathered her into a hug, and she sobbed on her shoulder.

"Oh, dear. Let it all out." Megan patted her back, stroked her hair.

"It's Harry," she said between sobs.

Megan's hand stilled, then dropped away.

"*Harry?*" She shifted away so she could look at Ana properly. "*What?*"

"Oh, nothing's happened," Ana said, sniffing and wiping her tears away. She was pulling herself together, regaining some composure. "All we've done is kissed, that's the honest truth. But he wants to divorce Katie and he wants me to end it with Percy. I think I'm in love with him, Megan."

Now that she'd blurted it out, she knew it to be true.

Megan took a large gulp of wine. "Holy shit. I knew he fancied you, anyone can see that. But this? Ana, for god's sake. Have you thought about poor Katie?"

"Of course. And Maria. But Harry says it's been over for years, and he's going to do the right thing by them both."

Megan's expression was sober. "Harry's a womanizer, Ana. One's never enough."

The words came as a shock. "I know all about Merry, I've spoken to both of them about it. It was never serious—"

"And Bennie?"

"Who?" Anna stared at Megan, bracing herself for something she desperately didn't want to hear.

"She was the first one. A Soho barmaid. It went on for at least two years. They have a son. Harry never sees him; Bennie asked him to stay away. We never talk about it. I actually found out from Charles."

The shock made Ana shaky. How could Harry not have mentioned this?

"Harry told Charles all about your bloody sister too. Even about the *special talents* she learned in France. And there have probably been others, Ana."

Ana stared at the carpet, feeling sick.

"Look. You know I love my brother to bits, and I sort of understand his behavior. He's pretty sensitive underneath all that self-confidence. He has to be Mr. Charisma for the job. We both had a ghastly time when our parents and Art died. It's a massive thing to lose three people you love, especially when you're a teenager. I compensated for that by shagging every man with a pulse, and he's done something similar."

"He told me how difficult things were," said Ana. "He said he was too young to deal with it all."

"Probably, but don't make excuses for him, Ana. He's behaved terribly. I wouldn't want you to be the next distraction; plus he's your boss, for god's sake."

"I think he's changed."

"He told you that?"

She needed to move this on. It would take time to process everything Megan had said. "Charles wasn't exactly whiter than white, was he? Look what happened to *his* wife! She ended up in rehab. But you weren't slow to move in on that particular married man, were you? Touch of the pot calling the kettle black?"

"Touché. OK, that's kind of a good point. But I'd known Charles all my life. I don't think you know the real Harry."

Ana sighed. "All I know is that I can't stop thinking about him. But you're right—I don't want to be his next bit on the side. If I'm giving up my future with Percy, it has to be for more than that, and he's stepping up."

"What do you mean? Harry wants to marry you? Are you serious?"

"He hasn't actually said that, and Katie won't agree to a divorce, so there'll be a long wait. But once he's separated, then we can be together."

"And your career? How's that going to go down with everyone at Rose?"

"I've proved I'm good at my job, so the fact that I'll be with Harry should be irrelevant."

"Ana, listen to yourself. You think people would treat you the same if you were Harry's—what? Live-in lover? Do you . . ."

She stopped at the sound of the key in the lock. "Oh god, Charles."

"Good evening, my lovelies! I come bearing . . ." Charles halted as he took in Ana's face, streaked with tears. It was probably the first time he'd seen her anything other than composed. "What's going on?"

Megan looked at Ana, who nodded. "The wedding's off."

"You're kidding."

"No," said Megan. "Long-distance relationship's not doing it for Ana, but she doesn't want him to come back. She's dumping him."

"Poor old Perce. Can't say I'm surprised, though." Charles sat down and put a bag of takeaway on the coffee table. Curry smells leaked out, making Ana feel even more nauseated.

"How so?" said Megan.

"A certain reluctance to talk about Percy, or the wedding. A general waning of interest, let's say. Tell me Harry boy hasn't got anything to do with this, Ana?"

Ana's eyes widened. "I—"

"What makes you say that?" interrupted Megan.

"He told me he's got the hots for Ana. OK, those weren't his actual words. It was more along the lines of sorting out things at home so he could have a proper crack at you."

"Nothing's happened," said Ana.

"I'm sure it will," said Charles. "Harry always gets what he wants. If you're set on being the next love interest, just make sure you go into it with your eyes wide open."

He disappeared into the kitchen.

"Bloody hell," said Megan. "Why didn't he say anything to me about it?"

"I'm sorry," said Ana. "This is causing so much mess." But Charles's words had lifted her heart. Harry had said he was sorting things out so he could move on to her with a clear conscience.

"Well, Ana, I suppose it would be fun to be sisters-in-law. Good luck with that wait, by the way."

Finishing it with Percy was horrible.

He came over from Dublin thinking they were going to be finalizing the wedding arrangements. Instead, Ana sat him down and told him she didn't love him enough to marry him.

They talked and talked, Ana explaining that their time apart had given her a different perspective on their relationship, that she realized now that they wanted different things out of life.

Percy cried. When he told her yet again that he'd move back to London, would take her career more seriously, she couldn't bear to lie anymore and finally blurted it out: "There's someone else. I'm so sorry."

The shock on his face was hard to bear. She looked down at her hands, twisting them in her lap. "I haven't been unfaithful, please believe me. We've only kissed. God knows I didn't mean for it to happen; I was horrified when I felt myself falling for him. I tried so hard to make it work with you, to not think about him. But it was hopeless."

"Who?" He was crying again.

"I can't tell you. He's married. He's leaving his wife, but we've got to be very discreet, there's so much at stake."

"A married man?" The tears stopped. "This isn't you, Ana. Look, if all you've done is kiss . . . I can come home, we can still—"

"No, Percy. We can't. I love him. I loved you, too, very much. Always believe that. But this is something else. It's on another level. I'm so sorry, but I can't help it."

Percy stood up, anger finally breaking through. "You're not the girl I fell in love with. She'd never behave like this. A married man? Good luck with that. They *never* leave their wives. You just trashed your future, Ana."

He headed out the door, slamming it behind him.

Ana stuck her head around her office door and hollered at the design team: "Turn it bloody down!" Meat Loaf was singing that he'd do anything for love, but he wouldn't do *that*. Again. The song had been at number one for weeks, and for some reason Ana found the words deeply unsettling.

Harry had been in the States again, and she'd heard nothing from him. He'd told her he'd keep his distance, but it was messing with her mind. She was tetchy and jumpy and needed to talk to him. And kiss him.

He was expected back today. She looked at her watch: noon. She picked up the phone. "Is Harry back? I need half an hour," she said to his secretary.

"What's it in regard to, please?"

God, the woman was like a bodyguard. Janette irritated Ana beyond measure, with her floral dresses and little bolero cardigans, her hair in a ponytail that swung annoyingly as she walked. She was obviously besotted with Harry, and he treated her like a pet poodle. The whole thing was nauseating.

"It's a managerial matter."

"I'm sorry, Harry's diary is full until Friday."

"Put me through."

"Harry's on the phone. Can I take a message?"

"Get him to ring me." She put the phone down.

Five minutes later, it rang. "It's Harry."

A thrill rippled through her at the sound of his voice. "Hi, welcome back. Can I have half an hour? I feel like we need to . . . catch up."

"Of course." He lowered his voice. "But better make it a quick ten minutes or my good intentions will be going to hell again."

"That's what I want to talk about. Your intentions. I've finished with Percy."

There was a brief silence. "Good. How did he take it?"

"Not well. I didn't tell him about us, of course."

"No. Right, well, come up. I'll push my next meeting back."

Ana couldn't resist a smirk as she walked past Janette's desk. The secretary pursed her lips and looked busy.

Harry raised his eyebrows as she shut the office door behind her. He stayed behind his desk, and she sat down opposite. "How was New York?"

"Very . . . vertical. Shouty and loud. I love it—so would you. I'll take you there." He finally smiled. "I'll buy us a penthouse."

Ana's golden future suddenly hung in front of her, like a big apple. She smiled back. "In the meantime, can we organize a night out or something? I'm feeling all at sea now the wedding's off. I need to move forward."

"Of course. I'm moving into the South Ken flat as soon as the house is sold; you can come over. Merry's staying in Scotland, as I'm sure you know."

Ana was taken aback. The place where her sister and Harry had spent stolen afternoons having "fun," as Harry insisted on calling it? *Really?*

"Ah. Doesn't appeal? Don't worry, there's nothing left of Merry there, and I'm having it redecorated."

"But still . . ." She left that hanging in the air.

"I suppose it's quite small," he said. "Should probably think about finding somewhere else."

"What's happening with Katie?"

"Leaving London. She's going to live with her friend Cassandra—you remember Charles's ex?"

Ana thought back to the drunken woman in the overly tight dress at the launch party. "Yes, I remember."

"Cass is a born-again teetotaler. A bit of a bore, to be honest—the old version was far better value. She's going to Wales. Setting up a—what's she calling it? A wellness retreat. A Welshness retreat, perhaps. At one with the sheep? I have Welsh ancestry, incidentally, but that's not something I generally admit to."

Ana laughed. Harry's views on anywhere west of the Cotswolds or north of Watford were akin to Terri's views on southerners.

"Cass is a new woman," he continued, "a very organic one. She's persuaded Katie to go with her, to work as a counselor. Katie's decided it'll be a fresh start, and thinks it'd be nice for Maria too. Though frankly, it's all New Age bollocks. I'd rather Maria went to boarding school."

"So . . . back to us?"

"Right, yes. We'll need to work out how and when to let people know. Thank god Megan and Charles have been discreet."

"I need to tell my parents, because of the wedding."

"Good, yes. Do that. Build me up."

"Mum's already a fan." But Ana wondered how much her mother knew about what had happened to Merry.

At last, Harry walked around to where she sat. She looked up at him, and he stroked her cheek, cupped her chin. "We'll be together soon," he said, and bent down to kiss her.

It was like an electric shock. Fighting the desire, she pulled away. "Publicly. As a couple."

"Right." He frowned slightly.

"I've given up a lot for this relationship," she said. "I don't want people thinking I'm just another notch on Harry Rose's bedpost." She stood up, and in her Manolo Blahniks, her eyes were almost level with his. "I should go, before your . . . typist gets suspicious."

"Be nice to Janette. She's a sweet thing, and useful to have onside."

Ana gave a small laugh.

Harry walked over to the door and opened it. "Thanks, Ana," he said, loudly enough for his secretary to hear. "I'll see what I can do."

She left, feeling the twin lasers of Janette's eyes sear her back.

CHAPTER 26

Harry

December 1993

The house was sold, and Katie and Maria had gone to Wales. His lawyer, Tom Wolston, advised not making a fuss if Harry wanted to see his daughter regularly.

Saying goodbye had been surprisingly painful. Cassandra had been giving Katie "counseling," though she had precisely no qualifications in that area. Frankly, Harry couldn't stand this new version of Cassandra. What was it with people who'd been through rehab and felt the need to evangelize their newfound knowledge of how to cope with life? Now Katie had been sucked into the whole ridiculous nonsense, talking about divesting herself of Harry's "negative influence" and their "toxic relationship."

While Harry would always remember Katie fondly, she was trying not to remember him at all.

From one problem woman to another. Harry had needed to talk to Merry about the South Ken flat. She'd been almost incoherent, alternately shrieking and crying, telling him he'd ruined her life and she'd make him pay. He'd put the phone down and told Wolston to speak to her on his behalf.

Now, it was only a matter of time before word spread about his split with Katie. He needed to preempt the gossip. Tonight was the office Christmas party, the time when tittle-tattle turned exponential. Tonight he'd bite the bullet.

He beckoned Janette into his office and asked her to shut the door. She looked surprised, and not a little excited.

"Janette, I know I can rely on your discretion."

"Of course, Harry." The seriousness of her expression was rather touching.

"Katie and I . . . we're separating. Perhaps you already know."

"I don't listen to office gossip, Harry. But I'm very sorry to hear that."

"We've sold the house, and I'll be living in town. There will be gossip, of course, about the reason for our separation. It's an irretrievable breakdown caused by Katie's ongoing battle with depression, which I'm no longer able to help with. It's amicable."

"Gosh, Harry, I'm sure you've done your best to make her happy. These things are always sad, but if you're making each other miserable, well . . ."

"Quite. Thank you, Janette."

It was a dismissal, but she didn't hear it that way.

"My sister was stuck in an unhappy marriage for years. She was afraid to leave because she didn't want to be alone, and because of the money situation. When they finally split she was that much happier, and then she met this really nice man called Ken. I'm sure the same will happen to you, Harry."

"Perhaps."

"If you ever need to talk . . ."

"Thanks. That's sweet of you. Where would I be without you? Better get on with it, though, eh?"

"Yes, of course, Harry. Loads to get through before the party tonight. Can't wait! And you can rely on me. Mum's the word."

Ana

It was four o'clock, and work had been abandoned for the afternoon. Wine was already flowing, and the girls were trooping, a few at a time, to the loos, emerging transformed and glittery in clouds of perfume.

Ana cleared her desk, pondering the evening ahead. From tonight, she and Harry would be official. Out and about as a couple. And although neither had spoken the words, it was understood she'd be staying over at his place. The prospect hung between them like a delicious fruit. For the past week, every look, every glance they'd shared, had scorched a path through her. A tremor of anticipation rippled down her body. Again.

Knowing all eyes would be upon her, she'd chosen her dress for maximum impact. Because now, not only would she be Rose Corp.'s style queen, she'd be queen consort too. She'd spotted it in *Vogue* and had brokered a deal with Versace—a chunk of advertising space for the loan of the dress. It was gold lamé, and it shimmered with a life of its own. The neckline was draped low, and it was slit to the thigh. Her makeup would be gold, too, and she'd wear her hair loose, poker straight. She was aiming for nothing less than goddess.

Ana switched off her computer, unhooked the hanger from her office door, and headed for the ladies.

Harry

Harry was at the Hippodrome early. It was company tradition that he welcomed everyone personally as they arrived.

Janette was one of the first, looking pretty. She'd gone to town with her makeup and was wearing a dress that was far shorter than her usual style. She kept pulling at the hem, as if everyone was trying to see up it.

"Hello, you look lovely," said Harry affectionately. He leaned forward to kiss her cheek.

Enormous blush.

"So do you! Happy Christmas!" she said in a high voice.

"Nice dress."

"You don't think it's too short? I went shopping with Lesley from human resources. She talked me into it."

"Is there such thing as a too-short dress?" said Harry cheekily. "Enjoy the party, sweetheart. Don't drink too much."

"I won't!"

A few more arrived, and then a flood, and he carried on being jovial Santa Harry.

Terri appeared, in head-to-toe black. She'd done something spiky with her hair, there was a black velvet choker around her neck, and her eyeliner was deliberately smudged.

"You look terrifying," said Harry. "Save a dance for me later. Something by the Cure, perhaps."

"Very fookin' funny, Harry . . . holy shit."

"What?"

"It's a walking bloody Oscar."

Ana was coming through the doors, shimmering in a dress made of something filmy and gold that clung to her perfect body. A smooth, glistening leg peeped through a split up one side, and her hair fell to her waist like a glossy black curtain.

Harry's composure flew right past her and out the door. Suddenly all he could think about was exploring inside that split.

Terri spoke in his ear. "Harry. Get a grip."

"What? Yes, get a grip, man. It's only a golden goddess."

Nate was with Ana, and Harry went to greet them. Ana was wearing gold eye makeup, and more gold glittered on her cheeks.

He kissed her below the sparkle.

"Hello, art people. That's quite a dress, Ana. Does it turn to rags at midnight?"

"I might have gone home by then. Depends if I find my prince."

"Princes are vastly overrated. Company bosses are far better value."

"'Someday my boss shall come.' Doesn't have quite the same ring."

"Oh, I don't know." Harry grinned.

Ana blushed as she realized the double entendre.

"Also less liable to turn into frogs when kissed," added Nate.

"I don't know about that either," said Harry. "But I'm willing to put it to the test. Ana?"

He kissed her again, this time on the lips. He'd intended a quick peck but found he couldn't pull away.

"Harry, have you not heard of sexual harassment?" said Terri, after many seconds had passed.

Ana ended it.

"Sorry," said Harry. "Got carried away. But then . . . Christmas."

"Can I have one?" said Terri.

"Fuck no, you might turn me to stone," said Harry.

"What makes you think I was talking to you?" said Terri, winking at Ana.

"Come on, Terri," said Nate. "Let's go and play."

Harry slipped an arm around Ana's waist. The gold material was thin and slithery, and he could feel the warmth of her skin beneath. "Let's go find the bar. I've had enough of the meet and greet."

He kept his arm there as they went through to where the dance floor was already pumping. Harry ordered champagne for himself, Ana, Terri, and Nate, then raised his glass toward them. "Merry Christmas, all. You're top girls and boys, and I love you dearly. A toast to 1994. I have a feeling it's going to be spectacular."

His arm was still around Ana's waist. Terri stared pointedly at it, then at his face, then cocked her head to one side. "Blatant favoritism, if you ask me. Just because she looks like Aphro-fookin'-dite."

"Doesn't she just," said Harry, and lifted Ana's hand to his lips. Her nails were gold too. "*Ding dong*. It's the belle of the ball."

"Harry . . ." said Ana, the question in her eyes.

"Nate, Terri, I'm happy for you two to be the first to know. Ana and I are a thing. An item. Whatever you want to call it. Feel free to light the gossip wildfire."

"You what?" said Nate. "Ana?"

"As you know, Percy and I split up," she said, as if she were delivering a company report. "Harry and his wife have separated too. So—"

"So no more eyes meeting across a crowded room but being too cautious to do anything about it," interrupted Harry. "But as far as work goes, it's business as usual. Nothing will change."

Terri snorted, and Harry sensed a hostility in her reaction far beyond what he'd anticipated. What was that all about?

"Terri. You didn't like it when I more or less ordered you to employ Ana, but I was right, wasn't I?"

"Can't deny it."

"Well, Rose won't be losing Ana because she's dating the boss. OK? Get used to it and move on."

"Right you are, boss. Message understood."

Harry hoped it was. It might be business as usual, but he knew how sensitive Ana was about any implication her meteoric rise was down to anything other than talent and hard work.

"Nate, darling, come and shake your delicious booty with me," said Terri.

"My pleasure. Lead on, Macduff."

Harry and Ana were as alone as they were likely to be in the next hour or two.

"Come back to the flat with me tonight."

"And spend Saturday in this?"

"Definitely. I think you should wear it every day, in fact."

"It has to go back to Versace."

"So I'm not allowed to rip it off?"

"No. Slow unzipping will do just fine."

Harry went quiet for a moment, then took her hand again, holding it in his lap.

"Right now, I'm in danger of another wholly indiscreet show of affection." He stroked her palm. "What shall we do about this, Ana?"

Her eyes, their gold lids glistening in the dim nightclub lighting, held his, and it was like being sucked into a whirlpool.

"Dance?"

"Yes. Dance."

All eyes were on them as Harry led her to the dance floor.

They kept a respectable distance apart as they moved to the heavy beat of New Order. Ana's dress flashed in the disco lights as she danced sinuously, feeling the music.

If he didn't touch her soon, he'd implode.

Then "Last Christmas" came on, and he pulled her into his arms. In her heels she was almost as tall as him. He looked into her eyes, and it took an enormous force of will not to kiss her again, to resist obliterating every last millimeter of space between them. "Let's go after this one."

"Harry, you're the boss, it wouldn't be right. Let's give it another hour."

It was the longest hour of his life. They separated after the slow dance, then spent time mingling, Harry trying not to look at his watch.

Finally they were out among the Christmas throngs of Leicester Square, looking for a taxi. The atmosphere was infectious, people singing, wearing tinsel, kissing people they shouldn't have been kissing.

"What's in there?" Harry asked, noticing Ana's oversized handbag.

"Tomorrow's clothes," she said with a grin.

"Oh really? Did you think I'd be so easy?"

He gathered her into his arms and kissed her hungrily. The noise and bustle of Leicester Square faded away and there was only Ana; her soft lips, her silky hair, her body warm as he slipped his arms inside her open coat.

"I want to look for a taxi, but I don't want to stop kissing you," he said.

"Find a taxi and kiss me some more."

One pulled over and a trio of girls in tiny Santa dresses spilled out, giggling.

Harry talked to the driver, then turned to the girls and grinned. "Happy Christmas, Santa ladies."

"Oooh, come with us, handsome!" replied one of them. "You can unwrap me anytime!"

"He's with me," said Ana.

"All right, don't get your knickers in a twist," said a second Santa. "If you're wearing any, that is. Probably not."

Harry guffawed, but Ana wasn't amused. She got into the taxi.

He turned to the girls and shrugged. "Sorry, Santas. Another time, maybe."

He was still grinning when he joined Ana.

"Harry, really," she said.

"Bah humbug, Ana," he replied, and took her in his arms.

They kissed all the way to Knightsbridge, Harry's hand creeping inside the split in Ana's dress, making its way higher, making her gasp, until she put her own over it. "Stop, Harry," she whispered, "before I reach the point of no return."

"Keep the change. Merry Christmas," Harry said to the driver.

"Cheers, mate. Won't be as merry as yours, I'm guessing." He winked. "Bloody gorgeous."

"Good night, Mr. Rose," called the night manager as Harry led Ana to the penthouse lift. "I hope you've enjoyed your evening."

"I have indeed, Ali," he replied. "And this is Ana. You'll be seeing a lot of her from now on."

She was looking around her; he saw the penny dropping. "This isn't . . . ?"

"No. I haven't bought this yet," he said, putting an arm around her waist and guiding her into the lift. "I wanted to make sure you approved first. Let's call tonight a test drive."

The doors opened directly into the enormous open-plan living area, a minimalist sea of white, with floor-to-ceiling windows looking out across the city.

"This is incredible," she said, looking around her.

"I thought it was very you. Drink?"

"Bed?" she replied, throwing her coat on a chair.

"How very wanton of you. But OK, then."

He led her by the hand into the bedroom, pressing a button to draw the curtains.

"You can unzip me now," she said, standing close, her breath tickling his cheek.

He turned her around and pushed her hair aside, sweeping it over one shoulder. Her exposed neck was irresistible, and he bent to kiss it. She smelled of vanilla and musk.

Ignoring the zip, his hands slipped around to her front, cupping her breasts, and she moaned softly, tipping her head back.

His breathing quickened and he brought his hands back, taking hold of the zip and slowly lowering it. Her beautiful back was revealed, reminding him of the time when he'd ached to touch it, at the launch party. He'd waited so long.

The dress slithered to the floor, forming a puddle of gold, and now she was standing in her tiny lace panties and high heels. He trailed a finger down her back, and she shivered under his touch.

She turned around and began unbuttoning his shirt.

"Too slow," he said, and pulled it over his head.

As they kissed, her fingers traced a path down his chest, then stroked him softly through his trousers. She unzipped him, and her fingers found their way through.

Soon they were naked, skin to skin, and she pulled him to the bed.

As they lay down he paused above her, searching her eyes, seeing his own hunger reflected in hers. Then he stopped thinking and there was just the touch of her, the scent of her, the sound of her moaning gently, whispering his name. He'd never lost himself so completely in a woman before, never experienced such passion. This was beyond anything he'd ever known. She kept her eyes locked on his as he entered her, making her gasp, and the heat in their dark depths took him to greater heights, then to someplace in his subconscious, beyond time, deeply recognized, strangely remembered. She cried out, finally closing her eyes as ecstasy flooded through him and he buried his face in her hair, muffling his cry.

They lay still and quiet for a while, their limbs entwined.

But not for long. They made love all night, their desire insatiable, their brief snatches of sleep interrupted by one or the other wanting more. Ana was like a woman possessed, kissing him with a ferocity he'd never known, matching his rhythm, digging her nails into his back.

So much for the Ice Queen.

"Going to have to rethink that nickname," he said, during a lull.

"What, Ice Queen?"

"If only they knew."

"You melted me. I'm a puddle now."

"And I'm drowning in it."

Next morning found Harry scrambling eggs and making coffee in the kitchen, like the stereotypical bloke in a rom-com after a big first night.

And just like the stereotypical girl, Ana appeared in the doorway dressed in the shirt he'd been wearing the night before. He took in her tousled hair, her sleepy eyes, her smile. If possible, she looked even sexier than she had last night.

"Come back," she said.

He looked at his pan of eggs. "But three hens and I worked hard to make your breakfast."

"Not forgetting the cock."

Harry chuckled as he turned off the stove and scooped her up in his arms. "Saucy wench."

CHAPTER 27

———◦◦◦◦◦———

Ana

Ana lay on the bed in a post-orgasm coma. Her limbs felt like lead, and her mind was filled with Zen-like calm. Satisfied. For now.

Harry had matched her, led her, whereas Percy had always followed. Harry was skilled, anticipating what she wanted—needed—with uncanny accuracy.

The unwelcome thought that Merry had paved the way intruded on her bliss, but she flicked it away. What had she expected? Harry had history. Rather that than an inexperienced guy with no imagination. She couldn't have it both ways.

She sighed with pleasure, remembering every detail of the night before, from the most sexually charged dance of her life, to the kiss in Leicester Square, the taxi ride, and the long, long night of passion. She'd never felt so alive.

It was Saturday, and the weekend stretched ahead, full of promise. They would do all those things people did on first weekends. Breakfast in bed, sex, walks in the park, more sex, more food.

She slid out of bed, feeling the life return to her limbs, and put Harry's shirt back on, walking through to the kitchen.

"No. This time I'm cooking the eggs," said Harry. He was dressed in jeans and a T-shirt, his feet bare. "I need to replenish my energy. Currently running on empty."

How could a man look so beautiful on zero sleep? She slid her arms around his waist and leaned her head on his back. "Eggs would be lovely. How good are you at cooking eggs? Our future together depends on your answer."

"I'm the boss. At eggs too."

Later Harry showed her around the penthouse. "Shall we keep it, then?"

"You want us to move in together already?"

"Would you rather go on sharing with Megan and Charles? Don't you feel like a gooseberry?"

She'd miss those two. But she wouldn't miss the sound of Megan's moans in the night, when Ana had been so full of longing for Harry.

"I wonder when they'll get married?" she said. "I suppose Charles's divorce will take a while."

"Cassandra will be only too glad to divest herself of the negative energy she hasn't purged via coffee enemas, or whatever it is they offer at Welshness."

"At what?"

"Her retreat in Wales, for losers in leather sandals. I'm worried they'll turn Maria into a witch."

"I thought Katie was Catholic. How does the New Age stuff fit in with her beliefs?"

"God only knows," said Harry.

"Funny."

"I don't care what Katie does. I just don't want Maria to turn against me."

"I might be her stepmother, one day."

"Jumping the gun, aren't you? We've got to make it through years of living in sin first."

"Sounds delicious. Lovely, lovely sin."

"Indeed. So, you want to come live in sin with me, then?"

"I do."

. . .

On Monday, as Ana made her way to her desk, heads swiveled, some surreptitiously; others, like Terri's, overtly.

Nate was the first to drop by. "Good party, wasn't it?"

"Yes . . . and yes."

"What's the second yes for?"

"Yes I confirm I'm having a proper thing with Harry."

"That wasn't my actual question, but thanks for telling me."

Why was he looking uncomfortable? He'd seen them together at the party.

He pulled up a chair. Why was he pulling up a chair?

"Ana. A bit awkward, but—"

"What is it, Nate?" She regarded him coolly.

"You know I've taken a personal interest in your career. You're the best designer I've ever worked with."

So far, so warm glow.

"Don't blow it by shagging the boss. A married man with a kid."

What the hell?

"Nate, it's not like that. He's left his wife and I'm moving in with him."

"Yeah, right."

"Yeah, it is right."

"What . . . really?"

"Really."

"Well, bugger me. I don't know what to say."

"How about congratulations?"

"OK. That. Sorry, I'm a bit gobsmacked. The first I knew there was anything going on was Friday night. Although, I did notice him hanging around your office. And you did get promoted unfeasibly quickly."

Ana frowned. "That was before there was anything between us. Never question that."

"Sorry. OK, then. I'd better . . ." He sidled out of her office.

She felt uncomfortable. She had such respect for Nate, and he'd never look at her in the same way again. Before, she'd been his star designer. Now, she was the boss's . . . what was she? Girlfriend? Live-in lover? Had "coming out" at the Christmas party been such a good idea after all?

Terri was the next to drop by. "Ana. That photo shoot at the Tower of London in Feb. You booked Randi to do the makeup, but I need her for Kate Moss. OK if we find you someone else?"

"Fine."

"So, um . . ."

"Yes?" Her tone didn't invite confidences. She hated to be the subject of office gossip.

"You'd rather I got to the point."

"I'd rather you didn't say anything about it."

"I'm a journalist. That's not going to happen. I'm in charge of the *Rack*, I'll torture it out of you if I have to."

"Yes, we're together. End of story."

Terri said nothing.

"You're still here."

"I don't know why I care, because you're a cold fish. But I do mind what happens to you."

"I don't need you to. I can look after myself."

"Hm. You and Harry, then. What's the story?"

"Why would I share it with you?"

"You might need me to deal with the office gossips, for one. If no one knows what's going on, they'll just make it up. As far as they know, he's a happily married man and you could be a home-wrecker. Everyone loves Harry. They'll think you seduced him. Let's face it, that dress wasn't the last word in subtlety."

Ana turned to face Terri. "I didn't seduce him. We've been friends for a while. He's been having marriage problems for years. Finally he and Katie have split up. She's gone to Wales and he's divorcing her as soon as he can, which is ages away because she's Catholic and won't agree to it. In the meantime he's moved to a flat in town, and I'm going to be living there with him. Soon."

"Holy fuck, that was quick. Out with the old, in with the new, eh?"

"Not that quick. We've waited ages. We've done everything properly. Now, if you don't mind, I need to get on with all this." She waved her hand at the pile of work on her desk.

"OK. Well. That's all quite surprising, but I wish you luck. Hope it doesn't come crashing down, for your sake."

She left.

Why were Nate and Terri worried about her future? Did they honestly think she couldn't look after herself?

The King Henry VIII was heaving with villagers. The noise level was deafening, as Christmas Eve revelers sang along with Slade's "Merry Xmas Everybody" blasting from the jukebox. Tinsel was strung across the oak beams, and the delicious cinnamon-spiced aroma of mulled wine filled the pub.

"Let's have two of those," Ana shouted to Merry, pointing to a blackboard. On it was a chalk drawing of a glass of steaming red wine and the words *King Henry VIII's Favorite Wassail! Only £2:50 per glass.*

Why was this pub named after the tyrant who'd beheaded Anne Boleyn, the locality's most famous historical figure? That didn't seem terribly supportive.

"I'll get them," called Merry. "See if you can find us a square foot of space."

Ana saw faces from her childhood—people she'd been at junior school with. She wondered whether to join two girls she remembered who were standing at the bar. It would be preferable to being alone with Merry, who was full of nervous energy, like a coiled spring.

Her sister had arrived home yesterday. Ana had caught today's four o'clock from Victoria and had spent the train journey (not to mention the past few weeks) wondering what to say to her, rehearsing it in her mind. She'd wondered—would Merry be back to her old self?

As soon as Ana had dumped her case on the hall floor, the answer became clear. Merry had appeared and wrapped her in a hug, then burst into tears. Her hair was back to its old shade of honey blond. Or at least, the top half of it was. The rest was grown-out bleached, and the soft curls had gone limp and straggly. She'd lost weight, and there were dark rings beneath her eyes.

"How do you think Merry's looking?" her mother said, her voice worried, when they'd had a moment alone after dinner. "It's so sad, what's happened to her, losing Will."

"It'll take time."

"At least you seem to be doing fine, Ana, considering you were meant to be getting married about now."

"It was for the best, Mum. Like I said on the phone, the holiday romance didn't really work in real life."

"Yes, well. Let that be a lesson to you. Think carefully before you commit yourself again."

Perhaps now wasn't the time for an update.

"Why don't you two go to the pub later? You don't want to be stuck here with us on Christmas Eve."

No, she wanted to be with Harry. But he was spending Christmas with Megan and Charles, then driving over to Wales to see his daughter.

Ana elbowed her way to a space near the fireplace and, while she waited for Merry, thought back to the night before. Harry had taken her for dinner at the Ivy, and it was their first proper "date" together. Although aware Harry was well known, she'd been taken aback at the level of interest as people whispered behind their hands, pretending not to gawp. And dining with a person of such influence had been a revelation. Under the attentive eye of the maître d', waiters had hovered like personal slaves, ready to top up their glasses or brush a crumb off the tablecloth.

The home secretary had stopped by their table, and Harry had exchanged a backslapping bear hug with Kenneth Branagh and an air-kiss with Emma Thompson. This all seemed to be business as usual for Harry.

As the evening progressed, however, she'd forgotten about the others in the restaurant as Harry told her what the past week had meant to him, how she made him feel. Then he'd taken her hand, stroking her palm, sending waves of heat racing through her body . . . and dropped something into it. She'd looked down to see a little box wrapped in gold paper. "Merry Christmas," he'd said, the flame between them reflected in his eyes, flickering, playing on those long, dark gold lashes. "Go on, open it."

The ring sparkled in the candlelight, an enormous ruby set in two circles of diamonds.

"It's bloody difficult, choosing for a style icon, but—"

"Harry, it's perfect . . ."

Ana wrenched her mind back to the present and craned her head toward the bar. Merry was still waiting to be served. Not so long ago, the crowds would have parted like the Red Sea, and some hopeful man would have asked her what she was drinking. But Merry's flame had gone out, and now she was just another girl fighting to be noticed.

Finally she arrived with the drinks, and they clinked their glasses together. It felt nice to be out of London. Ana felt Harry's absence as an ache, but the breathing space was probably good for her, and the Merry situation needed sorting.

"Bloody hell, that was a mission," said Merry. "So, dear sister, let's skip straight past my train wreck of a life and ask what's going on with yours. I was sorry to hear you dumped Percy. He seemed nice. Unlike a certain *shit* I was stupid enough to get involved with." She spat out the word.

"Pretty busy at work." Should she say something now? Or would that ruin Christmas for everyone? She didn't want to be responsible for familial drama.

"How long are you going to stay in Scotland?"

"For a while. I'll have to come down occasionally, for board meetings, but the McCarey's team doesn't need me and I was only ever interested in the wine part."

"Won't you go a bit mad, stuck up there?"

"Truth? I can't face coming back to London yet. Too many memories. I will eventually, when I'm ready for Operation Destroy Harry Rose. But that's going to be major drama, so I've got to make sure I'm strong enough. Oh, by the way, I know he's your boss, so that's obviously between us. We're family, so I can rely on you, right?"

A sense of impending doom crept over Ana. "What do you mean, Operation Destroy Harry Rose? You mustn't do anything rash, Merry. Just put it all behind you and move on."

"That's easy for you to say. You've never had your heart broken by a coldhearted bastard. And don't forget, 'Hell hath no fury.' We must be deserving of our scorned-woman reputations." Her eyes were glittering, and she gnawed at the side of her thumbnail.

"Stop it, Merry. You know he's a powerful man. You don't want to make an enemy out of Harry Rose. Get over him."

"I'll *never* get over him, Ana. He's ruined my life. Yes, it started as a fling, but I fell in love with him, and he said he loved me too."

Did he?

"Truth is, he loved blonde sex-bomb me, but when I turned into sad me with a dying husband, he didn't want to know. He needs to pay for the way he cast me aside like a—a used tissue. Maybe in the *News of the World.*"

"You're not serious. It'd hurt you more than Harry. Think of your reputation. You were married too."

"There speaks the perfect loyal employee. Just watch me, Ana. I can see it now: *Love Rat Harry Dumps Tragic Widow.* They'd love it. The broken promises, the sleaze, the lies. The press like nothing more than bringing down a hypocrite, a whiter-than-white good bloke."

Ana felt nauseated. "You mustn't, Merry." It came out as a croak.

"Oh, but I must! It's the only thing keeping me going at the moment. Like you say, one's at risk of mental illness, being cooped up in a castle."

Right now, she did indeed look like the madwoman in the attic.

"Please, Merry, for my sake, then. Harry might sack me, especially if he found out I knew what you were planning."

"Who'd tell him? Not me."

"Just . . . don't!"

"Sorry. My mind's made up. He's going to pay for what he's done."

Ana snapped. "For god's sake, Merry. Have some self-respect! You seduced Harry. It was *you* who instigated the affair. Then you hooked him with your blonde-bimbo routine and your special French . . . things. You were the classic bit on the side. It was *never* going to be anything more. As if someone like Harry would marry someone like you! Just let it go. Harry doesn't deserve that."

"Why are you defending him? Oh, of course. That ambition of yours. Suck up to the bloody boss rather than defend your own sister. Whatever happened to blood being thicker than water? You're a cold, calculating cow. I'd hate to be you."

"You can't expose Harry. You just can't." Her voice was pleading.

Merry went still as understanding dawned in her eyes. She turned white.

"No. You wouldn't do that to me. You . . . and Harry?"

Ana hadn't meant it to be like this. Her anger evaporated, and she reached out to touch her sister.

Merry quickly raised her arm, hitting Ana's out of the way.

Heads turned.

"Merry, please. I was going to tell you. I was waiting for the right moment, I didn't want to spoil Christmas."

Ana saw the fight leave Merry and despair take its place. Her sister's eyes filled with tears, and she slumped against the fireplace.

"Merry . . ."

"Go away. Just leave me alone."

"You won't go to the press, though . . ."

"Is that all you care about, Ana? What's happened to you?"

CHAPTER 28

Ana

February 1994

Ana stood on the Tower of London embankment, leaning on the railings above the Traitors' Gate. She was early for today's Blur photo shoot. The *Hooray!* team often had their music playing at work, and Ana was looking forward to meeting the band.

Terri, of course, preferred Oasis.

The brown waters of the Thames slapped against the ancient walls as a tour boat chugged past. She pushed her hands deeper into her coat pockets and tucked her chin into her scarf against the chill, peering down at the centuries-old gates beneath the stone arch. This was the way in for traitors in Tudor times. She could almost hear the quiet splash of oars, sense the fear of those who'd passed beneath this bridge.

A loud *caaark!* made her jump, and she turned to see a raven perched on the wall beside her. It looked her in the eye, and she shivered, remembering they were omens of bad luck. "Shoo!" she said, flapping her hand at it.

"Abandon hope all ye who enter . . . or whatever it is. Kind of creepy."

Jake, *Hooray!*'s chief photographer, had appeared at her side, rubbing his hands together. "It's brass monkeys today. Whose bright idea was it to shoot outside?"

"Mine."

"Oh. Well, I guess it'll look cool, London band at the Tower."

"It's your job to make it look cool. Randi will take care of the red noses."

"Right. Shall we make a start, then?"

Five minutes later, Blur piled out of a car. Ana couldn't help smiling. They were incredibly cute.

A member of the Tower staff showed the team and the band to the room they'd been allocated. Ana, Jake, and Ana's assistant Mark left them to it, and went to look at the locations Mark had previously scouted.

They made their way along a gravel path next to an expanse of lawn. On all four sides rose the Tower walls.

"I thought we could start here," said Mark, pointing to a plaque. "It's where they chopped people's heads off."

Ana moved closer to the small memorial, reading the names on it. As she did, she experienced the strangest sensation, as though there was something crawling beneath her skin.

WILLIAM, LORD HASTINGS. LADY JANE GREY.
QUEEN ANNE BOLEYN . . .

Now Ana felt nauseated, faint. "Excuse me," she said, and went to sit on the nearest bench.

"You all right, doll?" called Jake.

What was going on? She was overcome with dizziness; it felt as if the Tower walls were closing in on her. She put her head between her knees.

Jake sat down beside her. "You're not pregnant, are you?"

"Watch your mouth, Jake."

"Sorry, forgot my place there for a moment."

He didn't sound sorry.

She took some deep breaths and sat up straight. Thankfully, the world seemed to have stopped spinning. "I'm fine. Let's get on with it. But bin the memorial idea, it'd look crass."

They made their way back to the team.

"It's freezing out there," said Ana to the stylist. "We'll need Randi on standby to sort out red noses."

"It's not Randi, it's Liv." The stylist nodded at the makeup girl across the room.

A flash of irritation. Why had no one told her of any changes?

"Why? I booked Randi before Christmas. I specifically wanted Randi."

The room fell quiet as her voice rose.

"Why the hell don't people do as I ask?"

Mark coughed. "Terri needed Randi for Kate Moss. She said she agreed it with you ages ago."

Ana was breathing fast. This room with its grim stone walls was giving her claustrophobia. She sat down suddenly on a chair, taking deep breaths.

Now she remembered the conversation with Terri. "Sorry, all. I'm not feeling great today. Go ahead, I'll catch you up."

As they left, she wondered what had got into her. No doubt they all thought she was getting up herself. It was common knowledge she was Harry's girlfriend, though her demeanor didn't invite that particular topic of conversation, even with Terri and Nate, who now treated her with a degree of wariness that made her rather sad.

She was obviously more stressed than she realized, losing her head over inconsequential things. Living with Harry was wonderful, and she was never happier than when she was on his arm, out and about. London society now knew about his split with Katie and that Ana was his new partner. But there was a degree of sniffiness; Katie had been popular, back in the day.

She stood to leave, glancing out the window, smiling as she saw Blur larking around on Tower Green below.

Harry

August 1994

Rosenews.co.uk was going to be a trailblazer. In a matter of weeks, Harry's growing empire would be the first in the UK to put news online.

His team predicted that advertising uptake would be slow at first but would quickly build. The internet was growing across the world like a creeping plant, branching and dividing exponentially, its shoots tickling new hosts, sending down suckers. Already, every department at Rose rang to the shriek of computers logging on via their new modems.

This evening, Harry would be giving a presentation to advertisers, at the Southbank Centre. Janette was looking stressed, her cheeks pink as she worked through her to-do list, interrupted regularly by Harry wanting changes to his PowerPoint slides.

"Sorry, just a couple more," he said, perching on her desk.

"That's fine, Harry. Sorry I'm so slow. I'm still learning this software."

"Don't apologize. You're a treasure for putting up with my technological incompetence. I'd be utterly lost without you, dearest Moneypenny."

As Janette gave a delightful giggle, Ana walked in. She frowned as her eyes flicked between them, and asked, "Harry, what time should I be there tonight?"

"It's a sales thing, for advertisers. You probably wouldn't enjoy it."

"I'll come," said Ana. "I want to hear all about the website. You know—like I said?"

Harry remembered she'd expressed interest in the new venture, but he hadn't seen it as something she'd be suited for.

"OK, come if you want. Starts at six. I'll be going early with Janette."

She glanced up and gave Ana a proprietorial smile.

"Right," Ana said. "I have things to finish, but I'll do my best."

. . .

The presentation was well received, and as advertisers got stuck into the wine and finger food afterward, the buzz was all about the internet.

As Harry listened idly to the conversation of two ad execs who were probably ten years younger than him, he experienced a twinge of regret. Truth be told, he was sure that personally, he'd always prefer his news in print. He couldn't ever see himself logging on to a computer for his fix. But those around him were gung ho about the changes, so he wouldn't be sharing his personal preferences. God forbid he should be seen as a dinosaur.

He caught sight of Ana across the room. She was looking svelte and sophisticated, as always. They had recently been dubbed "London's Most Glamorous Couple" by the *Evening Standard*. She loved these functions, where she could waft around enjoying the attention, in particular the obsequiousness of those now below her on the social and business scale. Which was usually just about everyone.

As he watched her, he reflected on their time together—it had now been more than half a year. Life was mostly good, if sometimes exhausting. Ana was one demanding woman. She was great company, with her sharp intelligence and keen interest in the business—although he had to rein her in every now and again, remind her she was an art director, not a company director. And that was all he wanted her to be, for now. He was aware Rose staff were having trouble dealing with her queenly ways as it was. When she was more accepted, then he'd think about how he could involve her in the new directions the company was taking. Maybe.

Bored with the two ad execs, he decided to join her, but then realized she was talking to BWG's Connor Black. The agency spent a reasonable amount of money with Rose publications, but no longer handled Rose Corp.'s own advertising. Once Percy was exiled, Harry had sacked them. He'd avoid Connor for now; he'd never liked the man.

"Harry?"

He looked down to see Janette beside him.

"Yes, Janette."

"Someone from the *Standard* wants a quote from you about the website—that guy over there, if you have a moment."

"Fine. And . . . Janette?"

"Yes, Harry?"

"Thanks for all your help today. You've been great." He gave her an affectionate smile and touched her arm.

This time, her flush spread all the way down from her cheeks to her chest. "It's always a pleasure, Harry. You know that."

Ana

Bad Harry, leading that secretary on. Ana had clocked him from across the room, throwing a compliment her way like a man chucking a dog a bone. She could see the blush from here.

"Sorry?" She'd missed what Connor Black was saying. In fact, she didn't really care about his views on whether the move online was going to hurt or benefit news organizations. He was one of those advertising guys who said whatever they thought sounded cool, whether they believed it or not, using words they probably made up. In a fake Cockney accent.

"I said, Percy North's back in town."

"Oh!" This was a surprise. "Really? I'm not in touch with him anymore."

"No, I don't suppose you would be." Connor winked.

Ana resisted the temptation to cut him down to size. She was supposed to be nice to advertisers tonight.

"It didn't work out for him in Dublin. He wants his old job back. I might just give it to him. I think he probably deserves it, don't you?"

"But isn't the Celtic Tiger really kicking off?" said Ana. "Didn't he like Dublin in the end?"

"He was bored. There wasn't much for him to do—we handle most of it from here. Harry just wanted him out of the way. And now we know why. Naughty Harry." His eyes traveled down her body.

Harry had fired BWG, so Ana presumed he wasn't Connor's favorite person right now. Then she registered his words. "What did you say? Harry—"

"Percy was the only reason we won the Rose account in the first place, love. He gave us the business on the condition we sent Percy away, somewhere as far from you as possible. Poor old Percy." He kept his eyes on hers, narrowed, waiting for her response.

Ana managed to hide her shock. She didn't want to give this odious man the satisfaction of witnessing her discomfort.

"That's Harry for you!" she said briskly. "All's fair in love and war, and all that. Connor, would you excuse me? I need to powder my nose."

"Of course, love. Have one for me."

Jesus.

In the ladies, she sat down in a cubicle, her mind racing. Harry had engineered Percy's exile to Dublin with Machiavellian cunning. In the process, he'd hired and fired an agency, all because of her.

She hadn't thought about Percy in months, but now she allowed herself to remember the man she'd loved before her infatuation with Harry had taken hold. Before he'd cast his line and reeled her in.

Pictures came into her head, of happy, relaxed times with the person she'd thought of as her soul mate. For a moment she felt a deep sadness.

Then she thought about what Harry had done, how carefully he must have planned it. How much must he have wanted her?

A jolt of desire ran through her.

She exited the cubicle and washed her hands, then touched up her lipstick. Looking good.

As she was leaving, Janette came in. There was a hint of dismay as she saw Ana, then she smiled. "Hi, Ana! It's gone really well. Harry's very pleased!"

Ana caught a whiff of her perfume. Anaïs Anaïs, unless she was mistaken. How very Boots.

"Good. But it's time for him to come home now. I'm bored, and . . . well, horny, actually." She winked.

The secretary's jaw dropped, and Ana swept past. Smiling to herself, she headed toward Harry, aware of heads turning as she passed.

He was talking to a striking blonde wearing an indecently short, black, wet-look skirt teamed with knee-high white boots. Her pale pink lips were set in a deliberate pout as she looked up at Harry from under false eyelashes, which she was most definitely fluttering.

"Hi," Ana said to Harry, ignoring pretend Twiggy. "This thing finished at eight, didn't it? Shall we make a move?"

"Ana, this is Veronica," he replied, giving the blonde a charming smile. "Turns out she was at school with Megan. They made much mischief together."

Veronica's eyes flicked to Ana, then returned to Harry.

"Really," said Ana, her tone uninterested. She didn't attempt to fill the silence that followed. Her eyes traveled down Veronica's body, not so quickly that she might miss the appraisal, but not slowly enough for it to look rude. "That's an interesting outfit. Are skirts of that . . . type back in? And . . . white boots?"

"Veronica works at *Vogue*," said Harry. "If *she's* wearing one, then skirts of the micromini type are most definitely back. And I for one say hallelujah to that." He made a clicking noise, like he was encouraging a horse, and winked at Veronica.

She smiled playfully. "If you're a fan, wait until you see our October issue. Kate Moss in sixties gear. The photos are brilliant. Mario took them."

"Oh, well, *Kate* could make a bin bag look iconic," said Ana.

Veronica raised her eyebrows slightly, then turned back to Harry.

"I have to go. Tell Megan to give me a call. I'd love to catch up on all the . . ." Her glance briefly fell on Ana. "Gossip."

Harry grinned. "Will do, sweetheart. Take care."

As Veronica sashayed away, Harry turned to Ana. His eyes were cold. "Don't *ever* do that again."

"So I was supposed to just ignore the fact that some slut in a fetish skirt was sending 'shag me' vibes to my . . . my—"

"'Boss' is the word you're looking for. This is a work function. For god's sake, Ana, where's the professionalism you pride yourself on? You acted like a jealous wife. *Vogue's* bloody important, you know that."

It was difficult to say which of them was more furious as they made their way to the taxi rank. Setting off for Knightsbridge, Ana stared out the window, while Harry discussed the Tories' "Back to Basics" campaign with the driver.

They arrived home, and Harry went through to the kitchen without a word.

Ana changed into a thigh-length robe, leaving on her black lacy underwear. She tied the belt loosely, allowing the top to gape open, then went back into the living room and sat on the couch. She picked up a magazine. It was *Vogue*. She put it down and picked up a *Tatler*.

Harry came in with a whisky and a plate of toast and switched on the TV.

This was stupid. They were grown adults.

"Harry."

"What?" He munched his toast as he watched the news.

"I'm sorry."

He looked over, his eyes taking in her lingerie.

Now that she had his attention, it was time to go on the attack. "I spoke to Connor Black tonight."

"You have my sympathy."

"He said Percy's back in London."

"Oh?"

"He also said you told him to send Percy somewhere far away, or they'd lose the business."

Harry didn't even have the grace to look uncomfortable. "I might have had something to do with that, yes. I didn't want him working on the Rose account."

"Which they wouldn't have won if you hadn't wanted Percy out of the way—correct?"

He laughed. "It's a fair cop, guv. But it worked, didn't it? And I saved you from a life of tedium and unimaginative sex—your words, the sex part, by the way."

Ana went over and took Harry's plate from his hands, putting it down on the table.

"That's my toast, woman. Never separate a man from his late-night toast."

She slid onto his lap. "Harry, what you did was evil, but strangely, when I found out, all I wanted to do was come home and ravage you. That was what I was about to suggest when that tart was chatting you up. It's a shame you feel this compulsion to flirt with every bit of micro-mini that comes your way."

His hand slid inside her robe and began to explore. "Ana, jealousy is never appealing. Try and be nice—to Janette too."

Ana snorted. "God, she's annoying."

"She's a treasure, and she bakes me cakes." He stroked her breast, brushing her nipple.

She straddled him and loosened his tie. "Why do I find it such a turn-on that all these women want you, Harry?" Grabbing the tie, she pulled him close and kissed him.

"Because you're a competitive creature," he said, undoing her belt.

Their disagreements were becoming more frequent, but the making up was as intoxicating as ever.

CHAPTER 29

❯❯❯❯

Ana

November 1995

Two ushers raced to reach Ana first as she made her entrance into the Hurlingham Club's Palm Court. "Bride or groom?" asked the winner.

Light filtered down through the glass dome, illuminating the sea of colorful hats below. The buzz of conversation floated up to meet it.

"Bride, I suppose," said Ana.

She spotted Harry next to Charles in the front row and took an aisle seat two rows behind. She waited for them to turn around and notice her. In her red leather Chanel, she was difficult to miss. Ana had spotted the suit during Paris Fashion Week and had immediately known it would be perfect for Megan and Charles's autumn wedding.

Charles laughed heartily at something Harry said. She smiled. Charles didn't look at all nervous, which was par for the course. Neither of those boys was short on self-confidence.

If they hadn't yet noticed her, others had. Glances were coming at her sideways. She could imagine the whispers. *Harry's girlfriend—the one he got rid of Katie for.* It was only to be expected. Many of the guests would be Harry's relatives who would have attended his wedding to Katie. And of course, everyone had loved dear Katie.

When Ana had seen the red Chanel, she thought she might as well go the whole scarlet woman.

Meanwhile, Charles's relatives would no doubt be comparing home-wrecker Megan to Cassandra, who according to Harry had been a jolly good sort before she'd gone all New Age.

Ana peered around discreetly from beneath the brim of her hat, looking for faces she recognized. A group of girls tottered in, all blond highlights and high heels. Probably Megan's workmates. Directly across from Ana were aunt and uncle types. She recognized Harry's uncle Richard, who was still on Rose Corp.'s board. He saw her and nodded, but there was no smile. His wife noticed, ran her eye over Ana, and whispered something. Richard turned away.

And then she noticed Katie. And . . . Cassandra? Of course. Charles's and Harry's daughters were bridesmaids.

If Cassandra hadn't been sitting with Katie, Ana wouldn't have recognized her. Her hair had grown long and was loose around her shoulders, and there were flowers in it.

Katie sensed Ana's scrutiny and turned slightly, meeting her eye. As recognition dawned, she looked quickly away again. She said something to Cassandra, who craned her neck to give Ana the full once-over. Surprisingly, she smiled.

Ana dropped her eyes.

Harry turned around, finally. He was looking dapper in his morning suit, his gold-patterned waistcoat a splash of color against the gray and white. He grinned, before his eyes traveled over the other guests.

There were calls of "shh!" as a string quartet began to play. Everyone turned to see Megan, a vision in white tulle, floating down the aisle, a beatific smile on her face. Behind her came the posse of bridesmaids, including Harry's daughter, who wore an intense frown as she concentrated on not stepping on Megan's dress.

As the ceremony began, Ana experienced an upwelling of emotion. She remembered Megan as she'd been in France, flitting from one relationship to the next. Now look at her. She'd been with the same guy, a lifelong friend twelve years her senior, for all this time. And there was Charles, whose roving eye had driven his first wife to drink, now promising fidelity to the girl who'd held a special place in his heart since she was a child.

They were so right together, so content.

Would Ana and Harry ever achieve that? Watching Megan and Charles made her realize what hard work her relationship with Harry had become.

At the office, people were wary of her. In the loos, Ana had overheard Lesley from human resources (best friend of Janette) liken Ana to Camilla Parker Bowles, the saintly Katie being "just like Diana, really." And Harry was still fobbing her off every time she raised the subject of a more managerial role.

They were out several nights a week, at mostly work-related functions, and Harry was always too busy networking to pay her much attention. On the remaining nights he preferred to stay home and relax, watching TV or reading a book.

Sex was now a bedroom-only affair, after their initial can't-wait-that-long rampages. And, often as not, it was initiated by her. The only thing that guaranteed his attention was another guy showing too much interest.

It was time to move things on.

As Charles kissed his bride and the guests burst into applause, she wondered whether to speak to Katie, to see if she could get her to budge on the wait for a divorce.

At the reception, Ana was seated with Megan's work friends. After her initial annoyance at being some distance from the top table, she accepted that—technically speaking—she came under the heading "friends."

The girl on Ana's right was gushing over Ana's suit. "It's absolutely spectacular. Where did you get it from? If you don't mind me asking?"

"It's Chanel."

"Oh wow, Chanel! And how do you know Megan?"

"We used to share a flat, and—"

"That must've been fun. I work with her, we have such a laugh. I'm so happy for her. Charles is a lovely bloke. It's sad her parents aren't here, though, being dead, I mean. But at least her older brother is. The very rich and not exactly ugly Harry Rose. Isn't he a dreamboat? Shame he's married. Megan said he's separated from his wife, though. So maybe there's hope. I—"

"I'm Ana, Harry's girlfriend. Once the divorce comes through, we're getting married."

That shut her up.

Then: "Oh, of course. Penny dropping here! The one Megan organized the wedding for, then it got called off because . . . right. Sorry."

The girl picked up her glass of wine and took a prolonged sip, staring straight ahead.

"I work for *Hooray!*," said Ana. "Of course we've got exclusivity on today's photos."

"Jake! The photographer. I've met him a few times at events I've done. I remember him mentioning you now . . ." She stopped abruptly. "He's cool."

What had Jake said about her? She tried not to care.

Ana turned to the girl on her other side. "Hi, I'm Ana. How do you know Megan?"

A while later, as the waiters poured champagne for the toast, Harry stood up and tapped his glass with a spoon. The room went quiet.

"Back in the nineteen seventies," he began, "my sweet little seven-year-old sister proposed to my nineteen-year-old best friend."

There were "aaahs" and chuckles.

"Charles's response was, 'Ask me again in a few years.' Some twenty years later, she did. And here we are . . ."

Harry's speech was funny and full of affection, and as he finished, he wiped a tear from his eye, as did most in the room. Harry had charmed everyone, as per. He hadn't mentioned Ana at all, hadn't looked her way. She tried not to care about that either.

The dancing began, and Megan and Charles swayed together to "Love Is All Around." Harry led his daughter onto the dance floor, and people smiled as he made a big show of twirling her around.

Ana turned her back and made her way to the restrooms. She walked slowly, looking out the windows to the tennis courts, remembering the time she'd played doubles here. It had been the big Charles and Megan reunion, when it all kicked off. And Harry hadn't taken his eyes off Ana all evening. She tried not to compare then with now.

In the restrooms she took her time touching up her makeup, tucking stray hairs into her chignon. Two aunt types briskly came and went, giving her tight little smiles.

The door opened again, and Katie came in with Maria.

"Oh," Katie said, hesitating.

"Look, Mummy," said Maria. "It's like a bathroom in a palace!"

"Yes, isn't it lovely," said Katie.

Maria disappeared into a cubicle.

"Be careful with your dress!"

Katie sat down in an armchair. "Hello," she said. "We've never properly met, have we?" Her voice was calm; there was no undercurrent.

"No. How's life in Wales?"

"Good. It's beautiful where we are, really peaceful. I expect that sounds awfully boring to you, but we get a lot of people staying who need time out from their stressful lives, and it's great to be able to help them."

"You're a counselor?"

"Yes. And you? You're living with Harry, I hear."

"Yes." She decided to bite the bullet. "We want to get married, of course, but . . . Katie, I understand you're reluctant to divorce Harry. Would you consider . . . ?"

"I know it must be hard, Ana. I'm sorry, but I can't go against my faith. In God's eyes, we're still married. The law says Harry can divorce me and there's nothing I can do about that, but I'm not going to agree to it. Like I said, I'm sorry, truly."

"Look, Katie. Why make our lives difficult, when it's going to happen anyway? If it's because you think I stole—"

"No, this isn't about revenge or bad feeling. It's about my beliefs. And anyway, you didn't steal Harry. I had depression, and his way of dealing with that was to look elsewhere for . . . love. At the time, I blamed myself. But being away from him has made me realize, Harry was the one at fault. He could have helped me through it, but he didn't. He buried himself in his work and found women who were easier to be with—you know about Bennie? And your sister, obviously."

Ana nodded.

"The place Cassandra and I run, it's for women who need time out from modern life."

It looked like she was about to launch into "New Age bollocks," as Harry called it.

"If there's one thing I've learned through working there, it's that women blame themselves. I did. We've got to stop doing that. Look at the people here today. So many—especially the women, actually—have been offering sympathy for my marriage breakdown, and guess who they've been blaming?"

"Me?"

"Yes. Apparently you're a husband stealer."

"Well, they would blame me, wouldn't they? But I don't care."

"They're wrong. You're not a husband stealer. Harry betrayed me. Twice that I know of, maybe more. But is anyone saying how badly he behaved? No. Harry can do no wrong—everyone loves Harry. So, Ana, I'm not blaming you. I know how hard it is to resist Harry when he turns on the charm. No doubt he told you his marriage was over, and you weren't going to turn Harry down out of loyalty to a woman you didn't know, were you?"

Ana didn't know what to say. Katie—fragile, boring, mouse-wife

Katie—was in fact strong, self-assured Katie. And somehow, she was on Ana's side.

Katie smiled at Ana's confusion. "Does he still eat toast loudly in front of the late-night news?"

Ana laughed and nodded. For the first time that day, she felt herself relax.

There was the sound of flushing, and Maria reappeared.

"Maria, come and meet Ana. Wash your hands first, though."

The little girl looked up at her.

"You look so pretty," said Ana. "Did you like being a bridesmaid?"

"No," said Maria. "And this dress is silly."

The door opened and Cassandra came in. "Oh, hello, you two." She raised her eyebrows at Katie.

"Cassandra, you remember Ana?"

"Of course. How're you coping with Harry? God, I was always a bit jealous of Katie, Harry was so bloody gorgeous. Shame the rotten cad couldn't keep it in his pants, though."

"Cass!" said Katie. "Maria, why don't you go and find Arabella and Milly."

"Sorry," said Cassandra. "I've had a drink and I'm not used to it! No, Ana, don't worry. I can have the odd one now without getting blotto. It was the toxic marriage that was doing me in, not the booze. Gosh, that suit's magnificent. Not much call for Chanel in Wales, though. So anyway, you and Harry—how's that going?"

As Ana looked at the two women, she felt something shift inside. She wasn't wary of them anymore, and felt a sudden compulsion to blurt out all her problems and frustrations, the way she used to with Merry, or Megan, before her relationship with Harry had made those heart-to-hearts a thing of the past.

"You two . . . I can understand why you went off to Wales. You're lucky to have each other."

"You want to visit? Better than spending time worrying what Harry's up to!"

"Calm down, Cassandra," said Katie. "Ana's being very patient, waiting for Harry. I'm sure it's difficult enough for her already, without you making insinuations."

"Leopards and spots, Katie."

"But what about Charles?" said Ana. "He's changed his spots, hasn't he? If you don't mind me saying that?"

"We'll see," said Cassandra.

Ana thought about the two friends as she made her way back to the reception room. They'd built their lives around men who'd let them down. Now they'd moved on and were making new lives on their own terms.

Ana should be stronger, more like them. She needed to take charge. She'd waited around long enough.

CHAPTER 30

Harry

September 1996

Harry flicked through the *Times* as he sipped his first coffee of the working day. There was more fallout from the Charles and Diana divorce, now finalized after four years of separation.

Divorce, divorce, divorce. Harry couldn't escape the topic. This year's also included the Duke and Duchess of York—but not Harry and Katie Rose.

Tom Wolston had let him down. After Ana had ramped up the pressure, Harry tasked the lawyer with finding a loophole. He'd failed. There was simply no way, Tom said, if Katie contested the divorce. They would have to wait another two years, at least.

Ana was furious, pushing Harry to sack Wolston and find someone who could bend the law to Harry's will. Perhaps he should. The faithful old lawyer had been with Rose for years, his understated, old-school manner masking his ability to deal ruthlessly and efficiently with anyone who stood in Harry's way. But this time, Wolston seemed to be mixing up legal technicalities with the importance of doing as he was told.

Harry took another sip of his coffee.

Ana was obsessed with making their relationship official, and it seemed to be more about her position at work than her love for him. She somehow thought being his wife would consolidate her new role. Six months ago he'd promoted her to managing editor of six Rose titles, including the *Rack* and *Hooray!* It hadn't been easy, persuading the board, but he prepared a convincing argument. She'd been at Rose for four years, her work was consistently outstanding, and she was well respected by her colleagues, even if her demeanor ("quite haughty"— Janette's words) rubbed people up the wrong way.

He'd anticipated trouble from Terri, but she'd shrugged her shoulders and said, "She's welcome to it."

"You don't mind that it's not you?" he'd said. "I really don't want you in management, you were meant to be an editor."

"Management schmanagement," she'd said. "I'm happy where I am, and Ana won't bother me. However, a few grand extra to show your appreciation wouldn't go amiss."

"Your wish is my command. Genie boss will make it so. And I won't even make you rub me."

Harry buzzed Janette. "Can you come through when you're ready?"

"Of course, Harry! Won't be a tick."

Handling Mia Fox had been a different matter entirely. She'd sounded off about how she'd given her life to *Hooray!* and all this time had been answerable only to him. Now she was expected to take orders from a junior? And everyone knew the real reason why Ana was being promoted, and . . .

He'd tuned out at that point.

Mia was excellent at her job, but she wasn't irreplaceable. When she'd finally run out of rant, he'd said, "Mia, if you don't feel comfortable continuing in your role, we can look at transferring you to a different publication. Or perhaps across to online."

Defeat had settled around her shoulders. "It's not a good look, Harry," she'd spat out, "promoting your . . . lover, above more experienced staff. Do you think Ana will be respected in her new role? She's a great designer, but she's shit with people. Don't say I didn't warn you when it all comes tumbling down."

Nothing had crumbled, at least so far, but the move didn't seem to have made Ana any happier.

Janette sat down opposite, as she did every day about this time. Harry was firmly old-school. A man at the top needed a secretary with a shorthand notebook and a good pair of legs to perch it on. And Janette's were *very* good.

She crossed them, pencil poised. Her black tights made a gentle rasping noise.

Harry cleared his throat. "I need to go to Manchester to rally the troops up north. Can you organize it for early December? Talk to Barry up there."

"Sure, Harry." She finished scribbling, then uncrossed and recrossed her legs.

After a momentary pause, Harry added, "And you'd better come with me."

Her eyes flew to his, surprised, then she dropped them again and scribbled something else down.

He smiled inwardly. Janette didn't blush so much these days, but she was still easy to read.

"Barry's asked me to do a presentation about Rosenews to his advertisers. Far be it from me to point out that electricity isn't standard up north yet, never mind the internet."

Janette giggled.

"Anyway, you know how I am with technology—you can come and sort it all out for me."

As she left the room, he couldn't help comparing her shapely behind to Ana's rather flat, boyish bottom.

Janette

December 1996

The hotel receptionist handed over two keys. "Here we are, Ms. Morrissey. No relation to our own Morrissey, I take it?"

She giggled. "No! I have an auntie from Manchester, though."

"Let's go, shall we, Moneypenny?" said Harry.

They took the lift, Janette's skin tingling at her closeness to Harry.

"Barry's meeting me downstairs for a drink at seven," he said. "Why don't you join us at, say, seven thirty? Half an hour should be enough to get the business side of things out of the way, then we can spend the rest of the evening winding up Barry. He's a professional northerner who loathes southern softies like yours truly."

"Barry versus Harry!" said Janette as the lift bumped to a halt.

Harry's suite was on the corner, while her room was a few doors down. "See you at seven thirty!" she said, letting herself in.

She dumped her case on the floor and flopped down on the bed, flinging her arms out to her sides. There was a massive smile on her face, and her heart was racing.

After all this time, here she was, about to have a sort of date with the man she'd fallen in love with during her first week at Rose. Dare she hope he might be starting to see her as more than a bringer of tea, a typer-upper of letters, a sorter-outer of challenging software? Was she now a friend, at least?

He was confiding in her more and more, even complaining about Ana sometimes. And his eyes often traveled down from her face, appraising, noticing. And she adored the way he called her Moneypenny.

She knew it was foolish, but a girl could dream, couldn't she? *Pretty Woman* was her favorite movie of all time. (Not that Janette was at all a loose woman, of course.) And she enjoyed reading romance novels in which the nurse ended up with the surgeon, or the millionaire boss gently pulled out his secretary's hair clips and removed her glasses, and she swung her hair free, and he noticed she was, in fact, beautiful.

She sighed. *Down, girl!* She was simply meeting Harry and his colleague for a drink.

Ana's face came into her mind. Graceful, sophisticated Ana, who looked at Janette as if she were a piece of fluff to be flicked from one of her Chanel jackets. Well, Ana might be the epitome of style, but she was colder than a midwinter's day in Antarctica. And she wasn't married to Harry, she was only his girlfriend.

Three hours later, after changing her outfit several times (she was aiming for not too secretary, not too date night), plus three tries with hair and makeup, Janette made her way to the bar. She was wearing a little black dress from Next, with black court shoes and a pink bouclé jacket. Her lipstick matched the jacket. She hoped her Anaïs Anaïs wasn't too overpowering.

Yesterday she'd hovered for a good thirty minutes over the hosiery display in Selfridges. Was she crazy, thinking Harry might be interested? Harry Rose—rich, devastatingly handsome, powerful, and living with a style icon. A woman who never blushed.

When she bought the stockings, it was as if she'd taken something out of the box labeled *dreams* and put it in *daring to hope*. By the end of this evening, she'd be feeling either stupid, or . . . or what? It seemed beyond possible.

Harry was sitting with a large man with a florid complexion. Both men were casually dressed.

"Moneypenny," said Harry, rising out of his chair slightly. "You could have dressed up a bit."

"Sorry, I thought—"

"Joking, Janette."

She blushed.

"Forgive me, that was mean. You look very nice. Janette, this is Barry. Barry, meet my right-hand man."

"Is he always like this, love?" said Barry in a Lancashire accent.

"Oh yes," said Janette. "We have some fun in the office!"

"I'll bet you do," said Barry, his eyes traveling down her body.

Barry downed pint after pint, his cheeks going a little redder with each one. They talked business, while Janette sipped her drink and tried to look as though she understood what they were talking about.

Finally, Barry left, turning down the offer of dinner, as he had to "get back to the wife or there'd be trouble."

"Christ," said Harry. "And I thought I was a dinosaur. Come on, let's eat."

A waiter showed them to a cozy corner table in the dining room.

"How many years have we been together, Janette?" Harry said, his eyes flicking over the wine list.

"Four next week, actually!"

"Is it? Well I'd say that calls for champagne."

The evening was straight out of the dream box. Harry was the greatest company, telling entertaining anecdotes, then talking about his daughter, Maria, his problems with Katie; he even shared some of his future plans for Rose.

As she ate the gourmet food, not tasting it at all, the glow from the candle between them reflected how she was feeling inside.

Harry encouraged Janette to talk about herself, his deep blue eyes warm and interested. She told him about her family in Wiltshire, and about her love of needlework and embroidery. "But you must think that's so boring, Harry!"

"Not at all. Everyone should have a creative hobby, one that takes them out of themselves for a while. I like to write music. And poetry—but that's between you and me."

As she finished her coffee, she realized they were the only people left in the restaurant.

Harry put his napkin on the table. "Right then, we should call it a night. I have to speak to the good advertisers of Manchester tomorrow, and you, my dear Moneypenny, need to be PowerPoint ready."

As the lift made its way upward, she wondered if he could sense her tension. She was ready to explode with it.

"Good night, then," he said as they reached her door. He smiled, and there was a question in his eyes.

Wasn't there?

"I, um, well, there's a minibar, if you wanted a nightcap."

"You're blushing again." He raised his hand and stroked her cheek with the back of it.

"Oh god, am I? I wish I knew how to stop it."

"Don't ever. Your blush is utterly charming."

"No, it's so embarrassing," she said as her knees threatened to give way.

"It's lovely. Now, are you going to stand out here being embarrassed, or are you going to pour me that nightcap?"

Once inside, she was so nervous that she missed the glass as she up-ended the miniature. As she tried to mop the whisky up with a paper coaster, Harry came over, taking the glass from her hand. "I prefer my drinks stirred, not shaken, Moneypenny. But I don't really need another after all that bubbly."

"No, I'm a bit squiffy myself!"

He tucked a strand of hair behind her ear, and she nearly fainted with longing. Or was that just a line from one of the romance books? No, she really did feel awfully wobbly.

"You're so ridiculously sweet and adorable."

"Am I?"

"I don't think you realize. You're like an oasis of kindness and calm in the madness of my life. That's a bit purple prose, but you get the picture."

He ran his hand down her arm, making her shiver. When he reached her elbow, he slid his hand onto her waist. "I don't even know if you have a boyfriend."

"I don't." She didn't want to sound too available, so she added, "At the moment." She could hardly hear her own voice above the thumping of her heart.

His other hand moved up to her head, stroking her hair. "I like your hair up like this, it shows off your lovely neck." He bent and kissed it gently, where it met her shoulder, then trailed more kisses up her neck, getting closer to her jawline.

"Oh, Harry," she sighed. "I've imagined this for so long."

He pulled away slightly, and looked down into her eyes. "Please don't think of it as a boss-with-secretary cliché thing. You know how much I value you." He bent again and softly brushed her lips with his.

She was melting.

"Harry?"

"What?" he murmured.

"Will you . . . would you mind . . ."

"Would I mind what?" He kissed her again, deeply, and all the romance-book things were happening. The weak knees, the fireworks, the things that went on "downstairs" when a woman was kissed by the man she'd desired for at least twenty chapters.

"Would you unclip my hair?"

Harry gave a low chuckle. She felt his hand fumbling with her bun, then her long fair hair was falling loose, and she shook her head so it tumbled across her shoulders.

"Why, Moneypenny, you're beautiful," said Harry. "Turn round."

In a daze, she did as he asked, and he unzipped her dress slowly, then slid it down over her hips. She faced him again, and he smiled slowly as he took in the lacy underwear and stockings.

"Janette Morrissey, you dark horse you."

She put her arms around his neck, and he picked her up and carried her to the bed.

Harry was only Janette's second lover. The first had been at school, in the sixth form. She and her boyfriend had had a nice time learning the basics, but they hadn't exactly scaled the heights of ecstasy, as it had always been a rushed affair, time snatched during babysitting or when parents were out. Janette had never truly been able to relax.

So sex with Harry was a revelation. Waves of pleasure flooded through her as Harry trailed his fingers over her body, stopping to stroke the skin between the top of her stockings and her panties. His kisses moved down her neck to her chest, then back up to her lips, then down, and down some more . . . oh! She felt something inside her building, and lay inert, apart from a little writhing. Her one coherent thought, as Harry played her body like a harpist creating music fit for heaven, was that Ana would know what to do back, whereas she had no clue. But the momentary worry was swept away by the tide of ecstasy that suddenly swamped her, leaving her gasping in surprise.

"Nice?" he murmured, coming back up to eye level.

Then he was moving inside her, and to her amazement it was all building again, and then after a spectacular moment they were both lying on their backs, catching their breath.

"Marvelous," Harry said. He propped himself up on one elbow and looked down at her.

"I love you, Harry." There, she'd said it. Perhaps it was too soon, but after what they'd just done, he'd know anyway, surely?

"You do?"

"Of course. I don't expect you to love me back, but I'm here for you, whenever you need me, on whatever terms you want."

"I don't deserve that. You're an angel, and I'm . . . well, I'm often found wanting."

They cuddled and dozed for a while, then he sat up. "I shouldn't stay. I need to ring Ana. And you might not respect me in the morning."

She giggled, though the thought of him phoning Ana hurt her heart.

"That's fine, Harry. I'll still respect you." But would he still respect her?

He quickly dressed, then sat down again on the bed, taking her hand. "I know I can rely on you not to breathe a word, to anyone. Not even your cat."

"How did you know I have a cat?"

"Inspired guess."

"I won't, Harry. I promise."

Harry

In the taxi from Euston to Knightsbridge, Harry pondered on his evening with Janette. Quiet, adoring, sweet Janette, who never had a bad word to say about anybody. Janette, who had worn stockings and asked him to let her hair down, so they could properly play Bond and Moneypenny.

Who'd have thought it?

And now it was back to Ana, who would no doubt complain about the lack of cooperation at work, the tedious wait for his divorce—and she'd interrogate him about what he'd been up to in Manchester. Not that she'd ever suspect him of sleeping with Janette, whom she considered an annoyance rather than a threat.

What would it be like going home to someone like Janette, instead? Someone who'd cook him a delicious meal, followed by homemade cake; who'd massage his shoulders, ask him how his day had been. *Someone like Katie*, said a little voice inside his head.

When he opened the door to the penthouse, Ana was already home. She appeared in the living area, seductive in a red silk robe, her hair loose down her back.

"Darling, I'm so glad you came straight home."

He caught a whiff of something delicious from the kitchen. This was all highly unusual.

"What's going on?"

Ana smiled. "Well . . . I was going to wait until dinner. Yes, believe it or not I'm cooking. But what the heck, I can't wait that long." She wound her arms around his neck.

"For what?" He drew her close, feeling himself respond. "Me?"

"Yes, but . . . Harry. It wasn't planned, but I'm so happy about it. We're going to have a baby." She was searching his eyes, nervous, waiting for a response.

He could feel her words knocking on doors in his brain, forcing a foot in the crack, pushing their way in. Then his brain unscrambling them, working out what to do with them. Send out shock waves? Happy vibes?

He waited for his body to tell him how he felt.

"Harry?"

Joy. Unanticipated, overwhelming joy.

"Ana, you bloody goddess!" He swept her up and spun her around, then put her down gently on the white carpet, like she was made of glass. "Ana, that's the most incredible news. How—"

"Only five weeks. By my reckoning it's due in August. Are you pleased? Really?"

Ana rarely showed such vulnerability, and he experienced a rush of some deep, primal, protective instinct. "Come and sit down. I can't take this in."

"I need to check on the dinner. But . . ." She twined her hands behind his neck again, and her robe fell open. "It won't be ready for an hour or so."

"I know I shouldn't say this," said Harry later, stroking Ana's hair as she snuggled against his chest, "but I hope it's a boy."

"Why?"

"I guess every man wants a son, to play Lego with, take to cricket matches, pass the empire on to and all that."

"Harry Rose," she said, punching him lightly in the stomach. "You total dinosaur. Have the Spice Girls taught you nothing of girl power?"

"I like the one in the Union Jack dress."

"Ginger."

"Of course. And the posh one. She's a bit like you."

"Girls can do anything, Harry. This could be a daughter who grows up to change the world."

"True. Hey, Ana?"

"Mm?"

"I'm really hungry."

"Oh my god, the duck!"

Later, as Harry rang for a takeaway, he briefly thought about last night with Janette, and pushed away the guilt. Things were different now. Janette would understand.

CHAPTER 31

Ana

Ana and Harry shared their news first with Megan and Charles, who themselves had had a baby girl, Francesca, two months ago. Already Ana was picturing summers in Italy, their children splashing together in the pool of the sprawling Tuscan villa they would buy.

"You'll need to move again—this place isn't child friendly," said Megan. The former wild child was surprisingly into all things domestic.

She was probably right. There was so much white and so much glass. Having a child would mean relaxing her neat-freak tendencies. Did she mind that she'd need to change? She was mildly astonished to discover that she didn't.

"You should come and live near us," said Megan. She and Charles had moved to a pretty town house in Islington. Megan loved it there, but Charles, a staunch Tory, disliked the champagne socialists who'd colonized the area. The leader of the opposition, Tony Blair, was a neighbor, and apparently the gentrified street was full of "sun-dried tomato eaters."

"Chelsea would be more you, Harry," said Charles. "But you'll have to move fast. The Russians are buying it all up. They're coming off the plane from Moscow with suitcases full of cash. Of course, we're encouraging them to invest all their lovely rubles with us, but they're also snapping up property like nobody's business, especially round here."

"Where are they getting all their money from?" asked Ana.

"Asset sales, oil—much of it highly dodgy, but the bank hears no evil, sees no evil. Harry, far be it from me to talk business tonight, but seriously, let me know if you're looking for investors."

"Interesting," Harry replied. "Are your Russian buddies likely to be interested in satellite TV, perhaps in the sports area?"

"Undoubtedly. Especially if football's involved."

"Then we should have lunch next week—I'll get Janette to ring you and we can set the footballski rolling."

News of Ana's pregnancy made no difference to Katie's stance on divorce. Ana tried not to care that her child would be born "out of wedlock," as her father insisted on calling it when they told her parents the happy news.

They were in Kent for the weekend, and Ana and her mother were peeling vegetables for Sunday lunch.

"At least you won't be one of those brides waddling down the aisle in the nick of time," said Liz. "Such a vulgar look. Just make sure everything's in place for when the divorce finally comes through. You want to move fast when it's someone like Harry."

Ana stopped peeling and looked at her mother. "What do you mean, 'someone like Harry'?"

"Don't play the ingenue, darling. There will always be women keen to take your place, and men are easily led. You'll be up to your neck in nappies and exhausted from lack of sleep. It's all too easy to let things slide."

They already have.

Ana had been mortified when Harry stopped wanting sex, fobbing her off with one lame excuse after another. Finally he'd confessed to an irrational fear of harming the baby, following his traumatic experiences with Katie. It had been a relief to find out the reason. All she could hope was that after the baby was born, he'd be ready, if not desperate, to re-sume normal relations.

"I intend to employ a nanny, Mum."

"That's good. Just make sure she's not too pretty."

Really? What century was her mother from?

"Ana, we've never talked properly about Merry. Do you ever think about how she must be feeling?"

Ana's stomach dropped. Her sister had been on her mind, but she'd been putting off dealing with the situation.

"I thought not."

"It was just a fling, Mum. They were both married."

"He led her on. She thought he'd get a divorce and marry her, after Will died."

"He didn't lead her on, and he never said he'd marry her."

"Right, well. I've only heard her side of the story, but he broke her heart. And look what's happened to your relationship with her. Can't you make it up, darling? It's so upsetting for your father and me. You used to be so close."

Her mother was right. Ana missed her sister, and whereas Harry seemed to have wiped her completely from his conscience, Merry had been playing on hers.

"I thought you were a feminist, Ana. How does the way Harry treated Merry—and his wife, actually—fit in with that whole sisterhood idea?"

Her mother was pulling her up on her feminist principles. How had it come to this?

"Look, I'll get in touch. She'll probably hate me even more now that I'm having his baby, but I'll try my best."

"Good. There's one more thing, before the men get back from the pub."

"Well, they say bad things come in threes. Fire away."

"They aren't bad things, darling, I just worry about you. I met Helen

Worthington in town last week, and she told me Percy North's getting married. I wasn't sure if you knew?"

Ana had hardly thought of Percy recently. "That's nice, Mum. I'm pleased for him."

"No regrets? I was fond of Percy."

"Lucky escape!" said Ana's father, appearing with Harry in the kitchen doorway. Their cheeks were ruddy after their walk back from the Henry VIII.

"I concur," said Harry. "North was not worthy of such a prize." He kissed Ana, and she wafted the air, saying, "Pooh, beer."

"Obsequious chap, always insisted on calling me Sir Tom."

"That's because you scared him, Dad."

"The best man won, eh, Harry?" said Tom, clapping him on the shoulder.

"All's fair in love and war." Harry winked at Ana.

The men went to hang up their coats.

"What did Harry mean by that?"

Ana wasn't going to tell her mother the truth. She hardly wanted to acknowledge it herself. "Just the usual dick-waving stuff, Mum."

"I'm going to pretend I didn't hear that." And then she let out a loud snort. "Oh, gosh, that's funny. I've never heard that expression before. But seriously, darling, as soon as you hold your own child in your arms, you'll understand why I worry about you. It doesn't stop when they leave home. I'm sure Harry loves you very much, but just be careful. And if you *can* see your way to getting in touch with Merry, well, you'd make your mum very happy."

Ana dropped the final sprout into the saucepan and wrapped her mother in a hug. "I'll try, Mum, I promise."

Harry

September 1997

The intriguing thing about babies, Harry thought, as he returned his day-old daughter's intense gaze, was that at the very start of their lives, there was something ancient about them. He'd felt it before, with Maria. For that first day or two, it was like meeting an old soul in a brand-new body. A knowingness in their eyes, like they'd lived before, like they knew you. And then it was gone.

He remembered Katie saying it was because their eyes couldn't focus properly, they were making a huge effort to see and understand the blurry image filling their vision. That was why it was like having your soul searched. She was probably right. But when Harry stroked Elizabeth's cheek and said, "Hello there," it felt uncannily like he was greeting a long-lost loved one.

Ana smiled at them from her hospital bed. "A boy next time, maybe."

"Don't be daft, I couldn't be happier."

"She looks so much like you."

"You mean she's ginger."

"Golden-haired. I thought maybe we should shorten her name to Eliza, otherwise it's going to be confusing, with my mum."

"Eliza. I like it. Happy with that?" he said to the little bundle.

She continued to gaze at him, a slight frown on her tiny face.

"She says it's fine by her."

"Katie sent flowers," Ana said. "And . . . so did Merry."

"Merry? Does this mean the olive branch has been accepted?"

"I'm hoping so. I don't think she's ready to see you yet, but she's invited Elizabeth—Eliza—and me up to stay."

"That's good. Happy families again."

Harry put Eliza carefully back in her bassinet and sat down on the edge of Ana's hospital bed. Already, she was almost back to her immaculate self. He took her hand and kissed it. "You're incredible, darling." He grinned. "Not too posh to push after all."

"I'm a lot more sore than I look." She wriggled a little and winced.

"I have a small token of my appreciation." He fished inside his suit jacket and took out a key with a Porsche fob attached. "It's a 911. Red. I've road tested her; she's a dream."

As she took the key, openmouthed, he dropped a kiss on her head and stood. "Better go. Get some rest now, you deserve it. I'll ring you. On this." He fished in his jacket again and took out the latest Nokia mobile phone. "Press this button when it rings." One of the youngsters at the office had shown Harry how to use it, and they'd set the ringtone to the *William Tell* overture for fun.

Back at the office, Harry got very little done. People kept dropping by to congratulate him, and he wanted to show them all the Polaroids he'd taken of Eliza.

As the latest visitor left, Janette appeared. "Do you want me to shut the door, Harry? You'd probably like to finish your work so you can get off home."

"No, leave it. I can't settle to it anyway. Did I show you the photo?"

"Yes you did. She's so beautiful."

"How about we wet the baby's head?"

"We should! Shall I see who's still here?"

Janette was so sweet. Even though she had feelings for him, she was still enjoying his excitement at being a dad again.

"How about a glass of champagne à deux, Moneypenny? We haven't had a good chat in a while."

"Oh! OK, then. That'd be nice."

It was a relaxed evening, requiring little effort from Harry as Janette chatted away. She spent the first half hour sharing her grief at the recent death of Princess Diana. The mood at the office had been somber for days now, everyone shocked at the untimely end of a person who'd been so much a part of their lives. His editors had been reviewing their dealings with the paparazzi, feeling uncomfortable about their complicity in creating the demand for celebrity photos. Many had slipped out to add to the sea of flowers at Kensington Palace.

"I keep thinking of that *Panorama* interview," said Janette. "She loved Charles all those years, but did he ever really love her?" She wiped away a tear. "Poor Diana."

"She was a gem," said Harry, who'd met her many times. He remembered her flirtatious smile, those big blue eyes looking up at him from beneath her fringe. She'd been funny, too, and exceptionally kind.

"I don't like that Camilla," said Janette. She didn't hold back on her opinion of Mrs. Parker Bowles as the third glass of champagne took hold.

Harry watched her, amused. Janette's style had changed over the past year. She now wore her hair swept up and had taken to wearing simple shift dresses. Harry suspected she modeled herself on Ana, perhaps subconsciously, as he knew she wasn't a fan. This more sophisticated look made it all the more exciting when Harry remembered what had been revealed that time he'd unzipped her little black dress.

His conscience prodded him. *What are you thinking? Your girlfriend and soon-to-be wife has just given birth to your child!*

True, but it had been months since he and Ana made love. The problem had been his, a response to the sad endings to Katie's failed pregnancies. It didn't feel right. Babies were too fragile.

If he hadn't had that moment in Manchester, he would let it go. Gone home with a clear conscience. But Janette was so *cute*, and that whole role-play thing she'd done kept coming back to tease him.

"I don't know about you, Moneypenny," he drawled as he waved the waiter over for the bill, "but I find dessert is best served on satin sheets."

The blush was back! But she smiled, and he felt her toe tickle his calf.

"Home, James," she said, and giggled.

It was just for fun, he told himself. He deserved a bit of that, didn't he?

Ana

Motherhood was overwhelming. Even with a live-in nanny, it drained Ana in a way nothing ever had, both emotionally and physically.

Harry was besotted with his little daughter. He changed nappies, got up in the night, took her for walks in the buggy. Watching them together made Ana happy but, on the whole, motherhood hadn't been great for their relationship. The return to bedroom normality was a relief, but there was something missing. She didn't look too closely into what that was, for fear of finding out.

She hadn't returned to work yet. They'd decided she could do with a decent break, after moving to their new Chelsea home and having a baby. So she didn't have much of interest to talk to Harry about. She even bored herself, as she described walks in the park, sleeping patterns, baby milestones.

After nearly five years, Harry's divorce had finally come through. Frustrated with Wolston's failure to bend the law, he'd sacked his faithful old servant and employed a ruthless lawyer by the name of Cranwell. He was an obsequious snake who made Ana's skin crawl, but he'd somehow managed to shave a few months off the waiting period. With her mother's warning ringing in her ears, Ana had made sure everything was in place for their wedding.

They'd decided on a civil ceremony at the Chelsea Old Town Hall, followed by a reception at the Ritz. Harry had suggested keeping it simple, thinking Ana would be too tired to organize a big affair. Megan was too busy to help, having just had another baby, Helena, herself. But although Ana was prepared to downsize from the glorious castle she'd chosen for the aborted wedding to Percy, there was no way she was going to relinquish any of the pomp and ceremony appropriate for her marriage to Harry Rose.

It was the long- (so very long-) awaited day, and Ana took stock of her feelings as she climbed the town hall steps. There was triumph; she'd finally made it, after all these years. She would be Mrs. Rose, wife of a powerful man whose influence was growing daily.

Happiness? That was there too. Though it was so entwined with triumph and relief that she wasn't sure it deserved its own heading.

She swept into the ceremony room on her father's arm, and triumph surged as she smiled at the eminent politicians, the business tycoons, a carefully chosen bunch of celebrities, as well as relatives and a small group from the office. She saw Maria, sitting with Megan. She must have been the only ten-year-old in history who'd asked *not* to be a bridesmaid, because she thought bridesmaid dresses were "stupid." Charles was best man, of course. Merry had made her excuses.

Harry turned, and she saw his intake of breath, heard others as she passed. She was wearing a simple ivory silk gown that forgave *nothing*. Her shoulders were bare, and the back was cut low. Her glossy black hair was piled on top of her head in curls, and she held a small bouquet of creamy flowers. She was the living embodiment of the less-is-more fashion philosophy.

She noted the look of dismay on Janette's face as she swept past. *Never mind, Moneypenny.* Oh yes, she knew about the silly little nickname that still made the ridiculous secretary dissolve into giggles.

But now Janette and all the others were behind her, and here was Harry, indecently handsome in a dark blue suit, looking at her like he used to all those years ago, when she was still a challenge.

The ceremony was short. When the celebrant said Harry could kiss his bride, he pulled her into his arms as though it was the first time, and happiness inched ahead of triumph.

She linked her arm through Harry's and they made their way down the aisle, past VIPs, grinning friends and relatives, and Janette, whose puffy red eyes were ringed with smudged mascara.

They honeymooned in Menton, in an achingly beautiful villa shared with Eliza, the nanny, and a local cook and housekeeper. Days in the pool with Eliza, sleepy afternoons when the heat was intense, a little light sex, delicious meals outside under the stars, walks in the old town.

"It's so divine here," said Ana. "I could happily live in Provence. Maybe we should buy somewhere."

"*La Vie en Ana Rose*," said Harry. "Funny you should say that. Welcome to your wedding present."

"And baby came too. Not your traditional bonkfest, then," said Terri, on Ana's first day back at work, a month later.

"Not exactly, no. But it was lovely."

"Glad to hear it. Welcome back, Mrs. Rose."

Terri was the only person who seemed pleased to see her. "Fuck, you're thinner than before you were pregnant. How's that even possible?"

"Lack of sleep, probably. For new and less-fun reasons. Terri—what happened to your 'fook'?"

"I'm turning into a southerner, innit? Anything you want to catch up on, babe, just buy me an expensive lunch and I'll fill you in."

Someone had taken over Ana's old office, and she'd been allocated space on the finance floor. It was much bigger and had a great view over the Thames. But the department was silent, the accountants' heads down, the only sound the tapping of keyboards and the ringing of phones, any conversation muted and murmured. Already she missed the buzz of the third floor, with its music and chatter, the creative vibe as people swapped opinions, ran ideas past each other.

Outside her door was her assistant Mark's desk. He'd already disappeared on one of his fact-finding missions. In her absence he'd been seconded to the sales department, and she suspected he was back there, gossiping with his mates.

Next to her computer was a pristine notepad with neatly laid-out pens. She doodled a little artwork on the pad, just to put her mark on something. She needed to speak to Harry. Her managing editor role was a non-job, a sop. With the benefit of hindsight, she saw that clearly now. She didn't want to be stuck up here shuffling papers while Rose forged ahead. She wanted to be part of it.

She picked up the phone. "Harry, please," she said to Janette, fiddling with the cord as she waited.

"I'm sorry, he's not here this morning. Can I take a message?"

"Where is he?"

A pause. "Shall I get him to ring you back this afternoon?"

"Does he have his mobile?"

"He's in a meeting. I'll tell him you rang."

Ana put the phone down. She'd tackle him tonight.

Harry

You know my opinion, Ana. Stick with what you're good at. We're launching a new title, aimed at the executive woman. You could be art director."

He really didn't need this right now. What he needed was to relax with the paper and a glass of wine, while someone cooked him a decent meal. Today's meeting with Charles and the Russians had been hard going; it was difficult to understand their thickly accented broken English. And there was an air of menace about them, in spite of the hearty smiles and backslapping. He hated to think where Sokolov's billions had come from.

Thank heavens for Charles, who was brokering the investment for a dedicated football channel on Rose TV, his small but fast-growing satellite TV offering. The next step was apparently to procure the best seats for Chelsea's forthcoming home game. Charles would need to come too, and in the meantime Harry intended to swot up on the offside rule.

"That's it?" she said. "*Art director?* You think I'd be interested in going backward?"

"Look, Ana. What is it you actually want?"

"A role with teeth, Harry. A seat on the board. A directorship. You know I'm capable."

"Leave it with me. Is there food? I'm starving."

"Tegan left a lasagna. Can you put it in while I go and check on Eliza?"

"Why don't you put it in and then check on Eliza. I'm bushed."

"So am I! I had to brief Tegan before I left for work, then I was worrying all day about how Eliza would do without me, as well as trying to adjust to being back at work. Have a bit of consideration."

He stood. "I'll check on our daughter. You put the lasagna in. If you can manage it."

CHAPTER 32

Ana

My honest opinion, babe?" said Terri, over lunch. "Leave Rose. Set up on your own. Harry's got a lot on his plate—he's deep into this satellite TV shit with the Russians. He's bitten off more than he can chew there, I reckon. Bet they're in the bloody Mafia."

"It's all aboveboard, Terri. Charles wouldn't involve Harry in anything dodgy."

"He's a banker, isn't he? They have the moral scruples of a horny Catholic priest in a roomful of altar boys."

"Terri!"

"Seriously—wait until you read next week's cover story. But I digress. Look, you're stuck between a rock and a hard place. If you don't complain, you stay in your non-job and all your talent goes to waste. If you do complain, Harry gets tetchy. Option three, set up your own design consultancy, and I for one will outsource work to you. Ana Rose Design. How classy does that sound?"

The beginnings of something she hadn't felt in a while bubbled inside Ana. A creative rush. Harry would surely give her start-up money.

"It's a good idea."

"Fucking right it is."

"Thanks a million, but please, not a word, until I've bounced it off Harry."

"You can do it, Ana. And now, my sweet, I have to go—I'm interviewing Tony Blair this afternoon. Can't wait to find out if this New Labour hype is a whole new way or a whole new load of bollocks."

"The Cool Britannia thing seems a bit fake, don't you think? But you must be so pleased to see the back of the Tories. Unlike Harry. He's apoplectic."

"I'm not sure. Blair's got shifty eyes. I don't trust him."

Ana broached the subject of Ana Rose Design with Harry that evening. He was distracted, knocking back more than his usual glass or two of red.

"I'd have to see the figures, projections. Put something together—a proposal. Make it look good, then the finance guys might take it seriously."

Well it wasn't a no, at least.

October 1998

Ana had to look hard to identify Merry, waiting in the arrivals area of Edinburgh Airport. It had been five years since she last saw her.

"I'm not as I was," her sister had said over the phone. "Think country matron."

Merry was wearing a tweed jacket and jeans, and her hair was loosely tied back. Rosy cheeks hinted at long walks across the heather with the dogs.

"It's so good to see you!" said Ana. "Here, hold your niece so I can give you a hug."

"Well, hello there, wee bairn. I'm your auntie Merry, and you are so adorable I might just have to keep you with me, locked up in a high castle tower." She pronounced it *too-er*.

Ana sensed a relief in Merry as profound as her own as they settled into the familiar comfort of their pre-Harry relationship, chatting on the scenic drive from Edinburgh to Kindrummon. Eliza was asleep, and didn't wake when they stopped at a picnic site overlooking the Cairngorms.

The air was chilly, but Merry fetched Ana a fleece from the car, saying, "Och, ye Sassenach softie, it must be at least eight degrees today—prrractically tropical."

Ana hunkered into the jacket and looked out across the mountains, their tops dusted with snow. Clouds scudded across the sky, casting quick-change light and shade across the hills and glens. The only sound was the breeze whistling through the grass.

It was lovely to be up here, with Merry and Eliza, and she felt the loss of the wasted years.

"So, sister," said Merry as they tucked into sandwiches. "Now that normal relations have been resumed, dare we risk dipping our toes into heart-to-heart territory?"

"Let's give it a go."

"How are things with you and Harry—truth only, please."

Ana sighed. "Truth. OK. I don't know. Tricky. Working for him has been difficult. I want to leave Rose Corp. and set up on my own, but I need Harry's financial support to do that. Otherwise, well, he's so busy. Gets home late, doesn't switch off at weekends. He's fantastic with Eliza, though. He loves her to bits."

"Does he love you to bits?"

"You can't keep that initial passion thing going forever, can you? Truth is, I think he wanted me a lot more when I didn't want him. I wasn't playing hard to get, I honestly didn't like him an awful lot. But then I got to know him better, and I liked him more. And then I fell in love with him."

"He's hard to resist. Any other women?"

The blunt question took Ana by surprise. "No! He doesn't even have time for me, how would he fit in another woman?"

"Good. Does Mum keep telling you Ways to Keep Your Husband Happy?"

Ana laughed. "Oh yes. The whole 'full makeup and a welcoming smile when they come home' thing. Dinner on the table five minutes later. Shame I don't cook. Harry loves to remind me what a good cook Katie was."

Merry gazed out over the mountains. "I still feel bad about Katie. I thought I was so clever, nabbing gorgeous Harry from his boring little wife. Now that I know how that feels, I often wonder about her."

Ana was more relaxed than she'd felt in years. Evenings were spent lounging in front of the fire in the drawing room, Merry's two setters stretched out on the rugs. The chef brought them dinner on trays, which they ate in front of the TV. In the mornings, while Merry saw to estate business, Ana would carry Eliza down to the loch, only a tiny portion of her face visible between a warm coat and woolly hat. She'd put her down and she'd wobble around, delighting in the pebbles on the beach, the waves, the waterbirds, her red curls poking out from beneath her hat.

Afternoons were spent rambling over the mountainsides with Merry, Eliza in the baby backpack. Sometimes they chatted; often they walked in companionable silence.

On Wednesday morning, just after Ana had returned from her walk, the bedroom phone rang. It was an ancient-looking thing with an old-fashioned dial.

It was Megan.

"Hi, darling! How lovely of you to ring. Gosh, you and Charles should come up here with your girls. It's glorious. I—"

Megan had started crying.

"Megan? What on earth's wrong?" Her heart dropped. Had Charles reverted to his womanizing ways?

Finally Megan managed to speak. "Don't tell Charles. Or anyone, not even Harry."

"You're scaring me. What's going on?"

"I found a lump."

Ana sat down on the bed, staring unseeingly at Eliza's goofy smile. "Don't panic, Megan. People are always finding lumps. They're almost always benign. Don't worry yourself sick, get it checked."

"I did. It's malignant."

"Oh no. How . . . I mean, what—"

"Don't know yet, but I needed to tell someone."

"Why not Charles? You two are so close."

"I don't want to say anything until I have more answers for him. I've got a scan Friday morning—"

"I'm coming with you."

"But you're up there."

"I'll only lose a day. You can't go through this on your own. I'll call you as soon as I'm back. And, darling, try not to worry. You know how good the specialists are these days."

They ended the call. Shakily, she picked up Eliza and hugged her close.

Ana gave the taxi driver a generous tip as he helped her unload all the gear she'd needed for taking Eliza to Scotland.

"Home, Eliza!" she said, enjoying the elegant facade of their Chelsea house.

She hauled the bags into the hallway and was about to go into the kitchen when she heard a noise from upstairs.

She froze.

It came again.

After her initial panic, she realized—that was no burglar.

As she silently climbed the stairs, she experienced an out-of-body moment, watching herself about to see something she didn't want to see, but unable to stop herself from getting closer.

The sounds became clearer, unmistakable. Moaning, gasping, rhythmic. The thumping of the bedhead against the wall.

Out of some ridiculous wish to protect Eliza, she diverted into the nursery and put the baby in her cot, where she was happy reuniting with her soft toys.

Ana went back onto the landing. The sounds were louder now, the banging of the bedhead faster, more frantic. Out-of-body Ana noted in-body Ana's feelings: fear, anger, despair.

She opened the bedroom door, just a crack, and peered in.

Janette, dressed only in stockings, suspenders, and high heels, was riding Harry like a jockey heading down the home straight, bouncing up and down, her breasts jiggling, her head flung back, now shrieking, "Yes! Yes! Oh YES, Harry!"

Harry was watching her in delight, his hands on her hips.

"*Faster*, Harry!"

Ana thought she might vomit. She kicked the door hard, and it crashed open the rest of the way.

Harry's eyes met hers and widened, and he leaped off the bed, tumbling Janette off him. Janette grabbed the sheet and held it up to her chest, white-faced.

"Ana, oh god, Ana, I thought—"

"Seriously, Harry?" she said, her voice full of contempt. "Your sad little secretary? Desperate times. I'll be downstairs, when you're done."

She shut the door behind her and returned to Eliza's room. She was already asleep, tired after the long journey. Her hands shaking, Ana gently pulled up the blanket and made her way downstairs.

Her mind was numb. She poured herself a wine and sat at the kitchen worktop, staring into space. Just one day ago she'd been so happy. How quickly things could come tumbling down.

She heard feet on the stairs, then the front door shutting.

Harry appeared in the kitchen doorway, dressed in jeans and a sweater, his hair tousled, his cheeks still pink.

"Ana, I don't know what to say. I'm so sorry, you shouldn't have had to see that."

"How long has this rather pathetic . . . thing been going on?"

"It's not a thing. It's just . . . only once or twice. I didn't mean for anyone to get hurt. I'm sorry."

"So you said. You know what, Harry? If it'd been someone like Merry, I might have understood. But *her*? She's a moron. Why—"

"She's not a moron. I realize she doesn't have your style or your sharp brain, but she's kind, and she understands me."

"Did you really just say that, Harry? She *understands* you? Because she types your letters and knows how you like your coffee? And have you told her your wife *doesn't* understand you? Well? Have you, Harry?" Her voice rose, and finally the fury rushed in. "ANSWER ME, Harry!"

"I don't remember saying those exact words."

Ana picked up her wineglass and threw the contents at Harry. When they fell short, she threw the glass.

"You BASTARD!"

He ducked, and it smashed on the wall behind him. Then she picked up a plate from a pile draining by the sink, and threw that.

"You UTTER fucking BASTARD!"

As she picked up another, Harry left the kitchen and shut the door quickly. The plate smashed against it.

The red mist dissipated and she doubled over, crying great, heaving sobs. She couldn't forget Harry's expression of joy as he'd thrust into Janette. With Ana, his face only ever showed intense concentration.

She sank onto a stool and rested her head on her arms, tears soaking her sleeves. Her heart was breaking, shattering into pieces like the fragments of glass and china all over the floor.

A while later she sat up and took some deep breaths. Then she opened the kitchen door, swiping her wet cheeks with the palms of her hands.

"Where are you?" she called.

"Drawing room."

He was sitting in an armchair, staring into space. "I love you, Ana," he said. "Can we talk about this?"

"I want a divorce."

"Ana, it was one mistake. Every marriage has its ups and downs. Things haven't been good for a while, you know that. We can sort it, though. Do you want me to fire Janette?"

"Do what you want, Harry. I can't spend my life worrying what you're up to every time my back's turned. You were unfaithful to Katie, and now you've been unfaithful to me. For all I know, Janette could be one of many. I can't trust you anymore. I'm calling my lawyer tomorrow. Oh, not tomorrow, actually, because I'll be with your sick sister. Did you know about that? No, thought not. Well, when you feel like thinking about someone other than yourself, you SELFISH BASTARD, perhaps you'd like to give her a call. But not yet, because she needs to talk to Charles first. Do you see, Harry, how when women need someone to rely on, it's never a man?"

Trying not to care about the shock on Harry's face, she left the room.

CHAPTER 33

Harry

December 1998

It was that time again—the Rose Christmas party. Fatboy Slim was rocking the dance floor, and Rose employees were, as always, embracing the Christmas spirit. Harry smiled indulgently as he watched them.

His mind went back to five years ago, to his first night with Ana. And what a night it had been. There would never be another like it.

Why did he want Ana most when he couldn't have her? Now that she was colder than a morning shower at Eton, all he could think about was making up with her. It would happen, and it would be epic.

What kind of dysfunctional relationship was that?

In the meantime, they'd reached some sort of uneasy truce. Ana hadn't mentioned divorce again, and Harry had made an effort to help with plans for her design consultancy, recognizing that this, at least, was a sensible way forward.

At home they were polite, and he was doing more than his fair share of caring for Eliza when the nanny wasn't on hand. He loved cozying up with his daughter, singing her songs, tickling her, playing with her toes. Her gurgling giggle was the sweetest sound in the universe. Eliza was of a far sunnier disposition than Maria. While his first daughter had been a watchful child, Eliza was all smiles, and learned things at a rate that convinced Harry she was a genius.

"This girl's going to grow up to be some kind of superwoman," he'd said to Ana, during a slight thaw in relations. "Perhaps she'll be the next Maggie Thatcher." He was still a fan, even though the Iron Lady's reputation had taken a battering since her heyday.

He noticed Janette, sitting with the other top-floor secretaries. She quickly looked away as their eyes met. He felt bad. They hadn't talked properly since Ana had burst in on them. But he knew she'd understand.

Right now, he couldn't think beyond winning Ana back.

He spotted her, talking to Terri. She outshone every other woman in the room, dressed in a silvery sheath that did nothing to dispel her Ice Queen image.

He excused himself from the group he was talking to and went over.

"Hello, ladies. Looking glorious this evening."

"Harry," said Terri, dressed in her trademark black. "Not at all appropriate to talk business, but just letting you know we'll be contracting out some of the *Rack*'s production work to Ana. So hurry the fuck up and get her started."

"I second that motion," said Ana. She smiled at him, and his heart lifted.

"Come and dance," he said as the music slowed.

She hesitated, and Terri said, "Don't mind me."

Harry held out his hand, and Ana took it. The crowd parted as the Rose king and queen headed to the dance floor.

"How is it I've never fired Terri for insubordination and potty-mouthed language?" Harry said.

"Terri's brilliant. I couldn't have survived without her."

"Ana . . ." Harry gently took her in his arms. "I can't survive without you. Please, please forgive me."

She looked at him levelly, her hands on his shoulders, resisting him. "I can't forgive you, no. And I'll never trust you again. But for Eliza's sake, and if you support me in my new venture, I'll stay with you."

Ana

The final year of the millennium began, and so did Megan's battle with cancer. The prognosis was encouraging, and Megan was coming to terms with what lay ahead. Charles was being a rock.

Harry hadn't handled the news at all well; he couldn't face the thought of losing his beloved little sister.

Megan's diagnosis had made Ana think about what was important in life. She'd decided to give Harry a second chance. He'd been trying hard, and things between them were probably as good as they would get from now on. Fueled by champagne and the Christmas spirit, Ana had thawed at the Christmas party. It had been worth it just to see Janette's face when she kissed him on the dance floor. The secretary had been crushed like a bug under Ana's Jimmy Choo.

Ana had let Harry back into her bed that night, and it was an enormously erotic reunion as she took charge, punishing him for his misdemeanor. By the time they'd finally fallen asleep, some kind of armistice had been achieved.

Harry had made Janette office manager and moved her to the opposite end of the floor.

It was Saturday night, and Tegan's evening off. Ana had just put Eliza to bed, and the house was silent. She closed the drawing room curtains, looking out at the street below, where wrought-iron lamps cast pools of light on the pavement.

Earlier today, Harry had gone to a football match with Charles and the Russian oligarch—what was his name? Smirnoff, or something. Harry wanted him to invest in Rose Corp.'s football channel and had taken him to see Arsenal play Manchester United. No doubt they were now at dinner somewhere eye-wateringly expensive. It was like trying to woo a princess.

The Russian was a football fanatic, and Harry had been swotting up on the beautiful game, being more of a rugger man himself. *Match of the Day* videos were stacked up around the TV. Harry had been looking forward to seeing "Man U." Even Ana knew the club was on a roll this season. David Beckham was playing. He and his soon-to-be wife, Victoria, had featured in the *Rack* recently, and Terri had had the clever idea of asking Victoria to interview David, instead of doing it herself.

"Good grief, Terri," Ana had said. "You must be the only woman in Britain to turn down one-on-one time with Becks."

The photos of the incredibly photogenic pair had been a dream, and Ana had longed to design the layouts. Oh well, she'd be back at it soon, doing what she loved again.

She fetched her PowerBook and sat down to work on her business plan. Charles was going to give it the once-over before it was presented to the board. She'd found the perfect premises, on the top floor of a converted warehouse in Covent Garden. The rent was high, but Harry's pockets were suddenly deep—one benefit of busting his affair.

She opened the document, brought up the Global Search and Replace window, and typed in "Ana Rose Design."

Yesterday, Terri had said, "Not liking that name anymore, babe."

"Why not? It was your idea."

"Changed my mind. Rose isn't your name, it's his. New millennium coming, Ana. We women need to step it up."

"So—Ana Lyebon Design? But I never call myself that."

Terri grinned. "How about Ice Queen Design?"

"Sounds like a skate-wear company."

"IQ Design," said Terri. "You're welcome."

As she clicked Replace All, she looked at her watch: seven thirty. She wasn't sorry Harry hadn't asked her to join them for dinner. The Russian was apparently going to invite them to his mansion, so she'd meet him soon enough. She'd play the corporate wife, but felt uneasy about it. The papers were full of the "New Russians," hinting at their connections to corrupt officials and criminal bosses. They made London's own breed of gangsters look positively cuddly. She wished Harry could have found a less menacing prospect.

Harry

As Harry looked for a taxi, he resolved never to take Andre Sokolov to a favorite restaurant again. His behavior had been excruciating, demanding off-menu dishes and obscure wines. Afterward, Harry had sought a quiet word with the maître d' for fear he'd never be given his preferred table again.

Andre was well on the way to sozzledom and was giving Charles hearty slaps on the back. "My wonderful English friends, is best day in your country I ever have. The night is but young! We go to Annabel's now, I think. Always many lovely young girls at this place."

Harry and Charles exchanged a glance. If Andre wanted Annabel's, Andre would get Annabel's.

They were shown to a table with a ringside view of the rich and the beautiful. Andre ordered vintage Dom Pérignon that undoubtedly cost more than all three football tickets, before heading off to the dance floor.

"Churlish not to," shouted Harry above the music, pouring two glasses of champagne.

"Successful day, wouldn't you say?" said Charles.

"Not to jinx it, but I'd say we have our partner. Here's to you, Charles, and I'd expect your bank to be suitably generous when it comes to bonus time."

Andre returned with his arms around two girls, and one more following behind. The brunette sat on his lap, while the two blondes squeezed in on either side of Harry and Charles. Charles gave Harry a small smile and shook his head a little. Harry wasn't sure whether it was a *no way* shake or a *what can you do?* shake.

"London girls not so beautiful as Russians," hollered Andre, "but much more fun times!"

"Dom Pérignon!" said the blonde next to Charles. "My favorite tipple."

"I'm Caitlyn," said the girl next to Harry. "And you're Harry Rose."

"That's right, how clever of you."

Colored lights from the dance floor swept across her pale hair, turning it purple, green, and red, and illuminating her face, which was model pretty. And very young. She couldn't have been more than eighteen or nineteen. Her dress screamed, *I'm ripe now—peel me!* It was low cut at the front and barely covered her thighs. Harry tried not to let his eyes settle on the twin globes spilling over her neckline.

No. He wasn't going down that road again. A blond temptress had led him by the nose before, and that hadn't ended well.

But by jove, she was gorgeous.

"Well, Harry Rose, I have a surprise for you." She flicked back her hair, which fell to her waist in a silvery sheet. He fought an impulse to stroke it, picking up his champagne glass instead.

Andre, he noticed, was embracing his own impulses. The girl in his lap was squirming in a most unsubtle manner—it was practically a lap dance—and the Russian's eyes were glazing over.

Caitlyn leaned in toward Harry, and the eyeful he received was surely no accident.

"Surprise?"

"We're related!"

"We are? How so?"

"Your wife's my cousin. Though she's quite a bit older than me, so I never really knew her growing up. My family are the poor relations."

"Really? What's your full name? I'll have to tell her I met you."

"Caitlyn Howe. But maybe you shouldn't tell her. Kind of depends."

Could she be any more forward? Girls of his generation had surely never been this uninhibited. Or maybe he'd just missed out on all that. He'd married so young.

"Darling, you're absolutely delightful, but I'm very much a married man. I'm simply here babysitting my Russian friend. So I'd love to sip champagne with you, even take a turn on the dance floor, but—well, 'tis all."

He took her hand and kissed it.

"Bloody shame, you're the hottest guy here by a mile."

There was a bright flash. The blonde next to Charles was snapping photos of Andre and his brunette, with a tiny digital camera. Harry hoped she wasn't going to attempt extortion at some later date. But somehow he suspected dallying in a London nightclub with young girls who weren't his wife wouldn't be high on the Russian's list of crimes.

"Harry! Charles! We go!" bellowed Andre.

There was a moment of disappointment, Harry acknowledging how much he was enjoying flirting with this delicious young thing, swiftly followed by relief that he wouldn't have to go once more into battle with temptation, or spend time arguing the toss with his old nemesis, conscience.

"Girls come too!" said Andre, and the brunette in his lap punched the air saying, "Yeah! Party!"

Charles rolled his eyes at Harry. The girl next to him was hanging on to his arm, and Charles's hand was on her thigh. Harry tried not to think about Megan.

"Andre," called Charles, "I need to go to the little boys' room and then we'll find a taxi." He caught Harry's eye and flicked his head toward the gents.

"Me too," said Harry.

"We have to go along with this," said Charles in the quiet of the washroom. "He's out for a seriously good time; we'll just have to suck it up. Maybe call Ana now? I'll tell Megan we're off to a late-night drinking club. I'll try and be Responsible Charles, but if I have too much wodka and turn into Arsehole Charles, please keep schtum, my chum."

"Of course, Charles. Far be it from me to judge—but do bear in mind who you're married to. Let's keep our Russian friend happy, let our hair down, but not disgrace ourselves."

"Sounds like a planski."

. . .

They caught a cab to Andre's mansion, where the Russian instantly turned one of the palatial reception rooms into a mini nightclub, with dimmed lighting, loud music, and a bar in the corner. Andre and his brunette soon disappeared up the grand staircase.

"He probably wouldn't mind if we went off home now," said Harry.

"Aw, come on, guys," said Storm, the other blonde. She began to dance, closing her eyes and running her fingers through her long hair. Then she opened them and beckoned to Charles. He joined her and put his hands on her waist, and they danced, their eyes locked, inching closer together.

"Feeling like a wallflower here," said Caitlyn, sitting beside Harry on the enormous leather couch. She put her hand on his knee. "Shall we join in?"

Harry brought Ana's face to mind. And Eliza's. And then there was Janette, and Katie and Maria. The vodka was making him sentimental. He loved them all, his women and his girls. He didn't want to hurt any of them, ever again.

He stood up. "Charles, I'm going to make a move. Ladies, I'm terribly sorry to spoil the party, but really, we only came here to keep Andre company. Can I call you a cab?"

Charles came out of his dance trance. "Yep. Ladies, you are an utter delight, but so are our wives."

December 31, 1999, 11:59 p.m.

Positions, everybody," called Harry, looking out the boardroom window. "Ten seconds and counting!"

Friends and colleagues crowded around, glasses of champagne in hand, anticipating the spectacular fireworks the government had promised, as the TV in the corner showed Big Ben at one minute to midnight.

Bong . . . Bong . . . Bong . . .

Harry put his arm around Ana, pulling her close. She looked up at him and smiled. "I wonder what's in store for us?" she said, and rested her head on his shoulder.

Bong . . . Bong . . . Bong . . .

Harry glanced over at his father's portrait on the wall. *I'm doing OK, aren't I, Dad?* He felt Ana pat him on the back.

Bong . . . Bong . . . Bong . . .

He looked across to Megan and Charles, standing arm in arm. His sister caught his eye and blew him a kiss. Harry's heart constricted, and he found himself offering up a silent prayer. *Please, make her better.*

Bong . . . Bong . . . Bong.

Then Big Ben was silent, and there was a strange, quiet, profound moment.

That's it.

They were in a new millennium. The door had closed on the past one thousand years, and on the twentieth century. No final additions, no tweaks. It was history, the past.

Then the room erupted in cheers as fireworks streaked into the sky around the new Millennium Wheel.

CHAPTER 34

Ana

March 2001

Ana looked at the Cartier watch Harry had given her last Christmas. Five minutes until her next meeting. She checked her email inbox; there was one from Terri.

> Hello, my lovely. My first-ever email. Let me know if you get it cos I don't trust this. Lunch?

Ana smiled and clicked on the Reply symbol.

> I can't get used to it either. Fully expect emails to disappear without trace in cyberspace. Lunch would be great—Tuesday?

She returned the screen to the floating IQD logo.

Ana was expecting a publisher looking to outsource production of a new series of cookbooks. If IQD won the business, she'd need to employ two more staff. The company was going from strength to strength, thanks to Ana's hard work and skill at picking a team that was talented and committed. They also played hard, and Ana would watch wistfully as they headed off to the pub after work. But she had Eliza to go home to, and occasionally Harry.

Eliza was three, and a delight. Ana missed her terribly on weekdays, and that had taken her by surprise. Maternal Ana. Who'd have thought it? While she loved her work, she was happy to be on her way home by six, anticipating opening the front door and hearing "Mummy!" as Eliza flew down the hallway, her red curls bouncing.

It looked as if Harry's proud-dad comments about his genius daughter were, in fact, true. Reports from her nursery school teachers spoke of remarkable learning skills and an extraordinary ability to rule the roost while remaining popular with all the other children.

Ana always tried to be home for Eliza's bath and bedtime. Unfortunately, Harry usually missed both. Andre had come on board with the football channel investment, and now they were putting together a bid for the Premiership rights. It was going to be a long, hard scrap.

Ana loathed Andre. He was a Russian bear personified—huge; appeared friendly and cuddly, but one slash of those claws and you were history. It was unfortunate he lived so close—invitations were tediously regular. Last summer he'd also muscled in on Harry and Charles's tennis games at the Hurlingham. Before Andre had come along, Ana liked taking Eliza up there on a summer's evening. There was no escaping the man.

His wife (his third, apparently) was a beautiful, bored-looking ex-gymnast. Ana was expected to make conversation with her while Andre knocked back the vodka and talked football with Harry, his "English brother."

Ana could tell Andre didn't like her. He was certainly a misogynist, and dismissive of any views she attempted to share. He probably thought women were good for only one thing. She suspected he played around during his wife's absences in Moscow. Was Harry strong enough to resist the temptations that surely came his way when Andre dragged him and Charles out on the town?

She turned her mind to more wholesome topics. Over the Christmas break, they'd spent enough time together to make plans for the future, and had decided Eliza should have a little brother or sister. But Ana was wary of "trying for a baby." Harry had told her how Katie's fertility problems had wrecked their love life, and things between Ana and Harry were shaky enough as it was. Aware of this, Ana had suggested she just came off the pill and they'd see what happened, no calendars involved.

And now, three months in to seeing what might happen, perhaps something had. She was four days late, and she'd bought a testing kit on her way to work. After this meeting, she'd be off to the ladies. If the test were positive, it would confirm what she already knew deep inside.

August 2001

I love how they get on so well," said Megan as she and Ana watched the cousins playing in the Diana Memorial Playground. "Careful on there! Keep hold of Helena's hand, Chess!" she called as the three little girls negotiated the gangplank to the pirate ship. "Here, pass me Po."

She went over and held out her hand.

"Don't drop him, Mummy!" Helena called as the red creature fell into Megan's arms.

"What's wrong with a good old teddy bear?" Megan said, returning to Ana. She held up the Teletubby for inspection. "I can't fathom the appeal, can you?"

"No," replied Ana. "At breakfast this morning, Harry was saying he needed to cut down on the bacon sandwiches. I rubbed my bump and said we were both Tubbybellies, and Eliza thought it was the funniest thing ever."

Their laughter caught the attention of two women on a nearby bench. Noticing Megan's headwear and Ana's bump, one immediately said, "Here, have this seat."

"Oh, please, you don't have to. We're fine," said Megan.

"Take it, we're going soon anyway," said the first mum.

"You're very kind, thank you," said Megan.

She was wearing a stylish newsboy hat with a deep peak, but it didn't hide the fact that there was no hair beneath it. Her golden curls had fallen out after her latest round of chemo, but it had started to grow back, and the test results, which had come in yesterday, were what they'd all been longing for: NED—no evidence of disease.

Tonight, the two families were having a barbecue to celebrate. Ana hoped Harry and Charles would manage to off-load Andre on the way home.

The three men had driven down to Southampton for the first Premier League match of the season. Harry had been looking forward to it all week, mostly because it would give him a chance to take his new Aston Martin for a run down to the coast.

Harry

It was too hot to be watching football, a game Harry associated with frozen pitches, thick gloves, and scarves, and the visible breath of spectators. He was glad when the final whistle blew and they could move back inside from their VIP seats.

"Is thirsty work!" said Andre, who'd been making the most of the corporate hospitality. "One for road, my friends."

"Actually, Andre, Charles and I have plans—a family thing," said Harry. "Do you mind if we make a move?"

Andre's face clouded. "But I never see this part of England before. I think we first find somewhere to eat."

Harry had been ready for that. He raised his eyebrows at Charles and pulled Andre to one side. "Andre, Charles doesn't like to talk about this, but you know Megan's been sick? Very sick?"

"I know this, yes."

"My sister's treatment has been hard on all of us. This week we learned she's . . . well, they don't like to say 'cured,' but she's been given the all clear. So we're having a small celebration, just our two families. I'm sure you understand, we don't want to be late home for that."

The cloud lifted and Andre's eyes misted over. "Of course. Family is everything."

Harry gave Charles a nod and he came over.

"You want to come in my Ferrari again, Andre?" said Charles. "We'll get home a lot faster than Harry in his cranky Aston."

"Oh, we race!"

"Sorry, Andre," said Harry. "In England we have this inconvenient thing called a speed limit. And a police force that isn't open to bribery. Sadly."

"Pah. Still we can race," said Andre.

Charles grinned. "How about it, Harry? Last to the Stag on the River buys a round, quick pint before home."

Harry couldn't resist. "You're on."

Their route began on the M3, then cut across to avoid the roadworks that had slowed them on the way south. Harry's spirits soared as he sped along in his new baby, on an achingly beautiful late-summer evening. Above the golden cornfields, the sky was a deep blue. Megan was well, and Harry was going to be a dad again in a few months' time. Maybe this time it'd be a boy. Life was bloody great.

He was almost at the pub now, speeding at ninety-five along the Guildford bypass, the deep roar of the Aston Martin's engine filling his ears. If the police nabbed him, so be it. It was worth it.

In his rearview mirror, he saw Charles's red Ferrari for the first time since leaving Southampton. Thanks to a fortuitous series of green lights, Harry had gained a comfortable lead even before leaving the coast. He glanced in his mirror again—the Ferrari was gaining on him. He accelerated, pulling out to overtake an Audi.

He pulled back into the slow lane. Ahead, a weekend driver in a Ford Mondeo was hogging the outside lane; he'd have to pass it on the inside. He looked in the mirror again and made out Andre leaning forward, egging Charles on. He grinned to himself. But as he returned his eyes to the road ahead, he saw a blue hatchback pulling onto the carriageway from the slip road.

He was going to hit it.

Instinctively he swung right, straight into the Mondeo.

There was a terrific bang and the screech of metal, the squealing of tires. Time seemed to slow as Harry gripped the wheel, trying to regain control. But he was powerless as the Aston flew back across the road toward a hedge of tall trees. The last thing he saw before he lost consciousness was the tree trunk directly in his path.

CHAPTER 35

Harry

Life turns on such tiny moments of fate.

Harry's mind was wandering, woozy from drugs as he lay immobile after his second round of surgery.

If one of those green lights had been red, or he hadn't phoned Ana before leaving Southampton, or the M3 hadn't been covered in cones, then he wouldn't be here. And Ana wouldn't have lost their baby.

He remembered nothing of the accident two weeks earlier. His last memory was of swerving to avoid the little blue car, then nothing.

The Mondeo driver, a kind man by the name of Alan, had regained control of his car, in spite of the enormous swipe that had sent him careening toward the median barrier. He'd escaped with only whiplash. Alan confirmed to the police that Harry had been driving dangerously but otherwise hadn't wanted to cause any bother. Harry had sent him a check that would cover the cost of a new car—something rather more exciting than a Mondeo.

After the emergency services had cut Harry out of his Aston, he'd been taken to the Royal Surrey. One leg was crushed and he had severe internal injuries. He went straight into surgery and from there to intensive care.

Charles had driven back to London to break the news to Ana personally, then had taken her to Guildford. The surgeon had told them Harry might not last the night.

As they waited, hour after interminable hour, the stress became too much for Ana. She'd started to have contractions and was admitted to the hospital herself. Efforts to halt the early labor had failed, and by the time Harry was out of danger, the baby was lost.

When Harry came to, his brain fuzzy with medication, the doctors had explained that his shattered leg bones had been pinned together with rods and plates, and he would need ongoing surgery. It could take up to a year before he could walk properly again. In the meantime he'd be laid up for weeks, if not months, and could be left with a limp.

Later, a nurse had told him about Ana.

When he was stable, Harry had been transferred to a hospital closer to home. His first visitor after the move was Charles.

"Guess I'm gonna have to find myself a temporary tennis partner," joked his friend, looking at the metal contraption encasing Harry's leg. It resembled a Tudor-era torture instrument. "Bloody inconsiderate if you ask me." Then his smile disappeared. "Harry, I'm sorry—"

"Not your fault. Just shitty luck."

"At least you're still here, old boy. It was touch and go for a while there. How are you feeling?"

"Not too bad, until the painkillers start to wear off. How's Ana?"

Charles looked away, fixing his eyes on the machine beeping behind Harry's head. "Pretty upset, obviously, especially about the baby."

"Does she blame me?"

"I don't know. She knows about the race, and that you were driving dangerously." He looked at Harry again. "Your Tom Cranwell's on track to get you off with a fine, by the way. But Ana . . . well, you know how excited she was about this baby. She's bound to be upset, worrying about you and coping with that. But she's young. Plenty of time for another."

Where had Harry heard that before?

. . .

Ana had visited the next day, by herself. She didn't want Eliza to see him like this, she said.

It was brief, and awkward, and she didn't touch him other than to peck him on the cheek. After an initial "How are you feeling?" she didn't probe further into whether he was in pain or worried about his recovery. She didn't even ask any of the normal silence-filler hospital questions about the food or whether he had enough to read.

"I'm sorry," he said finally. "I'm so sad about the baby." His voice caught, and he held out his hand.

She ignored it, looking at him steadily for a moment before her eyes slid away to stare out of the window. "So am I, Harry. So am I."

"We can try again."

"I can't think about that. All I can think about is the life that never was."

"I understand. You'll need time."

"I don't want you seeing Andre outside of work," she said abruptly.

"What? Why not? The accident wasn't his fault."

"You act like a fool around him, Harry. And he's a bad person—you know he is. I know you need his money, but tell me, how much is that money worth? Your unborn child? Your family? You need to off-load him, get him out of your life."

"The race wasn't his idea."

"Then whose was it?" Her dark eyes bored into his.

"We just said last one to the pub should buy a round."

"Then Charles is an idiot too. And he's, what? Forty-five? And drinking and driving too? For Chrissake, Harry."

"I only had two beers at the match. That's the honest truth."

She sighed, the fight leaving her. "Whatever, Harry. It doesn't matter now."

. . .

There was a tap on the door, and Janette's head appeared around it. "Is it OK if I come in? I didn't know whether I should visit."

Harry's spirits lifted as she tiptoed in—a nonjudgmental friend. She was clutching grapes and a copy of Ian McEwan's *Atonement*.

"Come in, sweetheart, and try not to look too closely at this." He waved a hand toward the leg.

She talked about things at the office, and what was happening in the news, and her voice had such a soothing effect on him that he fell asleep, jerking awake later to find her sitting quietly, reading a magazine.

"Sorry, it's the drugs making me sleepy. You don't have to stay . . ."

"Do you want me to go? I'm sorry—"

"No. It's been lovely seeing you. Would you come again? And, Janette, I'd like you to move back to my office while I'm out of action. Take calls, answer emails, tell people what's going on with me."

"Of course, Harry. Nothing would make me happier. Oh, apart from you getting better really quickly, of course!"

"It's going to take a while. I'm not sure when they'll let me go home. Perhaps you could come in weekdays, at a time of day when . . . other visitors aren't here. You can bring in the paperwork, take a bit of dictation?"

"That sounds like a great plan."

And so it became his routine. Janette visited every afternoon, and it was the only bright spot in his day—that and his painkiller top-ups.

Andre came in a few times, filling the private room with his colossal presence. He talked football, mostly, but Harry couldn't work up any enthusiasm.

Ana visited on weekends, and for half an hour in the evening during the first two weeks, dropping to two evenings and Sunday afternoon on the third. She brought Eliza once, and he realized he'd missed her first day at school. He asked Eliza about it, but she seemed more interested in the complicated metal arrangement encasing his leg.

He found Ana's visits tiring. She fidgeted and avoided prolonged eye contact. Kisses were limited to a peck on the forehead. He didn't know what to say to her, how to make things right again. The loss of their baby hung between them, and he knew she still blamed him.

The nurse came in. The tall one with the kind eyes—Clare. "How are we today, Harry?"

"All the better for seeing you, Nurse Clare. And I'm sure we will be feeling much improved after a top-up of those lovely painkillers."

She picked up the chart from the bottom of his bed. "Not due for an hour or two yet. Can you manage?"

"How disheartening. Do I have a choice?"

"We don't want you leaving here an addict, do we? Now, time to change this dressing."

Harry's attention was abruptly diverted from Clare's agreeable body to his own leg as the pain made him gasp.

"Sorry, Harry, I'll be quick as I can. Look on the bright side—at least we know the nerve damage is healing."

He shut his eyes as she left the room ten minutes later.

"Harry?"

He opened them to see Janette by his bed. "Janette. Boy am I pleased to see someone who's not going to prod me or poke me or generally cause me unspeakable agony." He gave her a weak smile.

"Oh, you poor thing! Is it really painful?"

Janette's sympathy pierced his cheerful facade and he closed his eyes again, groping for her hand.

She took it and kissed it, then he felt her lips on his forehead. "This is so awful, my love. I hate seeing you like this."

"Another hour to wait for painkillers." He kept hold of her hand.

"The doctors know best, Harry. It's going to take time." She stroked his brow, then his hair, brushing it back from his forehead.

He sighed. It felt as if no one had touched him, other than to inject him, measure him, or bandage him, in weeks. He raised her hand to his mouth and kissed it. "You're an angel, Moneypenny."

The hand on his head stilled for a moment, then stroked his cheek tenderly.

"I just want to see you all better. More than anything." She leaned forward and kissed his forehead again, more slowly this time.

He opened his eyes and looked into hers, hovering just above him. "You wouldn't take advantage of a man who couldn't move, would you?"

She smiled. "Not unless he wanted me to."

He moved his hand to the back of her head and gently brought her close, until they were kissing. His head spun with the drugs and the pleasure of a sensation that wasn't pain.

Later, he had a quiet word with Nurse Clare, ensuring that—from now on—he wouldn't be disturbed during his assistant's visits.

Ana

Took me three hours to get through security at JFK," said Terri, who was just back from New York. "Everyone there's jumpy as a flea on a bouncy castle."

"A what?" said Ana.

"Sorry, metaphor fail. Jet lag."

A few weeks ago, the world had been rocked by the terrorist attack on New York's Twin Towers, and Londoners were on edge again too. Bomb threats were a normal part of life, but IRA attacks had dwindled, and since the Good Friday Agreement, people had finally dared hope for a lasting peace. Now it was back to bomb alerts and loop messages about unattended baggage.

For Ana, still mourning the loss of her child, this was turning out to be the year from hell. She said as much to Terri as she filled her in on recent events over their regular lunch.

Harry had come home. He was on crutches and, apart from the daily cleaning lady, was alone in the house for most of the day—Tegan now only babysat Eliza after school. With Charles and Megan's help, Ana had turned the dining room into a bedroom-office, and Harry was spending some of the time working. But he was still in pain, grew tired quickly, and as a result was in a constant bad temper.

"I know I'm being impatient with him," Ana said, "but I can't move past thinking this is all his own fault."

"You have to make allowances for boys, 'cause they're generally rubbish. That especially applies to overprivileged upper-class arsehole boys."

Ana laughed. "It's amazing you've worked for him this long, considering you've never liked him—have you?"

"Strangely, I'm fond of the old bugger. Couldn't stand him that first time I interviewed him, but there's something about Harry. Go easy on him, Ana. He's been a twat, but I think he's probably paid the price."

Ana mulled over Terri's words as they paid the bill and left. If Terri, who hated almost everyone, was speaking up for Harry, maybe it was indeed time for a little forgiveness. Blaming him for the loss of her baby was perhaps unfair. It had been his baby, too, and he'd been so excited.

She stopped in the street, causing a man following close behind to bump into her. He harrumphed, then as she turned to apologize, his eyes widened. "Sorry, my fault!"

She smiled. She still had it. And maybe it was time to give it back to Harry. She hailed a cab to take her home.

Fifteen minutes later she was opening the door to Harry's bedroom— quietly, just a crack, in case he was asleep.

He wasn't. Harry was seated in his armchair, his bad leg resting on a footstool. And on his lap was Janette, her head tucked into his shoulder. He was stroking her hair, and they were talking quietly.

CHAPTER 36

Harry

H arry, do you think, when you're better, we might still be able to . . ." said Janette, snuggling into his chest.

"I don't know, sweetheart. For now I'm just trying to get through the days. And you're making those days bearable. But we need to be careful. What time is it?"

Janette looked at her watch. "Two thirty. I should go." She kissed him, then stood up and smoothed down her dress. "Bye, Harry darling. Take care."

He closed his eyes. Janette's visits were the only thing that made him forget about the pain. His prescription medication just wasn't doing it anymore. He'd talk to the doctor about upping it again. He couldn't go on like this.

There were voices in the hall. Janette's voice, and . . . Ana?

"Get out of my house, you stupid moronic slut!"

"We were . . . it was work. Harry dictates letters—"

"How *dare* you insult my intelligence. Out!"

"But—"

"OUT!"

The front door slammed.

Oh god. What had Ana seen?

She came in and stood facing him, her eyes black flints.

"Ana?"

"You know what, Harry? You've been *insufferable* since your accident. You sit there feeling sorry for yourself while I work, run the house, organize Eliza, try and recover from my own loss, and all you can do is moan about something you brought upon yourself. And I was stupid enough to listen to Terri—she told me I should have a bit more sympathy. So I decided to come home and spend the afternoon with you. And who do I find has got here first? Jockey Janette, the secretary from Slutsville."

"Ana, I . . . we didn't—"

"Shut up, Harry. I don't care whether you did or didn't. When was the last time you held me like that?" Her voice broke, and he saw her tears. "We're done. Finished. It really is over this time. I want you to leave. And don't hobble after me on your stupid crutches, because I might just kick them out from underneath you. I'm taking Eliza to see the Harry Potter movie tonight. You can look after yourself."

She left the room, slamming the door behind her.

Harry sat for a long time, thinking, the room growing dark around him. He came to a decision. This time, he wouldn't try to win Ana back. He'd never felt about a woman the way he had about her, probably never would again. It had been a kind of madness, an infatuation. For the longest time he'd been unable to think about anything other than winning her. And when he had, it was glorious. But—he acknowledged the truth—over the past year or two, their relationship had become a battleground, and it was wearing him out.

Janette was a soothing balm, and he wondered again what it would be like to come home to her softness, her kindness, her love for him, every night.

If Ana wanted a divorce, this time he'd give her one.

"Harry!" bellowed Andre, his arms held wide. "How good is to see my English brother looking much improvement!"

It was New Year's Eve, and Harry was staying with Megan and Charles. He'd moved in the week after Ana discovered him with Janette.

"I'll get the drinks," said Megan, throwing a disapproving glance at the Russian's back. Like Ana, she wasn't a fan.

"Like old times, *da*?" said Andre.

"Indeed," said Harry.

"But you look much pale, my friend. You are not yet recovered?"

"I can walk with a stick. Don't worry, it won't be long before I'm whipping your arse at the Hurlingham again."

"Don't be fooled," said Charles, patting Harry on the shoulder. "He's being incredibly brave, but it hurts, eh, my old pal?"

"I won't lie, it's a tad sore," said Harry. "Doctors are being bloody stingy with the painkillers."

"What you need?" said Andre. "I get something not on your NHS menu, you know?"

"Good lord, Andre, what are you suggesting? A snort of Colombia's finest?"

"*Nyet*. Just something to help. I sort. No charge for dear friend."

Harry wondered whether it was all bluster, although he had no doubt Andre could source the dodgiest of goods with one click of his short pudgy fingers.

"I learn, you and Ana—you have parted your ways? Is true?"

"Sadly yes. She caught me in flagrante. Again."

"Where is this Flagrante?"

"He means bonking someone else," said Charles. "Ana's already filed for divorce. It won't be pretty."

"Cranwell's battening down the hatches," said Harry.

"Hm," said Charles. "Megan tells me Ana's gone with that lawyer who specializes in generous settlements for rich men's wives. I hope your man's up to the job."

. . .

A month later, Harry returned to work. The staff threw a welcome back party on his first afternoon. Janette baked one of her famous cakes, and there was champagne.

Harry knew he probably shouldn't have either. His girth had expanded alarmingly since the accident, the result of no exercise, too much comfort food, and bloating from all the drugs. True to his word, Andre had supplied him with a mountain of painkillers, which had been an enormous help.

Members of staff hadn't been able to hide their shock as he'd hobbled along the corridor, leaning on his stick, though they'd quickly fixed their welcoming smiles back in place. Not to worry. He was determined to get back to his old self, and the best physio in town was helping him get there. He would come off the drugs once his leg was properly healed.

On Harry's second morning back at work, his lawyer came to see him. Harry braced himself. He didn't enjoy the new Tom's company one bit, but needs must. He missed his old Tom—Wolston—the steady hand who'd steered Harry's younger self through the corporate maze. A stab of guilt jabbed him as he remembered pandering to Ana's demands that he should replace Wolston with someone more . . . twisted. Wolston had been a reliable old Labrador, whereas Cranwell was a pit bull.

"Thank you, Janette," Harry said as she showed the lawyer in. "Coffee, Tom?"

Cranwell glanced up at Janette as he took his seat opposite Harry, giving her a smile that bordered on the lecherous. "Nothing for me, thanks, dear."

As she left, he said with a knowing smile, "Ana's lawyer mentioned Janette. Perhaps I should close the door."

"What? Oh, I see. Of course." Harry and Janette were seeing each other outside of work but weren't yet "official."

They discussed Harry's progress, then Tom cleared his throat and said, "Regarding Ana's divorce petition—"

"I'm not contesting it, Tom. Just sort it out. Do your best on visiting rights—Ana won't object to that. And the smallest settlement you can get away with, obviously. She's making plenty of money herself now, and I've invested in her design company, she's not going to jeopardize that."

Tom fiddled with his tie. "Harry, her lawyer's coming in with all guns blazing. And he's good. Ana's demanding half of your assets, plus both houses. She says the Menton villa was a gift."

"Come on, Tom, they're just trying it on."

"I'm sure you'd prefer me to be frank."

"You're scaring me. What's on your mind?"

"As you know, I had a meeting with your finance man, Colin Hale, to get the big picture. Much of your personal capital is tied up in Rose. The thing is, Harry, you're already paying a substantial allowance to your first wife and your daughter Maria, and to Bennie Blunt for Henry. Now you'll have alimony for Ana and maintenance for Eliza too. Both houses will go to Ana if it comes down to the wire. Rose is stretched—advertising revenue is dropping and you've invested heavily in the football channel, which isn't likely to see a return anytime soon; losing out on the Premier League rights was obviously a setback."

"Couldn't be helped—I was busy trying to not die at the time."

"Sure. But you'll need to speak to your bank and your investors. You're overextended. And the Chelsea house is technically a company asset, so if Ana gets that, it's not going to help the cash flow."

Lawyers and accountants. Always the voices of bloody doom.

"Ana's not going to shaft me, Tom. I've invested in her design company, she can't afford to piss me off too much."

"Ana's already in a position to pay off that investment. She's doing extremely well."

"Well, she wouldn't be without my help. That's the bottom line."

"The bottom line, Harry, is that if it goes to court, and the court rules in her favor, your stake in Rose Corp. could be at risk, and your personal finances could take an enormous hit."

"For Chrissake, Tom. She wouldn't want to bankrupt me, I'm the father of her child!"

She wouldn't do that to him, would she?

"It's a starting point, Harry. That's all. But unless you talk her round, this is going to be a long-drawn-out and painful battle. We can play dirty as you like, but there's no guarantees."

CHAPTER 37

―∞―

Harry

It was the first warm evening of the year, and Harry, Charles, and Andre were sitting on the Hurlingham Club terrace sipping chilled New Zealand sauvignon blanc.

"Not a bad tipple, this one," said Charles, holding his glass up to the evening sunlight. "Here's to you—nicely played, Andre." The powerful Russian had beaten him 6–4, 6–3.

"Was good match," Andre replied. "And, Harry, you play soon too, my friend."

"Yep, I'm stick-free at last." That week, Harry had thrown it into the back of the cupboard of the St. Katharine Docks apartment he was leasing.

Megan had wanted him to find somewhere near them, but Harry had always felt drawn to the Thames.

The leg still ached, but he could walk on it properly now—his physio had worked wonders. He intended to kick the painkillers this summer, aware that the quantity he was taking was way out of proportion to the severity of the pain. But every time he tried to cut down, he'd get the jitters, couldn't concentrate, couldn't sleep.

"How is divorce coming, Harry?" asked Andre.

Harry's smile faded. He wasn't comfortable talking about his finances with Andre, aware that it was probably only their friendship keeping him from putting the Russian boot in. The latest figures for the football channel were abysmal.

"Excuse me, chaps, need to pay a visit," said Charles, leaving Harry to answer Andre's difficult question.

"Truth is, Andre, Ana's being difficult," he said. "That's the kindest way I can phrase it. It's not about the money—she's got plenty of that. It's all about revenge. Christ, I only had one affair in all the time we were married. One!"

"Pfft, English women. Her lawyer, I hear he is the best. How good is your Cranwell?"

"Suitably ruthless." But then he remembered Tom's misgivings. "I'm not sure he's up to this particular War of the Roses, though."

"You are on side of right. Rose Corp. was your father's life work, no? You cannot let angry woman ruin his legacy."

"Maybe I should find a lawyer who plays by different rules."

"These English rules I think are difficult to break. Too much in favor of wives. Is wrong. Wives are not ones who make money, so why wives get half the money? Is crazy. I would not tolerate. In Russia we have ways of dealing with troublesome wives who make unreasonable demands."

"You do?"

Andre gazed out across the grounds. And slowly drew his finger across his throat.

"Jesus, Andre. Tad extreme."

"In Russia we take seriously our family battles. Someone threatens to bring us down, like you say, is war. Has always been this way. In England it was too, I think."

"We haven't beheaded our enemies for quite some time, Andre. Or our wives."

"Not in public, Harry. In Russia we know how to do this, what is your word . . . discreetly. Ana, she make a big problem for you."

"She does. But—"

"I can handle this problem for you." He was still looking at the view.

"You *are* kidding? This is England. Wives generally aren't disposable."

Finally, Andre turned to him. "Harry. I much enjoy being business partner. You and Charles are my English family. But you think Russian money is like tap to turn on. You take Andre to football, you get money. You play tennis with Andre, you get more money. I am businessman. There is no more money for Rose until problem sorted. Your wife is problem."

Harry felt himself breaking out in a cold sweat.

"You give me nod, I make problem go away," said Andre.

"How?"

"Russian assets, especially military—many things we can get."

Charles was coming back.

"We haven't had this conversation, Andre."

Harry woke up from a nightmare, bathed in sweat. His legs were twitching and his heart was racing. He flicked on the bedside lamp and looked at the clock: three a.m.

He made his way to the kitchen, where he poured a glass of water and swallowed four pills, staring out the window at the black waters of the Thames.

Andre hadn't been serious. Of course he hadn't. Even Russians didn't go around bumping off other people's wives because they were hampering football-related plans.

Harry sank onto the couch, feeling his heart rate slow. He noticed his stomach spilling over the waistband of his pajamas. He was out of condition, dependent on drugs. His life was unraveling. He needed to take control. He'd find a new doctor and be frank about his painkiller addiction. Most importantly, he'd go and see Ana, get her to see reason.

Ana

It was a Wednesday evening, and Ana was the only person left in the office. Eliza was at a sleepover, so she was working late on a concept for a new client. She'd put background music on and was enjoying the solitude.

It was different from being alone at home, where she'd obsess about the divorce and what to do about Harry. Megan reported he was like a coiled spring, apt to explode in a temper over the most inconsequential things. She suspected he was addicted to painkillers, which were apparently being supplied by bloody Andre.

Ana wouldn't have given a damn, except, of course, there was Eliza to consider.

Tonight was her daughter's first-ever night away from home. Ana couldn't help wondering if she'd be all right. Eliza had been through so much upheaval this past year, with Harry's accident and the breakup. But she seemed remarkably resilient, as sunny and happy as ever, and excelling at school.

Ana jumped as the cleaner appeared in her doorway. She hadn't heard him come in.

He dragged his Hoover into her office and plugged it in behind her.

"Sorry for noise," he said. He sounded Eastern European.

"No problem."

In her final moment of consciousness, Ana was aware of the cleaner picking up her wastepaper bin. Then she felt a tiny prick in her neck. She spun around, shocked, and looked the man in the eye. Then everything went black.

Harry

Thursday morning, at about ten o'clock, Janette appeared in Harry's office doorway, her eyes wide. "Harry, it's the police."

His first thought was that Andre had been caught for some misdemeanor, and he was about to be dragged in.

"Can I get you a coffee?" Janette asked as the two officers approached his desk.

"Nothing, thank you," said the policeman. "Perhaps you could close the door on your way out."

"Mr. Rose," said the female officer. "It's about your wife."

Time seemed to slow down.

"Ana?"

"We're very sorry to tell you that she was found dead in her office this morning."

"Dead? No, that's not possible."

"There's nothing to suggest foul play, sir. It looks like natural causes."

Harry had lost the ability to think. His mind had gone blank.

"Mr. Rose, sir? Can we get you a cup of tea?"

"But . . . she can't be dead. She just can't be."

The male officer went to the door.

"Sir, I know it's a terrible shock," said the policewoman. "Can we call someone to come and be with you?"

"We're separated. Our daughter, Eliza. I'll need to . . . the nanny will have to—"

"Sir, if you let us have the nanny's phone number, we'll get in touch. Is there someone else we can call for you?"

"My sister Megan. She's Ana's friend. Oh my god, Ana. How did she . . . no, it can't be true."

This couldn't be anything to do with Andre. It just couldn't. Stuff like that didn't happen in real life.

He pictured Ana's beautiful face, and the emotion finally hit. He swung his chair around so it was facing away from the officers, and put his head in his hands, which were now shaking uncontrollably. Tears seeped through his fingers.

There was a tap on the door, and the sound of a mug being placed on his desk.

"Harry?" said Janette.

"Ms. . . ."

"Morrissey. I've been with Mr. Rose for many years. Could I ask—"

"Sorry, ma'am, we can't give you any information at this time."

Harry swung back, wiping his eyes.

Janette gasped. "Harry, whatever's happened?"

Harry and Eliza stayed with Charles and Megan for the rest of the week. No one could think further ahead. Handfuls of painkillers quieted the voice in Harry's head. The voice that was calling him a wife murderer.

He argued with it. They were still awaiting the autopsy results, and surely those would show this was a tragic case of . . . what? A heart attack? Brain hemorrhage? One of those, surely.

He mixed more pills with whisky and cried for his beautiful Ana, until Megan told him to pull himself together; she was hurting too. And he needed to get a grip for Eliza's sake.

The autopsy revealed an unusual cause of death—toxic shock syndrome. At first, everyone assumed it was a case of a forgotten tampon, but it appeared the bacteria causing the fatal condition had entered her body through a deep cut on her index finger, which the investigation suggested she'd acquired a few days earlier after a slipup with the office guillotine.

After the funeral, and a family conference, Megan, Charles, and Harry decided to accept Katie's thoughtful invitation for Eliza to join them in Wales for a while, until Harry had made firmer plans for her future.

In the weeks that followed, IQ Design was taken over by Ana's team in a management buyout, most of the substantial proceeds going back into Rose Corp., the sole investor.

Harry's leg continued to improve, and he began a daily regimen of Thames-side walks to build up its strength. His fitness increased, and his trousers were no longer too tight. Newly aware of the fragility of life, he reduced, little by little, the size of the daily pile of pills, although giving them up altogether remained a terrifying prospect. No way could he sleep at night without them.

Janette was an enormous help, her visits distracting him from dark thoughts, from his fear of the knock at the door that could herald the arrival of Scotland Yard. Or MI5.

Harry's first meeting with Andre after Ana's death was at the Rose offices, around a table with the Football TV team. Without the threat of the divorce settlement, they were able to proceed with an alternative plan for the channel. As well as lower division and cup matches, it would feature magazine-style programs heavy on nostalgia.

As everyone filed out of the meeting room, Andre was the last to leave, ahead of Harry.

"Harry, my English brother," he said, turning. "Time we saw a football game again. Life will be easier for you now, I think." And he winked.

CHAPTER 38

Janette

June 2003

"Bloody brilliant," said Terri. "You gotta see it, Harry."

Terri had recently interviewed Tracey Emin for the *Rack*, and was full of praise for her new exhibition. "I particularly enjoyed *Fuck Off and Die You Slag*." She smirked at Janette as she said it.

"Sounds delightful," said Harry. "Though I'm probably more of a Van Gogh man myself. Or one of the great portrait artists. Rembrandt, Hans Holbein."

"Oh, I love Van Gogh!" said Janette. "Especially the ones with all the stars."

Terri made a small noise in her throat. "Well, anyway, Harry, here's to you on your fortieth. May you continue to avoid an untimely death by a hairsbreadth for the next forty years too."

"An excellent sentiment," said Harry, raising his glass.

A few members of staff had been invited to Harry's office for Friday drinks to celebrate his birthday, which was the coming weekend. It was just heads of department, and Janette. Harry still found big parties too tiring. Janette could tell he was already in pain from standing for an hour or more, though he was too proud to sit down.

She'd make sure they left soon. At least Harry's troublesome leg meant she didn't have to endure these dos for long. Janette wasn't sure who found them more awkward—the staff, who were coming to terms with her being Harry's partner, or herself, trying to be that person.

Janette knew *exactly* who she felt like. One of her all-time favorite books was *Rebecca*. Right now, she was very much the second Mrs. de Winter, forever in her predecessor's tall, slim, elegant shadow, knowing she could never match up to her cool sophistication. Harry was, of course, the perfect Maxim de Winter—self-confident and erudite— while Terri was the mad Mrs. Danvers, forever watching through narrowed eyes, needling her with barbed comments, reminding Janette of her unworthiness to follow in Ana's footsteps.

Janette had never understood why Terri and Ana had got on so well, being such different women. Ana's smooth path to the top had been like Harry's—the result of a privileged background, expensive education, and impeccable social network. Conversely, Terri was from a working-class family and had fought her way up entirely on her own merits.

Anyone who'd come up against Ana had been dealt with via a withering glance and frosty silence, while Terri would tell people exactly what she thought of them using the strongest language.

Janette knew they'd laughed about her. The silly little secretary with a crush on her boss. And now that she and Harry were together, Terri's opinion of her seemed only to have worsened. Janette had appealed to Harry about Terri's attitude, but he'd only laughed and said she was a law unto herself, and he wouldn't have it any other way. "Don't worry, it's not just you," he'd said. "She hates everybody."

"Your girls coming up for your fortieth, Harry?" asked Terri.

"Yes. They'll be staying at my sister's. Six daughters between us—it'll be quite the madhouse."

"I can't wait to meet Eliza," said Janette. She was still in Wales with Katie, but Harry was hoping to bring her back to London soon.

He smiled. "You'll love her. She lights up the room, and I know I'm biased, but that's because she's incredibly bright."

"Takes after Ana, then," said Terri.

There was an awkward silence, then Janette said, "Harry, you're looking quite tired. Would you like to leave soon?"

"Who are you, his mum?" said Terri. "It's his fortieth, for fuck's sake!"

"I'll give it another ten," said Harry. "And in the meantime I need to . . . excuse me, ladies." He headed off in the direction of the restrooms.

Janette knew what he'd do when he got there. Harry's attempts to kick his painkiller habit seemed to have stalled.

An hour later they were back at the apartment, and Janette was sitting beside Harry on the bed, giving him a massage.

"You know what, Janette?" he said as she gently kneaded his leg. The scars had faded now, and his recent exercise regimen had returned his body almost to the size it was six years ago, in Manchester. As she slid her hands up his muscular back, she once again wondered how this spectacular man had come to be hers.

"What, Harry?"

"Of all the things I could be doing to celebrate my birthday, I can't think of anything better than this."

"Really? That makes me very happy. I know I'm not beautiful or clever, like your wives . . ."

"Janette, don't put yourself down. I don't want beautiful or clever. I want loving and kind and sweet . . ." He flipped over and propped himself up on his elbows. "And maybe, as it's my birthday . . ."

"The special underwear?"

"Well, that would be nice, but what I was going to say was, maybe you'd agree to be my wife?"

Harry

As they relaxed at Charles and Megan's after a birthday lunch, Harry and Janette shared news of their engagement.

Harry caught the looks on their faces. They didn't think Janette was a suitable third Mrs. Rose. He didn't care. He was sure when they realized how happy she made him, they'd understand. Being with Janette reminded him of his early days with Katie. Life was easy—no dramas, no point scoring, just a comfortable companionship and cozy times in the bedroom. Plus, Eliza needed a mother, and Janette would be perfect.

"Bit soon, isn't it?" said Megan.

Janette blushed, her eyes lowered.

"We're not in Victorian times," Harry said. "There isn't a compulsory mourning period. Why would we wait?"

"Fair enough," said Charles. "Congratulations, then. When's the big day?"

Harry was grateful to his friend for addressing the question to Janette.

"Oh, we haven't arranged anything yet," she said. "I don't expect it will be a big do, will it, Harry?"

"Can I be a bridesmaid?" piped up Eliza from across the room. "I'd like a pink dress, with sparkles and lace."

"I feel pink isn't always the wisest choice for us redheads, sweet pea," said Harry.

"Can I be one too?" chimed Francesca.

"And me!" shouted Helena.

"Janette might not want lots of bridesmaids, they don't want a fuss," said Megan.

"Oh, I think it would be *lovely* to have three little bridesmaids!" said Janette.

"Cassandra says we have to embrace our individuality," said Eliza. "So I think I *shall* have a pink dress."

"Good grief," said Charles. "*How* old is she?"

"Five."

"Knows her own mind, then."

Harry grinned. "OK. Pink bridesmaids' dresses for all—and let's do pink hair things and pink shoes and all the other pink things."

"YES, Daddy!"

"Yay!" cheered Francesca and Helena.

"How about I have a pink dress too!" said Janette.

"Don't be ridiculous," called Arabella from the sofa, where she and Milly were engrossed in a PlayStation game. "That would look totally gross."

"Well, she can't wear white," said Maria loudly, looking up from her book.

"Uncalled for," said Harry. She hadn't meant it as a humorous comment. Maria didn't do humor. Harry wondered how he and Katie had managed to produce this stern teenager who was surely destined for the judge's bench later in life.

"Why can't Janette wear white?" asked Eliza.

"Because she's living in sin with our father," said Maria. "And only good girls should wear white at their weddings."

"Holy fuck," said Milly.

"Milly!" chided Megan.

"Swearing is also a sin," said Maria. "And—"

"That's enough, Maria," said Harry. "Please keep such opinions to yourself, especially in front of the little ones."

"Well don't expect me to come to your wedding," she replied. "As far as I'm concerned, you're still married to my mother. Remember her? The one who never did anything wrong and never stopped loving you? You should look into your conscience sometime, Father."

"Ouch," muttered Charles.

If there was one thing Harry wanted to avoid right now, it was paying his conscience a visit. If he kept it at a distance, it remained clear. If he looked too closely, he might discover something in the shadows.

He looked across at the girls. Charles's Milly and Arabella—Things One and Two—growing up so fast, already thinking about which universities to attend. The three little ones: Eliza, Francesca, and Helena, their heads bobbing over Lego. And Maria, her early years spent with a mother suffering dark depressive episodes, then her parents splitting up. He'd always worried how she'd turn out, growing up at Welshness, but had the feeling Maria would have become this unsmiling, judgmental person, no matter what environment she'd been brought up in.

"I want you all there, team," he said. "Life's been difficult for us all these past few years."

"True," said Charles, and he squeezed Megan's hand.

"So we need a good excuse for a celebration. We'll make it special, and perhaps Rose pink themed, eh, Eliza?"

"Yes! Can we have pink cake?"

"Somebody stop this child with her Disney ideas," said Arabella.

"Harry's right," said Charles. "Things have been shite. But let's hope we've turned the corner. Harry's back on his feet and is going to be married again. So let's be happy for him, eh?"

CHAPTER 39

Harry

December 2003

Harry and Janette had a Christmas wedding. The "small do" ballooned into something bigger when Janette acknowledged that—really—she wanted the wedding she'd dreamed of since she was a little girl. More than once she referred to it as her "*Pretty Woman* moment, except I wasn't a . . . you know."

Her dress was palest pink, with a matching cape edged in white fake fur. She carried a fur muff and wore pink rosebuds in her hair.

Hooray!'s editor, Mia Fox, had suggested an exclusive wedding splash, but when Terri tipped Harry off that she'd probably make it a passive-aggressive attack on Janette, he vetoed the idea.

As they left for Heathrow, Janette tossing her bouquet straight at Lesley from human resources, Harry leaned back contentedly against the leather seats of the vintage Rolls and took Janette's hand. He was on his way to Barbados with his adorable new wife, Rose Corp.'s bottom line was healthy again, and when they returned from their honeymoon, they'd look for a new home suitable for a family. His leg pained him only occasionally, and he was down to just a handful of painkillers a day.

Third time lucky.

Janette

June 2004

Janette put a Tesco shepherd's pie in the microwave and poured herself a glass of pinot grigio. She'd just returned from dropping Eliza at Persephone Willoughby's house for a sleepover. She'd stayed for a glass of wine with the other mums but had escaped at the first opportunity, explaining she had to get ready for an evening out (a lie).

Janette wasn't comfortable with the yummy mummies. When she and Harry had first moved to Primrose Hill, Eliza joining them soon after, her stepdaughter had received so many playdate invitations that Janette had needed to open a social diary just for her. The mums were all keen for their children to become best friends with Harry Rose's daughter.

Most were collected from school by nannies, but the mothers would come home before Janette arrived to collect Eliza, and it would be rude not to accept the offer of a cup of tea. The choice of tea was important. She'd learned never to ask for "just normal." A preference for something more creative was expected, something organic that reduced one's stress levels.

Picking up Eliza also meant doing her hair and makeup and being dressed in the latest activewear. It was all quite exhausting. The next challenge would be how to avoid joining the PTA.

One by one, as the mothers learned she'd been Harry's secretary, possessed of no particular skill other than a talent for needlework (*sewing?*), there would be a moment where the balance shifted. She might be above them in the pecking order, but really, she was nothing special, especially compared to the spectacular Ana Rose, a regular on the society pages. She could see them wondering, how had a girl like her bagged a guy like Harry?

She missed life at the office and intended looking for charity work once the renovations were finished. Harry had given her carte blanche to redecorate the Georgian mansion, which was symmetrical, like a doll's house. She'd been busy choosing paint colors, and wallpaper for feature walls, inspired by *Changing Rooms*, which she usually watched before Harry came home from work. He'd offered to pay for a top interior designer, but she wanted to choose everything herself.

On the whole, Janette loved her new life. Eliza, while still pining for her real mother, had immediately accepted her as stepmother, and the two of them would cuddle on the sofa in the evenings to do Eliza's reading homework, followed by a chapter of Harry Potter.

Janette hadn't broached the subject yet, knowing it was a sensitive one, but she wanted to start trying for a child of her own. Harry had mentioned more than once that he'd love a boy.

He'd probably be home late tonight, she thought, as she took her meal into the drawing room and switched on the TV to watch the evening news. His new airline, Rose Air, had been launched that day. It would be the budget airline with a difference, flying daily to the UK's five favorite European holiday destinations—for starters.

Harry had been immersed in every detail, from the logo design to the selection of the "face" of Rose Air, Zara Lively, the stewardess who would appear in their advertising. The uniform was Rose red, of course.

And here he was!

"Harry Rose, head of media giant Rose Corp., launched a new budget airline today . . ."

Harry was standing with a handsome pilot and Zara Lively, in front of a Rose airliner.

Janette frowned. Harry looked pale, and she could see the sweat on his brow.

Later, she went into the bathroom and opened the cupboard. So many bottles. Were they all prescribed by his specialist? She knew he was trying to cut down. Was the doctor helping him with that?

She'd have a word this weekend.

Harry

After the photo call, Harry took the Rose Air PR team, plus the pilot and Zara Lively, for lunch. Terri had come along too, as the *Rack* was doing a piece on the launch, thinly disguised as a feature on the future of budget airlines.

Harry took a seat next to Zara, who'd just been asked for her autograph.

"How does it feel to be famous?" he said, flashing her a smile. She was still in her stewardess uniform. His eyes traveled over the unfeasibly sleek hair, pulled back into a shining bun, not an errant strand in sight, then to her lovely face with its precision makeup. It was all hugely appealing, in that it was crying out to be pulled down, messed up.

"It's freaking me out, seeing my own mug staring down at me from billboards," Zara replied.

"That is not a mug, sweetheart. If we're going for the drinking vessel analogy, allow me to say yours is a cup of the very finest porcelain." He unfolded his napkin and laid it in his lap, his hand lightly brushing her leg. Her tight skirt had ridden up, and his fingers connected with her black tights. A warm, familiar excitement crept along Harry's veins.

He looked up at her face, wondering if she was feeling it too, and was disappointed when she shifted her chair slightly away from his.

"Mr. Rose," she said, "if you weren't the boss, I'd say that's the cheesiest line I've ever been fed."

Feisty!

"Cheese. Right. You'd be . . . perhaps a wholesome cheddar. Tasty but relatable."

There was no charming blush. Instead she spurted out some of the wine she'd just lifted to her lips.

"And what do you think I would be?" he asked.

"Stilton!" called Terri from across the table. "Moldy and smelly, with visible veins."

There was a sudden hush. Eyes turned nervously to Harry.

"It was just a fucking joke, guys," Terri said. "No offense, Harry."

Not so long ago he would have laughed heartily and found a suitable cheese for Terri. Something laced with listeria, probably. But not today. His leg was aching after a long morning on his feet. Zara Lively, whom he'd personally chosen as the face of Rose Air, was not as expected. Not lively at all. There was no invitation in her feistiness, no answering gleam in her eye.

The silence stretched out, heavy with tension. Terri was still smiling, but there was something in her expression he'd never seen before. A wariness. Trepidation.

"None taken," he said finally.

Harry let himself in the front door. The faint squawk of the TV reached him from beyond the drawing room door as he hung up his coat and reflected on the day. The launch had gone well, and prospects for the airline were good. And yet he felt a strange disappointment, a sense of anticlimax. He recognized it for what it was. Today, for the first time in his life, he'd felt middle-aged. There had been a noticeable age gap between him and the others around the lunch table. Even the pilot had been ten years younger than him. The only other over-forty had been Terri, and—something else new—her customary pretend hate had held a trace of the real thing. What was going on with Terri?

The house still smelled of paint, although the redecorating was almost finished. He shook off the disquiet. *Forget about work.* This was what life was all about. Coming home to a loving wife and daughter, domestic tranquility after the cut and thrust of the rat race. So what if Terri had overstepped the mark, and Zara had failed to respond to his charm. Perhaps Zara wasn't interested in men.

What had he been thinking, anyway? Why could he not simply stay faithful to the woman who loved him, who'd created this lovely home?

(Although, while he tried not to judge Janette's color schemes through Ana's eyes, he had to admit the results weren't quite to his taste.)

He went through to the drawing room and wrapped his wife in a hug.

Later, in bed, he couldn't help thinking about Zara's impenetrable hair and tight skirt as he thrust into Janette. It didn't count if it was only in his mind, did it?

Afterward, he rolled off her with a groan.

"Leg?" said Janette, stroking his arm.

"Yep." He got out of bed. "I'll just go and—"

"Harry, I was thinking, perhaps we need to look at your medication. It doesn't seem to be helping much."

He looked down at her. "You're wrong. It's what keeps me going. But it won't be forever. The physio's getting me there."

Back in bed, she snuggled into his arms. "Harry," she said, "now that the house is all done, I was wondering . . . well, I've always wanted a child. *Your* child, Harry. A brother or sister for Eliza. Wouldn't that be lovely?"

Harry had a sense of time going in circles, replaying itself, over and over.

"I'd love a son," he said, "but let's just see what happens."

How many times had he said those words?

He tossed and turned for a while, his mind racing. Finally he fell asleep, and straight into a nightmare. He was on the pitch of a huge, empty football stadium. There was an unbearable loneliness and a sense of something terrible about to happen. Then out of the tunnel came Ana, dressed in a long white robe with a hood, and she was pointing at him. Blood poured from the finger she held out, and her eyes were dark sockets.

He woke with a terrified cry, feeling the cold sweat drenching his body.

"What is it, Harry?" murmured Janette.

"Nothing. Bad dream."

Janette was right. He needed to do something about the pills.

CHAPTER 40

Harry

October 2006

Harry was having difficulty concentrating on the concepts in front of him, for a new Rose Corp. HQ. But his distraction was for all the right reasons. He had a son. A bloody son! Little Eddie Rose, who'd entered the world with an apologetic whimper following his poor mother's forty-eight-hour labor.

Janette had wanted a home birth, but as the labor dragged on and she became increasingly exhausted, Harry had pleaded with her to transfer to the hospital. She'd asked for more time—another of her "dreams" had been to give birth in a big bed at home. But there were complications, and by the time an ambulance was called, Janette had been past caring where she was.

Finally, to everyone's relief, Eddie had arrived. But the placenta hadn't, and Janette was whipped off to theater to have it removed.

Harry had been left in the delivery room holding the baby, and as he met Eddie's solemn gaze, he felt it again, the sense of having met this little old soul before. "Hello there, old friend," he said.

Harry gave up trying to understand the complicated architectural drawings and sat back in his chair. It was eleven days since Eddie's arrival, and he was running on empty. He'd forgotten what it was like, being a new-parent zombie. He was getting on a bit for all this. Now that he had his longed-for son, he rather hoped this would be it, family-wise.

He yawned and stretched. He should probably take some time off, but these were busy times at Rose. The airline was going from strength to strength, and they'd added new routes to the States in the past year.

To help fund the expansion, Rose Corp. had bought up a number of failing companies, closing them down, laying off the staff, and selling their assets for a tidy profit. It was such easy money it had turned into something of a rampage, especially through the industrial north. Charles had jokingly called it the "dissolution of the factories."

The asset stripping had made Janette uncomfortable—all those jobs lost. She rarely expressed her views on his business, but on this she'd begged him to stop, after a *Panorama* documentary on the effects of a factory closure on a northern town had left her in tears.

Terri, too, had loathed this new direction, and had sneaked a feature into the *Rack* on the union boss who'd organized a well-attended protest march. With the accompanying black-and-white photos of derelict fac-tories and boarded-up local businesses, the piece had made for grim reading, and the media quickly picked up on the fact that plucky, prin-cipled Terri Robbins-More had taken a stand against her own boss, the powerful Harry Rose, who was suddenly losing the goodwill of the Brit-ish public.

Harry had been apoplectic, his bellowed fury reaching every corner of the top floor. Secretaries and receptionists had cowered, but Terri stood her ground. "Someone's got to prod your fucking conscience, Harry," she'd said. "Just read it."

While he didn't give a damn what a few bolshie rabble-rousers thought of him, he cared very much about his public image. And he knew that if he fired Terri, she'd be out there as a loose anti-Harry can-non. He read the article and was moved. He'd wound down the asset stripping and let Terri off with a stern warning.

Meanwhile, TV was doing well, and Rose's sortie into the provision of broadband, now that the market had opened up to competition, was promising. Later this week he'd be meeting with Charles and Andre to discuss streaming football live via the internet. Half of UK homes now had broadband, but the days when most would have the technology to watch live-stream football were still some way off. Years, probably. Harry intended to help make it happen.

Charles still handled many of Andre's millions, but Harry hadn't seen a lot of the Russian lately. Andre had fulfilled his dream of buying a football team. They weren't in the Premier League yet, but at the rate he was buying up the world's elite footballers, it probably wouldn't be long. Mercifully, Andre's obsession was keeping him busy, and Harry saw him only when they were invited to the same functions.

With all this expansion, Harry was overseeing the design of new premises to be built in Southwark. It was early days but, inspired by the Gherkin, he was talking towers with London's most innovative property developers and architects. One had even suggested something in the shape of a rose. Harry liked this idea but was also in favor of being the driving force behind London's tallest tower. It was going to be a tough choice.

His phone rang, and he looked at his watch: five fifteen. Perhaps he'd call it a day. He didn't pick up.

It rang again, and he looked through the open doorway to see Tina, his secretary, pointing at her receiver. "You need to take this, Harry," she called.

There was something in her voice.

He picked up the phone. "Harry Rose."

The woman introduced herself as "Henrietta, the mum of one of Eliza's friends." She explained, her voice shaky, that she'd brought Eliza home after a playdate, and had worried when no one answered the door and they heard the baby crying.

Harry went cold. "Go on."

"Eliza showed me where the spare key was kept, and we went in, and we found Janette unconscious on the floor. She was so dreadfully pale, and . . . oh it was awful, Mr. Rose. The paramedics said she's in . . . they called it postpartum shock. She's in the Royal Free. I'm still here with Eliza and the baby. He needs feeding. I'm not sure what to do."

She was waiting for instructions, but his mind had gone blank.

"Mr. Rose?"

"The Royal Free, you say?"

"That's right. I'm sure she'll be fine now she's there . . . Mr. Rose, we need to feed the baby."

"Just a moment."

He put the phone down on the desk and took some deep breaths. The panic started to recede.

Megan. She'd know what to do.

"I'll call my sister, then come back to you. She lives close."

Five minutes later Harry was on his way to the hospital, and Megan was en route to Primrose Hill, ready to stay over for as long as she was needed.

He sat by Janette's bed, unable to take in what had happened. She was linked up to all manner of beeping machines, drips, and tubes, unconscious, clinging to life, but only just.

The ICU doctor told him it was postpartum sepsis—her body's deadly response to an infection no one knew she had.

Sepsis? People didn't die of that these days, did they?

Apparently they did, but the doctors were doing everything they could.

Harry held her hand, spoke to her softly. He begged her not to leave him. She'd been part of his life for so long, always there, always caring, so kind, bringing him such deep contentment. He'd be lost without her.

He bent his head, resting it on her hand, soaking it with his tears, pleading with her to stay with him, and Eddie, their perfect boy.

Hour after hour he willed it. *Fight, Janette, don't leave us.*

Nurses came and went, checking, monitoring, bringing him cups of tea. At after two in the morning he finally dozed in the chair by her bed, still holding her hand. He'd had no medication since breakfast, no food since lunchtime, no proper sleep for weeks, and now the stress . . . his mind wandered in and out of consciousness, bringing disturbing dreams: shadowy figures in the room, murmured voices, a black silhouette in the corner. Another dark shape, a whisper: "She needs to die."

He jerked awake. It was four thirty in the morning.

Janette lived only one more hour, slipping away as she'd lived her life—quietly, without a fuss.

Harry's heart broke.

"You can't stay here alone," said Megan. "You clearly can't look after yourself."

The kitchen was piled with unwashed dishes and empty bottles. It was disgusting, but Harry couldn't bring himself to care. He'd told the cleaner to stay away, wanting to be by himself.

It had been—how long? Two weeks? He'd lost track of time since Janette died. His children were still at Megan and Charles's, and he hadn't been back to work yet. Alcohol and painkillers had dulled his mind, numbing the hurt to the extent that he was able to function, but only at home. He couldn't face the world.

She was gone. *Gone.* How did a person simply cease to exist?

Janette's parents had organized the funeral, and he'd sleepwalked through it. He could hardly remember giving the eulogy, or the tea and sandwiches afterward.

He was terrified of sleeping. He'd fall into vivid dreams that stayed with him throughout the day. Nightmares inhabited by pale ghosts— Janette, Ana, dead babies.

Paranoia was always lurking. A knock on the door or a ring of the phone could freeze him to the spot, convinced that whoever was there was not of this world.

He had blinding headaches, which handfuls of painkillers only reduced to a dull throb. Plain brown envelopes full of pills would be pushed through the letterbox every few days. Thank heavens for text messaging, though with his shaking fingers, tapping out a request to Andre's contact was a challenge.

"Come and stay with us. I'm worried about you," said Charles. "*Really* worried. Have you looked in the mirror lately?"

Last time he'd done so, he'd seen Ana standing behind him. He hadn't used a mirror since.

"No."

"Darling, you look like a ghost," said Megan. "Please, let us look after you. I know you want to be alone, but you've got to face the world sometime. We can help you."

Harry laid his head on his arms and started to cry. "Why her, Megan? I can't understand. Janette was such a good person. I should have made her go to hospital earlier. I should have—"

"Don't, Harry," said Charles. "It was a terrible thing, but it was no one's fault."

Megan began to cry too. "I don't understand either. The bad things that keep happening to your wives. It's like a curse. Why is fate being so unkind?"

"For fuck's sake, Megan," snapped Charles. "It's not fate, it's bad luck. Harry, you've got to get it together, for Eliza and Eddie's sake. Come back with us and we'll start thinking about how to move forward."

"I don't deserve you two," Harry said, sniffing.

"Course you do, old pal. None of this is your fault. Now go pack a bag."

CHAPTER 41

Harry

January 2007

W hat's that you're playing?" asked Harry, sitting down in an armchair. The deep leather cushion complained with a puff.

Milly and Arabella were on the sofa, both with laptops, discussing the hairstyles of the characters on their screens. Harry wasn't in fact interested in their game, but it was hard to know what to talk about to the younger generation.

The girls were both at college in London, and were here for Charles's birthday weekend. Maria had also now left Wales, and was studying theology at Edinburgh.

On learning of Janette's death, Katie and Cassandra had again offered to look after Eliza, and Eddie too, until Harry could organize a nanny for them. They'd anticipated this would take a week or two, but the little ones had now been gone nearly three months. Yet again, Harry realized how much he took Katie's good nature for granted.

Spending time with Charles's girls today had also made him aware, finally, how much he missed Eliza, and that he should be getting to know his baby son. What had he been doing all these weeks? It was time to bring them home.

"We're playing *Alt Life*," said Milly.

"I've heard of that. Do you design your own character?"

"It's an avatar," said Arabella, without looking up.

"As in the human manifestation of a Hindu deity," said Harry.

"As in someone you create on a computer, duh."

"But that's where the word comes from."

"Whatever."

Megan handed Harry a cup of tea and rolled her eyes at her step-daughter's response. "I'd forgotten what a mine of information you are," she said. "And, girls, don't dismiss Harry as an old fogy. If it wasn't for him, you might not be enjoying that high-speed internet connection. You'd be stuck watching *Ski Sunday*."

Arabella looked up and said, "Oh yeah, I forgot you do internet stuff. Cool! You wanna see, Harry? Hey, we could make you an avatar."

He went over to the sofa, the two girls shuffling along to make space between them. He squeezed in with difficulty. He'd put on weight again, but had been too wrapped up in his grief to do anything about it. The mirror still terrified him, so he'd also stopped shaving and had grown a beard. Terri had told him he looked like Henry VIII.

"Sorry to squash you, girls. I really ought to do something about this old fellow," he said, patting his spare tire.

"Oh, if you need diet advice, we know it all," said Arabella. "You've probably been comfort eating, right?"

"Me and Arabella do that, like, *all* the time," said Milly. "And stress eating. You've got a better excuse than us though. But yeah, might be time to lose a few kilos. Try giving up carbs. Just go for protein and veggies."

"Is cake carbs?"

The girls laughed. "No cake allowed. Or ice cream or biscuits," said Arabella.

"Or Nutella," said Milly.

"So what *can* I have for pudding?"

"An apple."

"Well, I have to say, you two are no fun at all."

"Your avatar can have as much cake as he wants," said Arabella. "Let's create an account for you, then you can play with us when you get home. We're usually online in the evening. It might take your mind off food—like, stop you from eating."

"That's actually a legit good idea," said Milly.

They created Harry's avatar and showed him how to play. He scrambled his surname and called himself Eros03. The tall, good-looking redhead in jeans and a check shirt resembled Harry at twenty.

Arabella grinned at Milly. "He's hot! I would."

The girls made him promise to meet up online that night. Their avatars were called Thing001 and Thing002.

"It was lovely to see you having fun," said Megan as he stood on the doorstep saying goodbye. "It's been a while. Perhaps it's time for Eliza and Eddie to come back."

"You're right, it is."

He waved from the taxi as it set off for St. Katharine Docks. Harry had hated being by himself in the huge, empty Primrose Hill house. Too many ghosts. He'd gone back to the river. Being near the Thames again helped.

The grief wasn't as raw now, but it would still blindside him at unexpected moments: a glimpse of someone who reminded him of her; a scent, a turn of phrase, a TV theme tune, a burst of music. He'd probably never watch another Bond movie in his life.

At least at work he could now hold the grief at bay. And he'd managed to reduce his daily painkillers from too many to count to single figures. He was still taking the sleeping pills, however—no way could he give those up yet. This past week he'd tried, but on the first night had woken several times, his sheets soaked in sweat, overwhelmed by a sense of dread.

Was he fit to look after his children again? Katie had said it would be no trouble to have them for a while longer. She was so saintly, he wouldn't have been surprised to see an actual halo hovering over her head. When she'd collected Eliza and Eddie after the funeral, he wondered for a moment why he'd ever let her go.

But yes, he *was* ready. In fact he was suddenly overwhelmed by the need to see his children again. He'd ask Megan to get in touch with the nanny agency.

Later, he went online and set off as Eros03 to find Milly and Arabella. He couldn't (the game was far more difficult without a youngster by his side), but instead found himself in a virtual tavern drinking virtual beer and chatting up a busty platinum blonde called Chloe0573. She had powerful thighs and a clever way with words, and they arranged to meet at the same time, same place, tomorrow.

After midnight, Harry forgot to take his sleeping pill, but nevertheless fell into a sleep that was deep and dreamless.

"They're all ready for their walk," said Lisa, the new nanny.

"Look, it's the Michelin Man!" said Harry, chucking Eddie under the chin. His little son, so well wrapped up he was practically rigid, gurgled in glee.

"Can I push him, Daddy?" asked Eliza as he maneuvered the buggy through the front door.

"When we get to the park. Thanks, Lisa. We'll be back later this afternoon."

The nanny agency had come up trumps. One of those friendly, fresh-faced Kiwis, that winning combination of laid-back and reliable. As long as she was allowed the occasional weekend off to explore the next on her list of European cities (taking advantage of a generous discount on Rose Air), Lisa was happy to stay home with the children anytime Harry wanted her to. But he wished she wouldn't call his son "Iddie."

"Oh, Harry," she said, "can I have a quick word about Iddie's vaccinations before you go? Mrs. Rose, Katie—I think she and the other lady . . . well, I get the impression they're anti-vaxxers—"

"I'd rather Eddie didn't contract a preventable disease," interrupted Harry. "I'd quite like him to make it to adulthood. Please go ahead, Lisa."

Harry hailed a cab and lifted Eddie in, still secured in the buggy, then strapped in Eliza. Thank heavens for black cabs. Single-handedly folding a buggy while holding a baby was a mighty challenge. Running a huge corporation often seemed simple in comparison to looking after two young children.

At Regent's Park they set off walking through an avenue of bare trees. The weak February sun shone through the branches, and the ground glistened with frost. It was a bitterly cold day, and the children's cheeks and noses were bright pink, their breath emerging as misty ghosts that flew off to play. Eliza seemed oblivious to the cold as she tore after a squirrel, her red boots crunching on the grass.

Harry smiled, watching her. Oh, to be able to live in the moment like that.

When they reached the end of the avenue, he sat down on a bench, parking Eddie beside him. The honk of a seal reached him on the wind, and he had a sudden memory of coming to the zoo with Katie and Maria all those years ago, and bumping into Bennie and Henry. It had been the beginning of the end of his marriage. That little boy would be eighteen or nineteen now. Would he ever show up on Harry's doorstep? What was he like? A sense of loss pushed its way in.

He realized . . . he was taking an interest in the world again, thinking beyond his own pain, his day-to-day existence. He felt like he might be heading back into the light. But if that light was going to shine on him, he needed to take himself in hand, kick the drugs and the whisky. And perhaps he should join a gym. Just this short walk across the park had rendered him breathless.

"Daddy, look at the squirrel!" Eliza gave them a happy wave, and Eddie chortled.

They deserved better than this broken man he'd become.

· · ·

After the children were in bed, Harry served himself only half of the pasta dish Lisa had left him, and poured a glass of water. Later, he logged on to the computer and started looking at property. Eliza and Eddie should have a proper home, with a big garden to run around in. He had a hankering to live in Richmond, somewhere not too far from the river. A sprawling, centuries-old property on the edge of Richmond Park caught his eye. It looked like a Tudor hunting lodge and was gloriously beautiful, with the added bonus of a tennis court and two swimming pools. Somehow it was calling to him. He noted down the details.

He was about to shut down the computer when the *Alt Life* icon caught his eye. He wondered if Milly and Arabella were online. If not, he could always look for Chloe0573. They had clicked on the "friend" thing at the end of the last session.

After a few false starts he managed to locate her, and he lost track of time as they chatted, having virtual dinner together and going out to a nightclub. It was bonkers, but he was having a wonderful evening and—oh, this was weird—he was starting to feel a strong attraction to this animated collection of pixels. Was it her appearance, or her conversation, or a mix of the two?

They walked out of the club into a beautiful night, the trees around them silvered by moonlight. In the distance was the inky silhouette of a towering mountain range. It wasn't the sort of view one would expect from a nightclub. But as Harry was learning, in the virtual world, anything was possible. Swept up in the romance of the moment, he chose Kiss from the dropdown menu. As Eros03 took Chloe0573 in his arms, fireflies flitting around them, Harry had to admit they looked good together.

He was astonished to find it was way past midnight when he logged off. Once again he'd forgotten himself, taken no pills, stayed off the bottle.

That night, the ghosts stayed away.

. . .

Over the following weeks, Eros03 and Chloe0573 met often, and as their online friendship blossomed into something more intimate, the real world began to overlap with the virtual one. But Harry drew a line. He relished the chance to be someone else—a man who wasn't a household name, who didn't come with tragic "dead wife" stories, who was baggage-free. One who could manage without drugs and alcohol. Eros03 was a rewind to an earlier Harry Rose, and he didn't want to come out from behind his avatar. At least, not yet.

Part of him wanted to believe the real Chloe0573 was indeed a strapping blonde with a superior talent for archery. But he was realistic enough to know she was more likely to be Sharon from Wolverhampton with a dull husband and three delinquent children (delinquent because their mother was too busy living another life to look after them properly).

As time went on, Harry was torn. Should he ask her to reveal her true identity, or carry on with the make-believe?

Then, one evening:

Chloe0573: DM me next time?

Eros03: What's DM?

When she explained, he didn't reply straightaway. Did he want to cross that line? In the end, curiosity got the better of him.

Eros03: Sure

Chloe0573: Cool! Look in your inbox!

Sure enough, when he logged on the following evening, there was a message. It was from "Anki."

Hi, Eros! I kinda feel like we're pretty close now, do you?
Don't wanna spoil the magic so just let's share the basics for

starters? I'm Anki and I live in Cleveland, Ohio, USA. I work
as a travel agent. I'd love to know about the real Eros, if you
feel ready to share? I'm gonna take a guess and say you're
not American because of the way you talk. Am I right? Xxx

Not from Wolverhampton, then. American. Anki? It sounded Scandinavian, or German. So maybe she did have white-blond hair and powerful thighs.

Hello there, Anki. You are quite correct, I am from across
the pond. Name of Harry. I live in London and work for
a large corporate. I'm a single dad (recently widowed,
I'm afraid) with three children: one grown-up, one small,
and one extra-small. I love fast cars and playing
tennis.

He didn't mention he was a widower twice over, for fear she might think him neglectful. What had Oscar Wilde said? To lose one parent may be regarded as a misfortune; to lose both looks like carelessness. Anki might make a similar assumption about Harry and his wives.

Oh, Harry, I'm so sorry to hear about your wife, that's very
sad. I'm recently divorced and I have no children. No special
talents, but I'm a reasonable cook. Although I'm a travel
agent, the farthest I've ever been is New York! I'm saving up
to visit Europe, it's always been my dream.

Harry was tempted to send her a ticket to London then and there. He chided himself. Anki wasn't Chloe. She was probably over fifty, large of waist, and loud of voice.

But he gave her the benefit of the doubt. Over the past weeks, via their avatars, they'd developed what felt like a genuine friendship. They shared a similar sense of humor and particularly enjoyed private jokes about some of the other avatars they interacted with. Anki was enormous fun and, he sensed, kind.

He invited Chloe0573 to join him in his new igloo in the Lands of the North.

Eros03: Would you care to snuggle with me under my fur rug? We can watch the northern lights through the strangely transparent ice window above our heads.

Chloe0573: This is cozy! Wouldn't it be amazing to see the real thing?

Eros03: When you've got your real-life ticket, I'll show you the sights of London.

Chloe0573: That would be awesome! I will save every cent.

Eros03: Will I recognize you by your white hair which reminds me of a palomino horse? Will you be wearing the metal-paneled skirt and pointy bra thing?

Chloe0573: You'll have to wait and see! And will you wear your tight blue jeans and check shirt?

Eros03: Sadly too tight. I need to eat less.

Chloe0573: Me too! Oreos are my downfall. Um, how about we swap photos?

Eros03: I will if you will.

Chloe0573: Maybe next time?

Eros03: Maybe.

But it was some time before Harry logged on again. Away from the intensity of the online conversations, and especially when he was in one of his dark moods, he wondered what he'd been thinking. Perhaps she was trying to scam him for money or angling to be an internet bride. Perhaps, somehow, she already knew he was a multimillionaire?

He was also working late most nights. On top of his usual load, plans for the new premises were moving forward. After extensive consultation with his team, he'd gone with the unfurling-rose concept. This was partly because word had reached him of another development, just up the river. At ninety-five stories high, it would be London's tallest tower. Not wanting to get into a phallic battle, Harry had decided his would be something different.

Then there was the matter of his own move. The Richmond Park mansion had been perfect, and he'd be exchanging contracts soon.

Also, he'd joined a gym. It was in Knightsbridge, and membership was so expensive it couldn't possibly fail. A personal trainer called TJ was easing him gently into daily exercise, and the gym's nutritionist was designing a diet that would help him shed the excess weight.

Last, but by no means least, he attempted to go cold turkey on the painkillers. Lisa was away, and he dropped the children for an overnight stay at Megan's, confiding in her as to the reason. She made him promise to phone if it got too difficult.

It was terrifying. He felt like he was dying. He *wanted* to die. It was like the worst case of flu he'd ever had, times ten, combined with suicidal thoughts and the feeling that nothing good would ever happen again.

And the ghosts came back. Black shadows, lurking in corners, behind doors. He could feel their pain, and their menace. Everything was his fault.

It was impossible. The only way to do this would be slowly, one step at a time. With help. He took a handful of painkillers and felt human again.

. . .

England was inching toward summer with the first warm days of the year. The children were in bed, and the balcony doors were open. The hum of voices floated up from the walkway below, mingling with the sound of the Thames softly lapping the sides of the marina.

For the first time in a while Harry clicked on *Alt Life*. A three-week-old message from Anki was waiting for him:

> Hi! Haven't heard from you in a while. I miss you! How's life in London, England?

He found Chloe0573 gardening the vegetable patch outside her log cabin.

> Eros03: Boo! Sorry I didn't answer your message. I've been very busy at work IRL and also moving house soon. How are you?

> Chloe0573: Howdy! I'm still saving! I think I might be able to come to London next year. I hope we can meet up for one of your famous British cups of tea.

> Eros03: That's exciting news! I think we will be the very best of friends.

> Chloe0573: I'm kinda hoping we might be more than friends (oh my gosh I am blushing IRL). I think we have a real connection going on. Hey, Harry, what do you look like? I have fair hair and brown eyes, regular height. I'm twenty-nine years old.

> Eros03: I'm six foot two. My hair is what they call strawberry blond. Eyes of blue. A bit heavier than I should be but working on that. Older than you but still in my prime.

> Chloe0573: So tall! I love a tall man. How about a photo?

> Eros03: Probably beyond my technical skills.

Harry waited while there was a brief pause.

> Chloe0573: Look in your inbox! That's me a little while ago. I'm
> trying to cut down on the junk food too!

Harry clicked on the photo. A pretty girl was standing in front of a
pirate ship, grinning at the camera. He recognized Disneyland. She had
wavy fair hair and was of average build. Just a regular girl. Harry liked
what he saw.

> Eros03: You look wholesome! Like healthy bread.

Anki explained how to attach a photo. He copied an old one from
the internet—in black tie, at some award ceremony, and sent it, hoping
she wouldn't recognize him.

> Eros03: That's me a couple of years ago. I'm a little larger now but
> should be back in trim soon. Also I have a beard now.

> Chloe0573: I love beards!

> Eros03: Excellent news.

> Chloe0573: I have to go now but it's been cool chatting. Good night,
> Harry xxx

> Eros03: Good night, sweetheart xxx

The next time they went online, Anki was on a mission. She hauled him to
her new purple couch, saying, "Let's make out!!" She told him Chloe0573
had done so once before but it had been gross, as the avatar she'd met
turned out to be kinky. There were a lot of those around, she said.

Eros03: Right you are, willing to give it a try.

Afterward, in a DM, he said:

Well, that was weird.

Yeah, but in a good way, right?

They got better at it after a few nights, by virtue of creative language that had Harry's pulse racing. After the fourth time, a red throbbing heart appeared over Chloe0573's head.

Chloe0573: Click on it!

He did as she said: Partnership request!

Eros03: What is this, pray?

Chloe0573: It's a proposal, honey. Will you marry me?

Carried away with the moment, Harry clicked Accept.

Chloe0573: Love you, Eros03! Now you need to go, cuz I got me a wedding to arrange!

CHAPTER 42

Terri

June 2007

As usual, Terri was at her desk an hour before anyone else arrived. It had been this way for sixteen years now, since Harry first lured her to Rose Corp. She relished the silence of the office as she worked her way through the tedious admin. Getting that out of the way meant she could spend more of the day doing the creative stuff.

Sixteen years was a heck of a long time, but she still loved her job, feeling no compulsion to move on. She'd established the *Rack* as the UK's leading current affairs magazine, up there with *Time*, and had no intention of relinquishing the reins.

Over the years, her opinion of Harry Rose had changed. Her initial knee-jerk loathing for the everything-on-a-plate public school boy had given way to respect—for his ability to stay one step ahead in business, and for the way he backed her up no matter how much she upset people. Which was a lot, and often. Eventually, she'd also come to enjoy his company. This was based mostly on the creative insults the pair threw each other's way. It was a fine sport indeed, and along with the mutual respect, a strange affection had grown between them.

Until recently. Of course, it wasn't surprising Harry had changed. The poor bloke had been through hell. First the accident, then losing two wives under tragic circumstances. It would be difficult for anyone to remain positive in the face of life throwing that level of shit at you.

But apart from the heinous asset-stripping episode, she'd never thought of Harry as a bad person.

She couldn't focus on her emails, and sat back in her chair, drumming her fingers on her desk, reflecting on the conversation that had been replaying in her mind in a relentless loop since yesterday.

She'd had lunch with the director of a new ad agency, from which the *Rack* was hoping to secure a healthy spend. She normally left such matters to the sales team, but Percy North had requested a one-on-one meeting.

When she saw him across the restaurant, she remembered—he was Ana's boyfriend before Ana had got together with Harry.

He hadn't changed much. His face was pudgier, but he still wore the same open-faced expression, somewhere between friendly and eager to please.

"Terri, it's been a while. What can I get you?"

"Is that a hearty red? I'll join you in one of those."

Percy seemed in a hurry to get the business part of the conversation out of the way. "Right, that's all good," he said, before they'd even started their meals. "I'll send our media team over."

"Right you are, Percy. Now why do I get the impression that's not the real reason you invited me here?"

He looked at her steadily, his eyes a little watery.

"Out with it, Percy."

"Right. Yep. First, I should mention my current situation, which isn't pretty but relates to everything. I'm getting divorced. The reason my marriage has been such a failure is because I've only ever loved one person, and she was stolen from me by your *fucking* boss."

"Ah."

Percy had an ax to grind, and it soon became clear he'd prefer it to be into Harry's skull. He claimed Harry had engineered Percy's move to Dublin, in some sort of business-for-banishment deal with his agency. With Percy out of the way, Harry had slithered in and seduced his fiancée.

Was it true? That sort of thing wasn't Harry's usual modus operandi. And yet . . . she cast her mind back. Harry had been infatuated with Ana, would have done anything to win her.

Ana.

She'd been the love of Percy's life, and Harry's, surely. And she was Terri's too, though Ana had never been aware of the true nature of her feelings.

Percy wasn't finished. There was a part two. He signaled to the waiter for more wine, his shirtsleeve falling back to reveal a chunky Rolex. He noticed her eyes on it and looked a little proud of himself.

"We use the same law firm as Rose. I met Harry's lawyer, Tom Cranwell. He has absolutely no discretion. Took me remarkably few drinks to loosen his tongue." He flicked back the lock of hair that had fallen across his eyes. The gesture annoyed Terri. The style was dated; his hair was far too long for a man in his forties.

For a moment, Terri appreciated how satisfying it must have been for Harry to whip this man's arse off to Dublin and steal his prize. And she knew why Ana hadn't followed him.

"Really."

"Yup. Cranwell said Ana intended to take Harry to the cleaners when it came to the divorce settlement. Basically didn't care if the bastard was ruined. If she'd been successful, he'd have needed to sell off a huge chunk of the business, and she demanded the two houses too."

"All of which was within the law. So?"

"How bloody convenient she died." He sat back, and there was a moment of triumph as he delivered his punch line. But then the swagger slipped, replaced by pain. He bent down to retrieve his napkin from the floor, and by the time he'd sat up straight again he'd regained his composure.

"Oh, for fuck's sake, Percy," she said. "What's this? Some sort of half-arsed conspiracy theory? She died of blood poisoning, or toxic shock or whatever they call it."

"Look, Terri. You're an investigative journalist. And you were her friend, right? She called you Cruella at first, but she really respected you."

Cruella. The sudden memory was like a dart piercing her heart. Ana had confessed to the nickname after she'd left Rose. They'd had a good laugh about it.

"You might want to check out how unusual that cause of death is, especially for a healthy young woman." He dropped his voice, looked around him. "And you might want to bear in mind that, according to Cranwell, Harry had some pretty dodgy associates at the time. His major investor, who was also a good friend, was a Russian."

Terri let out a bark of laughter. "Oh, so now we're in James Bond Land? Fuck off, Percy. Don't be ridiculous."

He went red and looked around him again. He tried to reiterate his theory, but she cut him off and stood up to leave. This was a stupid conversation, and one she didn't need to have.

Putting aside that it was the crazy ramblings of a bitter man, she just didn't want to prod the wound. Getting over Ana was still a work in progress. There had been no one since.

But now, in the quiet of her office, Terri allowed a chink to open in her mind. She indulged in a spot of what Harry irritatingly called "blue-sky thinking." Baskin-Robbins, who always got her scoop, argued with Terri Robbins-More, friend and unrequited lover of Ana.

She mulled over Percy's description of how Harry had removed him from the scene. What if he was capable of something even darker? Since losing Janette, he'd been moody, liable to lash out at staff in a way he never used to. The atmosphere on the top floor had changed. She'd put the moods down to his recent loss, plus she suspected his leg still pained him.

This new, unpredictable version of Harry Rose was a far cry from the charming man Ana had finally fallen for. But had he been there all along, hidden behind the dazzle?

She pulled her notebook toward her and scribbled: *Ana—coroner/ inquest.* Percy's conspiracy theory was out there, but on one thing he was right—she was an investigative journalist, and she owed it to Ana to make sure a crazy theory was all it was.

Harry

City's uneasy," said Charles as he sat with Harry on the terrace at Celtic Mists Wellness Retreat. "The Yanks have bollocked around with subprime mortgages and it could all blow up in their faces anytime."

"Won't affect you, though?"

"Everyone's nervous. We've started quietly unloading some of our high-risk stuff."

"Talking business? Nuh-uh," said Megan, putting a bottle of champagne and three glasses on the rustic wooden table. She was looking pretty in a simple pale blue dress with a beaded cardigan.

It was Katie's fiftieth birthday celebration, and Eliza had begged Harry to accept the invitation. There weren't many things he refused her, and while he'd protested at first, giving only "Wales" as an excuse, the arm-twisting had eventually worked, especially when Harry had learned Megan and Charles would be going.

Maria, Milly, and Arabella were here, along with a number of relatives and friends Harry hadn't seen in years. He'd brought Lisa along to look after Eddie, who was now staggering around like a little drunken person, hanging on to the legs of chairs and people—he didn't seem to differentiate between the two.

Cassandra wafted about like a cult leader, leaving inspirational quotes in her wake. Harry was finding the sympathetic smiles she kept bestowing on him increasingly irritating. Her partner, Matthew, of brown beard and sinewy limbs, was equally annoying. His whole attitude toward Harry implied, *You may be rich and powerful, but have you achieved inner calm?* Tosser. He kept referring to Cassandra's "old life" as if it had been one huge mistake.

"How do you like Matthew?" said Megan mischievously.

"Feeling a certain affront that I should be succeeded by someone so . . . organic," said Charles.

"From banker to wanker," said Harry.

"Careful, Harry. Such negative energy won't help you achieve inner happiness," said Megan.

"Nice spot, though," said Charles, looking out across the green hills, where inwardly happy sheep were grazing quietly.

"Katie wants a word, Harry," said Megan.

He picked up his glass and went over to where she was standing with Milly and Arabella.

"Eros03!" said Milly, poking him in the ribs.

He grinned. "Hello, Things."

"Eros?" said Katie.

"Don't worry, Hazza, your secret's safe with us," said Arabella, giggling.

"Let's go somewhere more private," said Katie.

She led him to a bench with a Celtic knot carved into the back, overlooking a fishpond.

"How are you, Harry?" she said, turning those kind eyes on him. There were new lines on her face, but none of them traced a frown. It seemed contentment had finally won out over depression.

"Standard answer, or the truth?" said Harry. Why did Katie always make him want to confess things?

"I thought so. I could tell something's troubling you. Anything you tell me is between us, you know that."

"Where to start? I miss Janette, my leg hurts much of the time, I'm dependent on painkillers. And I have trouble sleeping. Bad dreams. Guilt."

"Guilt for what?"

"For . . . just amorphous, nonspecific guilt. For stuffing things up, I guess."

"To err is human, Harry. Everyone makes mistakes."

"I'm sorry, about what happened to us. Especially about the other women. Clearly my twenties were my time of stupid. It was the decade of the blond floozy."

"God is forgiving, remember that. But past transgressions aside, what are you doing about the health side of things?"

"I've got a new leg chap, Dr. Butts. Ongoing physio too. I'm trying to cut down on the painkillers, but it's hard. I've joined a gym. Also hard."

"It sounds like you've turned a corner. How about . . . any new romance?"

"Not unless you count Anki from Cleveland, who I met online and have virtual dinner with a couple of times a week. And sometimes virtual nooky too."

She looked shocked. "Harry, for heaven's sake! That's—"

"Tragic? I know it must seem that way, but the lure of reinventing yourself online and having a relationship based purely on words . . . well, it's liberating, actually."

"I see. I can understand that, I think. Are you going to meet up in real life?"

"Maybe. But not a word."

"My lips are sealed." She took his hand. "Do you ever think back?"

He squeezed it. "All the time. Fate wasn't kind to us, was it?"

"I don't believe in fate, just in God's will."

"I got you something for your birthday." He took a prettily wrapped package from his jacket pocket.

"That's nice of you; you needn't have."

"Open it now; it's kind of personal. It's for . . . well, everything you've been to me. I don't really have the words."

She opened it up and took out a gold cross set with pearls, hanging on a fine chain.

"The chap in Asprey's said it's a copy of one owned by Catherine of Aragon. I thought it was very you," he said as she held it up. It twirled on the end of its chain, catching the sunlight.

"Too old fashioned?" he asked when she remained silent, but when he turned to look at her, he saw the tears running down her face.

A lump formed in his throat. "Hey, sweetheart. Don't cry." He put his arm around her, and she leaned her head on his shoulder. "I'll take it back and swap it for a plasma TV."

She gave a shaky laugh. "Sorry, Harry. It's beautiful. I don't know what to say."

"You deserve it. Have you never had another chap, Katie? I realize the chances are he'd be Welsh, but . . ."

She laughed again. "Stop it, Harry. The Welsh are lovely. But no, no one since you. I don't believe in divorce, if you remember. I made a vow before God. Cassandra doesn't approve of my fidelity—she tried to fix me up with this friend of Matthew's."

Harry snorted. "What does the bearded one actually do here?"

"You're bearded, Harry. I like it, by the way." She sat up and put the cross around her neck, and he did up the clasp for her. The moment of intimacy took him back.

"Yes, but mine is a fashion beard. His is a brown rice beard."

"He runs music therapy classes. Bongos, mainly. And acting therapy. He gets people to argue with each other, it's very purging."

"So people who're stressed because they spend time arguing come to Wales and argue some more?"

"Harry, your cynicism does you no favors. If you really want to be happy again, you need to open your mind a little more. Anyway, what I wanted to discuss with you was Maria. She's applied for lots of jobs, but she hasn't got anywhere."

"Probably terrifies the life out of interviewers," said Harry. Maria had hardly cracked a smile all weekend.

"It's just the way she is. She's a serious person. A deep thinker."

"So you want me to find her a job?"

"That's what I was hoping. I was wondering about an admin position, perhaps?"

"Leave it with me."

. . .

After Christmas, Maria started in Rose's human resources department. Harry offered to buy her a flat, but she took a room in a convent that provided accommodation for Catholic girls.

Harry's New Year resolution was to increase the regularity of his gym visits. At lunchtime on his first day back at work, aware that he was a post-Christmas cliché, he set off for Abs Fab, his Knightsbridge gym.

The club was so exclusive that its members were all already thin. It was more of a maintenance thing. He took to the bench press and began his prescribed number of leg raises. To distract himself from the agony, he surreptitiously watched the other gym goers. He hated the men on principle. The women were mostly beautiful, with their sleek hair, toned limbs, and gentle perspiration.

And their bottoms. He tried not to look, but they were exquisite, displayed in their Lycra, all peachy with only the slightest of wobbles as they moved from machine to machine.

His eye was caught by a particularly fine example perched on an exercise bike, the legs attached to it a blur as they pedaled their way to perfection. He was admiring the way the taut buttocks splayed across the saddle, then tapered up into a tiny waist, when he noticed their owner watching him in the mirror through big blue eyes. She was tiny, with a silvery-blond ponytail, her cheeks rosy from exercise, and Harry found he couldn't look away. This was mostly because she was arrestingly pretty, but also because he thought he'd seen her somewhere before.

He smiled.

The girl regarded him for a moment longer, then returned the smile before slowing down and dismounting. She took her towel, wiped it across the back of her neck, patted the bare skin above her tiny bra top, and then flicked it across her shoulder and walked off toward the changing rooms, glancing sideways at Harry as she passed.

Damn, but she was gorgeous!

Did she know who he was? Undoubtedly. A certain type of woman haunted these places, like spiders in a web. But Harry wasn't against the notion of being lured; it had been a long time. He wasn't on the lookout for another wife, but the prospect of a liaison was appealing.

He felt his spirits lift. He'd forgotten what it was like, the excitement of a new chase.

Over the following weeks, Harry didn't see the petite blonde again. He was disappointed, but it was probably just as well. She'd looked very young and, had he taken up with her, there would no doubt be many a raised eyebrow.

For now, his virtual relationship with his virtual wife would have to do.

In March, he received the news that Anki would be coming to London in May. Her flight was booked, as was a room at the Holiday Inn in Whitechapel.

> Eros03: Whitechapel? Interesting choice of accommodation. May I ask what inspired it?

> Chloe0573: I wanted to be as close to the city as possible!

> Eros03: Ah. The City of London is but a small part of the city of London. You want the city not the City. Just one of the British idiosyncrasies I look forward to enlightening you about. Can you unbook it? I'll find you an alternative.

He organized a suite at the Savoy, on the Rose account. She'd find out soon enough it was only pocket money to him. If things worked out, then the Savoy would be a fine venue for the start of their real-life relationship. If they didn't, then she still deserved a treat.

Anki

The 747 was on its approach to Heathrow, and Anki peered out the window to see the Thames snaking through London, glinting in the early-morning sunlight. She spotted the Houses of Parliament and the London Eye, which Harry had promised to take her on, and there was Windsor Castle! Her dream was about to become reality. Her heart was racing, and her stomach was tied in knots.

She checked her appearance in her hand mirror again. Gee, it was hard to look good after an overnight flight, even if you had been mysteriously upgraded to first class. Her careful blow-dry had lost its bounce and now hung limply around her face, still pale after the long Ohio winter. She pinched her cheeks. Her eyes, dry from the air-conditioning, were sore and a little red.

She tucked her hair behind her ears, then untucked it again. Tried to fluff it out a bit.

Within minutes they were taxiing on the tarmac at Heathrow, then they halted and the seat belt sign went off with a *ping*.

London! She was here.

As she lined up at immigration, her earlier butterflies gave way to sheer panic. What was she doing here? This was crazy. Meeting a man she'd befriended online, hoping their relationship would smoothly transition from virtual to real. Could you ever really know someone without meeting them in the flesh? Harry felt so real to her. He was funny, well mannered, knew so much about everything. He must have traveled a lot; had to be well educated too. Unlike her. Anki the Untraveled. Anki the Badly Educated. In her mind, Harry was somewhere between the avatar she knew—tall, slim, golden-haired—and Hugh Grant. He was going to be horribly disappointed with her.

She wished she'd chosen an avatar closer to her real-life appearance. Harry might be expecting a Scandinavian goddess to sweep through the arrivals doors, whereas she had no waist and no ankles, and her arms always let her down when she went sleeveless. Her hair was more mouse than blond, and she was way older than she'd been in the Disneyland photo.

Maybe she should turn around and catch the next flight home.

"Purpose of visit?"

"Um, vacation. My first time in your wonderful country. I'm so excited!"

The guy didn't even look at her as he handed her passport back.

She carried on to the baggage claim and was soon wheeling her suitcase through to the arrivals area, where hundreds of pairs of eyes scanned her as she proceeded between the barriers.

Harry had told her to look out for a sign with her name on it. And there it was: *Anki from Cleveland.*

Holding it was a tall, broad, bearded man with red-blond hair and piercing blue eyes, which hadn't yet met hers. He was older and heavier than in his photo. Although extremely handsome, he looked a little intimidating, and she wondered whether to pretend she hadn't seen him and walk on by.

Too late. His eyes met hers, and as they did, she saw his disappointment. She was mortified. But after the split-second assessment, he smiled and held out a hand. "Anki?"

"Harry!"

His face was transformed by the smile. And there it was, the glint of mischief she'd known would be there.

"Well, this is strange but fun, wouldn't you say? Welcome to London!"

And there was Harry's online voice, come to life!

"Yes, this is awesomely exciting, Harry! Wow, I'm actually here!"

"Allow me to whisk you away from the hellhole that is Heathrow. Your carriage awaits, as we like to say to our lady visitors."

The "carriage" was a luxurious chauffeur-driven sedan, and on the drive into London, Harry kept up an entertaining patter about Britain, past and present. He was extremely charming and had a lovely voice— oh, that accent!

They drove past some of the sights—Buckingham Palace, the Houses of Parliament and Trafalgar Square—before pulling up outside an expensive-looking hotel.

A liveried doorman helped her out, and she gazed around her, feeling horribly out of place. The Holiday Inn had been intended as a big treat to herself, but this?

"Harry, I can't afford this!" she hissed.

"It's on me," he said. "And no strings, by the way. Just a thank-you for being there for me in the evenings. My life's been a tad difficult recently, and you've helped me with that. You deserve a treat."

She didn't know what to say.

"Mr. Rose, welcome again, sir," said the receptionist. "The porter will show you to your suite."

"Anki, I'm going to pop home now. I thought you might prefer to rest, shower, and all those things. How about I meet you in the bar at six, then we can have dinner, take a walk to see the bright lights?"

"Sounds wonderful, Harry! I can't believe you've done this for me, I'm beyond thrilled."

"Right, well. I'll be off, then."

She watched him walk back to the entrance doors. There was a hint of a limp, and his head was slightly down, like he'd just received sad news.

It was no doubt his reaction to meeting her. Clearly, Harry was well off, and it looked like he was some big shot in London society. While she was plain old Anki, out of the USA for the first time ever. What was a guy like that doing playing *Alt Life*, let alone wanting to meet up with her?

The suite was breathtaking, and she kicked off her shoes and twirled around the room like a princess in a Disney movie.

She tried not to dwell on the fleeting disappointment in Harry's eyes.

What's the problem? I'm in London, with a man who feels like an old friend.

It was going to be great!

If he came back.

Harry

Anki was hideous. No, not hideous, just appallingly ordinary. Lank, mousy hair around a face with no definition, with nothing memorable about it. Watery, pale blue eyes, a tall but shapeless body in Walmart clothes.

Harry's initial dismay had been profound. Then he'd chided himself—how shallow was he? One should never judge a book by its cover. He knew Anki was a good person, kind and fun. So what if she wasn't a Scandinavian goddess?

He'd kept up the chitchat all the way into town. Anki's pleasure at seeing London and the Savoy was gratifying, and he decided to lock his disappointment away and make the most of his time with this unlikely friend.

Now here they were, stepping into their pod on the London Eye, just as she'd been dreaming about, she said. Harry looked down over his city at sunset, the lights twinkling in the dusk, the hum of traffic receding as they climbed higher into the silence. It was quite something, seeing London through the eyes of a first-time visitor.

"It's awesome, Harry," she said as the Houses of Parliament grew smaller below them, along with the barges and pleasure boats on the Thames.

"It is, isn't it?"

He pointed out the dome of St. Paul's, the iconic landmark that had famously watched over London during the Blitz, spared while the city burned around it. Then he was quiet, letting London work its magic on Anki. And on himself. He was aware of the sweep of time as he gazed down over history laid out below, from the few remnants of the Great Fire, through the Regency terraces, the Dickensian pubs and narrow backstreets, the former East End slums, now reborn as London's coolest postcodes. The city's dynamism, always reinventing itself, morphing, evolving, like some giant organic beast, the planners and authorities scurrying in its wake. The pomposity of Whitehall; the palaces, old and new; the churches and cathedrals, spires and domes. The gleaming towers of the City, their windows glinting in the evening sun. The grandfather of them all, the Tower of London, crouched beside Tower Bridge.

He was part of all this. It had made him what he was.

Harry saw Anki three more times before she set off on the coach tour that would use up the rest of her vacation. On her final afternoon, they strolled through St. James's Park.

"I googled you, Harry."

"Ah. The truth will out."

"You never told me you were this super-rich media guy."

"That's the beauty of the internet. Shouldn't have let you find out my surname, I suppose."

"I'm glad I did. You kinda make sense to me more now. I'm sorry you lost two wives. I guess all the money in the world can't make up for that."

"Quite. I haven't come to terms with Janette's death yet. Not sure I ever will. But I have the children, they're always a joy. OK, that's an exaggeration. Two of them are a joy, one's a worry."

She laughed. "Harry, you're a wonderful person. Can we stay friends? Still talk online?"

"Absolutely, sweetheart. Maybe we should desist from . . ."

"Making out?"

"Yes, that. Would seem a bit odd now, don't you think? So, no more hanki-panki with Anki?"

"I agree. Tell you what, I'll unpartner you. Like an online divorce. Then we can just be special friends."

"Perfect." He put a friendly arm around her shoulder. "Every cloud, right, Anki?"

"Quite," Anki said, in a clipped imitation of Harry's voice.

CHAPTER 43

Harry

July 2008

As Harry increased the speed on the treadmill at Abs Fab, he reflected on his conversation the previous evening with Charles. His friend had been distracted, fidgety, pale with worry. He claimed a banking crisis was about to blow that would send shock waves out into the UK economy, probably tipping it back into recession. Time could be up for those banks that didn't ask too many questions about the source of their clients' wealth. Which almost certainly included Charles's.

Harry was instantly sidetracked from his worries about Charles as the petite blonde he hadn't seen since the New Year appeared on the next treadmill along. Yes, it was definitely she of the silvery hair and tiny waist. She looked like the Barbie dolls Eliza had played with before Cassandra had convinced him they led to self-esteem issues.

He tried not to stare as she set off at a gentle pace, her ponytail swinging, and looked instead at his own reflection in the mirror. He was less than fourteen stone now, and the increased exercise had strengthened his bad leg, which had been hurting less. The only health cloud was his reliance on painkillers, which he'd get around to dealing with . . . sometime.

His gaze shifted to the view of the girl's generous bust bouncing up and down in a most delightful way. And . . . again, he was sure he'd seen her before.

He was so busy trying to work out where that might have been that he mistimed his pace and found himself speeding backward, falling off the belt into an undignified heap on the floor.

Barbie hit her emergency stop and rushed to his side. "Hey, are you all right?" she said, touching his arm.

"My pride is most painfully wounded."

She laughed, a sweet, tinkling laugh. "Happened to me when I was starting out. It's Harry, isn't it?"

He stood up. "It is. Have we met before?"

"Yes. Don't you remember?"

"Well, that's the thing. I can't imagine I'd meet you and then forget you. But I just can't place you."

"Annabel's. You and your friend were with the Russian guy. We went back to his place to party, but you went home to wifey."

"Of course!" He remembered now. It must have been eight or nine years ago. "Weren't you related to Ana? My late wife?"

"Yes. I heard she died. That was sad. She had a lot of style. I'm sorry for your loss."

"Thanks." Harry was quiet for a moment. He felt uncomfortable— he didn't like that she'd mentioned Ana and Andre together.

"You must miss her?"

"I do. She was a remarkable woman. I remarried, actually, but Janette died too, of complications after our son was born."

"Holy shit! That's so awful. It's not been a good time for you, then."

"You could say that."

This girl was exquisite; she reminded him of Brigitte Bardot. He told her so, while being aware it was a cheesy line.

"Who?"

"She was a French film star. Absolutely gorgeous."

"Oh, well, that's OK, then!" She was smiling at him in a way that made him slightly reckless. That made him believe he might be ready to take a step along the road to a new romance.

"Do you live round here?" he asked.

"No, I work just up the road, for a PR agency."

Harry rubbed his leg, which he realized was hurting after his fall. "Think I'll call it a day. I might get a bite of lunch in the café before I go back to the office. Fancy a sandwich?"

Ten minutes later, after a speedy blast under the shower, Harry was sitting opposite Caitlyn. She'd reapplied her lip gloss and smelled of something delicious.

"I don't need to ask what *you* do," she said, looking at him with those big blue eyes. "You're famous!"

"Hardly. At least . . ." Harry attempted to think of someone all the girls liked. "Not in a Colin Firth way."

Caitlyn snorted. "My grandma likes him."

"He's older than me, of course." Harry hoped this was correct. "Who on TV do you like, then?"

"The Kardashians."

"Hm. I'm not one for reality TV."

"I just love the family drama. And being real—that makes it more powerful."

"Is it real, though?"

They continued their chat for another half hour; Harry enjoyed batting the young versus not-so-young ball across the net, back and forth.

Then she took him by surprise. "You're a cool guy, Harry. I like you. Wanna go out sometime?"

"What?" he spluttered. "You mean, like . . . a date?"

"Yeah. I asked you once before, but you turned me down. Now you have no wife, so . . . how about it?"

Shouldn't he be the one asking? But her direct approach was rather refreshing.

"Well, why not?"

. . .

"I'm surprised you don't have a boyfriend," said Harry, popping an olive into his mouth. Caitlyn had suggested a Soho tapas bar for their date. It seemed girls preferred less-formal eateries these days.

He had to stop thinking of her as a girl. She was a woman. He had no idea how old she was, but it couldn't be more than thirty.

"I'm *kind* of with someone, but he's not good for me, you know? I'm going to dump him."

"Not good in what way?"

"He doesn't respect me. You know what, Harry? Blokes my age have no idea how to treat a woman. Give me an older man any day, with their nice manners." Her full lips curved into a seductive smile, and she reached across the table to touch Harry's hand.

His reaction caught him off guard. *That* hadn't happened in a while.

But it was hardly surprising. He hadn't been able to take his eyes off her since she'd walked into the bar, causing heads to turn like a Wimbledon crowd watching a Federer ace. She was wearing leather trousers with high-heeled ankle boots, and a lace-up blouse that exposed her shoulders.

And . . . around her neck was a delicate gold chain that twinkled in the light of the candle on the table. The pendant hanging from it had settled in her cleavage. There were no words to describe how badly he wanted to pluck it out, imagining his fingers brushing her breasts.

He cleared his throat. "Well, yes. Your generation doesn't seem as well versed in manners as mine. But when I say 'your generation'—I'm a little intrigued. How old are you, if you don't mind my asking?"

"Twenty-four. Nearly twenty-five. And you?"

"Quite a bit more than that."

She leaned forward, reaching for a mini kebab, and his eyes dipped to see the trapped pendant at closer quarters. He imagined how warm it must feel, lying there against her skin.

"I'll just google your age if you don't tell," she said.

"Cursed internet. Forty-five, then."

"Oh, that's not *old* old. In fact, that's absolutely the best age for a man, I reckon. Look at George Clooney. He gets better looking every year. And you're even more handsome than him."

"I won't deny it. Matinee idol is such a dated look."

She giggled delightfully. He poured them more wine.

They finished their meal and walked out into the warm Soho night. The streets were full of people who'd gone for a quick drink after work and then forgotten to go home. It was one of those seductive mid-summer evenings that did that to you.

"Can we do this again?" he said, putting a hand on her waist to guide her through the throngs.

"Tomorrow?" she said.

He laughed. "Not soon enough."

"Want to come back for a nightcap?"

He was fairly sure she didn't mean only a whisky. "I'd love to, sweetheart, but I have to catch the train to Richmond."

She pulled him by the arm into a doorway. "I thought you said you had a live-in nanny? You gotta live in the moment, Harry. Carpe diem."

"Caitlyn?" He moved in closer, ran his fingers down her arm.

"Yes, Harry," she breathed. She hooked the fingers of one hand between his shirt buttons and pulled him further toward her. He felt her nails on his skin.

"Your necklace."

"What about it?"

"The thing on the end of it . . ."

"It's a topaz."

"It's a stuck topaz."

"Is it?" She went to pull it out of her cleavage, but he grabbed her hand. "No. Let me."

He trailed his fingers slowly down her chest, pressing lightly on the swell of her breasts before sliding them into the cleavage, where they stroked her skin for a moment before plucking out the jewel.

"Jeez, Harry. That was . . . You gotta come home with me, you can't leave me like this."

"Like what?" he said, his voice low, his hand sliding behind her waist. Their bodies met, then their lips.

Harry felt his body come back to life, but after a few seconds gently took her shoulders and pushed her away. "Not here—one never knows when the paparazzi might be lurking. Don't want to be hoist with my own petard."

"Your own what?"

"I should go home, Caitlyn. Yes, I do have a live-in nanny, but I also have two children who expect me to spread Marmite on their toast in the morning."

He registered a fleeting expression on her face; part hurt and part . . . longing?

Then it was gone, replaced by a cheeky smile.

"OK, Dad. I'll let you off this time."

CHAPTER 44

⚊⚊⚋⚋⚊⚊

Caitlyn

I thought those went out yesterday?" said Florence Wells, head of Limelight PR, as she passed Caitlyn's desk. Caitlyn was stuffing face serum samples into courier bags, along with mermaid-shaped invitations to the launch of this breakthrough treatment that contained extract of sustainable sea grass. Or something.

She was ready with her excuse. "Sorry, I slunk off early last night— hot date I needed to get ready for. It was a maximum prep job. Hair, nails, skin buff, the works."

Florence halted. Florence liked to know everything. "Anyone I know?"

The smirk was coming, whether Caitlyn wanted it to or not. "Probably. Harry Rose."

"What! *The* Harry Rose? You're kidding me."

"Nope. We met at the gym. He fell off his treadmill and I picked him up. In both senses of the word, actually."

"But he must be—what? Twenty years older than you?"

"I *so* don't have a problem with that. And he's such a gentleman."

"Gosh," said Florence. "I met him once, years ago." (Florence was of indeterminate age, thanks to a skin clinic close enough for lunchtime Botox sessions.) "He looked like a Greek god. I hear he's made the *Forbes* rich list this year."

"Really?"

"Number eighteen, I believe. Are you seeing him again?"

"*Forbes*-so-lutely! Tonight, actually. I hope."

"Wow, good work, Caitlyn. Um . . . what about Frankie?"

Caitlyn's smile disappeared. "Look, it's one date. I'll worry about Frankie if and when I have to."

Caitlyn went back to stuffing envelopes. It was a good, mindless task, allowing her thoughts to roam free. Yes, it had only been one date, but she was sure Harry's interest was more than a passing fancy. He'd opened up to her over their tapas and had implied he was ready for another relationship after the death of his wife.

Of course, Caitlyn had googled Harry again as soon as she got home, in more depth this time. She'd examined the photos of Harry's three wives with interest. The first one, Katie, was attractive in a classy, understated way. Number two, Ana, was of course a style icon, all sleek raven hair and dark eyes. The third one was a surprise. Sweet faced, but ordinary. Caitlyn would worry about matching up to numbers one and two but figured she'd trounce number three.

She sealed another package and threw it onto the pile. It was early days, but Caitlyn dared to wonder if, this time, things would be different.

Most—no, make that *all*—of Caitlyn's personal relationships, from the day she was born, had been shit. Her drug-addicted mother had died when Caitlyn was five. Unable to cope, her father had sent her to live with her grandmother, an impoverished aristocrat whose life had got stuck in 1967, the summer of love. She lived in a crumbling mansion in what she called an eco-community, but they were just aging hippies and their families.

The children of Chesworth Manor had been left to their own devices, under the guise of raising them in an environment free of constricting boundaries, which included going to school only if they felt like it.

When Caitlyn was thirteen, a rock musician freeloading at the manor had taught Caitlyn the guitar. With her ignorance of societal norms, she hadn't realized it wasn't usual for a music teacher to sit his pupil on his lap and, after gaining her trust, sexually abuse her.

And where Mannox went first, others soon followed.

When they were fourteen, Caitlyn and her friend Storm ran away to London. Caitlyn picked up a little modeling work, which was also her ticket into clubs and B-list social events. Soon, she and Storm were frequently in the company of men who had no idea the girls were underage.

"Coffee, sweetness?"

Caitlyn was brought back into the moment by Anton, her office BFF, perched on her desk holding two takeaway cups.

"Thanks."

"What's up? You were a zillion miles away."

"I was just thinking about all the shitty relationships I've had and wondering if this guy I went out with last night might be a bit less shitty."

"Who! Do tell." Anton was more camp than a scout jamboree.

"Older man, but rich and handsome."

"Is he married?"

"Dead wife—wives. Two dead wives."

"Goodness. Sounds dangerous. Is he an ax murderer?"

She laughed. "It's Harry Rose."

"Oh. My. God." Anton's hands flew to his face. "You went out with Harry Rose? What's he like?"

"Nice. Gentlemanly. I invited him back to my place, but he had to get home to his kids."

"Aw, sweet! I need to know more. Lunch?"

"Sure."

Upmarket establishments like Annabel's had been good hunting grounds for Caitlyn and Storm. Foreigners tended to be more generous than locals, and Storm contributed to the rent by keeping them company.

Caitlyn preferred to stick with the modeling, but sometimes, if Storm hooked up with someone who was on the prowl with a friend, she'd make up the four for extra cash.

The girls were still only fifteen.

Things changed when Storm met Blair O'Connell, a "video producer," who introduced her to crack cocaine. The girls had grown up around people who were often off their faces on drugs, but while Storm followed blindly down that road, Caitlyn held back, her mother's fate forever in the back of her mind.

Blair had moved in without asking. Caitlyn tried to open Storm's eyes but failed. Eventually she gave up and moved out. Her modeling paid enough for the bedsit she found in Shepherd's Bush.

At a photo shoot for a new cosmetics brand, she'd met Limelight PR boss Florence, who, it turned out, had once stayed at the manor, when her feminist mother had run away in a bid to escape male repression. She'd soon returned home, declaring it was more "U-grope-ia than Utopia."

Florence had admired Caitlyn's pluck in making a life for herself and had offered her a trainee position at her agency. It was the first time anyone had praised Caitlyn for anything other than her looks, and she'd blossomed under Florence's encouragement.

Now she was a fully fledged PR executive. The money was good and the people were nice, and she'd been able to afford a one-bedroom flat on Ladbroke Grove. It was all a far cry from the squalor and anarchy of the manor.

The pile was done, and she carried the envelopes out to the front desk.

"Hi, Caitlyn!" said Zed, the dreadlocked receptionist. "I hear you got yourself a sugar daddy. Nice work, girrrl!"

"For god's sake," said Caitlyn, dumping the envelopes on the desk. "Anton?"

"Soul of indiscretion," said Zed.

The automatic doors behind her slid open, and a woman in a green apron walked through them, her neck craned around an enormous bunch of red roses.

"Delivery for Caitlyn Howe," she announced.

"That'd be me. Holy shit!"

"Are they from him?" said Zed.

Caitlyn snatched the envelope off the crinkly plastic, took out the card, and read it.

> *Not getting any work done for thinking of you. Till later,*
> *Harry x.*

"Nice one, doll," said Zed.

Caitlyn took the bouquet into the kitchen and snipped off the packaging. As it fell away she noticed a little pouch attached to one of the stems. Inside was a jeweled red rose on a fine gold chain. Were those real rubies? She stared at it, wondering if Harry did this for all his dates—or was this really the start of something?

She arranged the roses in a vase and put them on her desk. Their heavenly fragrance wafted around as she texted Harry. Thanks for the beautiful roses! Can't wait for 2nite. xxxxx

She noticed a message waiting on her phone. Her heart skipped a beat. It was from Frankie: Manchester sux. Back Sat.

It had been almost two years since she hooked up with Frankie Denham, the baby-faced manager of indie band Chaos. Frankie's pale skin contrasted with his spiky black hair and the enormous brown eyes of a nocturnal animal. But his sweet face belied the manipulative bad boy behind it. On a good day he was a charmer—fun and extravagantly generous. On a bad one he was cold and indifferent.

At least he'd never abused her.

Frankie wasn't a sensible choice of boyfriend, as Florence regularly reminded her. As well as managing the band, he was a small-time drug dealer, although he never touched the stuff himself.

Caitlyn never knew where she stood with Frankie, or how he felt about her. He was often away with the band, then he'd turn up on her doorstep after weeks of silence. And because of a little voice in her head that told her she didn't deserve any better, she let him in.

Her phone pinged. A reply from Harry: How early can you get away? I have a cunning plan.

There was nothing she couldn't get out of. Early as u like!

Harry: Let me know your address, I'll pick you up about 3. Bring overnight bag and posh frock.

CHAPTER 45

Harry

*R*elations between London and Moscow hit a new low yesterday, read Harry as he sat in the waiting room of Dr. Butts's Harley Street rooms.

He folded the newspaper and sat back, thinking. After Charles had shared his worries about the bank's Moscow connections, Harry instructed Rose Corp.'s financial director to flag any Russian investments that could be problematic, should they come under scrutiny from the authorities. Of course, he had one particular investor in mind. If they could buy him out, Harry's conscience might stop prodding him awake in the early hours.

A door in the oak-paneled wall opened and a nurse appeared. "Mr. Rose? Oh, Harry Rose! Fancy that!"

She seemed familiar. Fairish hair, twinkly brown eyes, the trace of a northern accent.

"You don't remember? How about if I say, 'Your special visitor's here, Mr. Rose.'" She tapped the side of her nose.

"Nurse Clare!" Harry rose out of his chair. "How wonderful to see you! How long has it been? Six, seven years? You were a bright spot in those dark days."

"Must be. I've been with Dr. Butts for a while now. Gosh, you were my favorite patient. You always had a friendly word and a joke, even when you were in pain. That was a dreadful injury you had, but the surgeons did a great job."

"They did. I just get the odd twinge now and again."

They stood smiling at each other, until Nurse Clare said, "I'd better stop holding you up—you can go through now."

"Thank you, Nurse Clare."

"Just call me Clare."

"OK, Clare. And I'll do my best to forget you emptied my bedpans and saw me in that bottom-revealing nightgown."

"Let's just say we have a special bond, Mr. Rose."

"So how are we going with the leg?" asked the doctor.

"Pretty good. I'm playing tennis again—life without tennis was a sad affair. Although it does ache afterward."

"Right, well hop up here and let's take a look. And let's have a chat about your latest medical results while we're at it."

"Must we?"

"They're much improved," Butts said, gently bending Harry's leg at the knee. "But the old blood pressure and cholesterol are still too high, and I have one or two other concerns. But don't worry, nothing that can't be fixed with a few of those 'lifestyle changes' they bang on about. Basically means cutting down on the nice stuff, especially the alcohol—I know it's a bore—and upping your healthy eating—even more of a bore."

At least there was no mention of the painkillers.

Afterward, Harry didn't return to the office. He'd blocked off the rest of the day and told Tina he was only to be contacted in case of emergency. This morning he'd driven into town in his DB9. He'd only had it a few months. After the accident he'd bought other cars, afraid of the memories another Aston Martin would bring back, but nothing had compared to the deep-throated roar of his old love.

He set off for Caitlyn's Ladbroke Grove address. He felt young again, heading off in his sports car to pick up a gorgeous blonde for an evening of softly lit romance, followed by . . .

As he paused at a set of traffic lights, engine purring, Harry wondered how this would go. It had been so long—almost two years. There had been no one since Janette.

His head was telling him: *Take it slow. She's a flirtatious girl of questionable morals, and—let's be honest here—she's likely more interested in your millions than in your conversation.*

But his heart—and body—were telling him to throw caution to the winds. Carpe diem, as Caitlyn had said. Outwardly she was sassy, self-confident, in control. But behind all that he thought he'd seen something of a little girl lost. Unexpectedly, Caitlyn had touched his heart.

An hour and a half later, they were driving through the sleepy Oxfordshire village of Great Milton, then pulling up outside the Manoir aux Quat'Saisons, all mellow, sun-warmed brick and tall chimneys.

"This do you?" said Harry, switching off the engine. Immediately the quiet of the English countryside settled over them, broken only by the trill of a skylark somewhere high above.

"Oh my gosh. When you said dinner . . . I'm not sure my table manners are up to this. At my *manoir* it was pretty much use your fingers or something fished out of the sink."

"Then it will be my pleasure to instruct you in which fork to use for your French-foraged field mushrooms."

He'd booked them a suite, and a table in the Michelin-starred restaurant for seven thirty. That was two hours away.

"I'd better hang up my clothes," said Caitlyn. "I can't look crumpled in one of England's poshest restaurants. I still can't believe you brought me here!"

He watched her exploring the room, opening cupboards and the minibar, exclaiming at the fruit and chocolates. As they'd left London behind, the girl-about-town had given way to a young person on an adventure. She was so appealing, her hair in a high ponytail, her trim body dressed in a pink shirt and white jeans.

She looked out at the gardens. "It's so pretty! Shall we take a walk outside?"

He hesitated for a moment. Watching her had stirred him. But he'd waited all this time. What was another half hour or so?

Caitlyn linked her arm through Harry's as they strolled past a bed of delphiniums. "Aren't they beautiful?" she said. "I've never lived any-where with a flower garden."

The calm of the countryside after the buzz of London was soothing. Harry felt himself unwinding, relaxing. They turned a corner and found themselves in a secluded walled garden. Caitlyn stopped and pulled Harry toward her.

"I don't want you to think I expect—"

"Sh," she said. "I know you're a gentleman, Harry."

He moved closer, then stopped. "Caitlyn, I don't think this is the sort of place that encourages snogging in the public areas."

"Then we'd better go in, hadn't we?"

It wasn't terribly successful. Harry was out of practice, and his leg twinged when he put weight on it. Noticing his discomfort, Caitlyn moved so she was on top, but in spite of her breathing his name as she closed her eyes, he doubted she'd found the experience satisfying.

He said as much, as they lay beneath the canopy of the four-poster.

"Can I be honest with you, Harry?"

"Oh dear. Are you about to give me one of those 'could try harder' reports?"

"No. I wanted to tell you . . . there have been quite a few men. I grew up in a place where they believed in free love. That basically meant the men were free to do whatever they wanted to the women. And that wasn't just the grown-up ones."

Harry had been stroking her hair. Released from its ponytail, it was soft, like silk. His hand stopped.

"So you see, my early experiences of men weren't great. Actually, my later ones haven't been great either. Mostly horrible, actually. Now it takes me a lot to trust someone. But I think I trust you, Harry. You're a decent bloke, I can tell."

She looked up at him, her eyes searching his. "Thing is, I know I go on about sexual freedom, but quite honestly I'm not that fussed. I've had so many bad experiences, a lot of the time I actually dread it, you know? So it's no big deal if your performance is below par sometimes. Quite often I'd rather just have a cuddle."

Harry didn't respond straightaway. "I'm good at cuddles," he said eventually. Then, preferring not to delve further into her past just yet, he said, "Anyway, I don't know about you, but I've worked up rather an appetite. And seeing as a table at one of England's finest restaurants is probably right now being laid with a confusing array of cutlery just for us, we should perhaps get ourselves down there."

"Use that one," Harry said, pointing to a small fork.

Caitlyn smiled. "I know, Harry. I'm not quite the street urchin I made myself out to be." She lifted a morsel of food to her mouth. "Oh my god. I have never tasted anything this divine in my *life*."

They were on the third of seven courses, *L'Oeuf*. This one was tiny but perfectly presented. A bit like Caitlyn.

"What even are morel and sabayon?" she said.

"No idea. The fewer words on the menu you understand, the better the restaurant, I always find."

Caitlyn snorted. "You are funny, Harry. I'm having such a lovely time."

He smiled indulgently. He was too. And he didn't mind the eyes surreptitiously turned their way as diners clocked Harry Rose with a stunning blonde young enough to be his daughter. Let them stare. The men would undoubtedly love to be in his shoes, while the women would be whispering about his midlife crisis.

Caitlyn asked him about his work, and Harry, ever looking to identify future trends, asked her what she liked to watch on TV. Her favorite programs were the reality ones, she said, where anyone could become famous just for being themselves. She loved *Britain's Next Top Model*, and *Big Brother*, had even thought about taking part. But the current series were feeling tired. Perhaps Harry should make something new? He should have done *The Apprentice*, she said. "You'd have been much better than Alan Sugar."

Harry sipped his wine thoughtfully. He'd seen Sugar in the UK series and had watched the US version too. He remembered Donald Trump describing reality TV as "for the bottom-feeders of society," before he'd gone on to star in his own series. Hypocrite.

"Hasn't everything already been done, though?" he said. "We've had the boardroom, the *Big Brother* house, the ones where people eat disgusting things on desert islands. What's left? *Britain's Top Accountant*? *MasterPlumber*?"

"I liked that one where the boss had to do the lowest job. It's good seeing people thrown into new situations, watching how they get on with others—it's all about the relationships. That's why the *Kardashians* is so good."

"But you appreciate it's not actually real. Bits of their bodies certainly aren't. Kim's bottom is highly suspect."

"You and your bottoms," said Caitlyn. "I saw you watching mine at the gym."

"I may have been," said Harry, with a wink. "So should I get my team onto it? Devise a quintessentially British reality show starring people who will end up hating each other and having highly watchable rows?"

"Yes! And, Harry, if you do, can I be in it?"

"Why on earth would you want to put yourself through that?"

"Doesn't everyone want to be famous? Even if only for a little while?"

"No."

"Yes."

"Your generation needs help."

They moved on to their fourth course, duck so delicious that Harry let out a little moan with each mouthful. Really, tonight had been a delight. The lively conversation; Caitlyn, looking lush in her red dress, the rose necklace against her creamy skin; the inspired food, outstanding wine . . . if not for his disappointing performance in the bedroom earlier, it would have been perfect. Perhaps later, now that his long sex-fast was behind him, he'd find his way back to his former glory.

Their second attempt was even more of a failure. It was true that Harry was feeling rather full, and had drunk more than his fair share of two bottles of wine, so the thought of an extended session was daunting. Nevertheless, he was full of desire for this lovely young woman, and as he explored her curves, hills, and valleys, his body responded in the expected manner. Until she whispered, "Now, Harry," when all at once something mortifying happened, and Harry found himself in the embarrassing position of having to be encouraged back to full strength.

He lay staring at the canopy, Caitlyn asleep beside him. After the high of the evening, he'd plummeted into despair. What had happened to him? If he couldn't perform properly for a luscious young thing like Caitlyn, did this mean he was forever doomed to bedroom failure?

He was overwhelmed with self-pity at this loss of his former self.

Caitlyn stirred beside him. "Don't worry, Harry," she whispered. "It's quite normal, I hear. You know, in older men. There's always Viagra."

Caitlyn

It had *almost* been true, what she'd told Harry about her take-it-or-leave-it attitude to sex. At least, the part about her taking a while to get over the abuse by Mannox and his successors was true. For the longest time she'd hated anyone touching her but in her first years in London had accepted it was part of the survival deal. She'd got through it by focusing her mind on nice things, like a tropical beach, or playing with a kitten.

When she'd begun to make money and a life for herself, she started to say no. Then one or two of the nicer men she'd dated had made it through the armor, and she felt something, responded in a way that told her this might actually be pleasant, if she worked on suppressing those negative memories.

And then she'd met Frankie, who finally lit her fire.

Could she have both Harry and Frankie? Frankie was bad for her, she knew that. But he had a hold over her she couldn't break. Harry was good for her. She'd felt herself sparkling under his gaze tonight. She knew it wasn't her mind he was attracted to, but he did seem to enjoy her company.

Why? She had no idea. She was no Katie or Ana. Had no education, no particular talent. And she was damaged goods. But perhaps Harry would help her put all that behind her, launch her into a new life of comfort and security—maybe even fame. He'd been pretty interested in the reality TV idea.

She snuggled further into the arms of this man who was so knowledgeable, confident, and worldly. His arms tightened around her, and she felt something new: safe.

CHAPTER 46

Harry

January 2009

You can't beat a real fire, thought Harry, feeding another piece of the dead Christmas tree into the wood-burning stove.

"One more time, Daddy?" said Eddie, from the sofa.

"Really? I'll be saying it in my sleep!"

Harry returned to sit beside his son. On this chilly winter's night, Eddie was snuggled into his fluffy green dressing gown. The pointy white teeth of the dinosaur hood framed his little face, which looked so much like Janette's it tugged at Harry's heart.

> *"The more it snows*
> *Tiddely pom . . ."*

As he read the Winnie-the-Pooh hum, Eddie joined in with the "tiddely poms."

Harry had worked from home that day, as England was in the grip of something that belonged in the Arctic. Or perhaps it was from Russia with love. The Russians were of course in the habit of bringing over things capable of causing paralysis.

Deep snow had caused much of England to grind to a halt, and in the process had transformed the garden and Richmond Park beyond into Narnia. Harry had spent the afternoon making a snowman with the children, and hauling them through the park on the sledge. It had been a carpe diem moment, abandoning the computer for the outdoors and acting like a kid, throwing soft little snowballs at Eddie and proper ones at Eliza, who was deadly accurate with return fire. It was time to get her some top-notch tennis lessons.

When they arrived home, their hands had been numb with cold, and Lisa had made them mugs of hot chocolate to warm them up.

"No marshmallows in mine," Harry had said, patting his tummy, and Eliza reminded him of the time Ana had called him a Tubbybelly.

"You remember that?" Harry had been surprised—she could only have been three or four.

"Yes, I don't remember doing many things with Mummy, but that was the day we went to the pirate-ship park with Chess and Helena."

Harry tended to block any thoughts of Ana that tried to wheedle their way in, but for once he allowed himself to remember. That had been the morning of his accident. They'd been making bacon sandwiches in the Chelsea house, the summer sun streaming in through the French doors.

Harry closed *The House at Pooh Corner*, and his thoughts of Ana. "Right, young stegosaurus. Time for bed."

"I'll take him, Dad," said Eliza, jumping off the armchair where she'd been curled up with her own book.

He experienced a moment's sadness at the new name—he wasn't Daddy anymore. Eliza was growing up so fast, already a mini version of the smart woman who was surely going to blaze a trail through whatever field she chose. In her school reports, her teachers had run out of adjectives to describe her abilities. Mostly they just began, "*Eliza continues to . . .*" alongside the usual bank of As and asterisks.

"Come on, Iddie," she said. Lisa's Kiwi pronunciation had become his nickname.

Eddie slid off the sofa, his slippers making a soft thud on the thick carpet.

Harry switched on the TV, where that night's episode of *Dirty Rascals*, his popular reality TV series, was about to begin.

"Oh, Dad, you're not watching that rubbish again?" Eliza said.

"It's work. I was supposed to be doing that today, remember?"

"Night night, Daddy!" called Eddie.

The news was still on, and it was mostly snow related. The other headline items were as grim as the weather outlook. More soldiers killed in Afghanistan; the government scrabbling to put bank bailout packages together.

Harry had hardly seen Charles recently. His friend had managed to keep his head above water, but the banking sector was in crisis, and the British public was turning on bankers like a bunch of outraged peasants with pitchforks.

The opening credits of *Dirty Rascals* came on. It was set in a castle—it had to be excruciatingly cold in there right now. His team had worked hard to find one they could use for the series, with the requisite features: moat, battlements, ancient working kitchen, garderobes with chutes leading to the pit . . .

Oh yes, the pit. It was already reality TV legend. Pit duty had been the downfall of several contestants, and made for compelling viewing.

After each episode, the public voted one of the contestants "King of the Castle" and another "Dirty Rascal." The king (or queen) got to allocate people to carry out the next day's tasks, while the Dirty Rascal was sent home. Castle jobs included cook, jester, archer, singer, and groom of the stool. Harry had drawn the line at bottom-wiping being part of the latter job description, even though his director had argued for complete authenticity. Instead they'd made it the groom's job to clean out the pit.

Caitlyn was doing well and had rated highly in the voting. However, yesterday's winner—today's queen—had clocked her as a serious opponent and had made her groom of the stool.

Harry knew she'd handle it just fine. She was a clear hit with the audience, and the PR office had been inundated with requests for more background information on the prettiest girl in the competition. Interviews, features, even job offers were stacking up. She'd be thrilled. Which was just as well, as living in a medieval castle, cleaning out sewage pits, and plucking chickens, all the while trying to get on with contestants chosen for the likelihood they'd hate each other, must be tough.

And there she was, dressed in her peasant costume, delicately shoveling the contents of the pit into a pail. She was stiff with cold but, aware of the cameras watching her every move, kept her grim smile in place. She made a lovely peasant. The authenticity of her costume, with its emphasis on laces and frills, was questionable, but she looked charming, and that was the point.

It was three weeks since the final, and Harry was on his way to Caitlyn's flat. She'd reached the final three, achieving the fame she'd hankered after. Harry was relieved she had lost out to the black guy with the big grin and generous spirit who'd won the hearts of Britain. Harry's relationship with Caitlyn was certain to become public soon, and he didn't want to be accused of rigging the result.

She'd been reluctant to invite him over until now, saying she was embarrassed by her flat. Well, if the talent agent she'd just signed with was as good as she seemed, Caitlyn would be able to buy something a lot fancier soon.

He parked up and knocked on the front door, stamping his feet to keep them warm. The weather was still bitterly cold, and Harry was wondering about a couple of weeks in the Caribbean. He'd been toying with the idea of buying somewhere over there, or perhaps a yacht. A recce, maybe. He could take Caitlyn with him.

She opened the door, and he held out the enormous bunch of red roses.

"Aw, thanks, babe!" She was dressed in a fluffy white jumper and jeans tucked into UGG boots, her hair loose around her shoulders. She was the same girl as before, but somehow more sparkly, buffed.

Over spaghetti Bolognese and a bottle of red ("Sorry, Harry, this is the extent of my culinary expertise"), she talked and talked about her plans, the offers she'd had. She looked so happy, he didn't feel inclined to warn her about the downside of fame. She'd find out soon enough.

"Oh, Harry, that was amazing!" said Caitlyn later. "I told you the Viagra would make you a new man."

And it had. Caitlyn's pink cheeks bore testament to his skill.

As he played with her hair, which was spilled across his chest, he was all at once overcome with emotion. She'd restored him, made him feel whole again. Before he could stop the words gathering in the impulse-governed part of his brain, they burst out in glee, saying, "Caitlyn, I love you, and you'd make me the happiest man alive if you became my wife."

The headline in *Hooray!* read: *HARRY ROSE AND HIS QUEEN OF THE CASTLE ANNOUNCE THEIR ENGAGEMENT!*

Harry smiled as he pressed Send on the email, giving Mia the go-ahead to run the piece. He was a happy man. However, thanks to his experience of Ana's divorce demands, he was seeing Tom Cranwell this morning to discuss a prenup. He believed Caitlyn when she said she loved him, but when one was as wealthy as he was, there was room for a little insecurity as to the reasons for that love.

They planned to marry on a Caribbean beach. It had been Caitlyn's idea to combine the search for a property there (perhaps an island) with their wedding—as long as it could still be in *Hooray!*

Mia was sending a team. Caitlyn would have her feature.

Caitlyn

August 2009

Well, as Jane said, 'It is a truth universally acknowledged, that a single man in possession of a good fortune, must be in want of a wife,'" said Florence, spearing kale with her fork. "Although you're probably more of a Lydia Bennet than an Elizabeth."

"What are you talking about?" said Caitlyn.

"Mr. Darcy. Colin F—never mind."

Caitlyn's boss had taken her to lunch to discuss the short list of interviewees they'd drawn up for Caitlyn's replacement. After the wedding, she was leaving to pursue the TV career that had opened up as a result of *Dirty Rascals*.

So far, all they'd discussed was Harry.

"Mister who?"

"I'll get you the DVD. Now look—what are you doing about Frankie?"

"Not this again. I'm onto it."

"But are you?" said Florence. "Darling, things are different now. You can't muck a man like Harry Rose about. Frankie needs to be an ex."

"I haven't seen him in weeks. Just a couple of texts." She didn't add that this was because he was on a tour of the States with Chaos.

Caitlyn had been putting off dealing with Frankie. After she'd finished *Dirty Rascals* he'd turned up, after weeks away, with a bunch of flowers. They were from the corner shop, but it was still a first-ever. He'd stayed for three weeks, coming and going in his usual lodger-with-benefits fashion. During that time he'd tried to convince her he should become her manager, in spite of Chaos's success—he could easily do both.

It had been the first time she'd refused him anything, and there had been major sulks, a couple of explosive rows. But she'd stood her ground.

She'd already made a verbal agreement with a major talent agency. He must understand that was the best thing for her career?

She'd told him how it had all begun, how during the date at the Oxfordshire hotel she'd sold Harry on the idea of the reality TV show.

"He gonna pay you for that?"

"It wasn't actually my idea—just that he should do a reality show. The concept was dreamed up by his team at Rose. They're cool people."

"But it wouldn't have got made without you feeding him the idea, right?"

"I like to think so."

"So he owes you, babe. Don't forget that."

"I thought you'd be more concerned about the fact that I've been sleeping with him, Frankie. I know you said no ties, but don't you mind at all?"

"You don't turn down the chance to be Harry Rose's bitch. Look where it's got you already."

How could someone with such a sweet face say such horrible things?

"I'm not his bitch. God, I hate that word. Look, if he *is* serious, you and me will have to cool things. He's old-school, you know? Won't want to share."

"Yeah, well. It's your body, not his. You get to share it with whoever you want."

"Earth to Caitlyn?" said Florence.

"Sorry. Yes, I will sort it out. It's just . . . I guess it's hard to break up with someone when you've never been properly together. Frankie just comes and goes. He's not really my boyfriend."

"But you still sleep with him."

"Well . . . yes."

"So just tell him, only friends from now on. No one's saying you can never see him again."

"Right. Good plan."

Florence leaned across the table and took Caitlyn's hand. She looked up in surprise. Hard-nosed PR trout Florence wasn't given to displays of affection.

"Caitlyn, when I met you, you were barely surviving. Now you've overcome an abusive background, resisted all sorts of crappy influences, and you're making something of your life. You've started to believe in yourself. And so you should—you're a great girl. Harry could take his pick, but he's chosen you, probably because he's seen the same things in you that I saw."

Was it true? Could Harry really see beyond the buffed, toned facade she worked so hard to maintain, and not be appalled at what lay beneath?

"I think he just likes my arse."

Florence laughed. "OK, well, it is a fine arse. Just promise me you won't do anything to stuff this up. You've got the chance for a stellar career *and* a happy marriage. You shouldn't let Frankie anywhere near your precious arse again. Ever."

CHAPTER 47

Harry

May 2010

Harry smiled as Caitlyn tore around the garden after Eliza, Francesca, and Helena, who were shrieking in delight. Eddie was running around in circles, not quite understanding the rules of the game but enjoying it enormously nonetheless.

It was a lazy Sunday afternoon, and Charles, Megan, and their two girls had come over for a barbecue.

"Fourth time lucky, eh, Harry?" said Charles as Caitlyn deftly sidestepped Helena.

Harry knew Charles and Megan remained unconvinced his marriage was a good idea.

"Fifth, if you count my online spouse Anki, she of the wild white hair and pointy breastplate."

"Honestly," said Megan, shaking her head. "I still don't have a good feeling about this, brother dear. But I hope it works out. You deserve a happy ending."

Out of nowhere, Harry's conscience prodded him. *Do I?*

"I just hope all this fame doesn't change her," Harry said. "She's a sweet thing, and I don't want her ending up like all the other basket cases in TV."

"The kids love her, don't they?" said Charles.

"Hardly surprising," muttered Megan. "She's still practically one herself."

"It's mutual," said Harry. "She's so good with them. It's the first time in her life she's had a proper family, would you believe? Her background would make your eyes water."

Caitlyn glanced over at him, and he smiled fondly.

"You're looking good, Harry," said Megan. "Is that her influence? Salads instead of pies?"

Harry chuckled. "Caitlyn's culinary repertoire consists only of spag Bol. But she's excellent at giving the new housekeeper instructions. Mrs. Downton's a treasure. You should get a Mrs. D."

"We won't be taking on more domestic staff anytime soon," said Charles glumly. "Looks like a banking bonus desert for the foreseeable. And everyone still hates us. We've dropped below drug dealers in the popularity stakes."

Caitlyn threw up her hands and said, "I surrender! And I declare Eddie the King of the Castle!"

"Yay!" said Eddie, throwing his arms around her knees.

Caitlyn

July 2010

Caitlyn's star continued to rise. She was about to take on the role of judge in a new talent-spotting program called *Rock God*. The initial rounds would involve touring the UK auditioning music acts, so she'd be away several nights a week.

The other judges were music producer Leroy Massey and nineties pop sensation Tommy Cultrane. The three were meeting with the production team before it all kicked off next week.

Caitlyn couldn't help but be aware of Tommy beside her—he was still stop-the-bus gorgeous. It would no doubt make the coming months more pleasant, having someone to flirt with, though with the paparazzi taking such an interest in her, she'd have to be on her best behavior. And as if she'd needed reminding, Florence had texted her: Tommy Cultrane!! Could life get any better? Look, but don't touch!

"So we're all good with the schedule, people?" asked Simeon, the producer.

They were.

"Cool. Thanks to our lovely Caitlyn, we have a sweet sponsorship deal with Rose Air, who'll be flying us around the venues. We'll reconvene in Manchester on Monday. Go, Team *Rock God*!"

The gossip started immediately. On the first episode, Tommy openly flirted with Caitlyn. She'd done nothing to encourage him, but that didn't stop the press talking about the "unmistakable chemistry" between them.

Simeon was delighted. Good relationships between the judges were key, he said. It was more about the judges than the bands.

It was a good job Harry was well acquainted with the ways of the British press, thought Caitlyn as she took her seat next to Tommy on the plane. They were heading to Edinburgh for the Scottish leg of the auditions.

She heard the click of a phone camera behind her and glared at the woman who'd just snapped her smiling at Tommy.

"It's just for me," said the woman.

"Can you delete it, please?" said Caitlyn. "I can do a selfie with you instead?"

"A what?"

"Here, give me your phone." Caitlyn took the picture, then deleted the earlier photo.

"Thanks, Caitlyn! I really love you!" said the woman.

People were weird.

She said as much to Tommy as she sat down.

"Yeah, too right," he said.

As his gray-green eyes met hers, something lurched inside her. He was too close. But not close enough.

"They think they know you but they don't," he said, smiling, and more bits of her lurched. "You're so tiny." The famous voice was deep and husky. "Funny how TV always makes people look taller."

"Yes. My husband's six two. I look a bit ridiculous next to him."

"He's a lucky man. Right, I think I'll catch some zeds. God, I hate flying."

"Yeah, it's quite scary, especially when it's bumpy."

"Scary? No, I meant it's boring. You're not scared, are you?"

"Not really, it's just . . . I haven't flown enough to get bored with it. I still get a buzz. I'm that person who looks out of the window."

"You want to swap places? I'm only going to be asleep, you should have the window seat." Tommy stood up and turned around, leaning back against the seat in front of him.

Caitlyn half stood and tried to slide past him, but it was a tight squeeze. She giggled as her nose bumped against his chest, then she moved her hips forward to clear the armrest, and they made contact with his jeans, and then . . . oh.

Seconds passed.

"You all right there?" he said, moving toward the middle.

She felt the friction of his hips against hers.

He looked down at her, his gaze suddenly intense.

She collapsed into the window seat, focusing on doing up her seat belt as her mind raced.

Tommy's leg was pressed against hers. "See you in Edinburgh," he said in a low voice.

. . .

She knocked him back twice, in Edinburgh and Newcastle, before succumbing in Birmingham. It wouldn't matter, would it? Just a bit of fun? It was all part of the not-real-life vibe of being away with this crew.

Confirming her opinion, Tommy breathed, "DCOL—doesn't count on location," into her ear as he nuzzled her neck in her hotel room.

He went back to his own room at five a.m. It had been a wonderful night, sex for its own sake with a pop idol, no strings attached. As Caitlyn thought about the appeal of that, it struck a chord. Wasn't that what the manor had been all about?

Can we ever truly escape our childhood? she thought as she finally gave in to sleep.

Caitlyn compartmentalized her relationships. Harry at Home—lovely, safe Harry. Tommy on Tour—rock god, sex god.

They were careful, but during the fourth week, the producer asked to see the pair privately.

"Guys," he said, shutting the meeting room door behind him. "I'm wondering if you two are about to piss off our major sponsor. Look, a quick bonk, fair enough. DCOL and all that. But is this more than a quick bonk?"

Caitlyn felt herself going red. "I don't know what you mean."

"Don't fuck with me, Caitlyn," said Simeon. "Or him." He jabbed a finger in Tommy's direction.

Tommy shrugged and looked unconcerned.

"The newspaper speculation I can handle," Simeon went on, "but when it starts to have a ring of truth, now *that* I don't like. You need to stop this now. Before Rose finds out."

"It's a fair cop, guv," said Tommy, grinning. "And yeah, probably not sensible. Can't blame me, though, right?"

In that moment, Caitlyn realized how stupid she'd been. She'd risked her career, possibly her marriage, for a fling with a has-been teen idol who didn't give a toss.

"I'm so sorry, Simeon," she said. "You have my word. It stops here. Now."

She went to call Harry. She needed her safe haven to tell her every-thing was going to be all right.

Caitlyn flew back to London that weekend, the first round of auditions complete. Harry picked her up from the airport, and as they chatted en route to Richmond, Caitlyn felt herself unwinding. Harry's reassuring presence calmed her.

"I'm so proud of you," he said. "The things you say when you're judging, they're really insightful. You're by far the best of the three."

"Do you really think so? I do enjoy it. People trying so hard to make it, putting themselves out there. Although . . . I think you were right. Fame is turning out to be a bit of a pain. I hope you didn't see . . . didn't mind. All that stupid stuff the papers were saying?"

"The *Times* doesn't tend to discuss the private lives of celebrity judges. And tabloid chitchat is all bollocks. I've been on the receiving end myself, and wouldn't use it to feed my wood-burning stove."

Arriving home, Eliza and Eddie threw themselves at her, and she hugged them tightly. This feeling of belonging was sublime.

"I've missed you guys so much!" she said. Being a stepmum was the greatest thing, and she couldn't wait to add to this little family with a baby of her own. Maybe they should start trying.

After a cozy family dinner, they had an early night. As Harry took her in his arms, she realized that for the first time in her life, she was properly in love. She'd never be unfaithful to Harry again.

The next morning, the story broke in the *News of the World*. Of course, this wasn't the Rose household's Sunday paper of choice, but Harry's secretary had emailed the piece to Harry, he said as he passed it to Cait-lyn across the breakfast table.

"Tell me what you make of it." He sipped his coffee, watching her carefully.

TOMMY AND CAITLYN—IT'S REALITY ALL RIGHT! There was a photo of the two of them kissing passionately in a corridor. She recognized it as the route up to the stage in Birmingham.

She felt the heat creeping up her neck. "I'm so sorry you had to see that," she whispered. "It was just a kiss. I'm sorry—"

"And the part where the people in the room next to yours could hear you—let me get the words right here—'bonking all night long, it kept us awake'?" His tone was now low, controlled. Furious.

Caitlyn looked again at the sheet of paper. Anything to avoid his eyes.

A hotel maid claimed to have seen Tommy sneaking out of her room, had counted up the empty condom packets: *Five!* That was made up, but as she finally raised her eyes, Harry's expression told her it wasn't worth splitting hairs.

"You've made a *fool* of me," he said, slamming the table with his hand.

Her plate of toast jumped.

"Harry, I love you. It meant nothing!" She was desperate to make him understand. "It's over. I'm so sorry."

His face twisted in contempt. "I'm sorry too—that I ever believed in you. That I thought you might have changed from that little slut I met at Annabel's."

In a flash, his disgust undid all the self-belief she'd built up.

"I *have* changed. So much. Harry, please. It's one stupid mistake."

"Yes, *my* stupid mistake, to think you were more than just another gold digger. Well, you've got what you wanted. You're famous, so now you can fuck right off back to the cesspit you came from. I wish I'd never set eyes on you. Goodbye, Caitlyn." He left the room, and she heard him climbing the stairs before a distant door slammed.

She sat in the kitchen, numb, immobile, staring at the table in front of her. The family cat, Wolsey, jumped onto her lap, and she picked him up and buried her face in his fur, and the tears came.

Eventually she stopped crying. What was she supposed to do?

The children were in the playroom, and Harry was probably shut in his study. She headed upstairs. All along the landing—or the first-floor gallery, as it was properly known—were Rose family portraits. As she passed, she sensed Harry's venerable ancestors looking down on her disapprovingly.

She sat on the edge of their bed, staring into space again. She seemed incapable of thought. Then, her mobile rang. Automatically she answered it.

"Caitlyn?"

"Who is this?" She shouldn't have picked up; it was probably to do with this morning's article. But only a few people had this private number.

"Tom Cranwell, Harry's lawyer."

"Oh, he—"

"I'm speaking on Harry's behalf. He'd like you to leave the house. Pack your bags, take nothing that isn't yours, and that includes any chattels."

Chattels?

"A car will pick you up; I'll give you half an hour. You need to decide where it's going to take you. Then you need to organize a lawyer. As you've established a successful career, thanks to Harry's support, there will be no settlement—and you signed the prenup. However, if you agree not to speak to the press about your private life with Harry, a reasonable fee will be paid under a one-off special agreement. Is that understood?"

Blood was rushing in her ears, her heart was pounding, her palms sweating. How was she even still sitting here? She wanted to curl up on the floor or run through the house screaming. But she couldn't move, her limbs seemed to have disconnected from her brain.

"Caitlyn?"

"Where can I go?"

"That's not Harry's concern. Do you have a friend in town?"

She thought. "No."

"There must be someone?"

"Only my old boss."

"Then I suggest you call him."

"Her. Not all bosses are male, you *wanker*."

Good. A spark. She was feeling something again.

"The car will be there in twenty-five minutes." He hung up.

Caitlyn made a conscious effort to do something, anything, to move this nightmare forward. How could she rewind it to the dream?

Harry. He loved her, she knew that. Surely he'd work through this, give her a second chance. He knew about her messed-up childhood, how she was still learning the rules and boundaries of adult life.

She stood up, took some deep breaths. The study was at the end of the gallery. She opened the bedroom door, walked along until she was standing outside it.

She tapped. "Harry?"

There was no response, so she tried again.

When there was no sound from within, she opened the door.

He was sitting with his back to her, staring at his computer screen, on which was a photo of Caitlyn, Eliza, and Eddie.

"Harry? Please, can we talk? Try and work this out? Let me show you how much I love you. I can't believe how dumb I've been. I'm so—"

"Out."

"*Please*, Harry."

He snapped. Whirling around, he stood up and took three steps toward her, his face twisted in anger. She could tell he'd been crying.

"I should have realized what you were, that first date. *I'll make you feel like a man again, Harry. And all I want in return is fame and fortune.* Then, as soon as the ring's on your finger, you go off and find a *real* man, one who can satisfy you without taking a pill first. And never mind that the dumb husband has kids who already love you—who cares about them? You're damaged goods, you said so yourself. Now get out of my sight."

Tears ran freely down her cheeks as all her walls came tumbling down. She looked up at him, searching for any sign that he still cared for her, minded what he was doing to her. There was none.

She turned and ran back down the gallery, sobbing.

The baggage tag from her honeymoon was still attached to her suitcase. Blinking back the tears, she opened drawers, pulled clothes off hangers, not bothering to fold anything. What was the point?

Where was she actually going?

With shaking hands, she picked up her phone and found Florence's contact details.

"Caitlyn! Hello, love. How's my favorite protégée?"

She couldn't say anything, couldn't get her words out.

"Caitlyn? Are you OK?"

"Have you s-seen the p-paper today?"

"Only the *Sunday Times*. Why, what scurrilous lies are they printing about you now? You know it's all rubbish, you worked in PR, darling. Don't worry, Harry won't believe a word."

"B-but he does, and it's t-true."

"What's true?"

"I s-slept with Tommy Cultrane and it's all over the *News of the World*. H-Harry's kicking me out and I've . . . I've got nowhere to g-go."

There was a moment of silence, then Florence said, "OK. It's best we get you out of the situation, let things calm down. You can come here for a few days."

When Caitlyn hung up, she was calmer. Florence was the closest thing to a mum she'd ever had.

Her phone pinged. A message from Cranwell: Car outside. Say nothing to the press.

She hauled her case downstairs and let herself out the front door. A crowd of baying photographers lay in wait beyond the front hedge. She ducked her head and pushed her way through them.

As the car drew away, she looked back at the beautiful redbrick mansion. There were no faces at the window.

CHAPTER 48

———✦✦✦———

Caitlyn

The press soon lost interest, and Florence helped Caitlyn find a flat to rent. Now that auditions for *Rock God* had been completed, the rest of the series would be filmed in town. It was only one day a week, so she found herself with time on her hands in which to brood on how she'd had everything she'd ever wanted and thrown it away for a fling with a has-been singer. She felt desolate, empty.

A few weeks after Harry kicked her out, she had a text from Frankie. Back from States. Where u living now?

As usual, they picked up where they'd left off. Caitlyn couldn't think of a reason not to. Frankie was like a bag of hot chips on a cold night. He warmed you up but was ultimately bad for you. Plus you felt kind of greasy afterward.

After a week or two, she mentioned the subject of rent. "Frankie, if you want to stay here, that's all good with me. But can you give me some cash? I have to be careful, you know? My agent says my brand's been damaged. And Harry's really powerful in the media. He might do that whole 'She'll never work in this town again' thing. So I have to watch the pennies."

"Bit of a cash-flow situation at the moment, doll. Anyway, if he's going to divorce you, you'll get some loot from that, right?"

"We've only been married five minutes. And I had to sign one of those prenup things. I won't get a cent."

"That sucks. Look, you gave up a good job to marry him. That's got to be worth something."

"I gave up the job to go into TV."

"But the two aren't unconnected, right?"

"He's got a top lawyer, Frankie. I don't even have a lawyer."

Tom Cranwell was moving things along quickly. Divorce papers had already been served on Caitlyn, but she'd done nothing with them. She'd returned none of Tom's calls and had ignored his texts. She knew she'd need to respond sooner or later, but a small part of her still hoped Harry would give her a second chance.

They'd just wrapped up the semifinal of *Rock God*. Tommy was warm and friendly to her, like he was warm and friendly to everyone. He wasn't a bad person, just an amoral one. Like her.

She was in her dressing room when a face from the past appeared around the door. "Caitlyn?"

"Storm? Oh my god, Storm!"

She was beyond happy to see a familiar face, one who knew pre-fame Caitlyn. She leaped up and they hugged, and there were tears on Caitlyn's cheeks—but not on Storm's.

"How did you find me?" she squealed.

"It wasn't difficult, Cates. You're friggin' famous now."

"It's so good to see you! I've had a horrible few weeks, this is the best thing."

"Yeah, I saw it in the paper. Don't blame you—Tommy Cultrane! Remember how we fancied him when we were kids?"

"Yes, but I shouldn't have gone there. My husband's chucked me out."

"He'll come round, though? God, girl, you're only human."

"I don't think so. Hey, let's talk about you instead."

"Sure. Shall we go to your place? Where you living now?"

"Camden. We could grab a bottle of wine?"

Then she remembered last time she'd seen Storm, passed out on the sofa with her loser boyfriend. "Before we go . . ."

"Yeah?"

"You're not with that guy still? Blair?"

"Nah. He died. Overdose. Idiot. I cleaned myself up after that."

"Oh. Shit. Well, thank god it was him and not you. One other thing."

"Yeah?"

"I've got this on-again off-again boyfriend, Frankie. He might be there."

Caitlyn wasn't altogether surprised to discover Storm had just been given notice on her own flat, for breaching the terms of her lease. It seemed the number of "guests" coming and going had raised suspicions, which had in fact been entirely correct. "I'm an escort," she said. "But they called me a prostitute! Bloody cheek. It's not the same thing at all. Half the time I just go along to events with blokes who need a glamorous date."

"And the other half?" asked Caitlyn as they sat on the sofa tucking into pizza.

"Well, a girl's gotta pay the rent somehow," said Storm with a wink. "But I'm choosy. Don't go with no mingers."

There was the sound of the key in the lock. Frankie was back.

"Well, hello," he said. "And who's this?"

"This is Storm, the girl I ran away from home with!"

"For real?"

Storm sat up straighter, flicking back her long hair. "And you're Frankie? So are you on again or off again at the moment?"

"Caitlyn upped and married some rich geezer, but I'm the one she really wants." He came over and planted a lingering kiss on her lips, but she noticed him watching Storm. "So would you be the friend she used to go on the game with? Gotta confess, I get frisky thinking about that."

"I didn't!" said Caitlyn. "I just . . . Guys used to buy us drinks, maybe give us a bit of cash, but it was us calling the shots, right, Storm?"

"Can't remember, to be honest. Was off my face most of the time."

"You a user?" said Frankie, helping himself to pizza.

"Strictly special occasions only, now."

"Frankie . . ." said Caitlyn, her voice loaded with warning.

He shrugged. "Never touch the stuff myself."

Storm stayed. Frankie stayed. They were a pair of parasites. The joy of seeing an old friend was soon overtaken by the realization that Storm hadn't changed, was still happy to live off Caitlyn while giving absolutely nothing in return.

The final of *Rock God* was a ratings blockbuster, and Caitlyn was signed up for the next series. In the meantime there were media interviews and advertising contracts, so she wouldn't have to worry about money.

But it wasn't financial security she wanted. She ached for what she'd lost. She'd felt wrapped in love, and now that blanket had been whipped away, leaving her cold, exposed.

Another letter from Tom Cranwell arrived. This time there were all sorts of legal threats she didn't understand. In fact, she didn't know some of the bigger, more complicated words—she'd never properly learned to read and write. Florence had taught her, kindly and patiently, so that she'd be able to do her job properly, but she still struggled at times.

Caitlyn found herself crying again as she thought back to how hard she'd strived and how Florence had believed in her. Even Harry had, for a while.

She hadn't been worth their efforts. Good people wasting time on bad.

When she'd calmed down, she showed the letter to Storm.

"You can't let him do this to you, babe. He owes you!" she said. "A man that rich wants a divorce, he pays the price."

Caitlyn explained about the prenup again.

"He's being a dick," said Frankie from across the room, where he was sitting sideways in an armchair, swigging beer from a bottle. "You be a bitch back. C'mon, Cates, it's time to get dirty. What you got on him?"

"What do you mean? He's as straight as they come. He hadn't slept with anyone since his last wife died."

"I met him, remember?" said Storm suddenly. "God, I'd forgotten all about it! That night at that Russian dude's place."

"Oh yes!" said Caitlyn. "Wow, that was so long ago. How old were we?"

"Can't have been more than fifteen. Maybe even fourteen," said Storm.

"Did you shag him?" asked Frankie.

"No," said Caitlyn. "He wasn't like that. Like I said, he's a good bloke."

"What was he doing partying with two fourteen-year-olds, then?" said Frankie.

"He and his mate were with that Russian guy, the one with the football team," said Storm. "He seemed to be calling the shots."

"Seriously? Andre Sokolov? Jesus, you two moved in powerful circles. Pity you didn't bonk Harry, Caitlyn. Could've done an exposé. Harry Rose, pillar of British society and shagger of underage schoolgirls."

"Who's to know he didn't?" said Storm.

"Can we just stop this?" said Caitlyn. "I like how Harry turned me down, even though he'd never have dreamed I was underage."

"Wait," said Storm. She disappeared off to the spare bedroom, where her belongings were sprayed all over the floor, and returned with a plastic bag. She emptied it onto the table.

"What's this?" asked Caitlyn.

"My photo collection. The sum total of my crappy life, in a crappy carrier bag. There are some of the manor—look." She passed one to Caitlyn.

The manor kids. Dirty, feral children, grinning at the camera. Caitlyn saw herself and shuddered, quickly threw the photo back on the table. This was nothing she wanted to remember.

"Here we are." Storm passed another photo over.

Her heart lurched. "Oh my god, I remember this."

In the foreground was Andre Sokolov, the brunette he'd picked up sitting on his lap. Behind them, Harry had just kissed Caitlyn's hand, which he was holding close to his lips.

She remembered the moment. She'd just offered herself to him—her self-esteem still needed work back then—and he'd turned her down, saying he was happily married. But he'd done it so charmingly that it hadn't felt like a rebuff at all.

To someone who was none the wiser, however, the picture would show Harry Rose looking intimate with a teenage girl.

"Give it here," said Frankie. As he studied the photo, his smile widened. "Fourteen? Fifteen? Defo not sixteen?"

"Fifteen max," said Storm.

"Well, I'm reckoning the press will be very interested in this," said Frankie. "Proof that Harry Rose likes underage girls."

"But he didn't!" said Caitlyn emphatically. "He never even so much as kissed me!"

"That kind of detail we don't need," he said. "Do you want a divorce settlement, or don't you?"

Caitlyn was on her way to meet her agent, Patti, who wanted to know the terms of her "special agreement" with Harry. The one that said she would get a lump sum in return for remaining private about her marriage. The terms were in one of the incomprehensible documents Tom Cranwell had sent through, and rather than try to interpret them herself, Caitlyn had decided to show them to Patti, who was champing at the bit, wanting to negotiate a tell-all with a magazine.

The taxi was halfway there when a text came through. Caitlyn was startled to read Harry's name on the screen. Her hands began to shake as she opened up the message.

Pls come to Rose offices. We need to talk. Today?

It was as if someone had unblocked a main artery—she felt a warm glow spreading through her body. *Harry wants to talk.*

She allowed the idea of a reconciliation to sidle in. Since the split she'd been attempting to shut down her feelings for Harry, as the loss of his love was too painful. Now they surged back.

She replied: Can be there in an hour.

He responded immediately: See you at 2.

She gave the taxi her home address—she wanted to change into something more appealing—then rang Patti to postpone.

She let herself in and went straight to her bedroom. As she peeled off her jeans and jumper, she registered a rhythmic noise coming from the far side of her bedroom wall.

She grew still, listening. The sounds were unmistakable. It was nauseating, but why would she be surprised?

Caitlyn marched out of her bedroom and threw open the spareroom door. Frankie and Storm were naked on the bed. Storm's eyes were open, and she was watching his face. Her own was bored. As she noticed Caitlyn, she smiled. "Frankie, you might wanna stop."

Frankie met Caitlyn's eyes, but he didn't stop. "Hey, beautiful, you're back. Wanna join in? Plenty here for two."

Caitlyn backed out of the room, then rushed to the bathroom and threw up, again and again, until she was dry retching.

Five minutes later she was dressed and out of the house, looking for a taxi, sipping from a water bottle to try to rid herself of the foul taste.

She must focus on Harry. Maybe she'd soon be out of that "cesspit," as he'd called it, and back in the beautiful Richmond house, with her lovely family. If only Harry would give her a second chance.

As Caitlyn approached the reception desk at Rose Corp. HQ, she could feel the eyes on her. She was recognized everywhere she went now, but here the vibe was different. She was the cheating wife of their beloved king.

"I'm here to see Harry Rose," she said to the receptionist, who was all tailored jacket and nice nails.

"Who shall I say is here?"

The woman definitely knew who she was.

"His wife."

The receptionist's eyes held hers for longer than was necessary, before she picked up the phone. "Tina, Mrs. Rose is here to see Harry." There was a pause. "Yes, Caitlyn Howe." She replaced the receiver. "Harry's secretary will be down shortly."

She was kept waiting for fifteen minutes, during which time those passing by did a double take, then pretended they hadn't.

"Caitlyn."

"Hello, Tina. How are you?"

"This way, please." Harry's secretary set off toward the lifts, her heels tap-tapping on the polished marble. The sound seemed loaded with disapproval.

As they waited, more people joined them—it was the end of lunch-time, and staff were returning to their offices. She felt their eyes on her, and kept hers on the descending numbers above the lift.

Finally it arrived and she moved inside, turned around.

Entering the lift was a small, stern-faced young woman. Out of the corner of her eye, Caitlyn saw the double take.

"You!" The voice was gruff, cross.

Caitlyn turned slightly and registered the disgusted expression on the woman's face.

"You've got a cheek, showing your face here. What sort of a woman are you? You—"

"Shut the fuck up, Maria," said another woman, dressed all in black, her red lipstick contrasting with her pale skin and dark hair.

Someone at the back of the lift snorted.

Caitlyn stared straight ahead but could feel the first woman's eyes boring into her.

"You were never really married to him, you know. He's still married to my mother in the eyes of God."

Caitlyn turned in surprise. Now she remembered Harry saying his eldest daughter worked at Rose. "Maria?"

The lift doors opened, and Maria strode out without a backward glance.

"Take no notice, she's a nutter," said the woman in black. "I'm Terri, editor of the *Rack*. I'd love to interview you, Caitlyn, but that probably wouldn't sit too well with him upstairs. When it's all calmed the fuck down, I'll buy you lunch."

The lift stopped twice more, and then only the three of them were left.

"You messed up, but who doesn't?" said Terri. "Let's just say our Harry's not exactly whiter than white when it comes to fidelity in marriage. A certain stench of hypocrisy. This is my floor. Here, take my card. Call me sometime."

The doors opened, letting in a burst of sound from the offices beyond, before shutting again.

The carpets on the top floor were thicker, the secretaries shinier. There was a reception desk with an elaborate display of red roses.

"Wait here," said Tina, and then she left.

A woman with enormous eyes and a long plait said, "Can I help you?"

"I'm here to see Mr. Rose."

"Please take a seat. Can I get you a coffee?"

At least this one wasn't hating on her. "I'd like a glass of water, please." She could still taste the bile.

She picked up a copy of *Hooray!* but put it down again, as her hands were visibly shaking. *Breathe*, she told herself. *It's Harry you're seeing. Kind, safe Harry. Your husband.*

The receptionist handed over the water. "Follow me, please."

She led her to a meeting room, and Caitlyn's stomach twisted as she spotted Harry, standing behind a man with slicked-back dark hair seated at a long table.

Harry only glanced at her before taking a seat beside the other man. Then he fixed his gaze out of the window, his expression stony.

Caitlyn's heart plummeted.

"Do sit down," said the man. "I'm Tom Cranwell." He didn't offer his hand.

Wordlessly, she took a seat opposite them.

"Harry?" said Tom.

"Deal with it, Tom," he said, still looking out the window.

"Right. Caitlyn, I assume you know why you're here?"

"I . . . I thought Harry might be willing to give me another chance?" She looked over at him, but he didn't move his head. "Harry?"

"Now why would you think that," said Tom, "when you're attempting to blackmail my client?"

Her gaze snapped back to Tom. "Blackmail? What do you mean?"

The men were silent.

"You mean the lump-sum thing? I thought *you* were going to say how much that was. It was your idea."

"The lump sum was, yes. And I assume this latest demand is the brainchild of your boyfriend, Mr. . . . ." He looked down at the papers in front of him. "Denham."

Caitlyn went cold. "Frankie? He's got nothing to do with anything. Frankie's history."

"If he's your ex, why is he asking for a ludicrous sum of money on your behalf?"

"I don't know what you're talking about."

"Ms. Howe, please don't play the innocent."

He fished something out of the pile and pushed it across the table to her. It was the photograph, attached to a typed sheet of paper.

She looked at it, confused, then up at Tom. "I don't know anything about this."

"I don't believe you."

She picked it up and read:

> £250,000 in used notes. Deliver by hand to
> 54A Brick Hill Road, Camden at 11 a.m. on
> Wednesday 3 December. If it doesn't happen,
> copies of this photo will be sent to the press with a
> statement from Caitlyn Howe to the effect that she
> was fifteen when she first had sex with Harry
> Rose, in 1999. There are witnesses who will
> confirm this.

It took her a while to process the words. Eventually she looked up at Tom and said, "I know nothing about this. You have to believe me. It's Frankie; he saw the photo. It was his idea, I never agreed to it. And anyway, it's not true. We didn't have sex that night."

"You say it was his idea. So you knew about it," said Tom.

"Yes, but like I said—"

"Why should we believe anything you say, Ms. Howe? We know you're a liar. That is your current address?"

Caitlyn couldn't think straight. How could Frankie have done this without her knowledge? She squeezed her eyes shut, took some deep breaths.

"This Mr. . . . Denham. You've known him how long?"

She opened her eyes again, felt tears pricking at the backs of them. "Three or four years? And only occasionally—he's away a lot."

"What is his profession?"

"He manages a band. Chaos."

"Apt," said Harry. "Inspired by your life?"

It was a relief to hear his voice. It gave her courage to speak up.

"Harry, you know I'd never do something like this. I've split up with Frankie. I can't stand him. He's a parasite. I've been trying to get him to leave, but—"

"Caitlyn, I have no interest in your grubby little life." As he finally met her eyes, she saw the wounded bear within. She wanted to reach out, to comfort, to try once more to explain. But as she went to stand, he said, his voice cold with suppressed rage, "I'm going to leave now. Tom will be telling you that unless *Rock God* replaces you immediately, Rose Air will be canceling their sponsorship."

He headed toward the door. "And as you know, Rose Corp.'s influence in the media is not insubstantial. Therefore don't be surprised if work dries up for you."

He stopped, his hand on the door handle. The wounded bear was gone, and now there was only contempt. "Honest to god," he said, "I don't know what I was thinking, marrying you. And you can tell your low-life boyfriend that if he even *thinks* about sharing that photo with the media, not only will I know about it and stop publication, but the Russian gentleman in the photograph, who likes to keep strict control over his image, would be only too pleased to make sure that one of Mr. Denham's small-time drug deals goes horribly wrong. Deaths in that line of work are of course only too common."

Caitlyn felt the blood drain from her face. "Harry, you have to listen to me, please!"

But he was already walking out the door.

"HARRY!" she shouted, losing control. She started to cry.

"Ms. Howe, calm yourself," said Tom. "Let's get this cleared up so we can all get on with our lives, hm?"

She turned on him. "I'm telling you, I had nothing to do with this. You're a lawyer. Aren't you supposed to defend people until they're proved guilty or something?" She swiped the tears from her cheeks.

"Not *quite* how it works." His smug smile made her want to slap him.

He walked around the table and came to stand behind her. "Now look. If you tell Mr. Denham to drop his demands, we'll take no further action. I suggest you hurry along and meet up with your agent to see what you can salvage of your career. Although, if you take my advice, you'll start retraining in some other field. Something like . . . let's see. Pole dancing?"

She stood up, making an effort to stop the tears, not wanting to give him the satisfaction.

Tom didn't move, looming over her. She could hear him breathing.

"Oh, and don't forget to sign those papers," he said. "Otherwise you'll find yourself in court."

She went to head for the door, but he didn't move aside. She looked up into his face. He licked his lips. His breathing was heavier. He raised his right hand and touched her arm, stroked it.

"Come, come, Caitlyn. It's just a divorce. You're young and you're . . ." His eyes traveled to her chest. "*Very* sexy. You'll find some other sugar daddy. In the meantime, perhaps *I* can help you."

She shrugged off his pudgy fingers. "Excuse me, I'd like to go now."

"Of course," he said, his voice smooth. He finally moved aside, and as she walked past him, she felt his hand on her behind. He patted it, then squeezed it. "I can see why Harry enjoyed you," he said. "Good luck."

Caitlyn let herself back into the flat. There was no one home. The silence was overwhelming. The emptiness of it all.

Harry had been right. Her "grubby little life" was sordid and the flat reflected that, strewn with dirty plates and takeaway cartons; smeared glasses with brown and yellow dregs in the bottom, and a smell of something gone sour. Storm and Frankie had dragged her down, and she no longer had the strength or energy to kick against them. What was the point?

She sank onto the arm of the couch and fished out her phone, tapping out Florence's number.

No reply.

She was alone in the world. She had no one. She was nothing.

She had to get away, couldn't face seeing Frankie after what he'd done. She grabbed her bag and left, hailing a cab and giving the driver Florence's Stockwell address.

She redialed, and this time Florence answered. Briefly Caitlyn explained—she'd had a bust-up with Frankie and needed a few days to get her head together. Could she stay again?

"How many times have I told you, Caitlyn?" Florence's voice was exasperated. "You've gotta kick him out. It's *your* flat, not his. Get rid. Now."

"I will, but I need to get myself together first. I've had a terrible day, I really need to talk to you about it."

"It's not a good time, Caitlyn. We have people coming round for dinner—one's a prospective client. Look, call me tomorrow."

"Florence, please, I—"

"Not now. Sorry, I really have to go. Take care." She hung up.

Caitlyn leaned her head back and closed her eyes. For a few minutes she didn't move. Finally she opened them and saw they were crossing the Thames. It was already dark, the lights of London reflected in the inky blackness below.

Caitlyn asked the cabdriver to pull over.

"What, here, love?"

"Yes. I've changed my mind. I'll walk to the station and take the train back."

"I voted for you in that castle thing," he said. "What you up to now?"

She paid him. "Nothing. Nothing at all. Keep the change."

"Resting, eh? Well, good luck."

Caitlyn stood staring over the parapet of Waterloo Bridge, her coat hood pulled up against the cold. All around her people were hurrying home, to their families, wives, flatmates.

Dirty old river . . . people so busy . . . The old Kinks song was one of her favorites.

London. It had sucked her in, made her a queen, then chewed her up and spat her out. Florence had been wrong—she wasn't a survivor.

She waited until the crowds thinned, before climbing over, letting go.

—◦◦◦—

CHAPTER 49

Harry

The top floor was abuzz with preparations for that night's reception. Caterers were setting up tables, the PR people were arranging information packs and name badges.

Plans for the new Rose building had finally been signed off. Harry was peeved that the Shard just up the riverbank had a head start, but they weren't far behind.

The building would be shaped like an unfurling rose, with the outer petals open to the sky. Inside, offices would radiate out from a central atrium where light would flood down to a rose garden. Rose Corp. would occupy roughly a quarter of the office space, and there would be public areas—a café with sweeping views of the Thames, and an art gallery. A scale model would be the centerpiece of tonight's function.

Harry slammed his office door against the noise. He should have been looking forward to tonight—he was creating a legacy for himself and an icon for his beloved city. But yet again, a woman was messing with his head.

He tried to focus on the spreadsheet in front of him, but Caitlyn's face pushed its way into his mind again. He couldn't forget the look in her eyes, how the hope in them had turned to anguish as he'd blanked her.

She'd walked into the boardroom looking like a little girl lost. The sparkle of recent months had faded, revealing the vulnerable girl beneath. And when he'd realized she thought there might be a reconciliation, he'd bled inside. The children were missing her terribly. As was he.

But the blackmail attempt by her "ex" had confirmed the truth—that he'd been taken for a ride. Caitlyn's betrayals had made him feel like a middle-aged fool.

He'd needed to mine that fury to remain strong yesterday. There could be no way back for them.

Harry was hurting badly, inside and out. He couldn't sleep from the stress of it all, and his leg was playing up. He'd upped the pills again. Pills to sleep, pills to stop the hurting, pills to perform in bed, pills simply to function. How was he ever supposed to give them up?

His phone buzzed. He ignored it. He'd told Tina he didn't want to be disturbed—what part of that was so hard to understand?

It buzzed again.

He slammed his hand on his desk and looked up, ready to mime slitting his throat. But through the doors he saw two police officers.

For god's sake. Could Cranwell not deal with the whole blackmail issue without dragging him into it? He paid the man enough.

There was a tap on the door. He ignored it, but it opened and Tina's face peered around. "Sorry to disturb you, Harry. The police would like a word."

"Can't someone else talk to them?" he snapped.

"Sorry, they say it needs to be you."

She showed them in and left the room.

He didn't offer them a seat. "I take it this is about Caitlyn and her . . . associate?"

"I'm afraid it does concern your wife, Mr. Rose," said the male officer. "But there's no one else involved, as far as we know." He looked at the female officer.

"Mr. Rose," she began, "I'm very sorry to tell you that a body was found in the Thames this morning. We believe it's your wife."

Pain shot through his leg. "In the Thames? What do you mean, a body?"

As the officer's words sunk in, the room seemed to tilt.

"I'm sorry, Mr. Rose. She'd been dead several hours by the time she was found."

The policewoman's voice seemed to be coming from far away.

"Early indications are that she jumped from a bridge. We'll be able to give you more information when our investigation is properly under-way. We'll need you to formally identify her. As her next of kin—"

"We're . . . we were separated. Getting divorced."

"There doesn't appear to be anyone else we can ask, Mr. Rose."

She looked so young; a pale, sleeping girl, and Harry's heart broke all over again. How alone must she have felt? His conscience whispered terrible things. He shut out the voice, but he couldn't stop the tears.

That night, in the restless half sleep before the pain woke him, the ghosts came back, and he knew that, this time, they wanted revenge.

WHY DID CAITLYN JUMP? screamed the headlines. Her bubbly per-sonality had won her many fans, and opinion columns were full of spec-ulation as to why someone so full of life could have wanted to end it all. Was it her split with Harry that had pushed her over the edge?

Harry went to ground, working from home. When Eliza quizzed him, he tried to fudge the truth about Caitlyn's death, but she was thir-teen now, and it was impossible. Her stepmother's death was the hottest topic of gossip at school.

Once again, Eliza astonished him with her insight and maturity. "People who really want to be famous are usually insecure, Dad," she said. "I bet she had an unhappy childhood."

For a moment he couldn't speak, remembering what Caitlyn had told him. "She did," he said finally, giving her a hug. "When did you get to be so wise?"

"I was sad for some of my childhood too. I missed Mum, and it was horrible that she died. Then Janette died too. But I always had you, so I don't feel like I want to be famous. Poor Caitlyn, I liked her a lot."

Harry left the funeral arrangements to Cranwell, instructing him to make it small and discreet. No colleagues from *Rock God* or *Dirty Rascals*. He couldn't stomach the thought of actor tears.

The police managed to track down Caitlyn's father, Howie. Harry remembered her describing him as a "waste of space," always broke, begging for handouts from relatives, and giving "precisely zero amounts of shit" about his children. Eventually he'd moved to Thailand to avoid his creditors.

One didn't have to be Poirot to work out what had brought him home. When Howie pleaded insufficient funds for a plane ticket, Cranwell had wired him the money plus more for his expenses. The sorry wretch had touted his story around the tabloids, in spite of the fact that he hadn't seen his daughter since she was five years old. On the morning of the funeral, the headline in the *Sun* read, *CAITLYN'S DAD: I'LL NEVER FORGIVE MYSELF.*

It was two months after the funeral, and the long, miserable winter was dragging on. Harry had spent a quiet Christmas at home with Charles, Megan, and the children. He'd drunk far too much and had carried on doing the same since. He wasn't going to the gym anymore—too many Caitlyn-related memories—and was taking more pills than ever.

It was eight thirty in the morning, and Harry was waiting for Maria in a Thames-side café close to the Rose offices. She'd asked to meet him, and he'd suggested breakfast. He'd only recently started eating out again, but was still aware of the eyes focused on him. "Suicide" was an easy word to pick up when people were whispering about you.

He ordered a full English and opened the *Times*.

"Father."

"Hello, Maria." He stood and kissed her cheek. It was cold from the chill February air. She had a new short haircut; it was fittingly severe.

As she took off her coat, he was filled with a mixture of fondness and exasperation. Fondness for the little girl he'd known before she went to Wales. Exasperation for this humorless creature who judged everyone and found them wanting. Especially him.

She ordered eggs and tea without looking the waitress in the face. How did that attitude go down in the human resources department?

"There are two things I want to talk about," she said.

"Fire away." There was no point in attempting preliminary small talk.

"Tom Cranwell."

"What about him?"

"We've had a complaint. More than one, actually. I can't go into detail because of staff confidentiality, but the general picture is sexual harassment. And verbal harassment—innuendo."

"You have proof?"

"The reports are stacking up. It can't be tolerated. Incidentally, Suvarna, the receptionist on your floor, saw him assault your ex-wife as she was leaving. And . . . I saw Caitlyn that day. I regret being a little short with her now."

"What? He *assaulted* Caitlyn?"

"Suvarna saw him pat her on the bottom, and then he groped it. And he's done the same to her."

"Jesus Christ."

"Please don't blaspheme."

Harry took a bite of sausage, thinking. These claims weren't a big surprise—anyone could see Cranwell was a lech. But he'd thought the man wouldn't be stupid enough to act on his odious impulses, especially not on company premises.

Harry had been feeling uncomfortable with the lawyer since the blackmail attempt. Tom knew too much. This could, in fact, be good timing.

"I spoke to our department head, Lesley," continued Maria. "She wants a formal written warning from you, as he's not technically a member of staff."

"Leave it with me. You said there were two things?"

"Yes, Father. The other one's personal, and it's . . ." She trailed off, fiddling with her napkin. She wouldn't meet his eyes.

"Yes?"

"It's Mother. She's been unwell."

"Oh. I'm sorry to hear that. But no doubt Welsh Wellness will work its magic."

Maria breathed in sharply. "Why do you always have to be so . . . *facetious*? I'm telling you Mother's sick, and all you can do is make snide comments about her life."

"Sorry. Is it depression?"

"No, Father. She was having stomach pains. Her doctor sent her for tests and it's cancer. She's starting chemo next week."

The jolt to Harry's heart was fierce. He lowered his knife and fork, his appetite gone. "Oh no. Maria, that's terrible news. How is she?"

"Oh, you know Mother. Brave. Still worrying about everyone else, never herself."

"Maria—what I can do? Anything. Anything at all."

"Pray."

CHAPTER 50

Harry

April 2011

"Bloody Mary?" said Charles to Maria.

"I don't drink alcohol, Uncle Charles."

"Ah, sorry. I'd forgotten. Hm. What royal-themed alternative can we come up with for you?"

"A tomato juice would be fine."

"How about a Virgin Mary—the nonalcoholic version?"

Maria gave him a death stare. "Why would I want a drink that trivializes the name of the Holy Mother?"

Maria really wasn't getting into the spirit.

"Righty-ho," said Charles. "Three Bloody Marys, one tomato juice, four orange juices."

"I'll give you a hand," said Harry, heaving himself out of the armchair. Easier said than done. He dropped back as his leg protested, and tried again.

Charles pretended not to notice his difficulty and carried on into the kitchen.

The two families were watching the royal wedding on TV. Prince William was marrying Kate Middleton, and London's habitual gray and green was overlaid with red, white, and blue. Chess and Helena had strung up Union Jack bunting, and all the children were wearing home-made crowns.

"Who was Bloody Mary again, Dad?" asked Eliza.

"England's very first queen. A seriously scary lady."

"Are you sure she was the first? What about Boudicca?" asked Eliza.

"Ah, the fearless Celt. A redhead, of course. So many of our great leaders have been redheads, have they not?" He winked at the children. "Boudicca was queen of a tribe, not the whole of England."

"Why was Mary scary?" asked Chess.

"She got rather carried away when it came to religion. Burned heretics at the stake. Hundreds of the poor blighters. And my staff think I'm harsh."

He made another attempt to get out of his chair.

"It's OK, Harry. You stay where you are," said Megan. "Girls, can you help Dad with the drinks? Off you go."

Now there was just Harry and Megan, and Eddie busy with his toy cars over in the corner.

"Harry . . ."

He knew what was coming. "I know, Megan. I could be in better shape. Give me a break, though. It hasn't been a great year so far."

"Look, most people are too scared of you to speak frankly. But I'm your sister—"

"Scared? Don't be ridiculous."

Megan lowered her voice. "Maria says you've been losing your temper at work, bawling people out. Verbal abuse, she called it. This isn't you, Harry. What's going on? Is it Caitlyn's suicide? The pills? Have you not managed to cut down?"

"This isn't the time for this conversation."

"It's well overdue, Harry. How are we going to get you back on track?"

"All right, don't nag. I'm seeing the doc this week, usual checkup. I'll ask him to take me in hand, crack the whip."

"Promise?"

"Yes, yes."

"And . . . Milly and Arabella saw Katie over Easter. It sounds like she's not so good. Maybe you should go and see her?"

Something snapped inside him. He gripped the arms of the chair and leaned toward her. "Stop bloody telling me what to do! If I want your advice, I'll ask for it. Right now, I don't."

She flinched, then frowned. "Well, that's as may be. But take a look at yourself, Harry, and think about your children. Eliza and Eddie lost their mothers, now they've lost a stepmother they loved. And Maria might lose Katie soon. How do you think it would be for them, losing their father too? Because that's where you're headed. You're stressed, unfit; you've put on weight. God knows how many pills you're popping. You're heading for an early grave if you don't sort yourself out."

She paused. "Look, you're my darling brother and I adore you, and I hate seeing you go downhill like this. Please, for all our sakes, do something about it. Get help."

Harry's anger was overtaken by self-pity. Look what life had done to him.

"Daddy," said a little voice from across the room.

Eddie was too young to have understood any of that, wasn't he? Especially the part about dying mothers?

"Yes, Eddie?"

"Can we get a hamster?"

Harry looked at Megan, and after a moment they both laughed.

"Good idea, son. Let's get two. We'll call them William and Kate!"

Nurse Clare was a sight for sore eyes, thought Harry as she pumped up the band wrapped around his arm. She wore a pale blue shirt and trousers, so crisp and clean, and her fair hair was pinned up into a creative bun, one with plaits and things going on to make it less sensible.

"How have you been?" she asked, keeping her hazel eyes on the blood-pressure monitor.

"Good!" said Harry. "And you, Nurse Clare?"

"Hundred and sixty over a hundred and ten." She looked at him, her head on one side. "We've known each other awhile, Harry."

"Indeed we have." He sensed she was about to say something along the lines of Megan's lecture last Friday.

"So . . . how are you *really*? Between you and me."

He sighed. "Not great." It was a relief to say it. "Terrible, actually."

"Thought so. For a start we'll need to up your blood-pressure medication." She released the armband.

"Lovely. More pills."

"Has Dr. Butts talked to you about lifestyle changes?"

"My lifestyle has a habit of changing, whether I want it to or not."

"I understand. And sometimes we respond to those changes in ways that do us no favors. We drink too much, eat too much; exercise goes out of the window because we just don't have the energy. I'm twice widowed, Harry. I might have some idea of what you're going through."

Harry had been enjoying the empathy, the opportunity for a spot of wallowing, but her words pulled him up. "You are? I'm sorry to hear that, Nurse Clare."

"Just Clare's fine. Look, after you've finished with the doctor, let's have a chat about how I can help you with those changes. It's all about small steps. Nobody's going to ask you to completely give up wine or cheese. But we could devise a plan?" She gently held his wrist while she took his pulse.

"Don't you wear that upside-down watch anymore?"

"No. And we wear trousers, not little dresses, and no more silly hats. Times have changed."

"Haven't they just," he said. "So it wouldn't be inappropriate if I asked you to give me some dietary advice over lunch, rather than in this scarily clinical environment?"

She smiled. "I finish at twelve. We can make it a long one. Healthy, of course."

"So how did it go with Dr. Butts?" Clare asked, pouring them both a glass of water. "If you want to tell me, that is. I don't mind if you don't."

"You have access to my records, so you can find out the sorry state of affairs, correct?"

"True, but I'd never nosey on a patient unless it was for professional reasons."

"Well, my leg hurts because it has to support too much weight and I'm not doing enough exercise. If I don't lose a couple of stone the leg reconstruction may need reconstructing. High cholesterol. High blood pressure. Regular headaches, not sure why. Stress. Also insomnia. Shall I go on?"

"There's more?"

Harry hesitated. Should he tell her? She had such kind eyes.

"I'm addicted to painkillers. Have been for years. Dr. Butts doesn't know about that one."

"OK, let's think about how we can address this."

Their salads arrived, and she continued to question him gently about his life. She should have been a psychiatrist. Most of his problems, she said, stemmed from the way he'd dealt with events in his past. And it was likely that most of his health issues were reversible.

By the time they finished their green tea, Harry felt as if he'd already taken the first steps on her program to the renewal of Harry Rose.

They exited the restaurant into bright May sunshine.

"What are you up to now, Harry?"

"Back to the grindstone, I suppose. And you?"

"I might take a walk in Regent's Park, as it's such a nice day. Why don't you come with me, if you haven't got anything important on."

"Work-life balance?"

"Exactly."

. . .

Over the next few months, with Clare's help, Harry managed to shed the excess weight. The pain in his leg eased, and Doc Butts said he might not need another op, after all. Physically, he was almost back to his old self. He even shaved off his beard.

He'd finally managed to withdraw from the painkillers, but once he'd kicked them, he realized how they'd been diverting his emotions, switching them like a set of points on a railway line. When he should have felt grief, the pills had switched him to anger and dark moods. When he should have felt guilt—well, that had ended up at the same destination.

Now that the drugs had relinquished their control, the emotional pain came rushing in. He was floored by grief, full of remorse and guilt, prone to self-pity.

Katie died the following winter and was buried in an ancient Welsh churchyard. Harry wept by the graveside, while Maria held herself together, grim-faced.

"It's too soon, Katie was too young," he said to Cassandra afterward as they held each other tight. "I can't bear it."

So many he'd loved, gone. Their lives snuffed out before their time. Katie. Ana. Janette. Caitlyn. His mother, his father. Art. Summer and Max, his and Katie's stillborn children. Eliza's little brother or sister that never was.

"She was at peace," Cassandra said, gently wiping his tears away. She fished in the pocket of her skirt. "Here. She wanted me to give you this."

He waited until he was alone, sitting on a churchyard bench overlooking the Welsh hills Katie had loved. The tears came back as he saw the familiar looping writing.

Dearest Harry

I know I don't have long left. The love I still feel for you means I can't let go without some final words that I hope will protect your soul, which is more important than all those worldly things you chase after. You've always been led by your desires, but each time you got what you thought you wanted, it didn't lead to happiness, did it? In fact those other women brought you only grief. For my part, I forgive it all, and am praying to God that He will too. Please continue to be a good father to Maria. Finally, remember, Harry, it's always been you.

Your ever-loving wife

Katie

CHAPTER 51

Clare

June 2012

The Lake District was working its magic on Harry, as she'd known it would. They were staying in the house she'd grown up in, a stone manor on the fells between Kendal and Windermere. She'd inherited the property from her parents and had divided it into holiday apartments. She made far more money from their rental than she did from her nursing, and there was the added bonus of having a bolt-hole far from the Big Smoke. Clare loved London, but her inner northerner often demanded to go home.

She'd been meeting Harry regularly for lunches, dinners, and evenings at the theater for more than a year now, and had grown increasingly fond of him. She loved her job, but had been lonely in London since the death of her second husband, and found herself counting down the days until she was due to see Harry again. As well as being great company, he was no stranger to loss himself, and spending time with someone who understood was comforting.

She remembered the beautiful man with the shattered leg she'd nursed back in 2001. All these years later he was still a handsome charmer, but ill health, addiction, and personal tragedy had taken their toll. She'd helped him reverse the physical decline, but he still needed to sort his head out. She sensed many demons in there.

Recently, Harry's stress levels had been on the rise again. He'd been upset by the death of his first wife, and at work he'd been wielding the ax, he said, lopping off parts of the Rose empire that were performing badly. Some of those were up north, and the surviving workers were threatening strike action.

He'd phoned to cancel Friday's planned theater trip. "Sorry, Clare. There's a rebellion up north. I have to go to Manchester to sort it out. Wish me luck. I hate going up there, it's like another country. A horrible one where they all hate me."

That's when the idea came to her. "You're forgetting, I'm from Cumbria. Surely you love the Lake District. *Everyone* loves the Lake District, even if it's usually pouring with rain."

"I've never been. Why would I? I have a house in Bermuda."

"Right. I'll meet you up north. When you've finished in Manchester, you can come and stay in my apartment. You do have a pair of walking boots?"

"Will green wellies do?"

"No. Don't worry, we'll buy you some in Kendal."

"Is that where the mint cake comes from?"

"It is! We can get some."

"But it's horrible."

"Cumberland sausage?"

"Better."

Clare drove up on Friday, and Harry met her at the apartment after his meeting with the unions.

"How did it go?" she asked, showing him in.

"As expected. One of the shop stewards called me a ginger tyrant. I don't suppose you'd allow me a small beer?"

"Oh dear. Yes, I think perhaps I should. In fact, let's abandon the no-alcohol policy this weekend. At least—if you agree to climb a minimum of two fells."

"Fells? Why don't they call them hills, like a normal person?"

"Go and change, Mr. Grumpy. I'll pour you that beer."

. . .

Now they were on the apartment balcony, looking out across the mountains on a beautiful June evening. A buzzard wheeled high in the sky above them, and the only sound was the gentle calling of sheep on the hillsides. Clare gave a sigh of pleasure. She could feel the magic of the Lakes spreading like a balm through her veins. She hoped the same was happening to Harry.

She looked across at him. He'd closed his eyes and was leaning back, his long legs stretched out in front of him, his face tilted toward the evening sun. Now that his health was back on track, and he'd lost the beard, he looked ten years younger than the first time he'd appeared in Dr. Butts's waiting room. He could pass for a man of forty. A ridiculously good-looking man of forty.

He opened his eyes and smiled at her, and something shifted inside.

Picking up his beer, he looked out across the fells. "Hm, I see now, there's more to this place they call the north than mills, cobblestones, and stroppy workers."

"Wait until you're up on the fell tops. There's nowhere like it."

"Which one is the hill with the daffodils?"

"They're fells, but anyway, it was a lake they were fluttering beside."

"No, he was wandering o'er vale and hill. See, he said 'hill,' not 'fell.'"

"Well, 'hill' rhymes with 'daffodil.'"

"He could've written about bluebells. That would have rhymed with 'fells.'"

"You have a point. And I've always found that phrase 'lonely as a cloud' highly suspect. If there's one thing about Lake District clouds, it's that they're not lonely. They come in packs and obliterate the sky. You're lucky to see it clear like this."

"Thank you for bringing me here. It's very pretty, I'll give you that."

"It's the best place in the world."

"No, that's London . . ."

Harry

Progress was slow. Clare was taking him on a walk that included a "smallish" fell, a tarn (northern for small lake), a café, and Wordsworth's cottage at Grasmere. The view was picture-postcard pretty, but the walking uphill part was disagreeable.

"Come on, Harry," she said, waiting for him. "You gotta *earn* that Cumberland sausage!"

She was wearing jeans tucked into thick socks, regulation hiking boots, and one of those colorful rain jackets that were de rigueur up here.

"But it's sunny!" he'd protested as she'd made him buy one, along with his new boots.

"You really have no idea, do you? It could be near freezing and blowing a gale by the time we're up high."

So here he was, a ridiculous rambler, no doubt red in the face. He hoped none of the steady stream of walkers coming the other way—popular place, this—recognized Harry Rose, media mogul, under these absurd clothes.

Half an hour later they reached the top.

"Congratulations! You've conquered Loughrigg," said Clare. "Here's your reward." She passed him a Penguin biscuit.

They sat with their backs against the cairn (northern for pile of stones), their shoulders touching, admiring the view.

"OK, Barr. I'll concede, this is a rather lovely place."

Clouds were scuttling across the sky; light was chasing shade over the fells. Far below, Grasmere was a splash of blue between green woodlands and fields crisscrossed by ancient stone walls.

"I might even write a poem."

"I sometimes paint when I come up here," said Clare. "It gets you like that. Makes you want to capture it all, whether it's in words, pictures, whatever."

He turned to look at her. The fresh air had turned her cheeks pink. "You win. Up north is all right. I should bring Eliza and Eddie."

She took his hand. "You're a lovely man, Harry Rose."

"So are you. Woman, I mean. How are you not married?"

"Oh, I've already had two husbands. I'm in no hurry to go down that road again. I've made a good life for myself in London. I love my job, I've got nice friends. And I have you. Your friendship means the world to me."

"Me too. I think I'd probably be dead now, if it hadn't been for you."

They carried on toward Grasmere, and soon reached the tearooms, where they found a table outside.

"I've just realized something," said Harry, after a minute or two of companionable silence. "I haven't thought about work all day. And . . . I'm happy."

"The north will do that to you, Harry."

"Clare Barr does that to me."

Her smile faltered.

He suddenly knew—the time was right. "Clare. You know about my vices, my baggage, my questionable record as a husband. Could you ever see me as more than a friend?"

She took her time answering, and he was aware of the butterflies in his stomach.

"I think I could. But I do worry about what's going on up here." She tapped her temple. "You strike me as a troubled man. You've been through a lot. You might not be ready for another relationship."

"But what if someone else steals you from under my nose?"

"That's not going to happen." She reached across and took his hand.

"Promise?" He turned her hand over and stroked her palm.

"How about we give Wordsworth's cottage a miss," she said.

Harry lowered himself into a steaming hot bath. He hadn't let on to Clare how much his leg had been hurting by the time they'd made it back. All frisky thoughts had been pushed aside by the need to lie down and do nothing for a while. He sighed in contentment as the hot water worked its magic, soothing his aching limbs.

There was a knock on the door, and Clare asked, "Do you want a beer, Harry? Or a wine?"

"If I'm allowed. Beer, please."

"Oh, you are allowed. You did great today."

A minute or so later she came in carrying two glasses. She was wearing a black satin robe. Harry sat up and pulled up his knees.

"Harry, don't be silly. I'm a nurse. I see naked men all the time. I thought you might like a back rub." She squirted something from a bottle onto her palms, perched on the edge of the bath, and began massaging his shoulders. It felt so good. He closed his eyes.

"Clare, you're a goddess."

She dropped a kiss onto his head.

When her hands stopped, he didn't open his eyes.

Then he felt her lips on his. They were so soft.

Still he didn't open his eyes.

Another kiss, and this time she lingered. It was a long, gentle kiss, as if they were both experimenting, seeing if they felt anything.

When her lips went away again, Harry felt their absence. But still he kept his eyes closed, not wanting to break the spell, hoping they'd come back.

They did, and this time the kiss was deep, sensuous.

She finally pulled away, and now he opened his eyes.

"I could get in with you," she said, "but—"

"Bit of a tight squeeze?"

"Maybe the shower would be more fun."

Before he could reply, she kissed him again, this time with . . . yes, he'd call that passion.

She turned her back to him, undid the belt on her robe, and the black satin slid to the floor.

As Harry stepped out of the bath, he couldn't help thinking about his last time, two years ago, with Caitlyn. In spite of finding her irresistible, he'd still needed that little blue pill. Now, he had no little blue pills.

It was as if she'd read his mind. "It's been a while for you, Harry?"

"It has. I don't know if . . ."

"I'd imagine it was all the drugs you were on. Your body wouldn't have known if it was coming or going."

"No pun intended?"

"Come on, I'm getting cold. And just another kiss will do. Let's take things slowly."

She held out her hand and led him into the shower. Hot water coursed over them, and he felt himself come back to life as their kiss grew increasingly passionate.

No little blue pill was necessary.

CHAPTER 52

Harry

September 2014

The results were in—Scotland had voted by a whisker to remain part of the UK.

"Thank Christ for that," said Harry, switching off the TV in his office.

"Hypocrite," said Terri, from the couch.

"How so, Baskin?"

"You moan about Europe, but when our northern neighbor kicks against being ruled by a distant bureaucracy, you're all 'better together.'"

"Entirely different. Brussels interferes too much in British business. We'd be better off without them."

"Bollocks."

"You wait, Terri. If the Tories get in again next year, there'll be a referendum. I'd bet my yacht the British public vote to leave."

Terri stood up and held out her hand. "Shake on it?"

Harry hesitated. "It was just a figure of speech."

"No, come on. Bet me your yacht the British vote to leave Europe."

"How about a hundred quid?"

"Yacht."

"Small car?"

"Where's those famous balls, Harry?"

Harry's superyacht, *Janette*, was his pride and joy. And he wasn't a gambling man. But he was convinced this was coming. Britain had always been fiercely independent. Look at the history. Henry VIII had shaken off Rome—no remote pope was going to tell him whom he could and couldn't marry. Then there'd been Winston, rallying plucky little Britain to resist the Nazis, picking themselves up day after grim day as the bombs rained down, making a cup of tea and getting on with it.

"Right. You're on." He shook her hand.

"Fuck! Better learn my port from my starboard, then."

"What was it you actually came to see me about?"

"Ah yes. I wanted to run something past you. I know I don't usually, but this one's a bit different because of Rose's involvement. I'm doing an in-depth feature on Andre Sokolov. You know his team just won the Premiership?"

Harry tried not to react, took his time sipping his coffee and placing it carefully back on the desk. "When you say in-depth . . ."

"Well, obviously the man's a crook."

"He's no longer involved with our TV offerings. His capital was too suspect. We bought out his investments."

"So we don't need to worry about upsetting him. I lure him in with the football, then go for the jugular."

Harry wondered how to sort this one. No way did he want Terri anywhere near Andre. Her ability to extract confessions was on a par with the Spanish Inquisition's.

"You know I'm hands-off, but I'm going to say this time, bin it. You *do* need to worry about upsetting Andre. He's dangerous in the way only Russians are dangerous. If he thinks he's coming for a chat about his beloved football and you start asking where his billions came from, you could find yourself in very hot water."

"Wouldn't exactly be the first time. Isn't that what investigative journalism's all about?"

"OK, let's put it more bluntly. That hot water, if it were used to make a cup of tea, could see you on a slab in the mortuary following an inexplicable poisoning incident."

"Like Ana, you mean."

Harry felt the blood draining from his face. "How *dare* you. What sort of crass comment is that?"

"Sorry. I've just always found it weird, you know? Forget I ever said that. I'll go back to my cave." She headed for the door.

"Terri." His tone was icy.

She turned and met his eye.

"Kill the interview. I don't want you anywhere near that man."

Terri

It was a high-risk strategy, but it had worked. The look on Harry's face had got her further than all those dead-end leads she'd followed since Percy had shared his conspiracy theory with her.

The coroner's report, hospital records, and eyewitness accounts had led nowhere. A bacterial infection in a wound had caused toxic shock syndrome. Highly unusual, but it happened.

The last person who saw Ana alive was the office cleaner. The police had attempted to track him down, but he'd left the company, whose questionable employment practices didn't include checking immigrants' papers. The police felt his disappearance was more likely due to a fear of the authorities rather than any connection to Ana's death.

Nobody in the office remembered her injuring herself on the guillotine. But apparently it didn't need to have been an obvious wound. Small but deep would have been enough, like a slip of the bread knife.

And there it had dried up. Until Harry had sacked that odious creep Cranwell for sexual harassment. Tom was bitter, and only too happy to share his thoughts on Harry Rose with Terri. Yes, of course a journalist protects her sources, she'd said.

He'd told her Ana had demanded half of Harry's assets, which had mostly been tied up in Rose and were security for sizable Russian investment into the company. And about a meeting with Caitlyn Howe, that tragic girl Harry had married after Janette. There had been an attempt at blackmail by her lover, who'd claimed he had evidence that Harry's relationship with Caitlyn had begun years ago, when she was only fifteen. It had been a lie, apparently, but the interesting part was that front and center in the photo the boyfriend had provided as evidence was Andre Sokolov. Harry had apparently told Caitlyn that while he wasn't worried about the blackmail attempt, Sokolov might not be so unconcerned. There had been a death threat—Cranwell had heard it with his own ears.

Terri opened up her wallet and pulled out a photo of herself with Ana, taken outside a Covent Garden café. "I haven't forgotten you," she whispered. "It's not over yet."

She propped the picture up against her computer. In spite of Cranwell's revelations, her investigations had continued to lead nowhere. But Terri wasn't one to give up. She'd decided to say something to Harry about her suspicions and gauge his reaction. This morning, she'd had the opportunity.

Harry's face had said it all. His ruddy cheeks had paled; he looked like a rabbit caught in the headlights.

What had Harry done? And what was she going to do about it?

Harry

Obviously he couldn't sack Terri. God, but she was clever. He remembered back to the reasons he'd employed her in the first place. He'd wanted to keep his enemy close. She'd always known too much. Now, it seemed she'd made the connection between Ana's death and Andre.

Nothing could be proved. Andre would never confess, and there was no one else. And of course, Harry had never meant for it to happen. His failure had been in not recognizing Andre's intent.

All he could do was get on with life and hope Terri let it go. Why would she want to bring him down?

He turned his mind to pleasanter things. Clare had moved in, but they still weren't married. He'd proposed to her (again) last weekend, and although she'd refused him (again), he knew he was wearing her down. His children loved her, even Maria, and Clare was properly part of the family now. Charles and Megan approved too. Well, who wouldn't? Clare was intelligent, sensible, fun.

"Is she superstitious?" Charles had asked, after Harry confided he'd been turned down yet again.

"Not that I know of. Why?"

"The curse of Harry Rose's wives. Might be safer to remain Ms. Barr."

Harry had considered the comment to be in spectacularly bad taste.

Terri

July 2016

Damn it, Harry got to keep his yacht. Unbelievably, the idiot British public had voted to cast itself adrift from Europe, to go it alone like it was still fighting off the Nazis in World War II.

Terri threw another file into a cardboard box, then stopped to look around. After what seemed like a lifetime in this office, she'd be leaving it today. She couldn't help feeling sentimental.

There was still so much to do. Twenty-odd years' worth of stuff. Terri's untidiness was legendary. While clean-desk policies had been implemented, no one had been brave enough to suggest Terri complied.

"Ah, Eliza. Just the man."

Ana's daughter entered the office like a blast of fresh air. Her red curls were scraped back off her face into a high ponytail, and her deep brown eyes—Ana's eyes—were full of enthusiasm for her gap-year job helping Terri.

"It's so exciting to be moving into the new offices, after all these years hearing Dad banging on about how brilliant they're going to be."

"Well, if you want to get there quicker, you can empty that filing cabinet. Coffee first, though. If you'd be so kind?"

"On it!"

Terri was delighted to have Eliza on board. She was sharp as a pin, didn't mind doing the dogsbody jobs, and Terri imagined it would have made Ana smile.

Eliza returned with two coffees and made a start. "Terri, why don't you chuck some of this stuff out? All the walls are made of glass in the new place, so everyone will be able to see each other's mess."

"I ignored that email. I'm too old to change my ways."

Later, Terri returned from an editorial meeting to find Eliza sitting at Terri's desk, a file open in front of her. She recognized the papers, and the photo of herself and Ana. *Shit.*

"Terri, why have you collected all this stuff about Mum's death?"

Eliza was eighteen now. Didn't she deserve to know?

"Now's not the time."

Eliza must have seen something in her expression. "Nobody's doing any proper work today. Tell me."

So Terri did. But she ended by saying, "Look, love. I've thought about this long and hard. I'm almost certain it was done without your dad's knowledge. I've never found anything to link him personally to your mum's death."

"Why is there a photo of Caitlyn with the Russian guy and Dad?"

Terri hadn't realized she'd seen that. "Of course, she was your step-mum for a while."

"She was lovely. I hated Dad for kicking her out. I know why he did now, but he was pretty horrible to her."

"Yes, that was all very sad. Caitlyn had a dodgy background. She was involved with a drug dealer, and she shacked up with a friend who tried to sell her story to me. Name of Storm. Dreadful person, I sent her packing. Poor Caitlyn. She tried to pull herself out of it when she met your dad, but it's difficult to shed your past."

"Dad won't talk about her now, but he really loved her, I think."

"He loved all of them, Eliza. Unfortunately for them."

Eliza was quiet for a moment. "I don't think I'll ever get married," she said. "In fact, I might just stay a virgin all my life."

CHAPTER 53

Harry

January 2018

Harry glanced up from his desk, looking through the glass walls to the distant boardroom, where he could just make out the huge portrait commissioned to mark the opening of the Rose building. In it, Harry was standing, legs apart, in what Terri had mockingly called a "power stance." The artist had emphasized his broad shoulders and long legs, but it was a shame the mouth looked rather mean.

They'd been in the new building for just over a year now. The millennials on Harry's staff were forever Instagramming photos of themselves flying down the glass slide from the third floor to the atrium, or eating their avocado-centric brunches in the café overlooking the Thames. Which was all fine by Harry. He wanted Rose to be the coolest place to work.

He opened up the report on RoseHealth.com that had just popped in from the Greenhouse, his research and development department. It had been Eliza's idea to share Clare's "lifestyle change" expertise online. Clare had been all for it. She'd grown tired of Doc Butts's "twentieth-century approach to wellness" (that word again) and had left not long after her and Harry's wedding a year ago (a quiet affair, close friends and family only). Now she was casting about for something other than volunteer work to fill her time.

As Harry looked at the report, he could see it showed promise.

There was a knock on his door, and he waved Aleesha in.

"Mr. Latham's here, Mr. R—sorry, Harry."

Bugger. He'd forgotten Howe's ambulance chaser of a lawyer was due. He hated the calendar app on his computer, but a desk diary was so last century.

Five minutes later, Aleesha placed two coffees in front of Harry and the lawyer, and once again Harry was treated to a tantalizing glimpse of her cleavage.

"Thank you, Aleesha. Aha—real cups. Excellent!"

"Zero waste, Harry," she said, and winked.

"Still pulling the young girls, eh?" said Latham as she left.

"Get to the point. I'm a busy man."

Once again, the sniveling little lawyer trotted out his convoluted case, that Harry owed compensation to "Howie" Howe for the unreasonable behavior that had driven his daughter to suicide.

"Mr. Latham, unless you have something to add to the ridiculous accusations you leveled at me last time, I suggest you leave now. Why are you even here?"

"Mr. Howe now has evidence of verbal abuse, witnessed by your ex-lawyer. Mr. Cranwell is willing to testify that this would have significantly contributed to Caitlyn's decision to kill herself. If you don't want Mr. Howe to go to the press, I'd strongly advise an out-of-court settlement."

"Hm. That would be the same Mr. Cranwell who sexually assaulted Caitlyn at the Rose offices—as witnessed by a receptionist who was similarly harassed by him. I suggest you leave now, Latham. Goodbye."

The lawyer was sensible enough to do as he was told, and Harry was left alone.

An unwelcome image of Cranwell groping Caitlyn flashed into his mind, followed swiftly by a rush of shame. He should have believed her when she said she'd had nothing to do with the blackmail. Deep down, he'd known she was telling the truth. But at the time he was still too hurt by her infidelity to act reasonably.

Hypocrite, said the voice in his head.

He'd abandoned her, leaving her to be assaulted one last time, just before she ended her short life.

Maybe Harry shouldn't be worrying about this #MeToo business, after all. Maybe he should welcome it, if it could expose creeps like Cranwell. Supposing someone assaulted Eliza like that. He'd want her to hashtag the hell out of whoever it was.

The phone rang. "It's your sister, Harry," said Aleesha.

"Put her through." He was glad of the distraction.

"Megan! What can I do for you on this particularly grim and gray morning? Recovered from Christmas?"

"It's not Megan, it's Margot."

Good lord, number one sister? Why on earth was she ringing him? He hadn't seen her for years; she rarely left her Scottish castle.

"*Quelle surprise!* To what do I owe this honor?"

"It's been so long, Harry. My New Year's resolution is to do something about that. How about coming up for a weekend? I'm inviting Megan and Charles too. Bring the children. And your new wife, of course. This one's called Clare, I believe?"

A few seconds in and she was already passive-aggressively judging him.

"That's right. Well, I don't see why not."

"If you come before the end of the month, we can shoot pheasant. It would be nice for you to get to know Robbie better too."

Harry could hardly remember her husband. He pictured the dour laird who'd never laughed at his jokes.

"And our daughters—Mackenzie and Eliza are about the same age."

"Eliza's at university now. Eddie's eleven. Not sure either would be up for slaughtering wildlife, but I'm happy to put the wind up a few birds."

Later, Harry made his way down to the *Rack*'s offices, where Eliza was working again during the holidays. He found her perched on Terri's desk. The two seemed close—he was pleased she was getting some top-notch experience, but their relationship made him uneasy.

"Hey, Dad!" Her smile always gave him a lift. "What are you doing here?"

"Something strange happened. Your aunt Margot's invited us up to Scotland."

"Why?"

"Wants to reconnect with her family. Megan's invited too. Margot was always mean to Megan. I guess we should do as we're told. It was always dangerous to say no to Margot."

"I'd love to come! I'd like to get to know Aunt Margot."

Good old Eliza. People were always innocent until proven guilty.

"And your cousin might be there—Mackenzie. She's about your age."

"Cool!"

That night, the ghosts came back in a dream, muttering his name. Amorphous shapes, black shadows full of menace. There was a whisper: "It's nearly time."

He woke up with a shout.

"Harry, what on earth?" said Clare, switching on the bedside lamp.

"Bad dream." He was sweating. He could sense them there, in the corners of his mind. He had a terrible sense of impending doom. "Will I ever be free of it?"

"Free of what?"

"The past."

"You can't undo the past, Harry. But talking about what's bothering you might help."

"I don't even want to think about it."

"Then go back to sleep, love. None of us is perfect; we all have stuff on our conscience."

Eliza

Aunt Margot was as joyless as Dad had said. No wonder he didn't bother keeping up with her. And her husband was like some grumpy Scottish cliché. Cousin Mackenzie had gone to Glasgow for a Young Scots for Independence rally, so Eliza didn't even get to meet her.

The mountains looked beautiful covered in snow, but when you needed five layers of clothing to go out for a walk . . . actually, you needed five layers to stay inside too. The castle was freezing.

There had been only two bright spots so far. The first was seeing Dad and Megan pulling silly faces behind Margot's back, just as they'd done as children, apparently. The other was seeing Dad dressed up in tweeds and a silly hat, all ready for the pheasant shoot.

Over breakfast, Aunt Margot had filled them in on who was coming to the shoot today. Most of them started with *Mc*. Dad was looking forward to it, as were Megan and Charles.

How could they? Eliza, along with Clare and Eddie, couldn't handle the idea of killing things. They'd be going for a walk instead. Aunt Margot had looked down her nose at their "silly" opinions, launching into a lecture on how pheasants that lived their lives free on the moors were a far more ethical source of food than chickens raised in factory farms. She had a point. But still, killing for fun? No.

People started arriving, most of them in cranky old Land Rovers with dogs in the back. They assembled on the graveled area in front of the castle, before setting off on foot, guns at their sides.

Eliza shuddered. Poor birds. She was sitting on a stone bench, the cold numbing her bottom, lacing up her walking boots. Clare and Eddie were still inside, searching out scarves and gloves.

There was the sound of an engine, and another Land Rover appeared, drawing to a halt at the path the shooters had taken. A woman leaped out, dressed in a kilt, a green jacket, and headscarf. From a distance she looked like the Queen. Could it be the Queen? The royals seemed to like it up here.

The woman turned toward her and called, "I'm late! Did they go this way?"

"Yes—they left about twenty minutes ago!"

The woman fetched her shotgun from her car and set off in a hurry.

Eliza was ready to leave. *Come on, you two!*

It was too cold to sit still. She wandered over to the footpath and noticed something lying in the snow. Car keys. They must belong to that woman. She picked them up and set off after her. Clare and Eddie would be coming this way, anyway.

Coming out of the trees onto the moor, she saw the shooting party lined up ahead, their guns held ready as men and dogs went forward to drive the pheasants into the air.

The birds took off, fluttering and panicking, high into the blue sky. The crack of gunfire echoed around the mountains and several plummeted to the ground.

Eliza felt sick.

Where was the woman? She spotted her, still some way behind the shooters. Eliza carried on, trying to ignore the carnage ahead.

When she was within yelling distance, she slowed down. Beyond the woman she saw Dad, Charles, and Megan, guns at the ready, pointing high into the sky.

The woman had stopped. Her gun was at the ready too.

It was pointed at Dad.

Eliza waited for her to raise it, like the others, but she didn't. She was squinting along the barrel.

Panic rose in Eliza's chest. "Hey!"

The woman ignored her cry, intent on lining up the gun sight.

This can't be happening.

More deadly shots echoed around the mountains, and more birds dropped like stones to the moorland below.

The woman released a catch on the shotgun, then returned her hand to the barrel.

"No! Stop!" Eliza screamed, setting off at a run.

She stumbled slightly, regained her balance, and reached the woman just as she pulled the trigger. "No!" Eliza pushed her to the ground.

But she was too late. Harry sank to his knees. A dark stain spread across his tweed jacket, then he toppled over onto the snow. Screams rang out among the gunfire.

"Is he dead?" the woman said, her voice flat.

Eliza took off past her, desperate to reach her father.

She saw Megan looking at her own gun, as if making sure she hadn't shot her brother by accident, then staring at Harry in disbelief. A patch of red was growing in the snow beside him.

People were pulling out mobile phones, calling for help.

Clare. We need Clare.

Battling her instinct to run to her father, Eliza headed back up the path, filled with a sense of unreality.

Dad had been shot. *Shot.*

The woman was still there, sitting on the ground, a stunned look on her face. "Wait," she said. "I need to know. Is he dead?"

She must have been about forty-five, fifty. Her headscarf had come off, revealing fair hair streaked with gray.

Eliza ignored her and carried on running.

"I need to know!" shrieked the woman.

"Thank God," Eliza said as she saw Clare coming the other way. "Mum! Come quickly. Dad's been shot!"

Clare broke into a run, her face panicked. "How? Where?"

Eliza pointed, then ran back toward the crowd now gathered around Harry.

She was level with the woman again.

"*She's* not your mum. *Ana* was your mum."

Eliza stopped in her tracks. "What?"

Clare ran past, glancing at the woman, Eddie following.

"Ana was your mum." She looked Eliza in the eye, and Eliza saw madness and sorrow. "And she was my sister. Harry killed her. Harry ruined my life and he killed my darling sister. He deserves to die."

"Aunt Merry?" Her mother's sister sent birthday cards, but she was rarely mentioned when Eliza visited her grandparents in Kent.

"Yes, I'm your aunt Merry." She burst into hysterical sobs.

Eliza was about to set off again, when she saw Charles hurrying toward her.

"Eliza! Are you OK?"

"Uncle Charles! Is Dad . . . ? He's not . . . ?"

Charles drew level.

Aunt Merry was now sitting with her arms around her knees, her head buried in them, crying quietly.

"He's alive, Eliza," Charles panted. "A rescue helicopter's on its way."

———◆———

CHAPTER 54

Harry

*H*arry was on the operating table. His heart had stopped beating. He wasn't dead, and he wasn't alive. He was somewhere in between.

He could see them, below him. Surgeons, nurses. The ghosts behind them, deciding whether he should live or die.

"Karma, or redemption?" said one of the ghosts.

Harry opened his eyes and saw Eliza and Clare. "My guardian angels," he said woozily. "Where would I be without my girls?"

"Six feet under," said Charles, from the other side of the hospital bed.

The bullet had hit Harry in the shoulder. Eliza had reached Merry just in time to send her shot slightly off course. He'd lost a lot of blood, but Clare had known what to do.

"Eliza, Eddie, let's go and buy your dad some chocolate," said Megan. "If Mrs. RoseHealth Dot-com will allow that?"

"Definitely," said Clare.

"I'll come and grab a coffee," said Charles diplomatically.

Alone, Harry and Clare chatted for a while about how he was feeling. And then there was an awkward pause.

"Harry, I need to ask this," Clare said finally.

Harry's smile faded. His cheerfulness had been forced; the near-death experience had left him deeply disturbed.

"Merry claims you had something to do with Ana's death. It's not true, is it?"

"No." He sighed. He'd never be free of the ghosts if he didn't confront his conscience. "But I think . . . maybe I could have stopped it. And yes, I did have an affair with Merry, and yes, I did treat her terribly."

Clare was quiet for a moment, not meeting his eyes. "She's been arrested."

"Clare, I don't know how to move forward with this. Every time I try, things come back to haunt me."

He leaned back on the pillows and closed his eyes. At least he'd said it out loud. *Maybe I could have stopped it.* He felt the load lighten a little.

"Look, Dad. Terry's Chocolate Orange!" came Eddie's voice.

"Fuck, Harry," said another voice. "What have you done now?"

Harry opened his eyes to see Terri. "I just had a major relapse," he said. "Get back to work, Baskin. And, Eddie, you'd better give the chocolate orange back, if it's Terri's."

After a little while the others were ushered out of the room again. Terri wanted a word.

"Look, Harry. I know what there is to know. Clare says you're battling your conscience. I think I can help with that, but it's gonna hurt."

"Help? How? And don't say therapy."

"Let me write about you. Let's get it out there. It won't be pretty, but the truth won't land you in prison. And, Harry . . . while we're on the subject of confessions, I have one of my own. Well, not a confession as such. Just something to share."

For the first time in all these years, Terri looked vulnerable.

"I was in love with Ana. Probably as much as you were."

Harry tried to haul himself up, but the pain sent him back to his pillows. "*In love?* You mean . . . you're gay?"

"Oh, come on, Harry. How many years have we known each other?"

"I just thought you were immune to my charms."

"Fuck's sake. So when Percy North told me he thought you'd had Ana bumped off—"

"What!"

"Percy. He was tipped off by that tosser Cranwell. He told me about the Caitlyn blackmail thing too. In other words, Harry, you're busted."

"Cranwell's a liar, and he knows nothing about Ana's death. In any case, I can't let you print any of that."

"My opinion? Your dick's got you into shitloads of trouble. You've done bad things, but you're not a terrible person. If you don't face up to what you've done, you'll never clear your conscience—or have Eliza's trust. She knows, Harry."

"She *knows*?"

"Yep—that you're at least partly responsible for Ana's death. I told her about Sokolov. Look, I don't believe you were behind it. I've thought long and hard, and I think he organized it over your head, which you were stupidly keeping buried in the sand. I'm right, aren't I?"

Harry said nothing. *Eliza knows.* Finally, he nodded.

"Sokolov's not going to sing," she said, "and there's no other way to connect you with her death. So let me do the story. Clear your conscience. Then you can start over."

Fate intervened. On Monday morning, the news broke. The press had been talking to Darius Draper, estate manager at Kindrummon Castle.

The revelations about Harry Rose were shocking. Until now, apart from a wobble during the factory closures episode, the British public had held the man who'd become part of their tapestry in deep affection. There had been outpourings of sympathy for the tragedies he'd endured—four wives dead, all far too young. They'd been pleased for him when he married Clare, who seemed such a lovely lady, and horrified when they heard about the shooting accident in Scotland that had almost killed him.

Except, it wasn't an accident. Monday's *Daily Mirror* claimed it was a murder attempt by a former mistress, Miranda "Merry" McCarey, who also happened to be the sister of Harry's second wife, Ana.

> Merry's close friend Darius Draper said: "I had no idea she was planning this, but she's always said Harry Rose ruined her life. And recently she'd been acting very strangely, claiming he killed her sister. Percy North, who was engaged to Ana before she married Harry, came to see Merry and put all sorts of ideas in her head about a Russian assassin! When Merry found out Harry was coming up for a pheasant shoot, she got this look in her eye. I should have realized what she was planning."

HARRY THE HYPOCRITE! screamed the *Sun* on Tuesday, reminding readers how Harry's coldhearted behavior had driven lovely young Caitlyn Rose to throw herself off a bridge. She'd been friendless, with no family, in the grip of an evil drug dealer, and Harry had been her savior. Until he'd turned his back on her.

HARRY'S MOSCOW MURDERER? inquired the *Daily Telegraph* on Wednesday:

> Harry Rose's second wife, Ana, almost certainly didn't die of natural causes, claims his ex-lawyer, Tom Cranwell. Although Cranwell has no evidence to back up his theory, he told the *Daily Telegraph* that he believes a Russian associate of Harry's arranged her assassination after she demanded half of his empire as her divorce settlement. Cranwell, who was dismissed from Rose Corp. for sexual harassment, refused to name Harry's alleged Russian ac-

complice, but at the time there was considerable Russian investment in the media giant . . .

On Thursday, Zara Lively, former face of Rose Air, took to Twitter: **Harry Rose sexually harassed me #MeToo.**

Harry sank back on his pillows. Surely it was only a matter of time before "Harry's secret love child" made an appearance.

He was finished.

"I'll ask you again, Harry," said Clare. "Is it true—about your part in Ana's death?"

They were sitting in the living room on Sunday morning, curtains drawn against the press pack outside. The day before, Clare and Eliza had fetched Harry from the hospital. This was the first time she'd raised the topic of the media revelations.

"There may be a few truths. I'm sorry you had to find out this way. But the press have twisted everything, as per."

"These things they're saying—I'm still processing them. I can't take it all in."

"Then don't. I'll tell you what really happened."

Eliza came into the room. "Dad, have you seen the *Sunday Times*?"

"Funnily enough, I'm avoiding the papers today."

"You need to read this," she said, holding out her iPad.

The headline read: *THE TRUTH ABOUT HARRY ROSE?* He checked the byline: Terri.

"Go on, read it," said Eliza. "And then I want to talk about Mum. Ana. Properly. None of your usual bullsh—spin."

Harry processed Terri's words. Clare and Eliza sat watching him.

Terri painted a picture of a brilliant but deeply flawed man, one who'd made terrible misjudgments when it came to the women in his life. Harry Rose loved women, but he'd "loved" them in ways that had harmed them, been deadly, even. In spite of his track record, he still insisted he'd always tried to do the right thing, even when what he'd convinced himself was right clearly wasn't. And often that concerned how to off-load one woman so he could move on to the next.

Harry's refusal to acknowledge the error of his ways, to confront his conscience, had led to mental-health issues and addictions. But Terri believed he was finally facing up to his mistakes, was serious about redeeming himself in the eyes of his family and the British public. Did he deserve a second chance? Or was it too late?

What now for Rose Corp.? she asked. Harry's position at the top was surely untenable in light of the recent revelations. His daughters, Maria and Eliza, were heirs to the Rose crown and showed great promise. Maria was breaking new ground with her ethics policies at Rose, while Eliza had all her father's charm and brilliance, and none of his obsession with the opposite sex. In fact, reported Terri, she'd resolved to remain a virgin for the foreseeable!

Perhaps it was time for Harry to take a back seat.

Harry put down the iPad.

"Dad," said Eliza. "I want to know the truth. Did you know Mum was going to die?"

"No, Eliza. Truthfully, I didn't. Andre made a remark about Russians knowing how to deal with troublesome wives, but I didn't take him seriously. Obviously I should have done."

"Is that all he said?"

Harry didn't meet her eye.

"Well, Dad?"

"He offered to make 'my problem' go away. I never said I wanted that."

"But you never said you didn't."

"I don't remember the exact conversation. It was so long ago."

She balled her fists and shut her eyes, then made them all jump with a short, loud scream. "Dad! Will you listen to yourself? *Still* not taking responsibility!"

"Steady on."

"No, I won't. Right, this is what's going to happen. You took what I loved most from me, so maybe I should do the same to you. Terri's right. You truly want redemption? Then retire. Take yourself away from temptation, give up your power. Maria and I will take over, with Terri's help. Rose will be run by women."

Clare was nodding. "You may not have killed Ana," she said, "but you must accept some responsibility for her death. And Caitlyn's. And Terri filled me in on your treatment of Merry, and how you cheated on Katie throughout your marriage to her. Then there was Janette, who you were carrying on with just after poor Ana had lost her baby, maybe before. I'm trying to come to terms with all this, Harry. I'm not at all sure I can."

Eliza looked stricken. "Mum, please . . . don't leave. Eddie and I love you. We've lost too many mums."

"Darling, you know I love you and Eddie. I'll always be part of your lives. And I love Harry. But he hasn't been honest with me, he's kept so much hidden. I'd have to live with that. I'll need time to think."

"Clare . . ." said Harry. "I *can* change. I already have. Thanks to you."

"If you want redemption, you're going to have to prove that," she said. "And Terri's right. You can't possibly carry on as head of Rose Corp. after all these revelations. You should do as Eliza says—give up your power, step down. Let Rose be run by women."

Harry lay in bed, staring at the ceiling. The space beside him was empty.

How had it come to this? He'd lost everything. The British media had brought him down. Hoist with his own petard.

Clare had exiled him to the spare room and was talking about spending time by herself in the Lakes while she considered their future.

Eliza didn't know what to believe about his involvement in Ana's death; he'd lost her trust.

Maria—well, Maria had hated him ever since he left Katie.

Eddie was back at school, wondering if he was about to lose another stepmother.

And to have any chance of regaining what he'd lost, Harry was going to have to step down from Rose. Give up his raison d'être, his life's work, his father's legacy.

But if that was what it would take, then so be it. He'd win back their love, their trust. And he'd earn the right to return to Rose.

The redemption of Harry Rose starts here.

EPILOGUE

Eliza

July 2018

"Thanks, Rob," said Eliza as the intern handed out lattes in compostable cups. Still a prototype, they quickly broke down to become food for the roses in the Ana Rose Atrium.

The cups were one of the products being tested under the new Green Rose brand Eliza was setting up before returning to Oxford in the autumn. She would work at Rose during her university breaks, and Maria would be acting CEO until Eliza finished her degree.

Terri was mentoring the sisters while they settled into their new roles, and the three were holding their usual morning briefing meeting.

"He's cute!" said Terri, winking at Eliza as Rob left the room.

"Terri . . ." warned Maria, drawing her thick brows together.

"Joke, Maria. Where's bloody Aleesha?"

"She's dropping her son off upstairs," said Eliza.

Since Harry's retirement, they'd turned his vast top-floor office suite into a crèche. Staff could head up there whenever they needed to, and studies were already showing increased productivity and retention of female staff.

"Have you seen today's *Guardian*?" asked Terri.

"Yes. Go, us!" said Eliza. The piece—*HARRY'S DAUGHTERS PIO-*

NEER NEW ERA AT ROSE—highlighted the recent policy changes at the company, which were focused on equality and ethics. The article hinted at the dawning of a golden age for women in media.

Eliza's phone buzzed; Harry's name flashed up on the screen.

"Hi, Dad."

"How's the virgin queen?"

"Stop it." Harry still teased Eliza remorselessly about the quote in Terri's article. "Are you still in the Lakes?" she said.

"I am, yes."

Eliza switched her phone to speaker so Maria could hear.

"And is Clare with you?"

"Right here."

"And . . . will she be coming home with you this time?"

It was Harry's third trip to the north; on the first two Clare had told him she needed more time. Eliza's heart was in her mouth as she waited for his reply. They all missed Clare terribly.

Harry's words were unintelligible as a strong gust of wind obliterated his voice. It sounded as if he was en route to the South Pole.

"What, Dad? I can't hear you."

"I said, yes," Harry shouted. "Clare's coming home at last."

"Thank God!" Eliza replied. There was another blast of wind. "That's wonderful news. Where on earth are you?"

"On a hill. Fell. Great Cockup, actually. A metaphor for my life?"

"Honestly, Dad," said Eliza.

"Fuck's sake," said Terri.

Cast of Characters

(continued)

ART ROSE [Arthur, Prince of Wales]
> Harry's older brother. Thoughtful and quiet. Dated Katie.
> Died while still a teenager.

MARGOT JAMES (née ROSE) [Princess Margaret; married King James of Scotland]
> Harry's older sister; married to a Scottish laird. No sense of humor. Harry never sees her.

MEGAN ROSE [Princess Mary; queen of France before her marriage to Charles Brandon]
> Harry's beloved little sister. In love with Harry's (married) best friend, Charles.

MARIA ROSE [Queen Mary I; "Bloody Mary"]
> Daughter of Harry and Katie. Intense, serious, deeply religious. Terrifies people.

ELIZA ROSE [Queen Elizabeth I]
> Daughter of Harry and Ana. Vivacious and exceptionally bright; gets on with everyone.

EDDIE ROSE [King Edward VI]
> Cute son of Harry and Janette.

HENRY BLUNT [Henry FitzRoy]
> Son of Harry and Bennie.

HENRY ROSE [King Henry VII]
> Harry's father. Died while Harry was still at school.

ELIZABETH ROSE [Elizabeth of York]
Harry's mother. Also died while Harry was at school.

GERMAINE [Germaine of Foix]
Katie's stepmother. Formidable.

SIR THOMAS LYEBON and LADY ELIZABETH LYEBON
[Sir Thomas and Lady Boleyn]
Ana's parents. Live near Hever Castle, Kent.

"HOWIE" HOWE [Lord Edmund Howard]
Caitlyn's father. Useless. Ran away to Thailand to avoid his
creditors.

BENNIE BLUNT [Bessie Blount]
Harry's first mistress. Barmaid in a Soho pub. Lively London
girl. Looks like Madonna.

MIRANDA "MERRY" MCCAREY (née LYEBON) [Mary Boleyn]
Harry's second mistress. Blond sex kitten. Ana's sister. Married
to gay whisky heir Will; lives in a Scottish castle.

CHARLES LISLE [Charles Brandon, 1st Duke of Suffolk]
Harry's best friend. Old Etonian; merchant banker.
Womanizer.

CASSANDRA LISLE [no direct Tudor equivalent]
Wife of Charles Lisle. Good sort. Enjoys a tipple.

TERRI "BASKIN-" ROBBINS-MORE [Sir Thomas More]
Voice of Harry's conscience. Left-wing northerner with strong
sense of social justice. Editor of Rose Corp. magazine the
Rack.

TOM WOLSTON [Thomas Wolsey]
Harry's lawyer. Old-school.

TOM CRANWELL [Thomas Cromwell]
Tom Wolston's ruthless replacement. A lech.

ANDRE SOKOLOV [no Tudor equivalent]
Russian billionaire oligarch. Football mad. Murky
background.

OTHER ROSE STAFF
Richard York—board member and ex-chairman of Rose Corp.
Lesley—human resources. Best friend of Janette Morrissey.
Colin Hale—financial director.
Ben, Tina, and Aleesha—Harry's PAs.
Nate Romano—art director, the *Rack*.
Lizzie—art editor, the *Rack*.
Mia Fox—editor, *Hooray!*
Jake—photographer, *Hooray!*

PERCY NORTH [Henry Percy, Earl of Northumberland]
Ana Lyebon's fiancé. Account director for ad agency BWG.
Good-natured; bit of a poseur.

WILL "GORDON" MCCAREY [William Carey]
Gay husband of Merry Lyebon. Owner of whisky distillery
and Scottish castle. A lovely chap.

DARIUS DRAPER
Interior designer and estate manager of Kindrummon Castle.
Partner of Will McCarey.

DOC BUTTS [Henry VIII's physician Dr. Butts]
Harry's doctor.

MILLY and ARABELLA LISLE [Mary and Anne Brandon]
Daughters of Charles and Cassandra Lisle. Nicknames Thing
One and Thing Two.

FRANCESCA and HELENA LISLE [Frances and Eleanor Brandon]
Daughters of Charles and Megan Lisle.

FRANKIE DENHAM [Francis Dereham]
On-again, off-again boyfriend of Caitlyn Howe. Manager of
indie band Chaos; small-time drug dealer. A parasite.

TOMMY CULTRANE [Thomas Culpeper]
Pop idol; fellow judge with Caitlyn on TV talent show *Rock
God*.

FLORENCE WELLS [no Tudor equivalent]
Caitlyn's boss at Limelight PR.

ACKNOWLEDGMENTS

Sincere thanks to my fabulous agents, Vicki Marsdon and Nadine Rubin Nathan at High Spot Literary, for their wise guidance and for being my sounding boards. Ladies, you are such a joy to work (and drink coffee) with!

Thanks to the teams at Little, Brown UK and Penguin Random House in the US, especially Emma Beswetherick and Amanda Bergeron. Your insight, expertise, and enthusiasm for this book made the editing process a real pleasure.

To my two reader crews, for valuable feedback on the first draft. In New Zealand: Jane Bloomfield (particularly knowledgeable on aftershave), Suzanne Main, Catherine Robertson, Julie Scott, and Penny Yates; and in the UK: Sue Anders, Alison Rose, Alice Snowdon, and the Reynolds sisters—Ailsa, Ali, Fiona, and Kath. This book is dedicated to the fifth sister we all miss so much.

Thanks as ever to my wonderfully supportive (redheaded) family—Michael, James, and Helena—who put up with my vagueness and dereliction of duty while my mind was full of that other redhead.

A final thanks to the New Zealand Society of Authors, who kicked off Harry's epic journey from New Zealand to the UK and on to the USA.

Wife After Wife

Olivia Hayfield

Olivia Hayfield

A Conversation
with Olivia Hayfield

What made you decide to undertake a modern-day retelling of Henry VIII and his wives?

I've always been fascinated by the story of Henry VIII and his wives. I remember going to see *Anne of the Thousand Days* when I was a girl, and being outraged at Henry's treatment of Anne Boleyn. It stayed with me for years. I wanted to take that man down!

More recently, with certain powerful men in the spotlight regarding their attitudes toward women, I was reminded of Henry (something to do with the hair?). I started to wonder, what if Henry VIII lived today—were reincarnated, maybe? How would it play out? Supposing he'd grown up in the sixties and seventies, when feminism was blazing a path. And now, with the #MeToo movement. Perhaps it was time for me to give him his comeuppance by pitching him against modern-day versions of the women in his life, who wouldn't stand for his behavior this time around.

So that's what set me off. Except things didn't play out quite as I'd expected . . .

Henry was a notorious philanderer and tyrant—how did you handle these traits when developing Harry into your hero?

Once I started researching properly, I was surprised to learn that in the context of the times, Henry wasn't considered much of a philanderer at all (and I think it's always important to view things in historical context). His French counterpart, François I, was far, far worse (good grief, that man!), as were most of the European rulers. Henry was quite restrained, in his kingly way.

For Harry, I wanted the reasons for his affairs to mirror what may have motivated Henry VIII. Henry's problems with Catherine of Aragon—the need for a male heir—would have made sex a fraught affair. Things with Anne Boleyn would have taken a similar turn when she failed to produce a boy, but for Harry, I made it more about Ana's ambition and their problems working together. This also rings true to me—Anne Boleyn was a strong, ambitious woman with forward-thinking views, and while Henry may have found this appealing when he was in the first flush of infatuation, later on, when a male heir failed to materialize, perhaps it was all too much (poor snowflake). In my twenty-first-century version of the story, it's Ana who calls a halt to their relationship, not Harry. She isn't willing to stand for his behavior, kicks him out, and gets herself a pit bull of a lawyer.

As for being a tyrant, Harry has a couple of tyrannical moments, most notably his asset-stripping rampage through the industrial north. However, two women—Janette and Terri—make him examine his conscience and look again at his actions, and he changes tack. So again we have women tempering his behavior. Also, without the absolute power and the ongoing health problems, Harry Rose's temper is a lot better than Henry VIII's.

Was there a lot of research involved?

Yes, I love research! Antonia Fraser's *The Six Wives of Henry VIII* was my go-to reference source. I also read Alison Weir's books on Henry's wives, dipped into many history blogs, and watched *The Tudors* (but seriously, a dark-haired Henry?). I worked in London in the 1980s and '90s, so the scene setting (and pubs) is mostly from memory with a little help from Google Maps. I joined several Facebook groups devoted to the Tudors and am amazed at the size of the fan scene out there. So many people are fascinated by this period in history. With good cause!

The big surprise to me was how drastically Henry VIII changed over the course of his life. When he became king at the age of seventeen, contemporary reports describe an outstandingly handsome, charismatic, intelligent, well-read guy who wrote poetry and music and excelled at sports. He was known for his ability to put people at ease and to get on with everyone, and was a deep thinker. He was undoubtedly changed by having absolute power, and his health problems. Take those two factors away, put him in the twenty-first century, and what would he be like?

Were there many challenges along the way?

My main challenge was deciding how Henry VIII's second chance at life would end—karma, or redemption? I set out to give that man his comeuppance. But once I'd taken away those influences that turned him into the tyrannical monster of the sixteenth century, I was left with someone I couldn't help liking. Rather a lot.

And I wanted his wives to be strong women, so I had to give them good reason to love this man, to stick with him. Therefore I wanted the reader to empathize with Harry, to love him a little, to want to shake him by the shoulders and tell him to pull himself together, to confront his conscience, because he was worth saving. I hope readers will be glad he's spared by fate and given the chance to make things right with the women in his life.

The #MeToo movement has changed the way modern women react to womanizers such as Harry. How difficult was it to weave this into the story sensitively while staying true to Harry's historical self?

A big challenge! We see Harry at the start of the story as a confused man, and a worried one. He knows he's behaved badly, and millennial women make him uneasy. But he's also learned from his experiences, recognizes the harm he's done, and this is the difference between Harry and Henry. Harry has been positively influenced by the strong women around him—most recently his daughter Eliza—whereas Henry was king and could do what he wanted, and no one dared tell him he was a disgrace.

Who was your favorite wife and why?

I like Clare. Everyone likes Clare. So wise, intelligent, and kind. But also Ana, though she's quite frosty. I feel that after a couple of glasses of wine I could have a good time with Ana, that she'd thaw. I love poor Caitlyn too; she tries so hard to turn her life around but can't shake off her past. The story of Catherine Howard is such a tragedy, that poor teenage girl, sacrificed on her family's altar of ambition to a Henry who by then had nothing to redeem him.

Can you talk a little more about the role of women in the story? How important a role do they play in Harry's own character development?

The women play a huge part in Harry's character development. As well as the influence of his wives, we have his daughter Eliza getting him thinking about the #MeToo movement, and Terri, the voice of his conscience, calling him out on his behavior. Right from the start

Harry shows respect for the women around him—for Terri's sharp brain and courage, Katie's saintliness, Ana's talent, Janette's thoughtfulness and sweetness, Caitlyn's attempts to overcome her abusive background, Clare's intelligence and kindness—so he's not in any way a misogynist. These women save him from himself, which is why, in the end, I decided he deserved redemption rather than karma. It's for their sake as much as his.

Were there many bits of history that you were forced to ignore, take out, or tweak to suit the modern-day setting?

The main one was how to treat the two beheadings. I had to find ways for Ana and Caitlyn to die that Harry could be responsible for, rather than directly causing.

Another problem was longevity—people died young in those days! I decided to keep one or two people alive, notably Harry's son Eddie. I have him vaccinated, so that was easy (Edward VI died of TB). Harry's sister Megan (Princess Mary Tudor) survives cancer (she died at age thirty-seven in real life), and Katie has fewer stillbirths and miscarriages than Catherine of Aragon. And of course Harry sorts out his "lifestyle" problems, and his leg heals, so he gets to live on in good health. Slim. Still hot.

To keep up the pace, and to make sure the plot and timeline worked, I massaged the years and also tweaked the birthdates of a few characters. For example, Catherine of Aragon and Henry VIII were married for twenty-four years, and his later marriages came and went in a blur, so I've shortened and lengthened. In my story, Maria and Eliza are born ten years apart, whereas the age gap between Mary and Elizabeth was seventeen years. I hope die-hard Tudor fans will forgive my playing fast and loose with history in the name of plot and pace.

Henry VIII's story is familiar to a lot of people. Did this add a weight of responsibility to your writing?

Yes, I have had a few worries about taking liberties with Henry and his wives. However, I hope people will take my tale in the spirit in which I wrote it, which is a what-if reimagining, not to be taken too seriously. I hope readers will laugh, will love Harry in spite of themselves, will adore his wives, and will want to find out what happens next . . .

Are you working on another story at the moment?

I have written the sequel to *Wife After Wife*. How could I not? I was so swept up in the lives of these amazing characters and wanted to find out what happens to them. This follow-up is written from Eliza's point of view and centers on her relationships with her sister Maria, the exuberant, twinkly-eyed Rob Studley (Robert Dudley, Earl of Leicester and love of Elizabeth I's life), and her intriguing thorn-in-the-side cousin Mackenzie James (Mary, Queen of Scots). Harry is very much still around, but takes a back seat in this tale. However, we see him continuing his journey to redemption through his relationship with Eliza.

We also meet modern versions of some famous Elizabethan characters, notably Eliza's friends Will Bardington (Shakespeare) and Kit Marley (Marlowe), who write and produce TV dramas for Rose Corp.'s new production arm, RoseGold. This sequel is lots of fun but also had one of my first-draft readers sobbing at the end, which is exactly what I was hoping for!

Questions for Discussion

1. Do you think Henry VIII's story lends itself to a modern-day re-telling?

2. How well do you think Olivia Hayfield has managed to remain true to the historical truth?

3. Do you think Harry works well as the story's hero?

4. What role do Harry's wives play in Harry's own story arc?

5. Who is your favorite wife and why?

6. If Henry VIII were alive today, how would he have to temper his behavior toward women?

7. Can you comment on London as a character within the story?

8. Do you feel the story ended in the right way? Would you have ended things differently?

Olivia Hayfield is the pseudonym of British author Sue Copsey. Sue is usually in her office editing other people's books, while Olivia is often in her writing hut at the bottom of the garden.

After several years in London Zoo's press office, Sue became an editor at Dorling Kindersley. She later moved to New Zealand, where she continues to work in publishing. Sue has written several children's books, including *The Ghosts of Tarawera*, which was a Storylines Notable Book Junior Fiction Award winner. *Wife After Wife* is her first adult novel. She is married with two children.

CONNECT ONLINE

OliviaHayfield.com

Ready to find
your next great read?

Let us help.

Visit prh.com/nextread

Penguin
Random
House